Cr

TRAGEDY ON THE BRANCH LINE

By Edward Marston

TRAGEDY ON THE BRANCH LINE

EDWARD MARSTON

Allison & Busby Limited
11 Wardour Mews
London W1F 8AN
allisonandbusby.com

First published in Great Britain by Allison & Busby in 2021.

Copyright © 2021 by Edward Marston

A CIP catalogue record for this book is available from
the British Library.

First Edition

ISBN 978-0-7490-2604-2

Typeset in 12/17 pt Adobe Garamond Pro by
Allison & Busby Ltd.

Printed and bound by
CPI Group (UK) Ltd, Croydon, CR0 4YY

To my beloved daughter, Helena,
who rowed for Oxford against Cambridge
in the lightweight women's four in 1987

CHAPTER ONE

Cambridge, 1863

As soon as he woke up early that morning, Bernard Pomeroy hopped out of bed, crossed to the window and drew back the curtains. It was still dark outside, but lanterns dappled the Old Court in Corpus Christi College with pools of light, allowing him to see the driving rain sweeping it clean. Pomeroy was undeterred. The crew went out in all weathers, contending with adverse conditions they might well face on the day of the Boat Race itself.

Then he noticed a letter pushed under his door. Picking it up, he recognised the handwriting and tore the missive open. The message was short and desperate. His priorities changed instantly. After dressing at speed, he scribbled a note and slipped it into an envelope. Then he grabbed his hat, let himself out and clattered down the staircase as fast as his legs would carry him. Once outside, he sprinted to the lodge where the porter, Jack Stott, gave him a polite welcome.

'Good morning, Mr Pomeroy,' he said, touching the brim of his hat.

'Someone will be calling for me in an hour.'

'Yes, I know, sir. It's Mr Thorpe from King's. He comes every morning.'

'Give him this,' ordered Pomeroy, thrusting the letter into his hand. 'Make sure that he gets it.'

'Yes, sir, I will. But let me give you a word of warning, if I may. Borrow this, or you'll get soaked.'

He reached for one of the umbrellas in the stand, but Pomeroy had already darted out of the door. Accustomed to headstrong behaviour from the undergraduates, Stott gave an understanding smile. It would be something about which to tell his colleagues in due course.

Pomeroy, meanwhile, was hurtling along Trumpington Street. Through the gloom ahead of him, he could pick out the shapes of the cabs waiting at the rank. When he got to the front of the queue, he yelled at the driver.

'The railway station!'

'Very good, sir,' said the man.

'And be quick about it.'

'Yes, sir.'

Pomeroy dived into the cab and the horse responded at once to a flick of the whip. Though they were soon rattling along at a good pace, the passenger was tense and angry, cursing the academic establishment for insisting that the station was built over a mile away from the university so that the sight, sound and stench of steam locomotives could not disturb its cloistered calm. Bristling with impatience, he took the letter from his pocket and read it again. There were only two brief sentences, but they were enough. Pomeroy was needed. Nothing else mattered.

By the time they reached the station, he was in a lather of apprehension. As he paid the driver and ran towards the ticket hall, he didn't notice the man who was lurking under an umbrella and who came to life at the sight of Pomeroy. When the undergraduate got in the queue, the man stood directly behind him. They inched forward until they could take turns at the hatch. Like Pomeroy, the man bought a ticket to Bury St Edmunds. Unaware that he was being tailed, Pomeroy joined the crowd at the edge of the unusually long single platform, moving nervously from foot to foot and wishing that the train would come. He was completely oblivious to the rain that was blowing in under the canopy and to the fact that someone was standing only inches behind him. All his concentration was focussed on the plea for help.

It seemed like an eternity before he heard the distant sound of the approaching train. He braced himself to leap at the nearest door when the locomotive finally came to a halt amid a fanfare of hissing and clanking. The man behind him also readied himself. When the moment came, the crowd surged forward, but nobody did so with the urgency of Pomeroy. He literally elbowed people aside. So intent was he on being the first to board the train that he hardly felt the sharp prick on the side of his neck. Once in the compartment, he sat beside a window and stared out. The man who followed him took a seat diagonally opposite and unfolded his newspaper, pretending to read while watching Pomeroy out of the corner of his eye.

With the compartment full, the train set off and headed for the branch line to Bury St Edmunds. It soon picked up speed, but it was nowhere near fast enough for Pomeroy. He goaded it on under his breath, rubbing his neck occasionally as if troubled by insistent stabs of pain. He began to feel unwell, and his condition slowly worsened. The man with the newspaper saw him take out a letter and read it surreptitiously before pushing it back into his pocket. Pomeroy began to sway slightly. When the train stopped at Newmarket, several passengers alighted and headed for the exit. As his eyes filmed over, Pomeroy struggled to read the name of the station. His body felt weak, his brain confused.

Relieved when the train steamed out of the station, he rallied slightly, but it was only a brief recovery. He was soon feeling ill once more. He closed his eyes tight and prayed for the strength and determination he needed. Someone relied on him. He *had* to be well enough to do whatever was needed. Pomeroy simply had to honour his promise. As he tried to repeat it to himself, however, his words became a meaningless jumble and his control faltered even more. Seated opposite him, an elderly couple became concerned. They asked him if he was all right and if there was anything they could do to help.

'Just help me to get off at Bury St Edmunds,' he begged. 'That's all.'

For the rest of the journey, they continued to stare at him, but Pomeroy was unaware of their scrutiny. He was too busy trying to summon up what little strength he had left. They eventually reached his station and he hauled himself upright. When the elderly couple offered to help him, he waved them away. The train stuttered to a halt. Opening the door of the compartment, he clambered out and staggered along the platform, barely able to keep upright. After bumping helplessly into other passengers, he lost his footing altogether and pitched forward, drawing cries of alarm from some women nearby. The first person to bend over him was the man with the newspaper who'd travelled in the same compartment. Making sure nobody saw what he did, he slipped a hand into Pomeroy's pocket and retrieved the letter he'd noticed earlier. Then he turned the body over with apparent tenderness and felt a wrist for a pulse. He shook his head sadly.

'He's dead,' he announced. 'Call a policeman!'

CHAPTER TWO

As he walked along the towpath, Nicholas Thorpe was gritting his teeth. He hated being the bearer of bad tidings and knew that he'd get a frosty reception. Thorpe was a handsome, rangy, fair-haired young man with the grace of a natural athlete. Ordinarily, he'd be strolling beside Bernard Pomeroy, his best friend, the cox of the Cambridge crew. Neither of them would have dared to miss the mandatory stint on the river. As their coach never failed to remind them, it built stamina, refined their rowing technique and generated the camaraderie essential in a crew. Until that point, everything had gone so well, but their luck had now changed dramatically. The absence of Pomeroy – even for a single morning – was a serious blow. It would hamper their progress and lower morale.

Huddled under umbrellas, the rest of the crew were shocked to see Thorpe walking towards them on his own. Every one of the oarsmen knew what a key role their cox played. Pushing forward, they demanded to know where he was. By way of a reply, Thorpe handed Pomeroy's note to the tall, commanding figure of Malcolm Henfrey-Ling, the Cambridge president. Waving everyone into silence, the latter read the message aloud.

'*Urgent business elsewhere. Pass on my sincere apologies.*'

'What sort of urgent business?' demanded James Webb, the coach, a stocky, intense, beetle-browed man in his thirties with a shock of brown hair. His eyes were blazing with anger. 'Nothing is more urgent than beating Oxford.'

'I agree,' said the president. 'They've trounced us twice in a row. We simply must get our revenge this year.'

'Well, we won't do it without Bernard.'

'I agree. He's been a godsend.' He turned to Thorpe. 'What the hell is he playing at, Nick?'

'I don't know,' admitted Thorpe, 'but I'm sure there's a perfectly good explanation for his behaviour. Bernard wouldn't let us down unless there was a real crisis. According to the porter at Corpus, he left the college in a terrible hurry.'

'Have you any idea why?'

'No, I don't. It's so uncharacteristic of him. We all know how committed he is to winning the Boat Race.'

'Then where *is* he?' asked Henfrey-Ling.

'I wish I knew, Malcolm.'

'And who's supposed to take his place while he's away?'

asked Webb. 'He's left us in the lurch. We can't take to the water without a cox.'

'I suppose not,' said Thorpe, apologetically.

'Did he give you no hint that this was going to happen?'

'No, James – none at all.'

'I'll give him such a roasting when he gets back,' threatened the coach.

'It may not be his fault.'

'Yes, it is. He swore that he'd keep to the training schedule.'

'We all did,' admitted Thorpe. 'As for what we do now, James, I suppose that *you'll* have to be our cox today. There's nobody else here yet.'

'Nick is right,' agreed Henfrey-Ling. 'You'll have to take over, James.'

Webb was livid. 'How can I do my job as a coach if I'm actually *in* the boat?' he yelled. 'I need to watch from the towpath and see any mistakes. I need to shout instructions from the saddle of my horse.'

The president was firm. 'The decision is made, James.'

'I'm not suited for it, Malcolm. To start with, I must be three or four stone heavier than Bernard. Also, I've never coxed an eight before.'

'Then perhaps it's time you learnt to do so. This is an emergency.' He looked the coach in the eye. 'Would you rather we abandoned the outing altogether?'

'No, no, of course not.'

'Then let's get on with it, shall we?'

'Bernard would expect it of us,' said Thorpe, helpfully.

'Don't mention that man's name,' sneered Webb. 'He's the

one who created this frightful mess. It's unforgivable. Wait until I see him again. I'm going to kill Bernard bloody Pomeroy!'

'Cambridge?' repeated Inspector Colbeck.

'Yes,' said Superintendent Tallis. 'The telegraph was sent by the Master of one of the colleges there.'

'Might I know his name, please?'

'Sir Harold Nellington.'

'Then the college is Corpus Christi.'

Tallis was surprised. 'You *know* this man?'

'I know *of* him, sir. He's a scholar of great repute, an authority on Greek and Roman archaeology. Sir Harold is responsible for some of the best exhibits at the British Museum. You should see them sometime.'

'Don't be ridiculous. Visiting a museum presupposes leisure, and that's a luxury I never possess because I've dedicated my life to the fight against crime.'

They were in the superintendent's office. Colbeck had been summoned there to look at a telegraph that had arrived at Scotland Yard. When it was handed to him, his eye immediately picked out three words.

'*Foul play suspected*,' he murmured.

'Yes, that worried me,' said Tallis, tetchily. 'I don't like that word "suspected". I prefer certainties.'

'Sir Harold is being cautious, that's all.'

'We're snowed under with major crimes here in London, cases that keep my officers at full stretch. Am I justified in sending one of my inspectors to Bury St Edmunds simply because someone collapsed and died on a railway platform?'

'I believe you *are* justified, sir.'

'What if we're the victims of some mischievous prank?' asked Tallis, bushy eyebrows forming a chevron of distrust. 'Perhaps the message was not sent by Sir Harold at all but by someone posing as him?'

'I beg leave to doubt that, Superintendent.'

'You know what undergraduates can be like. You were one yourself. There's a madcap element in some of them. They love to taunt the police.'

'This request is perfectly genuine,' said Colbeck, handing the telegraph back to him. 'You clearly haven't heard of Bernard Pomeroy.'

'The name means nothing to me.'

'That's because you don't read newspaper articles about sport, sir.'

'I regard them as a complete irrelevance.'

'Pomeroy was mentioned in *The Times* only a few days ago. He's the cox in the Cambridge boat and is, by all accounts, a brilliant one.' Colbeck raised a teasing eyebrow. 'I take it that you have *heard* of the Boat Race, sir.'

'Of course, I have,' said Tallis. 'It's a damnable event to police. The last thing London needs is a massive crowd of drunken, overexcited people watching a couple of boats being rowed along the Thames. By the end of the Race, the spectators are in a state of complete delirium. It's a nightmare for us.'

'You exaggerate, Superintendent. The Boat Race has become an institution, and a valued one at that. As for the plea from the Master of Corpus Christi, I believe that we should respond to it. Foul play might well be involved.'

'What makes you think that?'

'Pomeroy has been described by rowing connoisseurs as nothing short of a genius. They argue that *he's* the reason that Cambridge has been made the clear favourites to win the Race this year. That being the case, the telegraph has given us both a motive and a prime suspect.'

Tallis blinked in surprise. 'What the devil are you talking about?'

'Nobody would earn a place in the Cambridge boat unless he was supremely fit because the Race is a gruelling test of physical and mental strength. When a young man in his prime – as Pomeroy clearly was – dies suddenly from no apparent cause, then his death is suspicious. Who would profit most from his elimination?'

'You tell me,' said the other.

'The finger points at the Oxford boat.'

'I'm not entirely persuaded about that . . .'

'That's because you don't understand how much winning the event means to the two crews involved in it,' said Colbeck. 'The reputation of their respective universities is at stake. They would do anything – absolutely *anything* – to secure an advantage. Removing a crucial member of the Cambridge crew could certainly be described as such an advantage.' He headed for the door. 'Sergeant Leeming and I will be on the next train to Bury St Edmunds.'

Their morning on the river had been a disaster. Though he'd been an outstanding oarsman in his time, James Webb was not an experienced cox. Because he never established complete control of the boat, it zigzagged its way along the Cam and all but collided with the bank on two occasions. The one thing he did do correctly was to make himself easily heard, bellowing out the changes of rate as if addressing a troop of soldiers on a parade ground. Pulling hard on his oar like the rest of the crew, Nicholas Thorpe feared that the boat might overturn at any moment. He had also been made to feel obscurely responsible for the absence of Bernard Pomeroy, even though it was as much a shock to him as to the others. When the crew dispersed, Thorpe ran all the way back to Corpus Christi College in the hope that his friend had returned.

But there was no sign of Pomeroy and no word of his whereabouts. Thorpe therefore returned to his own college in dismay. Hours after lunch he decided to go back to Corpus. A radical change had occurred. He could see from the porter's expression that something had happened.

'Is he here?' he asked.

'I'm afraid not, Mr Thorpe,' said Stott, quietly.

'Then where is he?'

'I suggest that you speak to the Master.'

'You *know* something, don't you?'

'All I can offer you is a wild rumour, sir,' replied the other. 'Since you're such a close friend of Mr Pomeroy's, I think you deserve the truth. Only Sir Harold can give you that.'

Thorpe was alarmed. 'Rumour?' he said. '*What* rumour?'

'It's idle tittle-tattle and not worth repeating.'

'Is it bad news?'

'I'll take you to the Master's study, sir,' said Stott. 'You'll have a job finding it otherwise.' Picking up an umbrella, he led the way out of the lodge. 'How was your outing on the river today?'

'It was dreadful.'

'This wind and rain couldn't have helped.'

'We had much bigger problems, believe me.'

'I'm sorry to hear that, sir. What sort of problems?'

But Thorpe didn't even hear him. He was in a complete daze, trying to adapt to the possibility that something terrible had happened to Pomeroy. The porter led him to the Master's lodging and handed him over to the secretary, whispering something in the man's ear and getting an understanding nod in return. The secretary, a mousy little man of uncertain age, went off at once, and Stott took his leave. Thorpe was too preoccupied even to thank him for his help. He was on tenterhooks.

When the secretary reappeared, he beckoned the visitor, then took him down a corridor before pausing to knock on a door. Opening it, he ushered Thorpe into the study and announced him by name. He then withdrew, closing the door behind him.

Thorpe was left standing in a low-ceilinged room replete with bookshelves and grainy photographs of archaeological specimens. Seated behind the desk was Sir Harold Nellington, a spectral figure in his sixties whose gaunt features were framed by a mane of white hair. The old man rose to his feet with difficulty and extended a skeletal hand.

'Mr Thorpe, I believe,' he said.

'Yes, sir,' replied Thorpe, crossing the room to shake hands with him. 'It's good of you to see me, Master.'

'I understand you were a close friend of Bernard Pomeroy.'

'That's right.'

'How long had you known him?'

'Many years – we were at The King's School, Canterbury together.'

'Oh, I see. That explains his obsession with Christopher Marlowe.'

'Marlowe was a scholar there in the 1570s.'

'It seems as if Pomeroy was following in his footsteps to some extent. I'm told that he was—'

'Forgive me for interrupting,' said Thorpe, blurting out the words, 'but I simply must know what's happened to Bernard.'

'Why don't we both sit down?' suggested Sir Harold, resuming his seat.

'I'd prefer to stand if you don't mind.'

'Please yourself.'

'There's a wild rumour, apparently.'

'I'll give you all the facts that are known,' promised Sir Harold, solemnly. 'It appears that Pomeroy left the college early this morning in what the porter described as a blind panic. He took a cab to the railway station and bought a ticket to Bury St Edmunds.'

'Why?' demanded Thorpe. 'He had no reason to go there. Bernard should have been down at the river with the rest of us.'

'Let me finish, please.'

'Yes, of course. I'm sorry.'

'When he arrived at his destination, he stepped onto the platform and walked along it before collapsing. Another passenger examined him, but . . . there was nothing that he could do. Pomeroy was dead.'

The news hit Thorpe with the force of a blow, and he reeled from it. As the implications of what he'd just heard flooded into his mind, tears began to course down his cheeks. He moved to a chair, sat down and buried his face in his hands. The Master waited a couple of minutes before speaking.

'The police got in touch with me,' he explained. 'When I first heard the news, I was as shocked as you are. Healthy young men like Pomeroy don't simply drop dead like that. I checked his medical record in our files. It's quite spotless. He was extraordinarily fit.'

Thorpe raised his head. 'What did the police say?'

'They fear that foul play may be involved.'

'You mean that Bernard was . . . ? No, sir, surely not – it's *unthinkable*.'

'Given the circumstances, alas, nothing is unthinkable. That's why I've taken steps to institute a proper investigation. What's happened is truly appalling, but there is one consolation.'

'I don't see it.'

'Pomeroy died on the platform of a railway station. That gave me a legitimate reason to send for Inspector Colbeck. Had the sudden and unexplained death occurred here in the college or down by the river, we would've had been in the

23

hands of the local constabulary. As it is – with luck – we'll have the best possible man in charge.'

'I've never heard of this Inspector . . . Whatever-his-name-was.'

'Colbeck. He's better known as the Railway Detective.'

CHAPTER THREE

As the two of them strode along the platform together, they aroused both curiosity and amusement. They were similarly attired, but the contrast between them could not have been greater. Robert Colbeck was tall, elegant and immaculate, while the shorter, sturdier Victor Leeming was hunched, dishevelled and slightly sinister. He was also having difficulty keeping pace with the long strides of his companion. From their appearance, nobody would have guessed that they were the most efficient detectives in Scotland Yard. They looked more like master and servant. Spotting an empty compartment, Colbeck opened the door and let Leeming get in first before he followed.

'Welcome to the Great Eastern Railway,' he said, sitting down. 'It's the first time we've been able to travel on it.'

'Don't expect a round of applause from me,' grunted Leeming.

'I thought you'd be interested. It was formed by an amalgamation of the five squabbling railway companies we encountered when our work took us to Norwich. They have at last had the sense to put their differences aside and unite.'

'I couldn't care less, sir.'

Colbeck looked at him. 'Why are you in such a disagreeable mood?'

'It's because we're making a pointless journey.'

'I dispute that.'

'All we know is that foul play is *suspected*.'

'That's all we need to know.'

'We have no real evidence.'

'You'll find it in the name of the victim.'

'But he may not *be* a victim,' insisted Leeming. 'He may well have died from natural causes.'

'Bernard Pomeroy was selected as the Cambridge cox.'

'So?'

'You've watched the Boat Race, haven't you?'

'Yes, of course I have, especially when I was in uniform and on duty at the event. Last year, I was lucky enough to take my boys along. When Oxford won, we cheered with the rest of the crowd.'

'Did you happen to notice the cox of the winning crew?'

'I didn't spare him a glance,' said Leeming, dismissively. 'Why should I? It was the others who did all the work, pulling on those heavy oars for over four miles. They looked half-dead at the finish.'

'The crew owed an enormous amount to their coxswain,' Colbeck pointed out. 'He steered the boat and coordinated the power and rhythm of the oarsmen. There's a huge amount of skill involved. Think how many steamers were on the Thames during last year's event. As well as keeping clear of the Cambridge boat, the Oxford cox had to negotiate a way through all that traffic in a vessel that's built for speed rather than manoeuvrability.'

'I never thought about it that way.'

'A good cox is like gold dust and Pomeroy, by all accounts, was an exceptional one. He was targeted.'

Leeming frowned. 'Are you serious, sir?'

'I was never more so.'

'But the Boat Race is a sporting event.'

'All's fair in love and rowing, Victor.'

'Do you really believe that someone would stoop to murder?'

'I wouldn't rule it out,' said Colbeck. 'On the other hand, we must bear in mind that his death may have nothing whatsoever to do with rowing. The article about Pomeroy in *The Times* spoke of his many other achievements. He's made a real name for himself at Cambridge. Clearly, he was a remarkable young man. That kind of success breeds envy.'

'I suppose it does.'

'Envy sometimes turns into something far nastier.'

'We've seen that happen many times.'

'I rest my case.'

Leeming brightened. 'So we may not be on a wild goose chase after all,' he said. 'It's a murder case.'

'I can guarantee it.' A whistle was blown, and the train suddenly jerked forward. 'Sit back and relax while you can, Victor. I sense that we have a daunting challenge awaiting us.'

It took a long time for Nicholas Thorpe fully to absorb the news. He just sat there in the Master's study and gazed blankly at a bookcase. Seeing how profoundly shaken his visitor was, Sir Harold Nellington made no attempt to disturb him. He bided his time until Thorpe seemed to revive slightly.

'Is there anything I can get you?' offered the Master. 'A glass of water perhaps, or something stronger . . . ?'

'No, thank you.'

'I have a tolerable brandy.'

'That's very kind of you, Sir Harold,' said Thorpe, hauling himself to his feet, 'but I must go. Thank you for being so honest with me about . . . about Bernard.'

After giving a nod of farewell, he let himself out of the room, went down the corridor and out of the Master's lodging. Once out in the fresh air, he broke into a trot, left the college and kept going until he eventually came to Trinity Hall. He was soon running up two flights of stairs and banging on the oak door of Malcolm Henfrey-Ling's room before opening it and stepping inside.

Henfrey-Ling was seated in a leather armchair opposite James Webb. Both of them leapt to their feet at the sight of him.

'What's wrong, Nick?' asked Henfrey-Ling. 'You're as white as a ghost.'

'I've just spoken to Death Knell,' said Thorpe.

'Who?'

'It's the nickname for the Master of Corpus, Sir Harold Nellington, and it turned out to be hideously appropriate.'

'Why?' asked Webb. 'You're not making any sense, Nick.'

'Bernard is dead.'

'Don't be ridiculous – he's the healthiest person in Cambridge.'

'He may not have died by natural means.'

Webb gulped. 'What . . . ?'

'Come and sit down,' said Henfrey-Ling, putting an arm around Thorpe and guiding him to a chair. 'If anybody else had burst in here with that news, I'd have known it was a cruel joke. But you're serious, aren't you?'

'Yes, Malcolm, I am.'

Webb was distraught. 'I just can't take this in,' he said.

'Let Nick tell us what he knows,' said Henfrey-Ling. 'I'm like you, James. I can't believe it, but that's because I *daren't* believe it. If we've lost Bernard, then we can wave goodbye to our chance of winning the Boat Race.'

'I feel so guilty, Malcolm. When he let us down this morning, I lost my temper and said I'd *kill* Bernard and, at the time, I meant it. Now . . .'

'Let's listen to Nick.'

Henfrey-Ling turned to the newcomer, and Thorpe took his cue. In a voice that was quivering with emotion, he told them exactly what he'd heard and how he'd been stunned by the news. They reacted with mingled horror and disbelief. Henfrey-Ling was the first to recover his voice.

'Whatever took him to Bury St Edmunds?' he asked.

Thorpe shrugged. 'I don't know.'

'You must have some idea, Nick.'

'I wish that I did.'

'I thought you and Bernard were close friends,' said Webb, accusingly.

'We are,' said Thorpe. 'At least, we were . . .'

'Did he ever mention Bury St Edmunds to you?'

'No, James, he never did.'

'So he was hiding something from you.'

'I don't accept that. Bernard was always honest with me.'

'Evidently,' said Henfrey-Ling, 'he wasn't *completely* honest. Jesus Christ!' he exclaimed, slapping the arm of the chair. 'Of all the things that could have happened, this is the worst.'

'You said that he didn't die by natural means, Nick,' recalled Webb.

'That's not certain as yet,' said Thorpe.

'But it's a possibility.'

'Sir Harold felt that it was more than that.'

'Then it raises the question of who was responsible.'

'It does, James,' said Henfrey-Ling, 'and we all know who might be behind this outrage. I never thought that Oxford would resort to desperate tactics like this, but it seems I may have been wrong.'

'We mustn't make unfounded accusations,' warned Thorpe.

'Bernard was deliberately eliminated. It's obvious.'

'Death Knell is taking the matter seriously. He's sent for a detective inspector from Scotland Yard. He's famous, it seems. There's nobody more guaranteed to solve the mystery. He's sure to uncover the truth and put our minds at rest.'

'Ha!' said Webb, derisively. 'And how is this famous inspector supposed to do that? Is he going to take Bernard's place and cox the Cambridge boat to victory?'

After changing trains at Cambridge, they travelled on the branch line to Bury St Edmunds. When they arrived, Colbeck went straight off to the hospital and left Leeming to interview the stationmaster. Stanley Moult was a vain, self-important man in his forties with a luxuriant and carefully groomed moustache that spoke of hours spent in front of a mirror with a pair of scissors. Leeming introduced himself and was taken straight to the stationmaster's office.

'Nothing like this has ever happened before,' whined Moult. 'I make sure of that. We have a reputation to keep.'

'I don't think it's fair to blame the deceased,' said Leeming, antagonised by the man's pomposity. 'It's not as if he died on your platform on purpose. You ought to show more sympathy.'

Moult bridled. 'Don't you tell me how to do my job, Sergeant.'

'Think about the victim instead of about your precious station. The young man will have a family and friends who'll be devastated by what's happened. How would you feel if a son of yours was cut down in his prime?'

'I'm not married.'

Leeming took out his notebook. 'Just tell me what happened.'

Drawing himself up to his full height, Moult stroked his moustache.

'I was on duty this morning,' he said, 'when the train came in. Passengers began to alight and head towards the exit. There was the usual commotion, then I heard some women scream.'

'Where were you at the time?'

'I was standing towards the rear of the train. Fearing that there was an incident of some sort, I hurried along the platform to take charge of the situation. I had to push my way through a ring of people. They were gazing down at someone sprawled out on the platform. Bullen was bending over him.'

'Bullen?'

'He's one of the railway policemen.'

'Then he's probably more use to me than you are,' said Leeming, closing his notebook. 'Where will I find Mr Bullen?'

Moult was affronted. 'I can tell you everything you need to know, Sergeant. I questioned Bullen closely.'

'I intend to do the same.'

'You haven't listened to *my* account yet.'

'Bullen takes priority. He was obviously more involved than you were. If you have anything of substance to add to what he tells me,' said Leeming, brusquely, 'I'll make a note of it. Railway policemen are there to respond to emergencies. That's what this one did, so I need to talk to him.'

'I'll complain about this to your superior,' said Moult, angrily.

Leeming smiled. 'The inspector will be interested to hear from you, sir.'

Opening the door, he left the office with the stationmaster at his heels. It didn't take him long to find Arthur Bullen. Wearing his uniform proudly, the railway policeman was standing near the exit, watching the last of the passengers trickle away. He was a middle-aged man of reassuring bulk, with watchful eyes set into a craggy face. When Leeming introduced himself, Bullen's interest quickened.

'You've come from Scotland Yard?' he said in surprise.

'We're simply looking into what happened.'

'I've already given my report to Mr Moult.'

'There you are,' said the stationmaster.

'I'd still like to hear it myself,' said Leeming, 'without interruption from anyone else.' He was pleased to see Moult smart at the reproof. 'I've got my notebook ready. Describe the incident in your own words.'

Bullen was crisp, straightforward and mercifully brief. He explained that, when he arrived on the scene, a stranger was kneeling beside the stricken figure. The man had made way for the railway policeman and watched while the latter checked for vital signs. A colleague of Bullen's then arrived and started to clear the crowd away. The dead body was covered with a tarpaulin, then removed to the hospital soon afterwards.

'That was at *my* instigation,' said the stationmaster.

'You did the right thing,' agreed Leeming. He turned to Bullen. 'Tell me about the stranger who got to the body first.'

'He was a handsome, well-dressed man in his thirties, Sergeant,' said the other. 'He stood out a little because he was . . . well, slightly tanned. I don't think he got that complexion in our weather.'

'If you ask me,' volunteered Moult, 'he was a foreigner.'

'Did you hear him speak?' asked Leeming.

'No,' said Bullen, 'but Mr Moult is right. He could have been from abroad. I didn't get the chance to talk to him. He stayed for a minute or so, then he sort of melted away.'

'That's a pity. Is there anything else you'd like to add?'

'No, Sergeant.'

'Your statement is exemplary. Thank you for your help.'

'*I* could have told you all that,' asserted Moult.

'First-hand information is always the most reliable,' said Leeming. 'You were just a spectator, sir.'

About to protest, the stationmaster was distracted by a yell of anguish at the far end of the platform. A porter had been in the act of loading some heavy luggage onto a trolley when the strap on one of the trunks snapped and the lid flipped open. Clothing began to pour out. Moult immediately set off to investigate.

'Now,' said Leeming, taking advantage of his absence, 'I had a feeling you had more to say but didn't wish to do so in front of Mr Moult.'

'It's true,' confessed Bullen.

'Is he always so interfering?'

'Yes, he is. Let's disappear while we can, Sergeant.'

Taking him by the elbow, he led Leeming out through the exit and along the pavement. When they stopped, Bullen checked to see that they hadn't been followed by the stationmaster. His voice then lowered to a conspiratorial whisper.

'There's something I kept to myself,' he said. 'If I'd told the stationmaster, *he'd* have claimed credit for it. That'd be typical of him.'

'Go on,' encouraged Leeming.

'I've seen him before.'

'Who?' asked Leeming. 'Are you talking about that stranger?'

'No, Sergeant. I mean the one who collapsed and died.'

'Do you have any idea who he is?'

'I don't, I'm afraid, but he was a young toff from the university. You could tell by the way he dressed and carried himself. They're all like that. I noticed him here a few times in the last month, and it was obvious why he'd come to Bury St Edmunds.'

'Oh?'

'There was a young woman waiting for him.'

'Ah, I see.'

'They hugged each other when they met, then went off together.' A smile flitted across his face. 'She was beautiful.'

A cab had taken Colbeck to Hospital Road where he got his first glimpse of what had once been an ordnance depot. Almost forty years earlier, it had been converted into a hospital, though he felt that it had the same solid, utilitarian, slightly forbidding aspect of a prison. It was surrounded by a lawn and protected by iron railings. When he explained why he'd come, Colbeck was handed over to Dr Oliver Nunn, a tall, stooping man with a gleaming bald head and a habit of holding his hands clenched together in front of him. He conducted his visitor along a corridor.

'As you see,' he said, apologetically, 'we have limited facilities here. We can't compete with the hospitals in London.'

'I'm not here to conduct an inspection,' Colbeck told him. 'I'm just grateful that he died in a town that actually possesses a hospital. Many of the victims whose deaths we investigate are killed in isolated places. We've pulled them out of lakes, cut them down from the trees on which they've been hanged or found them burned to a cinder in a disused farm building. You can imagine the condition they've been in.'

'That's not the case here,' said Nunn. 'The body is in surprisingly good condition, so much so that we found it difficult to establish the cause of death.'

'Have you reached a decision yet?'

'Yes and no. Let me show you.'

Pausing at a door, he unlocked it with a key and led the way into an anteroom. Nunn then took him through into a larger room where the body of Bernard Pomeroy lay under a shroud. There was a strong smell of disinfectant. Nunn drew back the shroud to the waist so that Colbeck could see the slim, well-proportioned body of someone who looked as if he were simply asleep. The musculature belonged to a young man who took great care of himself.

'I can't see a mark on him,' said Colbeck.

'That was our initial reaction, Inspector. Then we

noticed this lesion,' said Nunn, pointing to what looked like a tiny scratch on the side of his neck. 'We thought that he might have nicked himself with the razor while shaving.'

'Is that what you still believe?'

'No, we found a tell-tale mark elsewhere.' Lifting up Pomeroy's right arm, he turned it slightly so that Colbeck could see a puncture mark on the wrist. 'That's the clear sign of an injection.'

'Poison,' said Colbeck, grimly.

'The question is: how did it get into his body?'

'Well, it certainly wasn't self-administered. This young man had everything to live for. He had a wonderful career ahead of him.'

'We'll know more when there's been a post-mortem.'

'I'll be interested to know the details.'

Nunn drew the shroud back in place. 'Is there any other way we can help you, Inspector?'

'Where are his effects?'

'They're locked away in my office.'

'I'd like to see them, if I may.'

'You're welcome to do so, Inspector. Apart from his clothing, there was only his wallet. It contained nothing apart from some money and a few membership cards of university societies. Oh,' he recalled, 'there was one other item.'

'What was it?'

'Some sort of identity card. It gave his full name.'

'Can you remember what it was?'

'It's not one I'm likely to forget – Bernard Alexander Zanni Pomeroy.'

'I see what you mean,' said Colbeck. 'It seems that the young man has Italian blood in him.'

CHAPTER FOUR

Leeming had warmed to Arthur Bullen from the moment he'd met him. The railway policeman reminded him of the kind of uniformed constables with whom he'd walked the beat in his younger days – strong, committed, fearless, hard-working and eagle-eyed. Bullen was clearly a man for all weathers and all situations. He now revealed his intelligence.

'I've been thinking, Sergeant,' he said.

'What about?'

'Well, it was that young woman who used to meet him here.'

'Ah,' said Leeming, 'I bet that you're wondering why she wasn't there on the platform to welcome him today.'

'No, it wasn't that.'

'Then what was it?'

'She was so pretty that anyone who'd met her would remember her. She was slim, dark-haired and, well, graceful. There aren't many in these parts who could match her looks, I can tell you that. She and her friend probably caught a cab and went off somewhere for the afternoon. He always came back alone.' Bullen pointed towards the cab rank. 'Do you see what I'm getting at now?'

'Yes, I do. If the two of them *did* hire a cab, the driver would be bound to remember her. More importantly, he'd know where he'd taken them.'

'Yes, he would.'

Leeming chuckled. 'You think like a detective, Bullen.'

'It's common sense, really.'

'And you say you saw them together more than once?'

'It was three or four times, Sergeant.'

'If they took a different cab each time, there might be separate cab drivers who'd remember them. One moment, though,' said Leeming, thoughtfully. 'If an attractive woman picks up a man and takes him off somewhere for a relatively short time, it usually means that she was a—'

'Oh, no,' said Bullen, firmly. 'She was very respectable. I can spot the other kind straight away. We have a couple of them hanging around the station after dark.'

'You should see London at night. It's full of them.'

'This young woman – "lady", I should say – was very different.'

'In what way?'

'She was . . . wholesome.'

Before he could question Bullen further, Leeming saw

a bustling figure coming towards them. He drew Bullen's attention to the approaching stationmaster.

'I hope I haven't got you into trouble,' he said.

'Don't worry about Mr Moult. I can handle him.'

'He looks angry.'

'I'll tell him I was explaining to you how to reach the hospital.'

'That's a good idea.'

'Once I get him out of the way, you can start talking to cab drivers.'

Leeming grinned. 'I can't wait.'

Madeleine Colbeck was always delighted when her friend called at the house. Lydia Quayle was excellent company. She was a striking young woman with all of the social graces, yet she'd somehow remained single. It was a mystery to Madeleine.

'It's a pity you didn't come a few hours ago, Lydia,' she said.

'I didn't dare. Now that you're working on a new commission, you told me that you like to spend the whole morning in your studio.'

'It's true – but I make an allowance for people like you.'

'I don't want to come between you and your latest painting, Madeleine.'

'I'd happily forgive you. I did the same for Constable Hinton when he called.'

Lydia beamed. 'Has Alan been here?'

'Yes, he has, and the first thing he did was to ask after you.'

'Did he bring a message from Robert?'

'Alan insisted on operating as my husband's postman.

41

As you well know, whenever Robert has to disappear out of London, he always warns me where he's going.'

'And where is it this time?'

'Cambridge.'

'But that's not far away,' said Lydia, happily. 'He may be able to come home again at night.'

'That's what I'm hoping, Lydia. There's a suspicious death in Bury St Edmunds, but Robert thinks he'll spend most of his time in Cambridge.'

'It's a beautiful city. You must get him to take you there.'

'Oh, I don't know about that,' said Madeleine, shyly. 'I'd feel out of place.'

'Why?'

'Unlike you, I never had a proper education.'

'You've been largely self-educated and proved just how intelligent you really are. Look at the way you learnt so much about art. That took time and application. You actually sell your paintings now. I may have gone to an expensive private school,' said Lydia, 'but I don't have any skills that could bring in an income.'

'With your inheritance, you don't *need* an income.'

'Perhaps not, but you take my point.'

'You come from a different world, Lydia. I envy you.'

'Well, I envy you far more.'

'Why?'

'You have a loving husband, an adorable daughter and a doting father.'

Madeleine laughed. 'The doting father can be a problem at times.'

'At least you're on good terms with him. I was estranged from my father and there's only one member of the family with whom I keep in touch. It makes me feel very lonely at times,' admitted Lydia. 'You have a vocation. I just trundle along.'

'That's a ridiculous thing to say. If you say anything as silly as that again, I'll report you to Alan Hinton.'

'And are you sure that he asked after me?'

'He *always* asks after you, Lydia.'

Madeleine took hold of her friend's hands and squeezed them affectionately. They were seated side by side on the sofa in the drawing room. Having met under bizarre circumstances, they'd been drawn together. When Lydia's father had been murdered in Derbyshire, Colbeck had been in charge of the case and had – unofficially, but to great effect – involved his wife in the investigation. At the time, Lydia had been shocked, bruised and living with a possessive older woman. Madeleine had not only rescued her from an increasingly awkward relationship, she'd befriended her. Lydia was now an honorary aunt to Helena Rose Colbeck, Madeleine's delightful little daughter. It was a role that she relished.

'Why don't *I* take you to Cambridge,' suggested Lydia. 'I don't mean right now. Robert would hate it if we got under his feet while he's leading a murder investigation. We'll go in the summer and take my favourite niece.'

'I'd be like a fish out of water.'

'Nonsense – you'd love it!'

'That's what Robert said when he took me to Oxford, and I spent the whole time feeling quietly terrified. I didn't *belong*,

Lydia. Having been educated there, Robert was completely at ease. I felt like an outsider.'

'I hadn't realised you were so sensitive about it, Madeleine.'

'It may change in time,' said the other, hopefully. 'It took me over a year to get used to the idea of having servants, but I take it in my stride now. And I'm grateful that I'll be able to give my daughter all the things I was never able to enjoy myself. Anyway,' she added with a wicked smile, 'if you're that keen to take someone to Cambridge, why don't you ask Alan Hinton?'

It took longer than Leeming had anticipated. The first three cab drivers to whom he spoke had never picked up a young man with a female companion of startling beauty. When he questioned a fourth man, he made slight progress. Though he hadn't been hired by the couple himself, the driver had heard about them.

'Bert 'Ollis is the man you wants, sir,' he said. 'They hired Bert twice in a row. He told me she was so pretty he didn't want to charge them a fare.'

'Where might I find Hollis?' asked Leeming.

'Bert'll be along sooner or later.'

In fact, the other driver turned up almost immediately and joined the rank. After explaining who he was, Leeming asked him about the couple in whom he was interested. Hollis was a tubby old man with a large nose dominating his rubicund face. He showed his remaining three teeth in an open-mouthed grin.

'Oh, yes, I remembers them, Sergeant,' he confirmed. 'That's to say, I remember *'er* much more than *'im*. She were like somethin' out of a fairy tale. You know – proper little princess, she were.'

'Do you remember where you took them?'

'Oh, ar – I'll never forget.'

'Can you take me there now?'

'If you likes, sir.' His eyes sparkled. 'Who exactly is she?'

'That's what I'm trying to find out.'

Leeming climbed into the cab and closed the doors after him. Hollis cracked his whip and the horse set off at a steady trot. Bury St Edmunds was an old Saxon town half a mile away from the station. Having been there before, Colbeck had told him that it was a place of great antiquity set in the most glorious part of West Suffolk, but the sergeant was not there to admire the remains of its abbey or the many fine churches and houses that had survived the centuries. His only interest was in the place to which Bernard Pomeroy and his female friend had been taken.

Bury St Edmunds was a modest market town of over fifteen thousand people and, when they got there, it seemed to Leeming as if every one of them had come out into the streets with the express purpose of slowing down his cab. They had to pick their way carefully through the hordes before pulling up outside The Fox, the former house of a merchant, now converted into an inn. Timber-framed, rendered and with a tiled roof, it had a welcoming air. The sound of many voices drifted out. As Leeming descended from the cab, Hollis pointed at the building.

'This where is I took 'em, sir,' he said. 'Am I to wait?'

'Yes,' said Leeming. 'I'll need a lift back to the station.'

'They serves a good pint in 'ere.'

'I'm not allowed to drink on duty.'

'Maybe not, sir, but *I* am.'

Ignoring the hint, Leeming went quickly into The Fox.

Arriving back at the railway station, Colbeck fully expected to find the sergeant there. He looked everywhere but without success. Since he clearly had to wait, he went to the ticket hall and noted the times of the trains to Cambridge. When he came out onto the platform, Colbeck was accosted by a railway policeman.

'Were you looking for Sergeant Leeming, sir?' asked Bullen.

'Yes, I was.'

'I thought so. I saw the two of you arrive together. I'm told that you've come from Scotland Yard.'

'That's right. I'm Inspector Colbeck and you've obviously met the sergeant.'

'He took a statement from me.'

'Have you any idea where he might be?'

'Yes, Inspector, he's gone into town.'

Colbeck was taken aback. 'Whatever for?' he asked. 'He was supposed to wait for me here.'

'*I* must take the blame, sir,' said Bullen. 'When I told him what I knew, he waited at the rank and talked to the cab drivers. What happened was this, you see.'

Bullen gave him a clear and concise report of seeing Pomeroy visit the town on previous occasions. Like the sergeant, Colbeck was impressed with the man's vigilance, and he was intrigued to hear that Pomeroy had met a young woman on each occasion. What interested him most was the fact that the man who'd first bent over the body of the fallen undergraduate had slipped away unseen when the railway policeman had taken over.

'Did he actually touch the body?' Colbeck asked.

'Oh, yes, he turned him over to take a good look at him.'

'What did he do then?'

'He felt his pulse.'

Colbeck remembered the puncture mark he'd seen on wrist of the corpse at the hospital. He believed that he might now have an idea how it got there.

'Thank you,' he said. 'You've been very helpful.'

'I know how to keep my eyes peeled, Inspector.'

'I wish that all railway policemen were as observant as you are.'

'I love my job,' said Bullen, stoutly, 'and I do it as well as I can. Now, if you'll excuse me, I'll get back on duty.'

He turned on his heel and strode off. Watching him go, Colbeck decided that Bullen was a cut above the average railway policeman. He was not only more alert and able, he was entirely free from the resentment that Colbeck and Leeming routinely met from such people who felt that they'd been elbowed out of an investigation by Scotland Yard detectives who would go on to claim all the glory. Bullen was a realist. Accepting the situation without complaint, he was grateful to have made a small but possibly significant contribution to the case. He was now back on patrol once more, marching along the platform as if he were in his element.

Colbeck's surveillance of the railway policeman came to an abrupt halt. Out of the corner of his eye, he caught sight of Leeming, who had just entered the station. He turned to look at the jaunty figure coming towards him and saw the grin on the sergeant's face. His spirits lifted. Good news was on its way.

When her father arrived unexpectedly at the house, Madeleine was surprised. Caleb Andrews had been due to join them for dinner, not for afternoon tea.

'What are you doing here?' she asked.

'Well, that's a poor welcome,' he said, clicking his tongue. 'Can't a loving grandfather see his granddaughter whenever he wants?'

'Yes, of course he can.' They embraced each other warmly. 'Helena will be delighted. She's in the nursery.'

'Wait a moment, Maddy,' he said as she turned away. 'Before I go up to see her, let me tell you why I came.' He heaved a sigh. 'I'm very sorry but I won't be able to join you and Robert for dinner this evening.'

'Why not? Are you unwell?'

'No, it's nothing like that.'

'Then what's the problem?'

'I'd forgotten a promise I made to go to a retirement party for Gilbert Parry. We started work on the railway at more or less the same time and we've been friends ever since. He'd be very hurt if I let him down. Well,' he added, 'you know Gil. He's easily upset. Besides, he joined in the celebrations when *I* retired.'

'In that case, you owe it to him to go along.'

'You don't mind?'

'No,' said Madeleine. 'I don't control your social life and you love being with other railwaymen. It's just a shame, that's all.'

'You and Robert can have dinner together.'

'I'm not sure that we can. He's been sent out of London again, and there's no guarantee that he'll be coming home this evening.'

'Where has he gone?'

'Bury St Edmunds.'

'The Great Eastern Railway!' said Andrews, scornfully. 'They only came into existence last year and they're already a laughing stock. What sort of mess is Robert being asked to clear up this time?'

'I don't know the full details, Father. I just have this feeling that Robert won't be joining me for dinner this evening.'

'Oh, I see . . .'

'On the other hand, I may be pleasantly surprised.'

'If it's the GER, it's likely to be serious – a train crash at the very least.'

No,' said Madeleine, 'it's nothing like that. A young man got out of a train and dropped dead on the platform. He's something to do with the Boat Race. That's all I can tell you.'

'Well, it sounds very fishy to me.'

'There's no point in speculating about it.' She sighed. 'I'm so sorry you can't come this evening but, while you're here, you simply must go up and see Helena.'

'I will. But first, I must apologise again.'

She shrugged. 'These things happen.'

'It's this old memory of mine, Maddy. It keeps playing tricks on me.'

'You ought to write any commitments in your diary.'

'I always do,' he said, 'but the trouble is that I forget to look at it. That's why I keep making mistakes like this.' He kissed her on the cheek. 'I'll make it up to you.'

'There's no need, Father.'

'Yes, there is.'

He walked across the hall to the staircase. Madeleine watched him climbing slowly up the steps. As his only child, she was very close to her father and could read his mind with some degree of accuracy. Ordinarily, she'd have been faintly annoyed that he'd cancelled a visit to the house at such short notice. This time, however, she was seething with quiet anger, wondering why he'd lied to her so blatantly.

CHAPTER FIVE

Almost immediately after Leeming had arrived, the Cambridge train steamed into the station. The detectives chose an empty compartment so that they could converse at will. Colbeck talked about his visit to the hospital where he'd learnt that Pomeroy had probably been poisoned, though he stressed that that had yet to be confirmed. He also told Leeming about the information he'd got from Bullen that the man who'd first attended to Pomeroy had felt his pulse.

'That's when he could've injected the poison,' said Leeming.

'It may well be that he wanted to make doubly sure that he'd killed him. My guess is that he'd already administered a fatal dose into Pomeroy's neck. It caused him to stagger along the platform and collapse.'

'I thought the man who knelt beside him was a Good Samaritan.'

'Good Samaritans don't carry a stock of what appears to be quick-acting poison, Victor. I fancy that he might have been an assassin.'

'Bullen told me that he had a dark complexion – like a Spaniard or an Italian.'

'He was almost certainly Italian.'

'How do you know, sir?'

'It's because he was sent to kill someone with a strong connection to Italy.'

'Pomeroy is a British name.'

'That's because his father was British,' said Colbeck. 'But I'm certain he was the child of a mixed marriage. His full name was Bernard Alexander Zanni Pomeroy. And when I saw him in the hospital morgue earlier, I thought there was a hint of the foreigner about him.'

'Oh dear!' groaned Leeming. 'I hope this doesn't mean that we'll have to go all the way to Italy to catch the killer. I thought this would be a simple assignment and that we'd go home in time for a meal with our families.'

'This case has suddenly become more interesting.'

'I prefer those that are very dull and easily solved.'

'Yet you had a grin on your face when you got back to the station.'

'That was because I'd learnt about the young woman Pomeroy went to see. I was excited in the way I always am when I make what could be an important discovery,' said Leeming. 'I'm not so happy about it now.'

'Why not?'

'The excitement has worn off, sir.'

'There's still the thrill of the chase to enjoy.'

'Not if it takes us abroad. I hate sailing even more than travelling by train.'

'The murder was committed here,' said Colbeck, 'and may well be solved in the area. Anyway, since we've been here, I feel that we've already made slight progress. Now then, tell me what *you* found out.'

'At Bullen's suggestion, I talked to the cab drivers.'

'He's a good man, perhaps too good for the job he's doing.'

'I spoke to someone who took Pomeroy and his friend into the town twice in a row. So I got him to drive me to The Fox, the place where they went each time. It's an inn in Eastgate Street.'

'What did you learn?'

'Well,' said Leeming, 'the landlord had some difficulty remembering them at first. The place is always very busy. During a normal day, dozens of different people come in and out. It was only when I gave him a description of the woman that I jogged his memory. Because she was so beautiful, she stood out a little. He told me that she came in two or three times with a young man. I think it was Pomeroy.'

'What did they do?'

'They sat in a private room with other people who'd come for a meal. According to the landlord, they were so absorbed in each other that they never looked up. They just talked and talked. When they'd finished, Pomeroy paid the bill and they slipped away.'

'Did they strike the landlord as being . . . very close?'

'I think the landlord only had eyes for the woman, sir.'

'Bullen told you how attractive she was,' recalled Colbeck.

'Yes, but he also noticed Pomeroy. He did what any good railway policeman would do. Bullen didn't allow himself to be distracted.'

'He also seems to be a good judge of character.'

'That comes with time, sir.'

'It's not always the case, Victor. I've met policemen, with thirty years of experience in uniform, who still miss the signs of an obvious villain. They've never developed an instinct.'

They fell silent for a couple of minutes. Colbeck glanced out at the scenery they were rattling past while the sergeant grappled with a problem that was worrying him. Leeming eventually spoke up.

'I still feel that there's something strange about her,' he said.

'Oh – in what way?'

'If she was that eager to see Pomeroy, why didn't she go to Cambridge instead of bringing him all the way to Bury St Edmunds?'

'I wish I knew.'

'It's as if she didn't want to be seen with him at the university.'

'Oh, I think it may be the other way around,' said Colbeck. 'Pomeroy may have deliberately chosen the venue to get away from Cambridge.'

'It may just be that the woman *lives* in Bury St Edmunds.'

'That's a possibility.'

'She was the one who told the cab driver to take them to The Fox. That proves she knows her way about the town.'

'I agree.'

'It looks as if *she* was making the decisions.'

'But why was Pomeroy bothering to go there *today*?' asked Colbeck, pensively. 'On previous occasions, we know, he went in the early afternoon and was met at the station each time by this mysterious woman.'

'She wasn't there today, Inspector.'

'*He* shouldn't have been there either. Pomeroy should have been out on the river with the rest of the Cambridge crew. If they're anything like their Oxford counterparts, they'll be working fanatically every day to improve their speed and coordination on the river.'

'Maybe the assassin wanted to lure him out into the open.'

'The best way to do that, I suggest, would have been an appeal from this woman. When he got to the railway station in Cambridge, it may well have been that somebody was waiting for him. If Pomeroy was desperate to get to Bury St Edmunds, he'd probably have been off guard. However,' said Colbeck, abandoning his theory, 'we shouldn't let our imaginations run riot. There may be no link whatsoever between the supposed killer – if that indeed is what he was – and this woman. Let's not rely on guesswork. It has a curious habit of leading us astray.'

'That's true. We've made that mistake in the past.'

'Suffice it to say that we must keep an open mind.'

'Where do we go now, sir?'

'Our next port of call is Pomeroy's college.'

'I was afraid you'd say that.'

'This is no time to feel socially insecure, Victor.'

'Universities are like foreign countries to me. They speak a different language there. I'll be completely lost.'

'You'll do what you always do,' said Colbeck, reassuringly, 'and adapt accordingly. Bernard Pomeroy intrigues me. We must find out absolutely everything we can about this young man and acquaint the Master with what we've already discovered.'

The three of them were still rocked by what they'd learnt about the fate of their cox. Malcolm Henfrey-Ling was convinced that Pomeroy's death was connected in some way to the Oxford University Boat Club, James Webb was wondering who could replace Pomeroy in the boat and Nicholas Thorpe was mourning his best friend. Henfrey-Ling had an impressive physique, but he seemed somehow to have shrunk in size. Webb, by contrast, appeared to have grown in stature. Seated bolt upright, he was throbbing with fury. Until he'd taken over as the coach, the Cambridge boat had been under the supervision of a waterman from Henley, a rough and ready individual who understood the mysteries of the Thames and taught them how to adapt to the tidal flow on the day of the Boat Race. Webb was a very different coach. During his days as an undergraduate, he'd rowed in the Cambridge boat and tasted the indescribable pleasure of actually winning the Race. He was now a Fellow of Pembroke College where he was known for his excellent lectures on Mathematics, his forthright manner and his ability to drink beer at a faster rate than anyone else.

Webb and Henfrey-Ling were already looking to the future, wondering how they could survive such a serious setback. Thorpe, meanwhile, was still locked in the past, recalling happier days in the company of Bernard Pomeroy whom he'd admired for many years.

'He was going to take me to Italy this summer,' he said, sadly. 'I was looking forward to seeing his mother and his sister again.'

'His father died years ago, didn't he?' recalled Webb.

'Yes, he did, James.'

'Does he have family in this country?'

'Most of them live in Ireland,' said Thorpe. 'I know that his eldest sister is married to an Irishman and two of his uncles have estates there. Bernard and I visited one of them. He was very proud of the fact that his nephew was at Cambridge.'

'*I'd* have been proud of him if he'd won the Boat Race for us,' growled Webb.

'There would have been eight other people in the boat,' said Henfrey-Ling, sharply. 'You always seem to forget *our* contribution.'

'I'm sorry.'

'Having actually helped to win a Boat Race, you should know that it's a shared experience and that everyone in the boat deserves equal merit.'

'I agree – though I was only repeating your earlier comment. Losing Bernard has scuppered any chances we had of winning the Race this year, you said. That's not an attitude a president should take,' argued Webb. 'It's too defeatist. When we get together tomorrow, we're going to have a dispirited crew. It's your job to rally them and put some steel in their spines. If you're resigned to losing the Race, there's no earthly point in taking part in it.'

'You're right,' conceded the other. 'I must be more positive.'

'That article in *The Times* didn't help,' said Thorpe. 'It hailed Bernard as a hero. At the time, I was glad for his sake, but a lot of other people must have read the article, including some in Oxford.'

Webb sniggered. 'It's nice to know their undergraduates *can* actually read.'

'That's where these detectives should concentrate their search,' said Henfrey-Ling. 'There's villainy afoot and it's dark blue in colour.'

'I disagree. We can hate the Oxford crew all we like but, in our hearts, we know that they'd never do anything so . . . unsportsmanlike.' Henfrey-Ling laughed harshly. 'It's true, Malcolm. They want to beat us fair and square.'

'You have your opinion, I have mine.'

'Well, my opinion is this. We don't let Bernard's death rob us of something we've worked so hard to achieve. We use it as a source of inspiration.'

'He would have wanted us to do exactly that,' said Thorpe.

'We must concentrate all our efforts on rowing,' said Webb, clenching a fist, 'and make sure we don't get distracted by any criminal investigation. Not that we can put much faith in that,' he added, sourly. 'Detectives are only ordinary policemen in plain clothes. Think how limited our local constabulary is. It's full of half-educated brutes whose only real skill lies in breaking up a drunken brawl.'

'Inspector Colbeck won't be like that,' said Thorpe, hopefully.

'Yes, he will, Nick. They're all the same. Policemen belong to a lower order of creation. Nobody's ever taught them to think straight or to speak properly.'

When they went to the college to see him, Sir Harold Nellington reacted in the way that most people did at a first meeting with the two detectives. He was impressed by Colbeck's appearance and manner but troubled by Leeming's rough-hewn look and by his patent discomfort in a seat of learning. However, the Master's respect for both men increased when he heard how much they'd found out in Bury St Edmunds.

'That's remarkable,' he said. 'You've already made an impact.'

'There's a very long way to go, Sir Harold,' warned Colbeck, 'and we may well have to revise some of the assumptions we've made. What we *have* found, however, is the reason Bernard Pomeroy made a series of visits to Bury St Edmunds.'

'Is that where you'll hunt the killer?'

'Our work will start here in the university. Initially, we'll need to talk to Pomeroy's friends, tutors and fellow members of the Boat Club.'

'That can be arranged.'

'Good.'

'Have you been to Cambridge before?'

'I came here on two occasions as an undergraduate,' said Colbeck, 'with the rest of the Oxford cricket team. Fenner's is a delightful ground on which to play.'

'It used to be a cherry orchard.' The Master's gaze flicked to Leeming. 'Are you a cricketer, Sergeant?'

'I never had the chance to play the game,' replied the other, 'but, when I first joined the police, I was in a tug-of-war team. It's not as easy as it looks. There's a real art to it.'

'I'll take your word for it. My sporting days are long over, alas. Archaeology brought me untold pleasure, but it also ruined my knees and gave my poor old spine a permanent curve.'

'I've admired the exhibits you donated to the British Museum,' said Colbeck.

'Thank you, Inspector. I may soon become one of them. I certainly feel like a relic most of the time. It's as well I'm due for retirement next year. Now, then,' continued the Master, picking up a sheet of paper. 'While I was waiting for you to arrive, I did some homework so that you'd have some basic information with which to work.' He held the paper up. 'This will give you a clear idea of Bernard Pomeroy's career here at Corpus. It's been astonishing.'

'So I gather,' said Colbeck, taking it from him. 'Thank you, Sir Harold. This will be very useful.'

'His next of kin is his widowed mother, who lives in Tuscany. I've sent word to her, but it may take time to reach her in Italy.'

'What about the rest of the family?'

'As far as I know, very few of them live in this country.'

'We'll need someone to identify the body.'

'If we can't find a family member, we'll have to call on Nicholas Thorpe. He was Pomeroy's closest friend. They were at school together. Thorpe is at King's. He's also in the Cambridge boat, by the way.'

'That's helpful. He'll know just how good a cox Pomeroy really was.'

'What are my instructions with regard to the newspapers?'

'Tell them as little as possible. If they become too intrusive – and they will do, I'm sure – refer them to me. I'm used to fending off the gentlemen of the press.' He glanced down at the information he'd been given. 'I must say that his curriculum vitae is quite astonishing. In addition to everything else, it seems, Pomeroy was a brilliant actor.'

'Yes, it's true. Last year, his Hamlet won great acclaim. Next term, he was due to play the title role in a production of Marlowe's *Doctor Faustus*.'

'It's a challenging role.'

'Pomeroy loved a challenge, Inspector,' said the Master.

'So it seems.' Colbeck rose to his feet and Leeming followed suit. 'I have a favour to ask, Sir Harold.'

'What is it?'

'I'd like to see Pomeroy's room.'

'Yes, of course,' said the other. 'I had it locked so it's exactly how he left it. You can get the key from the porter.'

'I'd value a chat with him,' said Colbeck. 'In my experience, porters are usually the most well-informed people in the colleges where they work.'

The Master chuckled. 'It's true. Whenever I have problem relating to the day-to-day operation of the college, the first place I always go for advice is the lodge. Porters are unacknowledged philosophers and worth their weight in gold.'

After speculating endlessly on how and why their cox had died on a railway platform, the three of them turned to the problem of replacing him in the boat. James Webb was categorical.

'It *has* to be Andrew Kinglake.'

'No,' said Henfrey-Ling. 'He let us down badly last year.'

'He's learnt from his mistakes.'

'My vote goes to Colin Smyly.'

'He's too young and inexperienced, Malcolm.'

'You said that about Bernard when he first came on the scene.'

'That's true,' remembered Thorpe, 'and Bernard turned out to be better than Andrew and Colin rolled together.'

'But we don't *have* Bernard any more,' said Webb, irritably. 'We have to find a substitute and the obvious one is Andrew.'

'Colin,' insisted Henfrey-Ling.

'Andrew knows how to control the boat in difficult conditions.'

'Colin can do that equally well. Also, he has a knack of making the right decisions under pressure. That's what let Andrew down last year.'

'He's improved markedly.'

'He's worked hard, I grant you that. But he doesn't inspire confidence.'

'I'm bound to agree with Malcolm,' said Thorpe.

'Keep out of this, Nick,' snapped Webb.

'He's entitled to voice an opinion,' said Henfrey-Ling, 'and it's one shared by other members of the crew. Colin may be young, but he has a natural flair that Andrew lacks. Besides, at the end of the day, the choice lies with the president.'

'That doesn't mean you can ignore sensible advice from the coach.'

'I don't ignore it, James. I've listened to you for the last half an hour.'

'Malcolm is right,' said Thorpe. 'You've had a fair hearing.'

'Doesn't my judgement count for *anything*?' demanded Webb. 'I want us to enter the Boat Race with the best possible chance of success. That means we have to choose someone who's actually been through it all before and knows what to expect. Colin has flair but is untried. Do we want to rely on a novice?'

'My decision is final,' said Henfrey-Ling.

'Listen to reason, man.'

The argument continued and became increasingly heated. President and coach were not simply involved in a tussle over the choice of an individual. It was a battle for power. Henfrey-Ling wouldn't yield an inch and Webb refused to concede defeat. There seemed to be no way to reach an agreement. It was then that Thorpe intervened.

'For what it's worth,' he said, quietly, 'I know whom Bernard would have chosen. He always favoured Colin Smyly.'

Webb wilted and Henfrey-Ling heaved a sigh of relief. The dispute had been resolved. Bernard Pomeroy had spoken from beyond the grave.

CHAPTER SIX

When they got to the lodge, they saw that the porter was talking to a young man. While they waited until he was free to deal with them, Colbeck appraised him. Jack Stott was a short, wiry man in his forties with a mobile face capable of arranging itself instantly into any shape to suit the occasion. Listening to his young companion, he wore a respectful smile and nodded obediently. What Leeming noticed about the porter was how smart he was in his frock coat and top hat. It made the sergeant feel even more dishevelled and grotesquely out of place.

As soon as the young man left, Stott turned to the detectives, his features reassembling themselves into a mask of solemnity and concern. Having met them when they'd first visited the college, he knew exactly who they were.

'Can I help you, Inspector?' he asked.

'We'd like you to tell us about Bernard Pomeroy,' said Colbeck.

'There's a lot to tell, sir.'

'Just pick out the salient aspects of his character for us.'

'First and foremost,' explained Stott, 'he was a proper gentleman. He knew what we brought to this college and always had time for us. By "we" I mean me and the other porters, the scouts who look after the rooms, the cooks who feed them and the servants who put the plates in front of them. He treated us as real human beings whereas a lot of the others . . . take us for granted.'

'I believe he was a gifted sportsman.'

'That's right. If he wasn't rowing, he'd be out running or playing cricket, or doing something else better than the rest of them. Whatever he did, he was a winner at it. Boundless energy, that's what he has – or *used* to have, anyway. Mr Pomeroy is a terrible loss to us.'

'Was he popular?' asked Leeming.

'Everyone loved him, sir,' replied Stott, then his face clouded. 'Well, there were one or two people who didn't, I suppose, but even they would admit that he had something special about him.'

'Could you give us some names?'

'I wouldn't like to speak out of turn, sir.'

'Whatever you tell us,' said Colbeck, 'will be strictly confidential. We're not going to report you or anything like that. Every scrap of information is vital to us. If you liked Mr Pomeroy as much as you appear to have done, you'll want us to find out the truth about why he died so suddenly.'

'Oh, I do, Inspector.'

'Then we need your help.'

'Of course,' said Stott, guardedly. 'This is only my opinion, mark you, so don't place too much importance on it.'

'Give us a name,' said Leeming.

'Dr Springett.'

'Who is he?'

'He's Professor of Divinity and one of the Fellows here.'

'According to information supplied by the Master,' noted Colbeck, 'Mr Pomeroy was reading Classics. Why should he and Dr Springett have anything at all to do with each other?'

'They both had an interest in the same person,' said Stott. 'Don't ask me why. I mean, he's been dead a very long time. I know that he was here in Corpus many years ago, but things were very different in those days, weren't they?'

'Who are you talking about?' asked Leeming.

'Christopher Marlowe.'

'The Master mentioned that name.'

'Yes, Sergeant,' said Colbeck, 'and he did so with pride in his voice. Marlowe is second only to Shakespeare as a poet and playwright. They are the shining stars of Elizabethan drama. It's a signal honour for this college to be associated with him.' He turned to the porter. 'What manner of man is Dr Springett?'

'He's a true scholar, by all accounts,' said Stott, 'and, of course, as you'd expect, he's very religious.'

'Did he and Mr Pomeroy have differing opinions about Marlowe?'

'Yes, they did.'

'How do you know?' asked Leeming.

'I heard them having a fierce argument outside the lodge one day.'

'Was there bad blood between them?'

Stott's face was impassive. 'You'll find out.'

Everything about Terence Springett came in generous proportions. The corpulent body was matched by a large, pale, spherical head without even a wisp of hair on it. His eyes were huge, inquisitive and dark green. He had a booming voice to match his frame and a sense of importance more substantial than either. When the urgent summons came from the Master, he refused to be hurried. Sir Harold Nellington could wait. Springett had never forgiven the archaeologist for leapfrogging over him to take control of Corpus Christi. The Professor of Divinity had felt insulted when told that two candidates would be interviewed for the post of Master. Nevertheless, he'd been supremely confident of success. Ten years younger than his rival, he was both physically and intellectually more vigorous. His defeat had devastated Springett and turned Sir Harold from an agreeable colleague into a mortal enemy.

When he finally sailed into the Master's study, however, there was no sign of hostility or resentment. Springett was a study in benevolence, beaming happily and oozing goodwill.

'Thank heaven you've come, Terence,' said the Master. 'Do please take a seat. I have something of great import to tell you.'

'Really?' said the other, lowering himself carefully into an armchair. 'Have you decided to retire earlier than you'd intended?'

'I wish that I'd already done so.'

'Why?'

'It's because I like peace and tranquillity. All I hoped to do in my declining years was to enjoy serenity in the groves of academe.'

'What Horace actually said,' corrected Springett, pedantically, 'was *Atque inter silvas academi quaerere verum.* I'd translate that as seeking *truth* in the groves of academe, not searching for serenity.'

'Bernard Pomeroy is dead.'

His visitor goggled. 'I beg your pardon.'

'Earlier today, Pomeroy collapsed and died on a platform at the railway station in Bury St Edmunds.'

'Dear God!'

'There's worse to come, Terence.'

'I don't believe it.'

'He did not die by natural means,' confided the Master. 'There's a strong possibility – and I ask you to keep this to yourself for the time being – that he was murdered.'

'Why?' cried the other. 'Pomeroy had such a promising life ahead of him. Who could possibly wish to do him harm – let alone contrive his death?'

'That's a question I'm leaving to an expert, Terence. The moment I heard what had happened in Bury St Edmunds, I sent a telegram to Scotland Yard.'

Springett was puzzled. 'I don't follow.'

'If there has to be a criminal investigation, I wanted the best possible person in charge of it. That's why I asked for Inspector Colbeck.'

'The name is unfamiliar to me.'

'You'll soon become accustomed to it,' said the Master, 'and, like me, you'll be impressed by the man himself.'

'He's *here*? You've actually met him?'

'Not long ago, he was sitting in the chair you now occupy.'

'Are you telling me,' asked Springett, grappling with the notion, 'that the college will be at the heart of a murder inquiry?'

'I'm afraid that I am, Terence.'

'It's going to be damned inconvenient for us.'

'That's a cross we'll all have to bear. I shudder to think how awkward it's going to be when the word gets out. London newspapers will despatch their reporters at once. We'll be under siege. However,' the Master went on, 'we must hold our nerve. Inspector Colbeck promised to deal with the press if they badgered us too much and, even at this early stage, his investigation has already borne fruit.'

'In what way, may I ask?'

'I can't go into details, I'm afraid.'

Springett ran a palm over his bald pate. 'This is truly desperate news.'

'I know that you and Pomeroy had your differences . . .'

'They're irrelevant now, and I feel both embarrassed and ashamed to think of what was only a petty disagreement.

Bernard Pomeroy was a genius, there's no doubting that. His talents set him way above his contemporaries.'

'And they were not merely scholastic,' the Master reminded him. 'Apart from anything else, he was about to help us win the Boat Race.'

'That's an event that weighs very little with me,' said Springett. 'He'll live in *my* memory for other reasons. I'm both shocked and saddened. It means that we'll never see what would have been his towering performance in Marlowe's *Doctor Faustus*.' Eyes moistening, he shook his head. 'I was *so* looking forward to that.'

Having been given the key by Stott, the detectives walked across Old Court, went through a stone arch and climbed oak stairs hollowed out by generations of feet. When they reached Pomeroy's room, Colbeck unlocked the door. Leeming followed him into the study, a small, nondescript, cheerless room with a low ceiling. What greeted them were signs of a rushed departure. Papers had been scattered uncaringly on the floor and a chair had been overturned. A small wooden desk stood near the window to catch the best of the light. After taking in the whole room, Colbeck went across to the desk. On the shelf above it were some books. Leeming peered at their titles with a wrinkled brow.

'What language are these in, sir?' he asked.

'Greek and Latin.'

'Then they're no use to me.'

'This one might be more to your taste, Victor,' said Colbeck, picking up a volume that lay open on the desk. 'It's an edition of Marlowe's play, *Doctor Faustus*. To be more exact, the last speech in the play is on display. After he's delivered it, Faustus is taken off to Hell by Lucifer and Mephistopheles.'

'Had Pomeroy been learning the part?'

'From what we've been told about him, I'd imagine that he already knew it by heart.' He indicated the shelf. 'What do you notice about the other books?'

'They're in a language I don't understand, sir.'

'What else?'

'They're neatly stacked on the shelf.'

'Exactly,' said Colbeck. 'He clearly valued his texts enough to look after them. People who really love books – and Pomeroy was one of them – never leave them open like this one. It damages the spine.'

'You're right, Inspector.'

'This is the work of someone else, an intruder who wished to leave a grim message. Faustus is going off to Hell – and so is the actor who was due to play the part next term.'

'It all sounds rather creepy to me.'

Closing the edition of Marlowe's play with care, Colbeck put it on the shelf with the other books. He then glanced around the room.

'Let's see what else we can find . . .'

The blackboard had been set up near the station entrance in Bury St Edmunds so that anybody arriving there could not fail to see it. Arthur Bullen used the piece of chalk to write a message in capital letters. The stationmaster was unimpressed.

'You're wasting your time,' he said, curling his lip.

'It may jog someone's memory, Mr Moult.'

'Most people will be in too much of a rush even to read it. Besides, how do you know that anyone who was on the particular train this morning will be going back to Cambridge today?'

'It's because I recognised some of them. They work here and go back home on the same train every evening.'

'After a hard day's work, they won't want to look at what you've scribbled.'

'You never know.'

'In any case,' said Moult, jabbing a finger at the blackboard, 'you're asking for anyone who travelled in the same compartment as the young man who collapsed to report to you. Most of the passengers will have forgotten all about him.'

'The two women who screamed won't forget,' said the railway policeman, 'and neither would the people who almost tripped over him. I think this appeal is well worth a try.'

The stationmaster laughed. 'You're a bigger fool than I thought, Bullen.'

'We'll see . . .'

The search of his room revealed a lot about Bernard Pomeroy's character. While he took care of his books and of the essays he'd written, he was more slapdash about everything else. Instead of being hung on pegs, his clothing was left in a series of untidy piles. It was, however, of uniformly good quality, and Leeming observed that, if he'd paid so much for his wardrobe, he ought to treat it with more respect. Tucked away under the bed was a large rosewood box, polished to a high sheen. When he hauled it out from its hiding place, Colbeck found that it was locked.

'We'll never know what's in there,' said Leeming. 'He must have had the key with him.'

'No, he didn't,' Colbeck told him. 'I saw his effects and there were no keys among them. That means the one we need is hidden in the room somewhere – most probably in the desk.'

'If that's the case, sir, you'll find it easily.'

Leeming's confidence was justified. Knowing that Colbeck's grandfather had been a cabinetmaker, he was aware of how, as a boy, the inspector had watched him design and build elaborate desks for members of the aristocracy. Leeming had seen his companion locate and open secret compartments time and again in such furniture. Because it was relatively small and simple in construction, the present desk was far less of a challenge. It took Colbeck only seconds to find the spring that he sought. When he pressed it, a little door opened to reveal the missing key. He used it to open the box beneath the bed.

'You should have been a burglar,' joked Leeming.

'My conscience would never allow it.'

'What exactly is in there?'

'Correspondence, for the most part,' said Colbeck, taking out a sheaf of letters and glancing at them in turn. 'This is interesting,' he went on, pausing to read the first paragraph of one missive. 'It's from that friend of his, Nicholas Thorpe.'

'Is it of any importance?'

'Not really . . .'

'Can I read it?'

'There's no point, Victor,' said the inspector, sliding the letter back into the sheaf and taking out another. 'It's just a note about the boat crew. This, on the other hand,' he added, studying second letter, 'really *is* worth showing to you. It's a remarkable thing to find in the possession of an undergraduate.'

'Why?'

'I feel like a gold prospector who has just stumbled on a huge nugget.'

'What does it say?'

'See for yourself.'

Colbeck handed the letter to him and watched the expression on Leeming's face change from one of interest to one of complete bewilderment. The sergeant turned to him in despair.

'I can't understand a word of it, sir. Is it in Latin or Greek?'

'It's neither – what you're holding is written in faultless Italian.'

'Do you speak the language?'

'Not really – I have a smattering, that's all.'

'Then how do you know it's faultless?'

'I've seen the name of the person who wrote that letter and I happen to know that he's fluent in Italian.'

'Who is it?' asked Leeming, staring at the signature. 'I can't make it out. It looks like a squiggle to me.'

'That's because you haven't seen it before, Victor.'

'Have you?'

'Yes, he was kind enough to write to the commissioner, who showed it to me. It was a letter to congratulate us on the work that the Metropolitan Police Force did in protecting him and his colleagues.'

'Who do you mean, sir?'

'Our Prime Minister,' replied Colbeck. 'Now why should Lord Palmerston take the trouble to write to someone like Bernard Pomeroy?'

There were few things that Stanley Moult enjoyed more than the feeling of being proved right. He'd warned Bullen that chalking up a message on the blackboard would be a pointless exercise. As he looked across at the railway policeman on the opposite platform, he smirked. Nobody had even stopped to read the appeal for help. Moult had watched with satisfaction as travellers swept past the blackboard as if it was not even there. It was exactly as the stationmaster had predicted. Bullen should have taken his advice.

When a train steamed alongside the platform on which Moult was standing, he had to break off to make sure that everyone who wished to get off did so safely. He also kept a beady eye on the porters to make sure that they did their job properly. The stationmaster then sent the train off on the next stage of its journey. Once it was clear of the station, Moult was able to look at the platform opposite again. Expecting to see Bullen standing there in isolation, he was disappointed.

The railway policeman was having an earnest conversation with an elderly couple. When he saw the woman point towards the blackboard, Moult felt as if he'd just been punched hard in the stomach.

CHAPTER SEVEN

Nicholas Thorpe was in despair. In front of the president and coach of the Cambridge crew, he'd managed to keep his feelings largely under control. There'd been important news to pass on to them. As a result, they'd had to make adjustments to their thinking about the Boat Race. Thorpe had been buoyed up by the others. Now that he was back in his room at King's College, however, there was nobody to offer sympathy and support. He was utterly alone. The sheer hopelessness of his position made him burst into tears, dab at his eyes with a handkerchief, then twist it so tightly around his fingers that it caused him real pain. A lot more suffering awaited him, physically and mentally. Life without Bernard Pomeroy would be a protracted ordeal.

He didn't even hear the first knock on his door and the

second barely reached his ears. The third was altogether more firm and decisive. It couldn't be ignored.

'Go away!' he shouted.

'Is that you, Mr Thorpe?' asked a polite voice.

'I don't wish to speak to *anybody*.'

'In my case, I hope that you'll make an exception. I'm Inspector Colbeck from Scotland Yard, and I'm investigating the suspicious death of your friend, Bernard Pomeroy.' There was a long silence. 'Did you hear me, sir?'

'Yes, yes,' said Thorpe. 'Please give me a moment, Inspector.'

Dragging himself to a mirror, he did his best to wipe away the last of the tears and to smarten himself up. After taking a deep breath, he straightened his shoulders and walked to the door. When he unlocked and opened it, he regarded his visitor with frank amazement.

'Are *you* Inspector Colbeck?' he asked.

'Is that a cause for such surprise?'

'No, no, not at all . . . it's just that you're not what I was anticipating. One of my friends spoke very harshly about the police. He regards them as buffoons.'

Colbeck was amused. 'I've been called worse. If your friend knew that I graduated from Oxford with a degree in Jurisprudence,' he said, 'he might think more kindly of us.' He became serious. 'First of all, let me offer you my deepest sympathy. I know that you've lost your dearest friend.'

'Bernard was like a brother to me, Inspector.'

'Did he have any real brothers?'

'No, there were three sisters, that's all.'

'Where might I find them?'

'One lives in Italy with her mother and another married a cousin in Ireland.'

'What about the third?'

Thorpe pursed his lips. 'She died many years ago,' he said. 'His father is also dead. I can give you the addresses of Bernard's mother and of the sister in Ireland.'

'Are there no relatives in this country whom I could contact?'

'I'm not sure that there are, Inspector. The Pomeroys are scattered far and wide. Why do you ask?'

'It's imperative that someone confirms the identity of the deceased. I'm calling him Bernard Pomeroy because of some items found in his possession, but we can't be certain it's him until a relative or close friend views the body.'

Thorpe shuddered. 'Are you asking *me*?'

'Can you suggest anyone better?'

'Well, no . . . I suppose not. I just wonder if . . .'

'He is at peace,' said Colbeck. 'I saw the body myself and there is nothing unsightly about it. In that sense, you will not be shocked, though the very fact of his death is likely to disturb you, especially when it's presented so starkly.' Thorpe lowered his head. 'If you feel unable to face the task, there must be another friend who could take on the office.'

'No, no, Inspector, it's my duty.'

'Then let's be on our way.'

'Before we do that,' said Thorpe, 'I'd like to send word to the president of the University Boat Club. He ought to be made aware of the fact that you're here.'

'Have no qualms on that score, sir,' said Colbeck, easily. 'My colleague, Sergeant Leeming, is probably talking to Mr Henfrey-Ling at this very moment. He'll tell your president that the investigation is fully under way.'

Jack Stott had not only told him who the president of the University Boat Club was, he gave clear instructions about how to find him. After thanking the porter, Leeming had set off towards Trinity Hall. When he reached the college, he found an equally obliging porter who conducted him all the way to Henfrey-Ling's room. Leeming was now sitting uncomfortably in a well-worn armchair between the president and the coach. From the glances they shot him, he could see that they were less than impressed by his appearance and his proletarian vowels.

'It's yet to be confirmed that Mr Pomeroy *was* murdered,' he emphasised, 'but it is a possibility. That being the case, can you think of any person with a strong enough reason to kill him?'

'I can think of *nine* such people,' said Henfrey-Ling. 'They'll be the Oxford crew during the Boat Race.'

'Don't be absurd,' scolded Webb.

'The more I think about it, the more certain I become.'

'Ignore him, Sergeant. It's a ridiculous suggestion.'

'They're determined to *win*, James – by fair means or foul.'

'Then why are *you* still alive?' demanded the other. 'If I was coaching the Oxford boat and was desperate to weaken my rivals, I'd make the president of the Cambridge boat my target, not the cox. Bernard Pomeroy can be replaced. Nobody in this university can take over from you, Malcolm.'

'That's a fair point,' agreed Leeming. 'You're the leader, Mr Henfrey-Lang.'

'Ling,' corrected the president. 'Henfrey-*Ling*.'

'I'm sorry, sir, but your friend is right. If they really wanted to cause havoc in your crew, Oxford would surely attack its most important member.'

'That's you, Malcolm,' said Webb.

'It was Bernard,' insisted Henfrey-Ling. 'He was our secret weapon. Then some fool of a reporter wrote that article about him in *The Times* and our secret weapon was no longer secret. He was made to sound as if he could win the Race on his own. It put the wind up Oxford, so they decided to eliminate him.'

Leeming was unconvinced. 'I don't believe that,' he said. 'Intelligent young gentlemen such as you would never dream of going to such lengths.'

'*We* might not. They certainly would.'

'How do you know that?'

'Oxford has much lower standards,' said Henfrey-Ling, dismissively.

'On that,' Webb interjected, 'I must agree.'

'Don't say so in front of the inspector,' advised Leeming. 'He went to Oxford and is by far the cleverest person in the Metropolitan Police Force.'

'And who does *he* think is behind Bernard's death?'

'We must consider all possible options. That's what he believes.'

'There *are* no other options,' complained Henfrey-Ling.

'Yes, there are,' said Webb. 'You're just too blinkered to see them.'

'Don't talk such rot,' retorted the president.

'Forget about Oxford. I'm coming round to the view that the culprit might well be here in Cambridge.' Henfrey-Ling snorted. 'Think about it, Malcolm. We all know how popular Bernard was, but there are people who resented him deeply.'

'Such as?'

'Well, let's start with Andrew Kinglake.'

'Who is he?' asked Leeming.

'He was our cox in last year's boat,' explained Webb, 'and he was brushed aside when Bernard Pomeroy came on the scene. That really hurt him. Kinglake was livid. Thanks to Bernard, he'd been summarily discarded.'

'That's not quite what happened,' said Henfrey-Ling.

'I'm not accusing Andrew, I'm just pointing out that he has a strong motive. And he's not the only one. Most of us loved Bernard, but there were those with a good reason to hate him.'

'One name has been whispered in *our* ears,' volunteered Leeming.

'Oh? What was it, Sergeant?'

'Professor Springett.'

'Ah, yes, I'd forgotten him,' admitted Webb.

'So had I,' said Henfrey-Ling, thoughtfully. 'He and Bernard had a terrible row. They did everything but fight a duel. From what I remember, it was Bernard's fault. He took an almost Machiavellian delight in goading Springett. I laughed when I first heard about it but . . . well, the way that he ridiculed the professor was cruel.'

When he sat down for a meal, Terence Springett never stinted himself. He would eat heartily and make light of his relentless increase of weight. With alcohol, by contrast, he was abstemious, rarely imbibing anything stronger than cordial during the day. Before he retired to the comfort of his bachelor bed, however, he allowed himself to have a glass of his favourite malt whisky. Until that moment, his routine had never changed, but then, he'd never had such an irresistible urge for celebration.

After leaving the Master's study, he waddled happily back to his lodging and went straight to the kitchen. When he'd poured himself an exceptionally large glass of whisky, he lowered himself into his chair with a smile of contentment. A sense of triumph coursed through his whole body.

'Goodbye, Pomeroy,' he said, raising his glass in a mock tribute. 'Give my regards to the Devil!'

On the cab ride to Cambridge railway station, Nicholas Thorpe lapsed into a brooding silence that Colbeck had no wish to interrupt. Having read the letter that Thorpe had sent to Pomeroy, he knew that the relationship between them was deep and loving and stretched back over ten years. His companion was utterly disabled by grief. The kindest thing that Colbeck could do was to spare him any questioning. On the train to Bury St Edmunds, private conversation would in any case have been difficult because they were in a compartment with four other passengers. The inspector had to content himself with trying to link together the various pieces of evidence they'd so far uncovered into some sort of coherent whole.

Alighting at their destination, the two of them were about to head for the exit when they were spotted by the stationmaster. Moult came hurrying across to them.

'You're Inspector Colbeck, I believe,' he said, accosting him.

'That's right,' confirmed the other.

'I saw you talking to Bullen earlier on, then you later caught a train with Sergeant Leeming.'

'You're very observant.'

'It's a vital asset in my job, sir. I'm Stanley Moult, by the way.'

'How do you do, Mr Moult?'

'I'm very well, thank you. I just wanted you to know that I've made my own small contribution to the investigation.'

'Really?'

'I chalked up a message on a blackboard and set it up on the other platform. It was an appeal for anyone who travelled in the same compartment as the young man who died here earlier this morning to come forward.'

'That was very enterprising of you, Mr Moult. Has there been any response to the appeal?'

'Not as yet, sir, but I live in hope.'

He broke off as he realised that he had to attend to his duties and be ready to despatch the train. When the stationmaster excused himself, Colbeck took his young companion out of the station and along to the cab rank. They were soon travelling towards the hospital. Colbeck tried to warn Thorpe what to expect but got no reaction from him at all. The undergraduate remained in an impenetrable silence. Since he expected it to be a short visit, Colbeck asked the cab driver to wait for them outside the hospital. He then ushered Thorpe gently inside the building and went in search of Dr Nunn. Having found him, he explained the situation.

'A confirmation of identity would be welcome,' said Nunn. 'It's very kind of you to come, Mr Thorpe. You're performing a valuable service. Since no family member is available, you are an ideal replacement.'

Unable to rise to a reply, Thorpe managed a nod.

'Would you like me to come in with you?' asked Colbeck. 'Dr Nunn will be there as well, of course, but I'll be happy to offer you my support, if you feel it might be of use.'

'Yes, please,' murmured Thorpe.

'Then let's get it over with, shall we?' said Nunn.

He led the way to the morgue. Colbeck could see that Thorpe was in distress, fearful of what he was about to see and uncertain about his ability to cope with the challenge. They eventually stopped outside a door. The others gave him time to build up enough courage to view the corpse of his closest friend. Minutes went past. When he felt ready, Thorpe gave another nod and was taken into the room where the body was kept. At first, he couldn't bear even to look at the shrouded figure. It took a huge effort to shift his gaze to it.

'Tell me when you feel ready,' said Nunn, quietly.

Thorpe took a deep breath and bit his lip. His face was white, his cheek muscles tense and his brow glistening with perspiration. Both of his hands were bunched. After a second intake of air, he ran his tongue over dry lips, then gave another nod. Nunn drew back the shroud to expose the head of Bernard Pomeroy. One glance was all that was needed. Recognition was instant.

'That's him,' gasped Thorpe.

Then he dropped to the floor.

Leeming was pleased that their manner towards him had changed when they realised they'd underestimated him. When he'd first arrived, Henfrey-Ling and Webb had been distinctly unimpressed. As the interview continued, however, and as he plied them with searching questions, they had to revise their opinion. He took notes of everything they said and that made them measure their words with care. Professor Springett had already been identified as a possible suspect. In the course of the interview, two more names emerged. The first was that of Andrew Kinglake, the dispossessed cox. It was Henfrey-Ling who suggested another potential suspect.

'What about Simon Reddish?' he said.

'Who?' asked Webb.

'He's that arrogant little excrescence from St John's who thinks that he's God's gift to the acting profession. You must have seen him in that production of *Hamlet* a few months ago.'

'I rarely go to the theatre.'

'Then you missed an absolute treat. Bernard took the title role and was head and shoulders above everyone else on stage. It was a brilliant performance. Everyone adored it – except for Simon Reddish.'

'Wait a moment,' said Webb, 'I think I *have* heard that name before. Bernard mentioned it, didn't he?'

'He never stopped mentioning it to me,' said Henfrey-Ling. 'Reddish had the gall to think that *he* should have played Hamlet, and he told Bernard he'd have been much better in the role.'

'What a cheek!'

'Bernard came close to punching him. What really upset Reddish was that he was cast as Horatio, the closest of Hamlet's friends, a much smaller role. He had to stand there during the curtain call every night and listen to Bernard getting an ovation.'

'That must have upset him.'

'There was worse to come.'

'Was there?' asked Leeming.

'Yes, Sergeant,' replied Henfrey-Ling. 'Reddish wanted to get his revenge by landing the role of Doctor Faustus in the next production. Apparently, he boasted to everyone that he was tailor-made for it.'

'What happened?'

'Bernard was chosen over him yet again.'

'That must have annoyed him,' said Webb.

'It enraged him, James,' said his friend. 'Salt was well and truly rubbed into the wound. Reddish was incensed. He's desperate to have an illustrious career on the stage and accused Bernard of deliberately standing in his way.'

'Bernard was obviously a better actor. Reddish should have accepted that.'

'He's far too temperamental to accept anything. During the rehearsals for *Hamlet*, he was always having tantrums. He had to be warned about his childish behaviour and told to exercise more control.'

'Who will get to play Doctor Faustus now?' asked Leeming.

'Simon Reddish – no question about it.'

'Add his name to your list, Sergeant,' advised Webb. 'He sounds far more likely to have arranged Bernard's death than either Professor Springett or Andrew Kinglake.'

After writing the new name in his notebook, Leeming questioned the two of them about the range of Pomeroy's interests and wondered how the man could possibly have shone in so many different spheres of activity. Each of them talked fondly of him and said that he had flights of genius that set him apart from his peers. In the case of everyone else, having such a wide variety of interests would mean an inability to devote enough time to each one. Pomeroy could never be accused of doing that. His management of time had been astonishing.

'One last question,' said Leeming, pencil poised, 'everyone speaks of Pomeroy as having been a very handsome man. Was that true?'

'Very true,' said Henfrey-Ling.

'Then he must have attracted a lot of female interest. Was there anyone in particular who got close to him?'

'No, Sergeant. The one thing that Bernard *didn't* have time for was any dalliance with the fair sex. He considered that a distraction.'

'Did you ever *see* him with a woman?'

'Yes,' said Henfrey-Ling. 'Once was with his mother and the second time was with his eldest sister. Both of them came to England last year. Bernard had the right priorities. He'd never have achieved all the things that he did if he had a woman friend in tow. She'd have been a handicap. Don't you agree, James?'

'I do,' said Webb. 'I just can't see Bernard with a member of the opposite sex. They simply held no interest for him. Save yourself the trouble of searching for one, Sergeant. You won't find a woman in this investigation.'

Leeming thought about the anonymous friend in Bury St Edmunds.

Though he quickly recovered consciousness, Nicholas Thorpe was clearly not well. His body was trembling and his voice hoarse. He kept apologising for what had happened, but Colbeck assured him that there was no need for forgiveness. With the help of Dr Nunn, he eased Thorpe into the anteroom and made him sit down. Nunn disappeared briefly, then returned with a glass of water. Thorpe sipped it gratefully. When he felt better, he asked to leave, clearly disturbed by his proximity to the corpse of his friend. After thanking the doctor, Colbeck took Thorpe out of the hospital where the clear air seemed to revive the latter slightly. In the course of the ride back to the railway station, he finally began to talk about his friendship with Bernard Pomeroy.

As soon as they stepped onto the platform, Colbeck saw the blackboard with the public appeal written on it. He went across to study it. Arthur Bullen drifted over to him at once. When Colbeck introduced the railway policeman to his companion, Thorpe took an immediate interest in the man, pressing him for details of what had actually happened to his late friend. Having given his reply, Bullen turned to the inspector and indicated the blackboard.

'What do you think of this?' he asked.

'It shows commendable initiative,' replied Colbeck. 'The stationmaster deserves a pat on the back.'

'Why?'

'He told me that it was his idea.'

'That's not true at all,' said Bullen, firmly. 'When I set the blackboard up, Mr Moult was quite scornful. He said that nobody would even look at it.'

'Then it was quite wrong for him to claim credit.'

'It's no more than I expected. As it happens, he was proved wrong. I saw a number of passengers glancing at it. Two of them read the message carefully.'

'Had they been on that particular train?' asked Colbeck.

'Yes, Inspector – they were an elderly couple who sat directly opposite the young man we now know as Mr Pomeroy. They told me that he'd been taken ill during the journey.'

'That doesn't sound like Bernard,' argued Thorpe. 'He'd hardly had a day's illness in his entire life.'

'Let's hear exactly what this couple said,' suggested Colbeck.

Referring to his notebook, Bullen told them exactly what he'd learnt. Thorpe asked for more detail and, when none was forthcoming, pressed the policeman to give his report a second time. Bullen was happy to comply with the request. The moment he'd finished, a train arrived at their platform. Colbeck thanked Bullen for his help, then shepherded Thorpe aboard. On the return journey to Cambridge, both of them sat in silence, wondering about the significance of what they'd just learnt.

Victor Leeming, meanwhile, was following instructions. He'd been told to search for accommodation in case it was needed. Colbeck had promised him that they'd return to London that evening but that it might be necessary from then on to operate from a base in Cambridge itself. The sergeant therefore had the pleasant task of choosing a suitable pub where they could have a room each and enjoy at least a measure of quiet and privacy. At the fourth attempt, he believed that he'd found the ideal place.

Leeming had been told to meet the inspector at the railway station. Since there might be a lengthy wait involved, he decided to walk there so that he could see a little more of the city. Apart from anything else, it would give him the kind of leisurely exercise he rarely enjoyed. The rain had long eased off and the pavements were no longer treacherously wet.

When the station finally came within sight, he realised that he'd never had the chance to look at it properly. Even in the fading light, it was spectacular. Built of pale East Anglian brick, it consisted of an open colonnade of fifteen arches. There was a lateral arch at each end so that cabs and carriages could enter a long *port cochère* that was lit by large glass lanterns. The facade was topped by a striking Italianate cornice. Leeming was entranced. He had finally found something about the railway system that he liked.

In the event, he had less time to wait than he'd feared. The third train to come into the station from the branch line to Bury St Edmunds was carrying Colbeck and Thorpe. The latter was too preoccupied for conversation. After being introduced to Leeming, he excused himself and went on his way.

'It's been a trying experience for him,' explained Colbeck. 'When he saw his friend's body, he passed out.'

'He's not the first to have done that, sir.'

'How did you get on?'

'Oh, I think I've found the ideal place to stay.'

'I wasn't asking about accommodation. Did you learn anything useful from the president and the coach?'

'Yes, I did. I've got some new names.'

'That will please the superintendent when I report to him in the morning. He demands a sign of progress,' said Colbeck, 'and I fancy that we've made enough to appease him. Let's go home, Victor.'

'In the note I sent to her, I did warn Estelle that I might not be back this evening so it will be a nice surprise for her. What about you, sir? Did you tell your wife not to expect you back?'

'Yes, I did. Madeleine will also have a pleasant surprise. She'll have resigned herself to the idea of dining alone with her father.'

*   *   *

Caleb Andrews put on the jacket of his best suit and wished that it didn't have a faint whiff of mothballs. After doing up the buttons, he looked at himself in the mirror and was pleased with what he saw. He went downstairs, took his hat from its peg and set it carefully on his head. Then he left the house and walked briskly through the streets for almost a quarter of an hour. When he reached his destination, he needed a moment to compose himself. After clearing his throat, he rang the bell.

He heard footsteps hurrying down the passageway, then the door opened.

'Good evening!' said Andrews, raising his hat in greeting.

CHAPTER EIGHT

Instead of returning to his own college, Nicholas Thorpe headed straight for Trinity Hall. James Webb was no longer there, but Malcolm Henfrey-Ling was still in his room. The president gave his visitor a cordial welcome.

'I'm glad you've come, Nick,' he said. 'I've got so much to tell you.'

'I've brought news of my own. Inspector Colbeck came to see me.'

'Oh? What sort of person is he?'

'For a start, he's highly intelligent.'

'I wish I could say the same about his assistant, Sergeant Leeming. He questioned me and James earlier.' He indicated a chair. 'Let's get ourselves comfortable, then you can tell me exactly what happened.'

After they'd sat down, Thorpe told him about the visit to Bury St Edmunds to identify the body of Bernard Pomeroy. He admitted that he'd been badly shaken by the experience but said nothing about having fainted. What had lifted his spirits slightly was the meeting with the railway policeman.

'He'd chalked up a notice,' he explained, 'asking for anyone who'd been in the same compartment as Bernard that morning to come forward. An elderly couple did just that, Malcolm. They said that Bernard had become increasingly unwell on the journey. They offered their help, but he spurned them. When he got out of the train, he could barely stand up.'

'I've never known him be off colour, let alone feel ill.'

'Well, he was certainly ill on that train.'

'What else did this old couple say?'

'They claim that he was so anxious to get on the train in the first place that he elbowed everyone else rudely out of the way. Does that sound like Bernard to you?'

'It certainly doesn't.'

'He was always so polite and considerate.'

'What did Inspector Colbeck make of it all?'

'Like me,' said Thorpe, 'he wondered what had caused such a dramatic change in Bernard. It's made him even more determined to find out the truth. I trust him to keep his word.'

'Was he entirely open with you?'

'Yes, he was.'

'Did you find him trustworthy?'

Thorpe was surprised. 'Why do you ask that?'

'It's because of the way that Sergeant Leeming behaved,' said the other. 'He's much more akin to James's sneering description of policemen as uncouth and educationally limited. Actually,' he went on, 'he's cleverer than he looks. The sergeant grilled us expertly.'

'So what's your reservation about him?'

'He's holding something back, Nick.'

'How do you know?'

'It was his manner.'

'I didn't get that impression with the inspector. Besides, what can they know that we don't? They never even met Bernard. They have no idea what sort of person he was and what kind of life he led. They're still gathering basic information.'

'I wonder . . .'

'What did James think of the sergeant?'

'Much the same as I do – that he was a trifle coarse but obviously knew his job. Yet while he asked us a lot of questions, he never gave answers to some of the ones we put to him.'

'Did anything come out of the interview?'

'Yes,' said Henfrey-Ling, 'we gave him the names of two possible suspects.'

'I thought you believed that the Oxford crew was behind it all?'

'To some extent, I still do.'

'Who else did you name?'

'Andrew Kinglake for a start, because he hated the way that Bernard had replaced him in the boat, then virtually ignored him.'

Thorpe was dubious. 'Andrew is not that vengeful, surely.'

'I think he could be. He'd be working on the assumption that, with our cox out of the way, *he'd* take his place. Ironically, of course, that won't happen.'

'You mentioned *two* new suspects.'

'Yes, and the second one is a much more likely candidate.'

'Who is it?'

'Simon Reddish.'

Thorpe needed a few moments to think about the suggestion. When he eventually made up his mind, however, there was a ring of certainty in his voice.

'You're right, Malcolm. It *has* to be him.'

Having braced herself to dine alone that evening, Madeleine Colbeck was just about to sit down at the table when she heard a key being inserted into the front door lock. There was only one person it could be. Leaping up, she ran into the hall and flung herself into Colbeck's arms with such force that she knocked his top hat off. They shared a laugh.

'What a treat!' she cried.

'I wanted to surprise you.'

'You've certainly done that, Robert, and you've also rescued me from spending a very lonely evening here.'

'How can you be lonely when you have company?'

'Father is not here.'

'Why not?'

'I'll tell you in a moment. Let me help you off with your coat and take you into the dining room. I was just on the point of starting when you came in.'

'My timing was always perfect,' he boasted.

After allowing her to take off his coat, he hung it up with his hat, then followed her into the dining room. No place had been set for him, but it took Madeleine only seconds to organise one. Colbeck sat down beside her.

'What sort of day have you had?' he asked.

'My news can wait, Robert. I want to hear how *you* got on.'

'I think you could say that we've made a promising start.'

'Does that mean you're confident of solving the crime fairly soon?'

'I'm afraid not,' he said, pulling a face. 'It means that we have a complex puzzle on our hands. Victor and I will be kept at full stretch. In fact, I'm going to ask the superintendent for additional help.'

'Alan Hinton, perhaps?'

'There's nobody better, in my opinion.'

'Tell me what you've found so far.'

Colbeck gave her a brief summary of the case, knowing that he could trust her completely to keep the details to herself. After listening intently, Madeleine made some perceptive comments and asked a few probing questions. Her main interest was in the character and motives of the woman whom Pomeroy had met in Bury St Edmunds.

'How did she send for him?' she asked.

'We don't know that she did.'

'It's a logical explanation, Robert.'

'I've learnt to be wary of those.'

'This woman is going to be an important figure in the investigation. I sense it.'

'Is she an innocent party or a conspirator?'

'I'm dying for you to find out.'

'So am I, Madeleine,' he said. 'But why are you on your own this evening? You haven't told me why your father isn't here.'

'Which explanation do you want?'

'I don't follow.'

'Well, there's Father's explanation or there's mine. His story is that he forgot he was due to attend a leaving party for a friend of his called Gilbert Parry. I happen to know that it's a lie.'

'Are you certain of that?'

'There's no room for doubt.'

'Your father is always so honest with you.'

'Not this time, Robert,' she said. 'My memory is much better than his, and I remember clearly that he went to a party in honour of Mr Parry some three years ago. In other words, he's going somewhere completely different this evening and doesn't want me to know where it is. Why not? I'm his daughter. He tells me everything.'

'Did you challenge him?'

'No, I didn't. I'm beginning to wish that I had now.'

'This behaviour is very untypical.'

'That's that worries me, Robert. He told me an outrageous lie. I can't ever remember him doing that before.' Madeleine spread her arms in frustration. 'What is he hiding from me?'

Malcolm Henfrey-Ling had taken a bottle of port from a cupboard and poured two generous glasses. The alcohol seemed to fortify them for a long discussion about what had made Pomeroy dash off to Bury St Edmunds in defiance of a prior commitment on the river. When they were halfway through their second glass, the talk turned back to possible suspects. Henfrey-Ling still had vestigial fears that the Oxford University Boat Club was somehow implicated, but Thorpe dismissed the notion. On reflection, he was also unwilling to include the name of Andrew Kinglake among the suspects.

'He'd never do such a thing,' he insisted. 'He may have been jealous of Bernard, but he accepted that he could never compete with him as a cox. Above all else, Andrew wants us to win the Boat Race and knew that our chances of doing so would have been enhanced by Bernard's presence.'

'Andrew *does* have a nasty streak,' said the other.

'Which of us doesn't?'

'That's a rather cynical comment for you, Nick.'

'Admit it. We all have our faults.'

'Let's move on,' said Henfrey-Ling. 'We'll forget Andrew for the time being and concentrate on the others. You favour Reddish but I'm warming to the notion that Professor Springett deserves close examination.'

'I disagree, Malcolm. He and Bernard may have been engaged in a sort of scholarly vendetta but that's as far as it went.'

'I'm not certain about that.'

'What do you mean?'

'I remember the pleasure that Bernard got from attacking him in print. He really hated Springett. Also, they had a ferocious argument outside the lodge at Corpus. Bernard

101

told me that he'd won that as well. He reduced Springett to tears, apparently.'

'That was months ago.'

'It would seem like yesterday to Springett. What could be more humiliating for a professor than to be savaged in a magazine by an undergraduate? It's not the kind of thing that you can shrug off.'

'No,' said Thorpe, 'I suppose not. But I still feel that Simon Reddish has to be the prime suspect. There was animosity between Bernard and him from the moment they first met. Reddish couldn't bear to be overshadowed. His father is the famous actor, Oliver Reddish, and he's groomed his son to have similar success on the boards. I daresay that Reddish senior was shocked when Simon was rejected for the part of Hamlet and given only a supporting role.'

'Yes, you can't really catch the eye as Horatio.'

'Simon was even more infuriated at the last auditions. He'd set his heart on playing the title role in *Doctor Faustus* – and what happened?'

'Bernard was given preference yet again.'

'I rest my case.'

'Would he really want to get Bernard out of his way for good?'

'He would,' said Thorpe. 'I've met Simon Reddish a number of times and found him thoroughly objectionable. As an actor, he's very talented, but he's also a monstrous egotist. Reddish is burning with ambition. He'll do absolutely anything to get what he wants. That's why *he'll* be playing Doctor Faustus next term instead of Bernard.'

* * *

Simon Reddish was a tall, slender, handsome young man with dark eyes and wavy black hair that fell to his shoulders. As he stood in front of the mirror in his room, he declaimed a speech that he'd memorised weeks ago.

'*Ah, Faustus,*
Now thou hast but one bare hour to live
And then thou must be damned perpetually . . .'

Edward Tallis was habitually early when he went to Scotland Yard, so he was taken aback to see that someone had actually got there before him. Colbeck was waiting patiently in the superintendent's office. After an exchange of greetings, the inspector handed him a written report. Taking a seat behind his desk, Tallis read it with care and asked for clarification on a few points. He then set the report aside.

'You and Leeming have been busy,' he said.

'It's a case that demands swift action. There's a possibility that the killer might try to leave the country.'

'There's no mention of that in the report.'

'It's a feeling I have, Superintendent.'

'Ah, we're at the mercy of one of your feelings again, are we?' said Tallis, wearily. 'I need hardly remind you that they are less than reliable.'

'They always point me in the right direction, sir.'

'I beg to differ. However, let me ask you this. There's a glaring omission in your report. You hardly mention Pomeroy's family.'

'I've yet to find out very much about them,' admitted Colbeck. 'When I took Thorpe to Bury St Edmunds, I'd hoped to glean a lot of information from him about Pomeroy's background, but he was in too great a state of shock to help me. What I can tell you is that his father – Pomeroy's, that is, not Thorpe's – was a senior diplomat based in Italy. He met and married an Italian woman of noble birth in what was then the Grand Duchy of Tuscany. It was a love match, I fancy.'

'Why do you say that?'

'Mr Pomeroy converted to Roman Catholicism.'

'Ah, I see. Is that all you can tell me?'

'More or less – oh, except for the fact that the father died over three years ago.'

'What was the cause of death?'

'I intend to find out, sir.'

'Don't you have a "feeling" about it?'

'Not as yet,' said Colbeck, responding to Tallis's sarcasm with a smile. 'Before I go back to Cambridge, I have two requests to make.'

'If they concern money, restrain yourself. Our budget is not unlimited.'

'I need additional help, sir.'

'And neither is our manpower,' warned Tallis.

'Sergeant Leeming and I will operate in Cambridge for the most part, but it would be helpful to have someone I can despatch to places like Oxford and Bury St Edmunds.'

'Oxford? According to your report, it's unlikely to have the slightest connection with Pomeroy's death.'

'I'm still reluctant to rule it out as a possibility. All I wish to do is what you insisted – when I first joined the Detective Department – that I should *always* do.'

'And what was that?'

'Explore every avenue,' replied Colbeck. 'It was sound advice. When I first heard about this case, Oxford immediately popped into my mind. I've become more sceptical now, but it can't be ignored. I need to send him there.'

'Who?'

'Detective Constable Hinton.'

'He's already been assigned to another investigation.'

'Is it a *murder* investigation, sir?'

'No – it's a case of petty larceny.'

'Then you're wasting his talents, sir,' said Colbeck. 'Have you forgotten how well Hinton discharged his duties in Gloucestershire? He's an able detective and deserves something worthy of him.'

Tallis sniffed. 'I'll see what can be arranged.'

'My other request may involve the commissioner because he has direct contact with the government. I need to speak to the Prime Minister.'

Tallis blenched. 'Why on earth should you wish to do that?'

'It's relevant to our investigation, sir,' said Colbeck. 'I discovered a letter in Pomeroy's room that had been written to him by Lord Palmerston.'

'What did it say?'

'I'm not at all sure, Superintendent. It was written in Italian.'

'Is this some kind of joke?' demanded Tallis, angrily.

'I give you my word that it isn't, sir. In case you're unaware of it, the Prime Minister was once at Cambridge himself and stood unsuccessfully for the university seat at the age of twenty-one. Since he is also fluent in Italian,' Colbeck went on, 'it's not surprising that he wrote in that language to someone who was born and brought up in Tuscany. What I need to establish is what was in that letter, in case it has a bearing on the case. Is that unreasonable?'

'No,' conceded the other. 'I'll speak to the commissioner.' He stroked his moustache. 'On second thoughts,' he added, 'we may not need to trouble Lord Palmerston at all. Your report claims that this young fellow, Thorpe, is the closest friend of the deceased. Surely, *he* would have been told what was in the letter.'

'Not necessarily.'

'Pomeroy would have been bound to confide in Thorpe.'

'I suspect that it's one of the things that he kept from him. Thorpe, I fear, is learning that he was not as close to his friend as he'd imagined. He hadn't been told about the visits to Bury St Edmunds, for instance, and would be shocked if he realised that a woman was involved.' Colbeck moved to the door. 'Thank you for being so cooperative, Superintendent. I'll wait until Constable Hinton arrives in my office, then send him straight off to Oxford with his instructions.'

'Oh, I see.'

'If an appointment with the Prime Minister *can* be arranged as a matter of urgency, you can summon me back from Cambridge by telegraph.' He opened the door. 'Goodbye, Superintendent.'

Before Tallis could even open his mouth, Colbeck had left.

Because he was not looking forward to meeting the rest of the crew, Nicholas Thorpe arranged to arrive with Malcolm

Henfrey-Ling. On the way to the river, the president made an effort to sound optimistic about their hopes for the Boat Race, but all that Thorpe could think about was the debilitating effect that the loss of Pomeroy would have. They arrived to find the other oarsmen already there. Thorpe noticed the smug look on the face of Andrew Kinglake, a slight, bony individual with a pair of unusually large ears. Everyone else was subdued and withdrawn. They looked as if they were about to attend a funeral rather than test themselves on the river.

Henfrey-Ling had his speech ready. Delivered in a strong, confident voice, it was designed to dispel the communal gloom and fill them with determination. What they must do, he argued, was not simply to uphold the honour of Cambridge but compete for all they were worth in memory of their dear friend, Bernard Pomeroy.

'He may not be there in person,' he told them, 'but Bernard will be in the boat in spirit. He'll spur us on to achieve a resounding victory.'

It was a rousing speech and Thorpe joined in the applause. Henfrey-Ling had transformed the mood and injected a sense of purpose into the crew. While Kinglake was waiting to be installed as the substitute cox, Colin Smyly, his youthful rival, was standing at the edge of the group as if not really belonging to it.

'As from today,' announced the president, 'we will have a new cox in the boat. After a long discussion with our coach, I'm pleased to announce that I have selected . . .' He used a hand to indicate. 'Colin Smyly.'

Smyly was so surprised that he refused to believe it at first. When some of the others congratulated him, he realised that it was true and almost blushed. Kinglake, on the other hand, was scowling. Having been certain of taking over, he was shocked to the core at being overlooked, especially as he knew that James Webb would speak up for him. Yet for some reason, it seemed, he had not. The coach had betrayed him. After glaring at him, Kinglake gathered up his things and left without a word to anyone. Thorpe could see that he was pulsating with anger. Something about the way that Kinglake stalked off suggested that there would be repercussions in due course.

There were days when Madeleine Colbeck had a creative urge that sent her straight to her studio to begin work on her latest painting. Unfortunately, there were also times when her muse seemed to have deserted her, depriving her of energy and purpose. She was enduring the latter experience now, unable to raise any enthusiasm and using the excuse of bad light to stay away from the studio. When Lydia Quayle called in unexpectedly, Madeleine was delighted at the interruption.

'It's so lovely to see you again, Lydia,' she said.

'I didn't mean to interrupt. I just wanted to drop off that wonderful book I told you about.'

'Well, while you're here, I insist on your staying for refreshment. Ordinarily, I'd be slaving at my easel but that leaden sky casts dark shadows on the canvas.'

Taking her visitor into the drawing room, she sat opposite and studied the title page of the book she'd just been handed.

It was a copy of *North and South* by Mrs Gaskell.

'It's a wonderful novel,' said Lydia. 'Margaret Hale, the heroine, moves from the rural south to the industrial north and sees how harsh life is up there. I loved it.'

'Thank you very much. Before I took up painting, I used to read a lot. Robert loaned me books from his library.'

'It's *your* library as well now, Madeleine.'

'Yes, I suppose it is.'

'Speaking of Robert, have you heard anything from him?'

'I heard a great deal,' said the other, laughing. 'He came back for the night and is now on his way to Cambridge again. But I can give you tidings that are certain to please you.'

'Oh?'

'Alan Hinton is now involved in the investigation.'

'That's wonderful!' exclaimed Lydia. 'It's a real feather in his cap.'

'He'll be working *for* Robert but not actually with him. While Robert is in Cambridge, Alan has been sent off to Oxford.'

'Why?'

'I don't know the full details,' said Madeleine, anxious to talk about something else altogether. 'Alan will no doubt tell you everything in the fullness of time. Now that you're here, I'd like to ask you for some advice.'

'Is there a problem?'

Madeleine nodded. 'Yes, there is.'

'What is it?'

'It's something that happened yesterday with my father.'

'Then I'm hardly the best person to comment on it,' said Lydia, rolling her eyes. 'You love your father. I was afraid of mine. I can't ever remember enjoying his company. I was happiest when I was estranged from him.' She grimaced. 'Isn't that a terrible thing to say?'

'You did what you felt was best for you, Lydia. I admire that.'

'Tell me about Mr Andrews.'

Madeleine sat back and explained what had happened the previous day. She also told her friend how surprised her husband had been when he'd heard about his father-in-law's behaviour.

'Robert agreed with me. It's both unusual and worrying.'

'I think you're taking it too seriously.'

Madeleine was taken aback. 'What do you mean?'

'We all tell white lies from time to time.'

'This wasn't a white lie. It was a great big black one.'

'How do you know?'

'I could see that he felt guilty.'

'Your father is entitled to a life of his own,' said Lydia, reasonably. 'He's never entirely comfortable in a house like this with servants in attendance. Among his friends from the railway, he's completely at ease.'

'But that isn't where he was going last night.'

'Wherever it was, it was his business. I'm sorry that you're deeply troubled by what happened, Madeleine, but you mustn't expect to control his movements. You're his daughter – not his mother or his wife.'

Madeleine was nettled. 'There's no need to be so critical of me.'

'You asked me for my advice and I'm giving it.'

'I'd hoped for some support from you.'

'You can always count on that.'

'Then why are you claiming that *I'm* at fault?'

'That's not what I'm doing,' said Lydia. 'When I was here yesterday, I told you how much I envied you. A large part of that envy concerned your loving relationship with your father. It's something I was denied.'

'I was denied it to some extent as well,' said Madeleine, sadly. 'The truth is that I rarely saw my father when I was young because he worked long hours. It was only when my mother died that he and I got closer.'

'I've spoken out of turn,' apologised Lydia. 'Please forgive me.'

'You don't know the full facts.'

'I accept that.'

'My mother was desperately ill for a long time. When she knew that she was about to die, she grabbed me by the wrist and made me promise something to her.'

'What was it?'

'I had to look after my father.'

'That's as it should be, Madeleine.'

'You don't understand. It wasn't just a case of cooking his meals, washing his clothes and running the house. She knew my father's weaknesses. My mother didn't need to put it into words,' said Madeleine, 'but I understood what she was asking. I had to protect my father from being taken advantage of by . . . someone unsuitable.'

Elsie Gurr was a bespectacled little woman in her sixties with an air of determination about her that made her seem bigger than she really was. Wearing a smart coat and a feathered hat, she went into the churchyard and moved among the headstones until she came to one that held great significance for her. When she reached the grave she sought, she stood in front of it and read the chiselled details of her past life. She then closed her eyes and offered up a silent prayer. When she'd finished, she kissed the fingers of a gloved hand so that she could transfer the kiss to the headstone.

CHAPTER NINE

On the cab ride to the railway station, Colbeck told Leeming about the way he'd managed to get two important concessions from the superintendent. Knowing how obdurate Tallis could be, the sergeant was impressed.

'That was a stroke of genius, sir,' he said.

'I fled from his office before he had chance to change his mind.'

'Hinton will so grateful to you. When he learns he will be working with us on another murder investigation, he'll be thrilled.'

'To be honest, I don't expect him to find any startling evidence in Oxford, but someone needs to go there just in case.'

'Yet when we first heard about Pomeroy's death,'

Leeming reminded him, 'you said that the rival boat crew had to be suspects.'

'That was before we had some details about the actual murder and, more importantly, about Pomeroy himself. On the basis of those,' admitted Colbeck, 'I've been compelled to revise my judgement. Nevertheless, I'd like to hear what Hinton can find out about the reaction of the Oxford University Boat Club to this rather sensational development. One thing I *can* assure you. If their own cox had been killed, they'd immediately assume that Cambridge was responsible.'

'Why is there such hatred between the two universities?'

'They prefer to call it friendly competition.'

Leeming laughed. 'It doesn't sound very friendly to me.'

'Let's plan the day ahead,' said Colbeck, briskly. 'The first thing we must do is to settle into our accommodation. I will then pay a courtesy visit to the police station to let the local constabulary know why we're trespassing on their patch and to warn that we may need their help at a later date. As for you, Victor, I think you should have another chat with the porter at Corpus Christi.'

'Yes, he was very helpful.'

'Ask him for details of that argument he overheard between Pomeroy and Professor Springett. If the porter could hear them clearly in the lodge, voices must have been raised in anger.'

'What do I do then, sir?'

'See if you can interview Springett himself.'

'I'm not sure I'll enjoy doing that,' confessed Leeming. 'I'm much more at home questioning thugs and thieves and prostitutes. I've never talked to a Professor of Divinity before.'

'He's a human being just like you.'

'He belongs to a different world, sir.'

'My advice is to treat him like anyone else.'

'Do you think he'll have heard what happened to Pomeroy?'

'Oh, yes,' said Colbeck. 'There's a possibility that he might have known about his death before it actually occurred.'

Terence Springett was in excellent humour. For the first time in months, he was able to take a bracing walk along the riverbank. Hitherto, it had been a dangerous thing to do of a morning because he was likely to see the university boat flash past him with Bernard Pomeroy acting as cox. On one occasion, Pomeroy had even grinned wolfishly at him. The threat of that happening again had now been decisively removed, so he had the freedom to walk beside the Cam once more. He could also contribute an article to a learned journal again without the fear of being pilloried in an undergraduate magazine. As he strolled along, he heard the rhythmical swish of oars behind him and turned to see the Cambridge boat being propelled at a steady speed towards him. Seated at the rear of the boat and concentrating on steering it was a pale-faced young man who looked nothing like his predecessor. Springett was so pleased that he gave the oarsmen a cheerful wave.

Cambridge had public houses in abundance. The one that Leeming had chosen had the virtue of being within easy walking distance of Corpus Christi College. Having secured a room apiece for the night at The Jolly Traveller, the detectives went their separate ways. Following directions from the publican, Colbeck walked to the police station and introduced himself. When the duty sergeant heard who he was and why he was there, he summoned Captain George Davies at once. Coming quickly out of his office, the latter shook hands warmly with his visitor.

Davies bore an alarming likeness to Edward Tallis. He had the same square jaw, the same neat moustache, the same physical presence and the same military stance. Also, like Tallis, he looked as if he'd been born in his uniform. When he spoke, however, all resemblance to the superintendent disappeared. The captain was relaxed, pleasant and extremely approachable. Having been chief constable of the Cambridgeshire Constabulary for twelve years, he had long experience, a detailed knowledge of the area he policed and an encyclopaedic memory of the crimes that had been committed there during his tenure. Gesturing his visitor to a chair, he sat behind his desk.

Colbeck gave him a concise description of what had so far occurred.

'Are you *certain* that it is a case of murder?' asked Davies.

'Everything indicates it.'

'Technically, Bury St Edmunds – or Bury, as we tend to call it – is outside my jurisdiction.'

'Of course,' said Colbeck, 'but the initial attack on the victim seems to have taken place at Cambridge railway station. An elderly couple who travelled in the same compartment with the victim have described an individual who made sure he left the train immediately after Pomeroy. When they walked past the body on the platform, this man was crouching over him.'

'Do you have a description of him?'

'Fortunately, we do. An observant railway policeman by the name of Bullen was on duty. He examined the body and gave us useful information about this individual. Needless to say, the passenger soon vanished into the crowd. Anyway,' said Colbeck, 'I just wanted you to be aware of our presence in the city. We'll do our best not to step on any of your officers' toes.'

'That's considerate of you, Inspector,' said Davies. 'I'm glad to say that we've had blessedly few murders since I joined this constabulary. One of the victims, alas, was a young constable of mine, killed while on duty.'

'What happened?'

'We don't rightly know. Constable Richard Peak had been dealing with a drunken gang one night and vanished soon afterwards. His body was never found. That still rankles with me. However,' he continued, 'I wouldn't want you to think that the city is at the mercy of lawless villains – far from it. We keep everything firmly under control and, of course, we have the assistance of the university constables.'

'Yes,' recalled Colbeck with a grin, 'we had the same system in Oxford when I was an undergraduate there. The constables – or bulldogs – worked in conjunction with the proctors. I'm ashamed to say that they caught me late one night trying to climb back into my college.'

'What was the punishment?'

'There was a small fine and a lot of embarrassment.'

'I'm glad that you started obeying the law instead,' said Davies, chuckling. 'And thank you for explaining what you're doing here. If you need assistance, you only have to ask for it.'

'I need some right now, as it happens.'

'Oh?'

'Unless I'm mistaken, the university boat crew will have been on the river all morning. Where exactly might I find them?'

Victor Leeming was glad to see the porter again. He could talk to Jack Stott without any need for deference. The problem was to get him alone for long enough. People were coming in and out of the lodge all the time. Stott handled the various requests and enquiries with quiet efficiency. Leeming eventually had some time alone with him. He plunged straight in.

'Tell me about that argument you overheard between Mr Pomeroy and Professor Springett,' he said.

'It was loud, and they both waved their hands a lot.'

'What was actually *said*?'

Stott was cautious. 'I can't rightly remember, Sergeant.'

'Yes, you can. Your memory is excellent. I've watched you deal with well over a dozen students. You knew them all by name because it's part of your job. Nothing of interest escapes you. If two people are yelling at each other only yards away,' argued Leeming, 'you'd not only hear every word they said, you'd *remember* it.'

'Maybe I do, Sergeant – and maybe I don't.'

'What are you afraid of?'

'I've told you all I can,' said Stott, evasively.

'This is a murder inquiry, for heaven's sake! We need all the help that we can get. Stop wriggling, man.'

'You're putting me in an awkward position, sir.'

'Why?'

'There could be . . . consequences.'

'What sort of consequences?'

'It's better if I say nothing.'

'It may be better for *you*,' said Leeming, firmly, 'but it certainly isn't for me. Yesterday morning, Bernard Pomeroy was killed. You may have information that's relevant. Why can't you trust us with it?'

Stott took a deep breath. 'I love my job, Sergeant,' he said, 'and I do it to the best of my ability. If I got sacked from here, no other college would touch me.'

'Why should you get sacked?' Leeming saw the hunted expression on his face. 'Ah, I see. If you tell me too much, you're afraid that you'll pay for it. In other words, you're scared of Professor Springett.'

'He's got a temper on him. Last year, he had another porter dismissed because he claimed the man had been disrespectful. It was untrue. The porter caught him in a bad mood, that's all, yet he lost his job. He's been out of work ever since. The professor is cruel. If I tell you too much and it gets back to him . . .'

'I understand,' said Leeming, sympathetically, 'though I'd never disclose to him whatever you say to me. Since you

119

can't go into detail, just answer one simple question and I'll disappear. What was the argument about?'

Stott lowered his voice. 'Religion.'

Madeleine Colbeck was dismayed. Delighted when Lydia Quayle had arrived at the house, her mood had changed markedly by the time she bade her friend farewell. For the first time since they'd met, they'd had a real argument. Lydia had criticised Madeleine in a way that she'd never done before, and it was a sobering experience for the latter. Though they'd parted with an affectionate embrace, Madeleine was left to question her own behaviour. Without realising it, had she been trying to control her father's life? Was she too overbearing and too critical of him?

She became so worried that she'd been at fault that she forced herself to go up to her studio in order to lose herself in her work. But even with a brush in her hand, she couldn't escape the feeling of guilt. The fact that she was painting a railway scene onto the canvas only intensified that guilt because it was one that her father would recognise instantly. When she heard the doorbell ring, she knew that he'd arrived. After cleaning her hands with a rag, Madeleine went downstairs, unsure if she should confront her father about the lie he'd told or apologise for the unkind thoughts she'd had about him.

As he gave her a token kiss, Caleb Andrews was in high spirits.

'I'm so sorry that I couldn't come last night,' he said. 'It meant that you had to eat on your own for once.'

'No, I didn't. Robert came back for the night.'

His eyes ignited. 'Did he say anything about the investigation?'

'Yes, he did.'

'Well, tell me about it,' he urged. 'I'd love to know all the details.'

'They can wait. How did you get on at Mr Parry's house?'

'Oh, it was a good party. Gil was on fine form. But let's forget him, Maddy. I want to hear what Robert had to say.'

'All in good time,' she insisted. 'There's something we need to discuss first.'

She ushered him into the drawing room and closed the door behind them.

He was puzzled. 'What is it we're supposed to talk about?'

'I'm cross with you, Father.'

'Why?'

'I think you lied to me,' she said. 'You told me that you were going to a party to celebrate Mr Parry's retirement, yet I remember clearly that he left the LNWR three years ago. You should have thought of a better excuse.'

Andrews bristled. 'It wasn't an excuse, Maddy.'

'Yes, it was.'

'I *did* go to Gil Parry's.'

'Nobody has *two* retirement parties three years apart.'

'All right, maybe I got muddled about what the party was for.'

'There *was* no party, Father.'

He was outraged. 'Are you calling me a liar?'

'Well . . . I suppose that I am.'

'That's a shameful thing to do, Maddy. I'm your father.'

'Then why didn't you tell me the truth?'

'I *did* tell you the truth.'

'You were doing something entirely different last night.'

'Maddy . . .'

'Something you deliberately kept from me.'

'I kept nothing from you.'

'I don't believe you, Father.'

'Then you can go straight round to Gil Parry's house now,' he said with a challenging stare. 'Go on – I'll give you his address. He'll tell you what I told you in the first place. I spent yesterday evening under his roof.' He recovered what he could of his dignity. 'If you'll excuse me,' he added, 'I'm going up to the nursery to see my granddaughter. At least, *she* won't accuse me of telling lies.'

Madeleine was left in a quandary. Should she believe him, or was he telling her another lie? It was impossible to say. One thing, however, was crystal clear. In the space of an hour, she'd had separate arguments with two people she loved deeply.

It was disturbing.

Late-morning sunshine was showing off the colleges at their best and making the Cam dazzle. Colbeck took the route recommended by Captain Davies. When he saw the boat crew, he realised that they'd finished on the river and were recovering from their exertions. As he got closer, he saw that they were being addressed by a man he assumed must be their coach. Then they began to disperse. Nicholas Thorpe broke away from the others and trudged along the towpath with a towel wrapped around his neck. When he recognised Colbeck, he stopped in his tracks and turned to summon Henfrey-Ling and Webb.

Colbeck soon reached them and was introduced to the president and the coach. Both told him how pleased they were with the morning's outing. In spite of having a new cox, they'd somehow shaved seconds off their best time. Webb was smiling with satisfaction and Henfrey-Ling was patently elated. After chatting with Colbeck for a few minutes, both of them moved away. Still glistening with sweat, Thorpe fell in beside the inspector and they started the long walk back to King's College.

'At a guess,' said Colbeck, 'I'd say that the president is your stroke.'

'That's right, Inspector.'

'What about you?'

'I'm the bow.'

'So you're at either ends of the boat.'

'Yes,' said Thorpe with a tired laugh. 'If we're lucky enough to win the Boat Race, I'll be the first past the finishing post.'

'I'm glad that the morning went well for you.'

'That was Malcolm's doing. He inspired us with a wonderful speech that put new life and determination into us.'

'You must have missed your friend.'

'I didn't have time to miss Bernard. Once I got into that boat, everything else went out of my mind.' He hunched his shoulders. 'But I'm thinking about him again now and asking myself the same questions.'

'I'd like to add a few more, if I may,' said Colbeck. 'Do you feel able to talk about Mr Pomeroy?'

'Yes, I do,' replied Thorpe. 'And I'm very sorry that I was so preoccupied yesterday. You were very patient with me.'

'You needed time to adjust to what had happened.'

'Oh, I don't think that I'll ever do that.'

'We'll see.'

Thorpe grimaced. 'Looking at him on that trolley was bad enough, but I was horrified to hear that there'd be a post-mortem as well.'

'We need to be certain about the cause of death.'

'Does Bernard *have* to be butchered?' demanded Thorpe. 'Is someone going to open up that beautiful body of his?'

'It's a course of action we must follow,' said Colbeck, gently.

Thorpe fell silent and went off into a world of his own. Minutes passed before he realised that someone was walking beside him. He straightened his shoulders.

'What would you like to know, Inspector?' he asked.

Professor Springett was proving to be elusive. Leeming went to three different locations in search of him and each time he was told that the man had moved on. He eventually ran him to earth at the place where he'd been at the very start – his study at Corpus Christi. Before he went in to see him. Leeming reminded himself of what he'd been told about the professor. He was clearly a man who was unable to cope with criticism and who had a spiteful element in his character. A hapless porter had been summarily dismissed because of him. Springett used his power to the full.

Leeming knocked on the door of the study and, after a long wait, tentatively opened it and stepped inside. He found himself in a low room with undulating floorboards and an oppressive sense of the past. Bookshelves on two sides of the room were laden with tomes. A crucifix stood on the mantelpiece. There was an oil painting on one wall but, because of the general gloom, it was impossible to see what its subject was. When he looked at the professor, Leeming thought that he was asleep because the man's eyes were closed and his body was motionless. When he suddenly sat up, therefore, he made his visitor jump.

'I thought you were asleep,' said Leeming.

'I was saying my prayers and didn't wish to be disturbed.'

'Oh, I'm sorry.'

'You don't have the look of a man who understands the virtue of regular prayer,' said Springett, eyeing him up and down. 'I find it empowering. Now, who the devil are you, and why are you interrupting me?'

'I'm Sergeant Leeming, and I'm one of the detectives from Scotland Yard investigating the death of Bernard Pomeroy.'

The professor was indignant. 'Then why are you bothering *me*?'

'I believe that you knew the young man.'

'Everyone in this college knew Pomeroy because he made sure that we all did. People who court attention so relentlessly are not to be trusted in my view. That's why I kept clear of the strutting know-all.'

'We understand that you had a fierce argument with him.'

'What's that to you?'

'If you don't mind, I'd like to know the details.'

'Confound your impertinence,' said the other, hotly. 'It's none of your damned business.'

'I never expected a Professor of Divinity to use language like that.'

'You'll hear worse if you continue to irritate me.'

Unable to control himself, Leeming suddenly burst out laughing. His fear of the man disappeared completely. Instead of being a distinguished academic, Springett looked and sounded like a barrel of pomposity. Leeming quickly controlled his mirth.

'I see nothing to provoke amusement,' said Springett. 'The Master tells me that an Inspector Colbeck is also here.'

'He's in charge of the investigation.'

'Then I'll make a point of complaining to him about your behaviour.'

'It was the inspector who sent me here, Professor.'

'And were you ordered to laugh in my face?'

'No, I wasn't,' said Leeming. 'I'm sorry I did that.'

'Please leave me alone to continue with my prayers.'

'We've been thinking, sir, and we wonder if Mr Pomeroy's death was planned by someone who was aware of his movements on a daily basis. In other words,' he went on, watching the professor carefully, 'might it be that someone from this college had a hand in what happened to him?'

'Are you accusing *me*?' asked Springett, crimson with rage.

'Not at all – I'm just telling you how it looks from our point of view.'

'This is intolerable! How dare you come here to make

such vile allegations against me! Who put you up to this? Someone is spreading poison about me. Who is it? I demand to know.'

'Your dislike of Mr Pomeroy seems to be common knowledge, sir,' said Leeming. 'Do you deny that the two of you fell out?'

'That's water under the bridge,' said the other, petulantly.

'It may suit you to dismiss it, but we're bound to look into what happened between the two of you. That's why I wanted to hear *your* side of the story.'

'Then you shall, Sergeant. I can give it to you in a sentence. Bernard Pomeroy was an evil, malicious, vindictive individual who sought to destroy a reputation for a consistently high level of scholarship that I'd built up over decades.'

'I take it, then,' said Leeming, 'that you don't mourn his death.'

'Mourn it!' howled Springett, forcing his vast bulk into a standing position. 'I shall be celebrating the anniversary of the event for as long as I live!'

Alan Hinton had been overjoyed when recruited to work with Colbeck and Leeming on another investigation. When he was told what to do, however, he had a momentary sensation of panic. How could he go into a city he'd never been to before, single out eight oarsman, one cox and their coach, and establish if they had any connection whatsoever to the murder of someone whose death had struck a savage blow at the chances of their rivals winning the forthcoming Boat Race? It seemed an impossible task. Fortunately, Colbeck had gone on to explain how best to tackle it.

On his advice, Hinton had taken the train to Oxford and made his way to the office of *Jackson's Oxford Journal*. It was a periodical that had lasted for over a century and which had been read on a regular basis by Colbeck during his years as an undergraduate in the city. The office was situated in the High Street near the entrance to the covered market. Carrying baskets or bags of some description, people were streaming in and out of the market. Hinton went into the office and introduced himself to the editor.

Martin Caffrey was a genial man in his sixties with a ruddy complexion, a permanent smile and an outcrop of curly white hair circling two-thirds of his bald head like a bushy halo. When he shook hands with Hinton, his grip was firm.

'Take a pew, take a pew,' he invited before resuming his own seat. 'We rarely have an officer of the law in here. As a journalist, therefore, I take an immediate interest. I smell a story.'

'Oh, I can't promise you that, sir,' said Hinton, obeying orders not to give away too much of his true intentions. 'I simply came in search of information. I was told that you were the fount of all wisdom.'

'What a delicious compliment!' said Caffrey, chortling. 'From whom did it come, may I ask?'

'A detective inspector who studied here in his younger days.'

'Please tell me his name.'

'Colbeck – Robert Colbeck.'

'Colbeck, Colbeck, Colbeck,' repeated the other before snapping his fingers. 'Yes, I can place him now. He played cricket of the most sublime quality. Colbeck was a fine batsman. I recall him getting a century against our old enemy, Cambridge.'

'You have an amazing memory, sir.'

Caffrey shook with laughter. 'I revel in the sporting events of this university,' he said. 'When I'm not bent over my desk, I'm watching cricket, cheering on tennis players, enjoying the sight of swordsmen in combat or losing my voice at the Boat Race.' He saw Hinton's eyes light up involuntarily. 'Yes, I thought that might be what brought you here. You obviously don't realise that my copy of *The Times* arrives early enough for me to read it before breakfast. In short, I am well aware of the death of the Cambridge cox, Bernard Pomeroy.'

'I wouldn't wish you to get hold of the wrong idea, sir,' said Hinton.

'Have no fear – I'm not going to give it prominence on the front page of the journal. You're here to find out if anyone from our rowing contingent is party to this appalling tragedy. In my opinion, you're going up a blind alley. If, however, you *do* unearth some link between a dead coxswain and the Oxford University Boat Club, then I'll offer you my apology and give the story full publicity.'

'I was hoping to . . . be discreet.'

'That's exactly what you must be,' said the editor. 'It's not wise to ruffle the feathers of oarsmen. They're big, strong men who wouldn't take kindly to being wrongly accused of something as serious as this.' He rubbed his hands. 'Oh,

this is an unexpected treat for me. I feel as if I'm involved –
albeit in a very small way – in this year's Boat Race.' He leant
forward. 'What do you wish to know?'

'Who is the Oxford president,' asked Hinton, taking out
his notebook, 'and where might I find him?'

'His name is Vincent Pinckney and he's at Oriel.' He pointed
a finger. 'Cross the High Street and you're almost there.'

'Thank you, sir.'

'What else may I tell you?'

'Who is the coach?'

'Ah, now I'd better warn you about him. Liam Brannigan
is a fiery Irishman. Though he looks like a resentful coalminer
whose pick has been stolen, he is in fact a very good coach as
well as being a graduate of this university.'

'I'm very grateful to you,' said Hinton, jotting down the
name. 'Where might I find Mr Brannigan?'

'Pinckney will tell you that.'

'Then I'll take no more of your time.'

'But there's one more question to ask me.'

Hinton was baffled. 'Is there?'

'Of course – who is going to win this year's Boat Race?'

'I've no idea, Mr Caffrey, but I can see that *you* do.'

'Oh, yes,' said the other, beaming. 'I certainly do – Oxford.'

CHAPTER TEN

They met back at The Jolly Traveller and had a light meal together. Colbeck gave an abbreviated account of his visit to the police station and of his conversation with Nicholas Thorpe. From the latter, he'd heard a great deal about Pomeroy's family and their association with Italy.

'It's a country with a chequered history,' he explained, 'and, as you may know, took steps towards unification not all that long ago, thanks to the work of people like Garibaldi. Before that, it was a confusing collection of duchies, kingdoms, Papal States and so forth. Even during those years, we retained diplomatic links with the country. The British Embassy is in Rome, now established as Italy's capital, and there are also several consulates dotted around.'

'Pomeroy's father worked in Tuscany, didn't he?'

'Yes, he was based in Florence, reputedly one of the most beautiful cities in the whole country. In fact, he went on to become the British Consul there.'

Leeming was impressed. 'That sounds like an important job.'

'It is, Victor. It consists in protecting British interests there. According to Thorpe, the Consulate was also kept busy dealing with British visitors who got into trouble. Thomas Cook has been leading tours to places like Florence, Pisa and Naples on a regular basis so large parties have been descending on them. Apparently, it was something Pomeroy's father lamented. Some of the British travellers always managed to go astray.'

'I'd do the same, probably,' said Leeming. 'It's a grim fate, isn't it, being lost in a country when you can't speak a word of the language. And aren't there supposed to be a lot of brigands there?'

'That's principally in the south of the country. Tuscany is further north.'

'I see. What did Pomeroy's father die of?'

'He had stomach cancer and declined over a period of months.'

'Are they quite sure that . . . ?'

'Yes,' replied Colbeck. 'Thorpe was careful to confirm that. Alexander Pomeroy had been under the care of a reliable physician. There's no suggestion of anything sinister about his death.'

He went on to tell Leeming everything he'd garnered about the family from Thorpe. He also dwelt on the long friendship between Thorpe and Bernard Pomeroy. Having met at school in Canterbury, they'd been more or less inseparable.

'What did you make of him, sir?'

'He's a pleasant, sensitive, intelligent young man. That letter of his I read showed me how close he and Pomeroy were. Thorpe is modest about his own achievements because they're dwarfed by what Pomeroy did. Still,' said Colbeck, 'it's your turn now. How was your interview with Professor Springett?'

'It was hard work, sir.'

'What did you learn?'

'I learnt that he is delighted at Pomeroy's death.'

Leeming told him about Stott's reluctance to say very much about Springett beyond the fact that the professor had had another of the college porters dismissed. He went on to describe how he'd deliberately angered Springett.

'I wanted to make him lose his temper,' he explained. 'When suspects are angry, they often blurt out something they don't mean to. That's what the professor did. He suddenly looked and sounded like a guilty man.'

'I'll speak to him myself.'

'All you'll hear are complaints about me.'

Colbeck was amused. 'I had the feeling that it wouldn't exactly be a marriage of true minds.'

'I'll never forget the way he glared at me.'

'Would you say that he was vengeful?'

'Oh, yes,' replied Leeming. 'He's the kind of man who never forgives his enemies. He prefers to make them *suffer*.'

* * *

Jack Stott was sifting through some papers when he saw Springett coming towards the lodge with an air of hostility about him. Stepping out to greet him, the porter rearranged his face into an expression of polite inscrutability.

'Can I help you, Professor?' he asked.

'You certainly can, Stott. Have you spoken to those detectives?'

'They introduced themselves when they first arrived here,' said the other, 'and the inspector asked me about Mr Pomeroy.'

'What did you tell them?'

'I told them how he'd left the college in a rush early that morning. I offered him an umbrella, but he ran off into the pouring rain. It was only after they'd gone that I realised I was probably the last person from Corpus who saw Mr Pomeroy alive.' He pursed his lips. 'That shook me.'

'Have you spoken to either of them today?'

'I haven't seen the inspector, but I did have a word with Sergeant Leeming. He was anxious to speak to you, Professor, so I gave him directions to your study.'

'Is that *all* you gave him?' demanded Springett.

'It's all he asked for.'

'Are you quite sure?'

'The sergeant came at a time when I was very busy,' said Stott. 'I told him where to find you and he went off on his way.'

The professor subjected him to a long, suspicious, penetrating stare. Stott remained calm under examination. Eventually, Springett took a step closer and issued a rasping command. 'If either of them asks about me – especially if it's the sergeant – don't say anything whatsoever about my dealings with Pomeroy. Understand?'

'Yes, Professor.'

'I'll hold you to that. Remember what happened to the last porter who crossed me.'

'I treat the Fellows of this college with the respect that they rightly deserve,' said Stott, dutifully. 'You have my word on that.'

After studying him carefully for a few moments, Springett walked away.

Though she forced herself to work in the studio, Madeleine Colbeck was conscious that her efforts were doomed. She lacked both energy and inspiration. The row with her father still preyed on her mind. When she went past the nursery earlier, she had been tempted to go inside and apologise to Andrews. What held her back was the sound of her daughter's merry laughter from inside the room. Her father deserved time alone with his granddaughter and, by the same token, Helena Rose should be allowed to play with her grandfather without interruption. The two of them were happy in each other's company. Madeleine would be an intruder.

She listened for the sound of the nursery door opening, but it never came. That worried her. The longer she was forced to wait, the more difficult it would be for him to accept her apology. Madeleine knew her father of old. If he fell out with someone, his grudge against them used to harden and grow to the point where he was beyond reason. She blamed herself time and again for her folly in challenging him about his whereabouts on the previous evening. Lydia Quayle was right, she now accepted. Her father was not answerable to her with regard to any social arrangements he might make elsewhere. Madeleine should have held her peace.

Eventually, she did hear the nursery door open and dashed out to intercept him. Her daughter didn't make the situation any easier. As soon as she saw her mother, she ran to her, and Madeleine had to scoop her up in her arms.

'Did you have a nice time with Grandad?' she asked.

'Yes,' said Helena Rose. 'I did.'

'She's so full of beans,' said Andrews.

Madeleine smiled. 'You used to say that about me.'

'I must be on my way.'

'But I feel that I owe you an apology.'

'I have . . . things to do, Maddy.'

'Why not stay and have a meal with us?'

'I'd rather be on my own, if you don't mind,' he said. 'But I'll look in tomorrow to see this little angel.' Tickling the child, he made her giggle. 'Take care of your mother for me. Goodbye.'

And he went off down the stairs. Unable to stop him, Madeleine was rooted to the spot. Her father was still angry. He hadn't met her eyes or softened in any way towards her. The tension between them remained.

Alan Hinton was completely overawed by Oxford. He'd never seen so many striking buildings in such close proximity to each other. While the city had the distinctive atmosphere of a place of study, however, the majority of the inhabitants were ordinary people, unconnected in any way with the academic life. Town and gown lived side by side yet there was little sense of harmony. Hinton could imagine how the privileged scholars would look down on the local citizens, who, in return, would surely resent the intrusion of outsiders.

After leaving the office of *Jackson's Oxford Journal*, he walked to Oriel College in less than a minute. Its facade was arresting, and he stood for some time in Canterbury Square admiring it. Hinton then went in through the main entrance and spoke to the porter, a stolid, middle-aged man with a fringe beard and a pleasing local accent.

'I'm here to see Mr Pinckney,' said Hinton.

'You're one of many,' observed the other. 'He's a very popular gentleman.'

'Is he in his room at the moment?'

'There's only one way to find out, sir.'

'How could I get to it?'

'Mr Pinckney is in the Second Quad – that's the Back Quad.'

After taking precise directions from the porter, Hinton went off to what had originally been a large, well-tended garden. In the previous century, a demand for more accommodation for the undergraduates had led to the building of two free-standing blocks. Individually, the buildings were impressive examples of Georgian architecture and Hinton was struck by their extraordinary symmetry. No expense had been spared on the living quarters of the undergraduates.

Pinckney had a room in the Robinson Building, named after a bishop of Bristol and former Fellow at Oriel. Hinton walked towards the door at the extreme right. Unlike Leeming, he was determined not to be cowed in the presence of the educational elite. When he found his way to Pinckney's room, therefore, he rapped hard on the door. The noise produced a loud yell from inside.

'If that's Wainwright – clear off! If it's anyone else – come in.'

Hinton opened the door and stepped into the room. Vincent Pinckney was lolling on the sofa as he munched the last of a muffin. He was wearing little more than a shirt and a pair of trousers. His bare feet had a ghastly whiteness.

'Can I help you?' he asked.

'My name is Detective Constable Hinton. I'm from Scotland Yard.'

'Then you've come to the wrong place. I'm legendarily law-abiding.'

'I'm here to pass on some news to you, sir.'

'What kind of news?'

'Sadly,' said Hinton, 'one of the members of the Cambridge crew has died in what we feel are suspicious circumstances. His name is Bernard Pomeroy.'

'I don't believe it!' exclaimed the other.

Pinckney was on his feet at once. He was a tall, fair-haired young man with wide shoulders conveying a sense of power. His face was contorted by disbelief.

'Are you talking about their cox?'

'Yes, sir, I am.'

'When did this happen?'

'Yesterday morning, it seems. I can't go into details, I'm afraid. Given your position as the president of the Oxford Boat Club, we felt that you should be told.'

Pinckney's tone changed. 'Don't lie to me, Constable Hinton.'

'I've told you the truth, sir.'

'You came here in the hope of catching me out,' accused Pinckney. 'You wanted to see how I'd react to news that is of obvious advantage to us. In short, you dare to suspect us of involvement.'

'That's not the case at all, sir.'

'It's downright insulting.'

'It wasn't meant to be,' said Hinton. 'Inspector Colbeck, who is in charge of the investigation, was himself educated at Oxford. Do you think for one minute that he'd imagine his old university capable of such a crime?'

Pinckney was only partially mollified. 'I'm sorry,' he claimed. 'I really am very sorry – firstly, for Pomeroy's family but, secondly, for his Boat Club. We know only too well what a brilliant cox he was. His death has weakened the Cambridge crew immeasurably.' His voice hardened. 'What devilish swine could have plotted his murder?'

'I understand that we have credible suspects.'

'Yes – I'm one of them.'

'Pomeroy had enemies, it seems.'

'Am I at the top of that list or a bit further down?'

'Inspector Colbeck has more or less absolved you, sir.'

'More or less?' echoed Pinckney. 'That's not exactly a ringing endorsement of our code of ethics, is it? More or less, indeed! Neither I nor any member of my crew would dream of trying to gain advantage by committing such a heinous crime. What do you take us for?'

'I'll trouble you no more, Mr Pinckney. I'm sorry that you misunderstand the reason for my coming here.'

Before he could leave the room, however, the door was suddenly flung open and a bulky man in his thirties came in.

'You've come at the right time,' said Pinckney to the newcomer before turning to Hinton. 'This is our coach, Liam Brannigan. I'm sure that he'd love to join in this conversation. Please tell *him* what you dared to say to me.'

Hinton looked into the unforgiving eyes of the Irishman.

That afternoon, Colbeck took a train to Bury St Edmunds. Before doing so, he called in at the telegraph station to see if any message had been sent to him. Unfortunately, it had not, confirming his fear that even the commissioner of the Metropolitan Police Force would be unable to make contact with the Prime Minister. Colbeck accepted that his wish to speak in person to Lord Palmerston might never be fulfilled. He therefore turned his mind to the purpose of his visit.

Alighting at his destination with the rest of the passengers, he saw Arthur Bullen talking to the stationmaster. Colbeck made a point of going across to them.

'Ah, you're back again, Inspector,' said Moult. 'Can we help you?'

'The best way to help me,' said Colbeck, 'is by telling the truth. Why did you claim to have had the idea of putting up that blackboard? In fact, it was Bullen's brainchild, wasn't it?'

'Well, yes . . . in a way, I suppose it was . . .'

'You mocked me about it,' recalled Bullen. 'And yet it worked.'

'Two people did come forward to give us useful information,' added Colbeck, 'so the credit should go where it's due.'

After blustering for a few seconds, the stationmaster said that he had to despatch the train and walked quickly away.

'Thank you, Inspector,' said Bullen with a grin.

'You're the one who deserves gratitude.'

'It's good to see you again.'

'I'm making my third trip to the hospital,' explained Colbeck, 'then I'm going on to The Fox Inn. Do you know it?'

'Yes, I know it well. It's in the heart of the town. I have a drink there now and again, but the price of the food is a bit steep for someone on my wage.'

'Has anyone else come forward as a result of your appeal?'

'I'm afraid not.'

'Witnesses are never easy to find. They'll see something that happens right in front of them but – whenever we ask for a statement – they're afraid to come forward. Still,' said Colbeck, glancing up at the platform clock, 'I must be on my way.'

'Good luck at the hospital, Inspector!'

'I'd much rather I had it at The Fox.'

Colbeck left the station and took a cab on the now familiar route to the hospital. He found Dr Nunn in the latter's office and there was a friendly exchange of greetings. The doctor held up two apologetic palms.

'I know what you've come for, Inspector,' he said, 'but I'm unable to give it to you yet. You want the result of the post-mortem and it's incomplete. The pathologist confirmed that the cause of death was poisoning, but he was unable to identify it. We've sent for someone from St Thomas's Hospital in London. He's an expert toxicologist.'

'Then I'll await his opinion,' said Colbeck. 'To save me the trouble of coming all the way here again, you can make contact via the telegraph station in Cambridge. They've promised to send messages on by hand to the place where we're staying.'

'I'll do as you say.'

'And thank you for the way that you dealt with that young man I brought here yesterday. You were both kind and considerate.'

'That's part of my job, Inspector,' said the other. 'Mr Thorpe is one of many who've been overcome at the sight of someone they love lying in our morgue. How is he now?'

'He's over the worst of the shock, I believe.'

'Will he be able to face the inquest?'

'I hope so. I need to find out what date has been set. It's one of the things I have to do while I'm here. First, however, I must pay a visit to The Fox.'

'I can recommend their menu.'

'Oh, I'm not going there to dine, Dr Nunn,' said Colbeck, smiling. 'I'm in search of something far more important than a good meal.'

* * *

Since he'd been warned about Brannigan's fiery temper, Alan Hinton went on the defensive and tried to placate him. It turned out to be quite unnecessary. Though Pinckney continued to berate the detective, the coach was polite and reasonable. His educated voice with its Irish lilt was at variance with his menacing appearance.

'We're prime suspects in a murder case,' claimed Pinckney.

'Keep your voice down,' advised Brannigan.

'You heard what he had to say, Liam. He more or less accused me, as president of the Boat Club, of sanctioning an assassination. I ought to take him to court!'

'You'll do nothing of the kind, man, because you're jumping to conclusions like a demented kangaroo. Instead of yelling at Detective Constable Hinton, we should be thanking him.'

'Thanking him!' cried the other. 'Are you *serious?*'

'I was never more so. Our visitor has brought us important information that has a bearing on the Boat Race. We ought to be grateful. Sending him here was an act of courtesy by Scotland Yard.'

'That's *exactly* what it was,' Hinton chimed in.

'I apologise on behalf of both of us,' said Brannigan.

'Thank you.'

'Vince chose to misunderstand your motives.'

'No, I didn't,' insisted Pinckney. 'And you can leave me out of any apology.'

'Don't be so hostile. We're talking about the death – murder, possibly – of a brilliant young man with a promising future ahead of him. It's been snuffed out like a candle. Doesn't that *mean* anything to you?'

'Yes, of course it does,' said Pinckney, sulkily.

'Vince . . .'

There was a warning note in the coach's voice, and it made Pinckney's anger subside. Instead of railing at Hinton, he made what sounded like a sincere apology and promised to send his condolences to the Cambridge president. He also praised Pomeroy's skill and regretted that it would not be on show at the Boat Race. Brannigan was even more complimentary about the Cambridge coxswain, going into technical detail about his skill. He expressed great sympathy for the rival boat crew.

'How do you know so much about him?' asked Hinton.

Brannigan shrugged. 'What do you mean?'

'Well, according to the information *I* was given, this is the first time that Pomeroy would have competed in the Race. Cambridge had a different cox last year. He was brushed aside when they realised how much better Pomeroy was. In short,' said Hinton, looking from one to the other, 'neither of you could possibly have seen him in action. Why are you so well-informed about him?' Pinckney and Brannigan traded a glance. 'Ah, I understand now,' said Hinton. 'You had him watched, didn't you? I'll wager that you watched him yourself, Mr Brannigan.'

'There's no law against it,' said the Irishman.

'You *spied* on the Cambridge crew.'

'It's no more than they've done to us. When you go into a major contest, it's wise to know exactly what you're up against. It's also common sense. So – yes, I have had the privilege of seeing Pomeroy at work on the Cam. His control of the boat is outstanding.'

'Cambridge spied on *us*,' said Pinckney. 'We've seen strangers watching us from the towpath and taking notes.'

'One of those so-called strangers was James Webb, their coach. I remember him rowing in a Cambridge crew that managed to beat us. I was in the Oxford boat that day,' said Brannigan, 'and I still get sleepless nights about it. Webb is the kind of man who sticks in the mind. Like me, he's out to win. Losing isn't an option.'

'That's what it's all about.'

'So I see,' said Hinton. 'I hadn't realised it was so competitive.'

Pinckney was adamant. 'We do stop short of murder.'

'I give you my word,' said the coach.

'Apart from anything else, it's so unnecessary. Why should we wish to get rid of the Cambridge cox when we have the best crew we've had in the last ten years? Even *with* Bernard Pomeroy, we'd win by several lengths.'

'Ignore him,' warned Brannigan. 'Vince is a brilliant oarsman, but he does let his enthusiasm get the better of him sometimes. I've seen too many clear favourites come to grief. In one of the Races when I was in the Oxford boat, we established a good lead and were pulling away. Then our stroke caught a crab, and we were done for. Cambridge shot past us and that was that.'

'It won't happen to us this time.'

'We'll see.' He smiled at Hinton. 'Is there anything else you'd like to ask us?'

'I don't think so.'

'We've nothing to hide.'

'I'm glad that we had this chat,' said Hinton, 'and I'm sorry that I had to barge in on you.'

'You brought us significant news. We're grateful.'

'We're extremely grateful,' said Pinckney. 'My initial reaction was ill-judged. Please forgive me.'

'I will, sir.'

After bidding them farewell, Hinton left the room and made his way out into the quadrangle. It had been an informative visit. He'd been handicapped by his ignorance of rowing but had learnt a lot from the discussion. He'd also learnt that the Oxford crew were not party to any criminal tactics. They could be removed forthwith from the list of suspects.

When he'd arrived at the college, he'd walked straight to the lodge to speak to the porter. Hinton hadn't been aware of the noticeboard nearby. When he glanced at it now, his gaze settled on a sign – BOAT RACE NEWS. He walked across to the board and saw that, beneath the sign, was an item cut out from that morning's edition of *The Times*, describing the fate of the Cambridge coxswain. Hinton went over to the lodge and spoke to the porter.

'There's an item about the Boat Race on your noticeboard,' he said.

'That's right, sir.'

'Who put it there?'

'The person you've just been to see,' replied the porter. 'It was Mr Pinckney.'

Hinton was shocked. When he'd passed on the news of Pomeroy's death to the Oxford president, the latter had feigned ignorance of the event and so had the coach. In fact, the detective had told both of them something that they already knew. Hinton had been deliberately deceived.

Pinckney and Brannigan were probably laughing their heads off.

Colbeck had the good fortune to arrive at The Fox Inn when there was a lull. It meant that the landlord, a freckled man in his fifties with a drooping moustache, was able to give him more time than he'd accorded to Leeming. Colbeck therefore gathered snippets of information that had never been divulged to the sergeant. What he really wanted to do, however, was to talk to the person who had actually served the meals to Pomeroy and his female companion.

Alice Beynon was the landlord's daughter, a plump young woman with a kind smile and a dutiful manner. When Colbeck introduced himself to her, she was alarmed.

'I've done nothing wrong, have I?' she asked, worriedly.

'No, of course you haven't.'

'I always obey the law.'

'I'm sure that you do,' said Colbeck. 'There's no cause for concern. My questions are not about you but about someone you served recently.'

'There are scores of them, Inspector. I can't remember them all.'

'You'll remember this couple. Your father did.'

As soon as he described them, a smile blossomed on her face. Alice had good reason to recall them because each time she'd waited on the couple, the man had left her a generous tip. She'd not only been struck by the woman's beauty, Alice had also been impressed by what she'd worn.

'We don't get many dresses of that quality in here,' she said. 'I'd loved to have felt that material between my fingers.'

'Did you hear them talking to each other?'

'I heard them,' said Alice, 'but I couldn't understand a word. They spoke in this funny language that was very fast.'

'It was Italian.'

'They never stopped talking to each other. When I put their meals on the table, they hardly noticed me. They were so bound up in each other.'

'Did you hear their names mentioned?'

'Yes, he was called Bernardo and her name – oh dear, it's gone – let me think for a moment.' Her face brightened. 'Isabella – that was it, Inspector.'

'Did they seem close?'

'That depends on what you mean?'

'They were obviously friends. Were they anything more, do you think?'

'I did at first,' she said, 'then I changed my mind.'

'Why?'

'Well, Isabella kept telling him things and he kept nodding as if he was hearing it all for the first time. But don't rely on me. The truth is that I didn't understand a single word they said.'

'One last question . . .'

'What is it?'

'Do you have any idea where they were going when they left here?'

'Oh, yes, I do.'

'Well?'

'St Edmund's – I heard Bernardo say that in English.'

'Where might I find it?'

'Westgate Street,' she said. 'St Edmund's is our Roman Catholic Church.'

Caleb Andrews walked through streets of terraced housing with a speed and vigour that belied his age. When he came to the house he sought, he didn't have to knock on the door because it opened invitingly.

'Hello, Elsie,' he said with undisguised affection.

She glowed with pleasure. 'Come on in, Caleb.'

CHAPTER ELEVEN

Left behind in Cambridge, Leeming had been given the task of tracking down two of the undergraduates whose names had made their way onto the list of suspects. It would mean picking his way through the labyrinth of streets, lanes and winding passageways that constituted the university. At least, he consoled himself, neither of the young men would be as daunting to question as Terence Springett. His hope was that they'd be much easier to find than the truculent professor. It was certainly true of Andrew Kinglake. To his surprise and relief, Leeming located Pembroke College with relative ease. Having established where the former cox's room was, he knocked on the door.

'There's nobody at home!' a voice snarled.

'Mr Kinglake?' enquired Leeming.

'I don't care who you are or what you want. Please go away.'

'I'm Detective Sergeant Leeming from Scotland Yard and I'm part of the investigation into the unexplained death of Bernard Pomeroy.'

'Good riddance to him!'

'That's very harsh of you, sir.'

'You didn't know him as well as I did.'

'Open the door, please.'

'I'm in no mood for company.'

'Frankly,' said Leeming, 'I'm not interested in your mood.' He tried the door and found it locked. 'Do I have to bring someone with a duplicate key? If I do, I should warn you, we'll be having a conversation at the police station instead.'

'I had nothing to do with Pomeroy's murder.'

'How do you know that he was murdered?'

The question caught Kinglake off balance. After a long silence, he conceded defeat and rose to his feet. The door shook visibly. 'All right, I'm coming. You don't have to tear it off its hinges.'

He unlocked the door and stood back so that Leeming could enter. Each took a moment to weigh the other up. Kinglake then flopped back into his chair. Taking out his notebook, Leeming sat opposite him.

'That's better, sir. We'll make a genial host of you yet.'

'I don't need sarcasm.'

'Your needs don't matter to me, Mr Kinglake,' said Leeming, sharply. 'I know that you're nursing a disappointment because I was told what happened down by the river this morning. It's not the first time you've been dropped from the Cambridge boat, is it? Perhaps you should ask yourself why.'

'I *know* why, Sergeant. There's a conspiracy against me.'

'Let's talk about Mr Pomeroy.'

'He was at the head of it. Pomeroy was a snake-in-the-grass.'

'We were told he was very popular.'

'Yes, he was with his cronies like Thorpe and Henfrey-Ling, but I saw through him. I watched the sly way that he worked on people.'

'He obviously didn't charm *you*.'

'I hated him.'

'Hate is often a powerful motive for revenge.'

'I was every bit as good a cox as Pomeroy,' insisted Kinglake.

'Then why did you lose your place in the crew?' asked Leeming, opening his notebook. 'Let's start with the question that I asked earlier, shall we?'

'What question?'

'How did you *know* he was murdered?'

Elsie Gurr was a good listener. As they sat on the sofa in her living room, she let Andrews talk at length about the way that his daughter had accused him to his face. Elsie was full of sympathy.

'It must have been so hurtful,' she said

'It was, Elsie.'

'You told me she was very considerate as a rule.'

'I got the sharp edge of her tongue this time,' said Andrews. 'It came out of the blue. Maddy took me into the drawing room and called me a liar.'

'That's shocking, Caleb.'

'I just don't know what to do.'

'Well, the first thing is to stay away from there for a bit. I know you'd miss your granddaughter, but you'd be sending a message. Madeleine would realise just how much she upset you and want to make up.'

'I'm not sure about that.'

'She'll come round in time.'

'Maddy might but it's *me* I'm worried about. I'm just not ready to pretend that it never happened. I've got my pride, Elsie.'

'A father has the right to be believed and respected.'

'That's what I think.'

'Let's have a cup of tea,' she suggested, rising to her feet. 'I always feel that it helps in a situation like this.'

'Thank you. It's a good idea.'

After she'd left, he looked around the room. It was spotlessly clean and tidy. It was also much cosier than his living room and was filled with ornaments that added interest and bright colour. The only things that Andrews objected to were the mementoes of her husband Elsie kept on display. A former sailor, Joe Gurr had died a few years earlier. His grieving widow had put a photograph of him in uniform in the middle of the mantelpiece.

The presence of another man in the room was unsettling. Andrews felt that he was constantly under surveillance by the dead sailor. It was inhibiting. He decided that it was time to invite Elsie to his house. There'd only be the two of them there.

* * *

Faced with some probing questions, Andrew Kinglake controlled his temper and chose his words with care. Leeming's persistence irked him. It reached the point where he felt that he was being unfairly interrogated. He struck back.

'What did your father do, Sergeant?' he asked.

'That's none of your business.'

'Are you afraid to tell me?'

'No, of course I'm not.'

'Was he a street pie man, perhaps, a dock labourer, a costermonger?'

'He was a policeman,' said Leeming, proudly.

Kinglake's tone was haughty. 'My father is in royal service.'

'That's interesting, sir. We have something in common at last. My father was part of a police cordon protecting Buckingham Palace when the Chartists were afoot. There was a riot in Trafalgar Square that spilled over into surrounding streets. A group of drunken rioters descended on Buckingham Palace and taunted the police. The two groups soon came to blows. My father was killed by a brick that hit him full in the face so you might say that he died in royal service.' Leeming's smile was steely. 'Has *your* father ever risked his life for the Queen?' Kinglake was sullen. 'No, I can see that he hasn't.'

'I was just pointing out the social divide between us.'

'I'm well aware of it, Mr Kinglake.'

'Then you should be more respectful.'

Leeming's eyes twinkled. 'Would you prefer a bow or a curtsey?'

'Listen,' said the other, angrily, 'the main reason I came to this university was to fulfil an ambition. When my father was here at Pembroke in 1829, he took part in the first ever Boat Race against Oxford. It was rowed at Henley-on-Thames. My father was the Cambridge cox that day. It's my duty to emulate him.'

'But I thought you'd already done that,' said Leeming. 'You were in the Cambridge crew last year, weren't you?'

'We were beaten on that occasion. I vowed to be in a *winning* boat.'

'Mr Pomeroy had the same ambition.'

'I've actually *been* in the Race before and know how hellish it can be. Pomeroy didn't have anything like my experience. Oh, what's the point in trying to explain it to you,' he said, peevishly. 'You don't understand what the Boat Race *means* to us.'

'Yes, I do – it's a matter of life and death.'

'I gave my word to my father.'

'Which one of you had the idea of getting rid of your rival?'

Kinglake jumped to his feet. 'I resent that accusation.'

'Perhaps you'll explain why,' said Leeming. 'Before you do that, please tell me who won that first ever Boat Race – the one in which your father rowed.'

'Oxford,' muttered the other.

'So both of you – father and son – have been in the losing boat.'

'I wanted a second chance so that we could *win*.'

'At least *your* father is still alive, sir,' said Leeming. 'Mine died because an angry rioter hurled a brick that cracked his skull open. It was so unfair, really. My father was simply doing his job. In fact, he had a lot of sympathy for the Chartists. He agreed with some of the things they demanded.' He pulled a face. 'Life can be cruel, can't it?'

When Madeleine turned up unexpectedly on her doorstep, Lydia Quayle was at once pleased and worried, delighted to see her friend yet aware that only a problem could have brought her friend there. The frown on Madeleine's face was confirmation in itself that something had happened. Lydia listened patiently to her visitor's tale.

'Oh dear!' she sighed.

'Father was wounded to the quick.'

'I can well believe it.'

'After seeing Helena, he couldn't leave the house quick enough.'

'That must have been upsetting for you.'

'It was, I promise you.'

'Are you quite certain that . . . ?' Lydia shook her head. 'No, no, I shouldn't ask that. It's none of my business.'

'What were you going to say?'

'It doesn't matter.'

'Yes, it does, Lydia. I'm desperate for advice. Don't be afraid to give it.'

'You told me that your father had lied to you,' recalled Lydia. 'Are you quite sure that he was telling you the truth this time?'

'Yes, I am.'

'How do you know?'

'It was the way he responded,' said Madeleine. 'He was shocked that I'd even suspect him of misleading me.

156

He really *did* go to Mr Parry's house. There's no doubt about that. What he did admit was that it wasn't for the retirement party he'd mentioned to me. It was for another type of celebration.'

'How did you feel when he told you that?'

'I was mortified.'

'Well, my advice is simple. Don't let the rift get wider. That was the mistake I made with *my* father. I should at least have kept in touch with him. Instead of that, I just wanted to escape completely from the house.'

'Your situation was different, Lydia. Your father stepped in to break up your romance and did so quite brutally. If you'd stayed, you'd have been reminded of it every day. You made the right decision.'

'I still have qualms about it sometimes. However,' she went on, a hand on her friend's arm, 'let's deal with *your* problem. Go to him at once, Madeleine.'

'What do I say?'

'Make a full apology.'

'I'll *try*,' said Madeleine with a sigh, 'but there could be a problem.'

'Problem?'

'What happens if he won't accept it?'

On his return to Cambridge, Colbeck made a point of paying a second visit to the telegraph station. No message had come for him, so he took a cab to Corpus Christi College and made his way to the Master's study. Fortunately, Sir Harold Nellington was alone and able to see his visitor at once.

'It's a pity you weren't here ten minutes ago, Inspector,' he said.

'Why was that, Sir Harold?'

'I had Professor Springett in here, complaining about the way that he'd been questioned by Sergeant Leeming. He claimed that it was tantamount to a cross-examination.'

'It's clear that he's never been in a witness box in court. During my years as a barrister, I saw many cross-examinations. They can be ruthless and destructive. The sergeant would never be either of those things.'

'It might help if you said that to Springett.'

'I'll be glad to do so,' said Colbeck. 'Has there been any sign of the press?'

'We've had three reporters from London so far. I told them exactly what you told me to say. They're very eager to talk to you in person.'

'Earlier today, I spoke to the chief constable and left a statement that can be issued to any members of the press. They'll also have been told that I'll be at the police station this evening to answer any questions they might have.'

'My fear is that they'll bother Pomeroy's friends.'

'That's inevitable, I'm afraid. As his closest friend, Nicholas Thorpe will be the main target. I've advised him to say very little.'

'I accept that newspapers are entitled to gather information,' said the Master, 'but I don't want their presence here to hamper the preparations for the Boat Race.'

'I share that concern, Sir Harold.'

'Apart from anything else, the crew will be coping with their grief in the wake of Pomeroy's death. We don't want reporters pestering them.'

'They're only doing what they're paid to do, I'm afraid.'

Colbeck went on to talk about his visit to the hospital where the diagnosis of poison had been confirmed. What he didn't mention was the existence of a woman in Pomeroy's life who had met him in Bury St Edmunds more than once. It was a line of enquiry that he'd also keep from the press.

'We have identified some possible suspects,' said Colbeck.

'What enraged Springett most,' said the Master, 'was that he was being treated as one of them.'

'That was a misunderstanding on his part. We simply wanted to know more about the scholastic dispute between him and Pomeroy.'

'It was more serious than that, Inspector. The professor wrote an article about Christopher Marlowe's religious views. It was learned and well-researched. Pomeroy took a different view. Writing in an undergraduate magazine,' he continued, 'he tore it apart line by line. Springett was appalled. He demanded that I sent Pomeroy down at once, but I saw no reason to do that. Terminating an undergraduate's career here is a momentous decision to take. When all was said and done, Pomeroy's article was scholarly and well-written. I'm afraid that I'm not qualified to tell you which side of the argument has the greater merit. All I know of Christopher Marlowe is that he had the misfortune to be killed in a tavern brawl.'

'That may have been a case of bad luck,' said Colbeck. 'Pomeroy's death, by contrast, was the result of careful planning.'

Victor Leeming was beginning to enjoy Cambridge University. He was no longer unnerved by its distinguished history and abiding sense of privilege. Since he'd been there, he'd managed to hold his own against a Professor of Divinity and reduce an arrogant undergraduate to a gibbering wreck. As he set off in search of a third triumph, he was full of confidence.

St John's College was easy to find because it was close to Trinity Hall where Leeming had earlier spoken to members of the Boat Club. Once again, a helpful porter was able to give him directions.

'Mr Reddish, sir?' said the man. 'I'll take you to his staircase. You won't need to be told which room.'

'Why is that?'

'You'll hear the laughter.'

The porter's prediction was correct. As soon as they reached the relevant staircase, there were sounds of merriment from a room at the top of it. Climbing the stairs, however, Leeming could not hear the kind of hearty laughter that he expected. What drifted into his ears was a series of high pitched titters. When he got to the room, he knocked on the door.

'Come in!' called a voice.

Leeming entered to be scrutinised by four pairs of eyes. It was easy to pick out Simon Reddish. While his three friends reclined in chairs, Reddish was standing in front of the window as if holding court. His pose was studied. Even when Leeming introduced himself, Reddish didn't relax his attitude.

'I'm sorry, gentlemen,' he said to the others, 'I suspect that the sergeant wishes for a private conversation.'

'What have you been up to now, Simon?' joked one of the others. 'Are you going to be arrested for failing to return a library book?'

There was an outburst of laughter as the three of them left the room.

'I'm sorry to disturb you, sir,' Leeming began, 'but I've come to discuss a matter of great importance.'

'I know full well what's brought you to me,' said Reddish with a grand gesture towards the sofa. 'At least be comfortable while you're here.'

'Thank you, sir.'

Putting his top hat beside him, Leeming sat down and took out his notebook. Reddish remained on his feet and tossed his hair.

'You've come about poor Bernard, haven't you?' he asked.

'Yes, sir, I have.'

'Then let me save you a lot of time. Whatever others may have told you, I had the greatest admiration for him. We had so much in common, after all. We were both born thespians. We both had gifts that lifted us above our contemporaries. And we both had Italian connections.'

'Oh?'

'In my case, they weren't quite as strong as the ties that Bernard had, but they were there nevertheless. My family

161

owns property in Tuscany near Lucca. It's a place to which we retreat whenever opportunity arises.'

'I see.'

'Bernard and I had long talks about Italy.'

'Does that mean you speak the language?'

'I can get by,' said Reddish, loftily.

He turned his head so that his visitor could see a different profile. Leeming was reminded of Nigel Buckmaster, actor manager of a theatre company, whom they had met while investigating a murder in Cardiff. Reddish had the same compulsion to preen and to be the centre of attention. Leeming had the urge to pluck a few feathers from the swaggering peacock.

'I'm told that you objected strongly when Mr Pomeroy was given the role of Hamlet. Is that true?'

'It was a justified complaint. Bernard himself was the first to admit that I'd have brought more depth to my treatment of the part.'

'Unfortunately, he's not here to confirm that, sir.'

Reddish was offended. 'Do you doubt my word?'

'I'll ask the questions, if you don't mind,' said Leeming, firmly. 'When did you first become aware of Mr Pomeroy's death?'

'I can't give you a specific time, Sergeant.'

'Was it yesterday or today?'

'It was yesterday. The news was whirling around the university.'

'What was your immediate response?'

'I was shocked,' replied the other. 'Bernard Pomeroy dead and a hint of foul play – it brought me close to tears.'

'Were they tears of regret or of joy?'

Reddish bridled. 'What on earth do you mean?'

'Well, you stood to gain from his death, didn't you? I heard that Mr Pomeroy had been given another role that you wanted. Now that he's dead, it's yours.'

'Nothing was further from my mind. I'd certainly have been a finer Hamlet, but Bernard was the best choice for Doctor Faustus. He had a satanic side to his character that made him the perfect choice.'

'You'll now take over, Mr Reddish.'

'That's yet to be decided.'

Leeming studied him carefully for a few moments.

'Why are you the odd man out?' he asked.

'I don't understand what you mean.'

'Well, you claim that you were a friend and admirer of Mr Pomeroy. Why is it that everybody else tells me the opposite – that you hated him because he was a better actor and you had fierce rows with him?'

'They weren't in any way fierce,' denied Reddish. 'Bernard loved a good argument and that's what I gave him. It was all in fun, really.'

'What would have happened to him – if he'd stayed alive, that is?'

'Bernard? Oh, I know exactly what he'd have gone on to do.'

'He'd have made a living as an actor?'

'No, he'd have gone into politics. I suppose that there's a histrionic element to that. He had a fine voice, but it was never destined for the stage. It would have echoed around the House of Commons.'

'Are you *sure* that that was his ambition?' asked Leeming in surprise.

'I'm certain that it was. That was the difference between us, you see.'

'Difference?'

'Yes,' said Reddish with sudden passion. 'Talented as he was, Bernard was merely *playing* at being an actor whereas *I* am the genuine article. It's in my blood. Bernard was using Cambridge as a stepping-stone into politics, but I was inspired by a higher motive. My avowed aim is to perform the greatest roles every written for an actor – Hamlet, Othello, Macbeth, Tamburlaine, Doctor Faustus – and make them my own, forging a reputation that will burn brightly for centuries.'

In the limited space, it was an astonishing performance, full of anger, resolve and a ferocious pride. Leeming was tempted to applaud.

After a long discussion with the Master, Colbeck decided to visit Terence Springett in order to make his own judgement of the man. He found the professor alone in his study. After introducing himself, Colbeck was quick to offer an apology in the hope of staving off the protest that was clearly hovering on the other man's lips.

'The Master tells me that you found Sergeant Leeming's questions too intrusive,' said Colbeck. 'I'm sorry that you felt so upset but, in a case of this importance, I fear, we have to amass all the relevant information.'

'Does that mean you're allowed to level an accusation at an innocent man on the basis of a total lack of evidence?'

'Is that what the sergeant did to you?'

'Yes – he treated me as a suspect.'

'His account is rather different, sir.'

'Anyone who knows me will vouch for my moral probity and my devotion to Christian principles,' said Springett, vehemently. 'Nobody is more aware of the Ten Commandments and more committed to obeying them. *Thou shalt not kill* is engraved on my heart.'

'I've no doubt that it is,' said Colbeck, smoothly, 'and I can assure you that the sergeant does not believe for one moment that you are capable of killing someone. He was simply interested in finding out more about your feud with Bernard Pomeroy.'

'It's not germane to your inquiry.'

'I disagree. We are trying to build up a detailed picture of the murder victim, Professor. That involves talking to people who knew him well and can give us some insight into his character. Friends of his idolise him, but your relationship with him reveals another side to Bernard Pomeroy.'

'He was insufferable.'

'Since he was reading Classics, it's odd that you and he came into contact with each other.'

'Precisely,' said the other with emphasis. 'Along with his acting and rowing activities, his studies should have kept him fully occupied. Why did he make time to read an article that I wrote in an obscure journal?'

'How was he even aware that you'd *written* such an article?'

'Someone must have told him that it concerned Christopher Marlowe.'

'If he'd disagreed with your point of view,' suggested Colbeck, 'it would surely have been more sensible to contact you privately – more sensible and more respectful of your eminence.'

'That's exactly the point, Inspector,' said Springett, nodding eagerly. 'My door is always open. I welcome reasonable comment, but what appeared in his critique was neither reasonable nor respectful. It was a cold-blooded example of character assassination.'

'What prompted it, do you think?'

'Sheer wickedness on his part – a trait, I'd argue, he shared with Marlowe.'

'Do you have a copy of his critique, by any chance?'

Springett glowered. 'I *burnt* it, Inspector,' he declared, 'though I daresay that Pomeroy kept his copy so that he could read it again and snigger.'

'That's a false assumption,' said Colbeck. 'When we searched his room, we found no trace of any undergraduate magazine, nor indeed was there a copy of the journal in which your article had first appeared.'

'Oh, I see.'

'He was far too busy preparing for the Boat Race to snigger at you, sir.'

Faced with Colbeck's immaculate appearance and cultured voice, Springett found it difficult to sustain his anger. The inspector had offered him an apology and shown a degree of sympathy for him. His courteous manner was in marked contrast to what Springett saw as Leeming's boorishness. After inhaling deeply, the professor lowered his head.

'I'm at fault to some degree,' he confessed. 'Instead of brooding on it, I should have shown more resilience with regard to Pomeroy.' He looked up. 'The whole business is over and done with now, anyway, so I should be ashamed of speaking ill of the dead.'

'It was only natural, sir,' said Colbeck. 'You still bore the scars that he inflicted. I hope that they fade away completely in time.'

'So do I.'

'Well, I'm sorry to interrupt you. I'll leave you in peace.'

'Do you have *any* suspects in mind?'

'Names have been put forward, sir, and we're in the process of talking to the people concerned. But these are early days. A lot more hard work has to be done before we actually solve this crime. If you'll excuse me,' said Colbeck, moving to the door, 'I must be off to do my fair share of it.'

Madeleine decided to heed her friend's advice. Lydia's opinion had, as always, been an amalgam of common sense and instinct. Having met Caleb Andrews many times, she knew that he was inclined to harbour grudges. It was essential to make sure that he didn't nurse one about his own daughter. As she sat in a cab on the way to the house, Madeleine rehearsed what she was going to say, hoping that her visit would end with a warm hug from her father. If she chose the wrong words, she knew, the breach between them might widen.

When she reached the house, she asked the driver to wait in case there was nobody at home. She then knocked on the door and waited. There was no response from within. After peering through the window, Madeleine knocked even harder and stood back from the door. After a full minute, she accepted that her father was not there and climbed back into the cab.

As it rolled off down the street, Andrews tugged back the curtain in the front bedroom and peeped out.

CHAPTER TWELVE

After speaking to the press at the police station, Colbeck arrived at The Jolly Traveller at almost the same time as Leeming. They chose an isolated table, then took it in turns to describe what they'd learnt during the day. The sergeant talked about his spiky meeting with Andrew Kinglake where he'd learnt that the cox's father had represented Cambridge in the first ever Boat Race. Listening carefully, Colbeck made mental notes about the suspect. But it was the description of Simon Reddish that really interested him.

'He was in the same mould as Nigel Buckmaster, you say?'

'Yes,' confirmed Leeming. 'He spoke as if there were twenty of us in the room and waved his arms about like a windmill. Reddish knows how to hold your attention, I'll give him that.'

'Of the two, who is the more likely suspect?'

'Oh, it was Reddish, sir. Kinglake is angry enough to strike back at someone he has reason to hate, but it's the kind of anger that quickly burns itself out. Reddish is much more sly and calculating. He's livid that Pomeroy slowed down what Reddish sees as his brilliant career on the stage.'

'Also, there's his link with Italy.'

'Yes, that may be important.'

'It's strange that each of them has been strongly influenced by their fathers,' said Colbeck. 'Kinglake is desperate to succeed where his father failed, and Reddish wants to surpass his father's notable achievements in the theatre.'

'Sons often try to copy their fathers. It's what *I* did.'

'And I'm eternally grateful, Victor. You're a natural policeman.'

'Thank you, sir.'

'Well, you've unearthed a lot in your interviews. I'm glad that you didn't let either of these uppish young men push you around.'

Leeming grinned. 'I'm getting the hang of dealing with them now, sir.'

'While we can't dismiss Kinglake altogether, it's apparent that Reddish is the one to concentrate on. I keep thinking of that edition of *Doctor Faustus* we found left open in Pomeroy's room. Kinglake would have no reason whatsoever to touch the play,' said Colbeck, 'but Reddish certainly would. The speech we saw on display is one that he will actually deliver on stage now that his rival has been swept aside.'

'He told me that he was a *real* actor. He'd dedicate his life to it whereas Pomeroy wanted to go into politics.'

'That's interesting. Unfortunately, it will never happen now.'

'No, I suppose not,' said Leeming, sitting back. 'Anyway, it's your turn now, sir. Tell me how *you* got on today.'

'Oh, I learnt something new and possibly significant. The woman who was seen with Pomeroy at The Fox Inn was called Isabella.'

'How did you find that out?'

'I spoke to the landlord's daughter. She served them. It seems that they talked in Italian and Isabella kept calling him Bernardo.'

Colbeck went on to give full details of his visit to Bury St Edmunds and of his later discussion with the Master of Corpus Christi College. Leeming's ears pricked up at the mention of Professor Springett.

'Did he say anything about *me*, sir?'

'He said a lot, Victor – none of it complimentary.' Leeming laughed. 'I spent most of my time trying to calm him down. He pretended that he'd got over the row that he had with Pomeroy, but he clearly hadn't. We must keep him in mind.'

'Do you want me to speak to him again?'

'No, no,' said Colbeck, quickly. 'I promised him that I'd keep you on a leash.'

'He looked so guilty to me.'

'I caught him in an angry mood. On reflection, however, my feeling is that Professor Springett is unconvincing as a killer.'

'He could have been in conspiracy with Reddish.'

'No,' said Colbeck, 'I don't feel that there's any pact between them.'

'They both hated Pomeroy and wanted their revenge. Perhaps they hired a third person – the one seen at the railway station by Arthur Bullen – to do their dirty work for them.'

'Reddish and Springett are unlikely bedfellows. That's not to say that we cross out their names altogether. We must keep each of them in mind.'

'What's our next move, sir?'

'I think that someone has just dictated it,' said Colbeck, rising to his feet as he saw Alan Hinton coming in through the door. 'We're going to have a companionable drink together and listen to our colleague. I fancy that he's brought us some news.'

Malcolm Henfrey-Ling was a young man with initiative. When he took over as president of the Cambridge Boat Club, he appointed a new coach, changed the training routine and established a more rigorous attitude to fitness. He also stressed the importance of bonding as a group. As a consequence, the oarsmen spurned the beer cellars in their respective colleges and drifted along to the Boat House instead. Nicholas Thorpe was one of the first to arrive, not because of any urge to see his friends but because he found that being alone was a trial. Unable to work, he simply sat in his room and mourned his dearest friend, suffering in silence and trying to fight off despair. He felt the need to find relief in the company of others.

When he got there, he found a small cluster of oarsmen

chatting together. The first person who approached him, however, was someone he hadn't expected to see.

Andrew Kinglake gave him a warm handshake.

'I'm sorry about what happened earlier,' he said. 'I've apologised to everyone else here and I now want to tell you face-to-face that my behaviour was childish. One should always accept the president's decision.'

'What you did was understandable,' said Thorpe, 'and an indication of how eager you are to make amends for last year's disappointment. I'm glad that you feel able to come back to us, Andrew.'

'It's so kind of you to say so.'

'I'm sure that everyone feels the same. You're one of us.'

'That's what Malcolm said to me a few moments ago.' Kinglake lowered his voice. 'Listen, I haven't had the chance to say this to you, Nick, but I'm terribly sad about what happened to Bernard. I know how much you must miss him.'

Thorpe sighed. 'I feel as if I've suffered an amputation.'

'He was a brilliant cox. I've always acknowledged that.'

'Don't undervalue your own talents.'

'I'm trying to be realistic. In view of the mistakes I made in last year's race, I can see why Colin Smyly was chosen instead of me. Before you arrived, I made a point of congratulating Colin. I'm sure he'll rise to the occasion.'

'We still have you in reserve, Andrew.'

'Yes, that's true.'

'There are weeks to go before the Boat Race. Anything can happen in that time. Colin could be injured or struck down by an illness. It's comforting to know that we have a first-rate cox ready to take his place in the event of an emergency.'

'I don't believe that I'll be needed.'

'You never know.'

'Take a look at Colin. He's a picture of good health.'

'Bernard was the same,' said Thorpe, sadly. 'He was the perfect all-round athlete. Who would have thought that his rowing career would come to such an abrupt end in a railway station? He was murdered. There was speculation about it in some of the morning papers.'

'Have you been bothered by reporters from London?'

'Yes, I have. From now on, I'll keep one step ahead of them.'

'They cornered Malcolm, apparently.'

'Then I hope they let him speak for the rest of us. To be candid,' continued Thorpe, uneasily, 'I don't think I could cope with the sort of questions they'd fire at me. As you can imagine, I still feel shaken by it all. That's why I came here. I needed somewhere to hide.'

Between occasional sips of his beer, Alan Hinton told them about his visit to Oxford. Colbeck was pleased to hear that his advice about seeking help from the editor of *Jackson's Oxford Journal* had proved its worth. He was duly touched that the man had remembered him because of his batting prowess on the cricket field. For his part, Leeming was impressed that Hinton had adjusted so quickly to the university atmosphere in Oxford that he himself had found so oppressive.

'It was a bit daunting at first,' admitted Hinton, 'but I kept telling myself that I was there for a purpose and the fear slowly ebbed away.'

'You did well, Alan.'

'I agree,' added Colbeck. 'I thought you'd find nothing remotely suspicious and yet you did. It was good work.'

'The president and the coach lied to me,' said Hinton. 'They pretended to know nothing about Pomeroy's death, yet they were clearly aware of it. Why couldn't Pinckney be honest about it when I first arrived? He and Brannigan tried to trick me.'

'Luckily, it didn't work.'

'No,' said Leeming. 'They just wanted to get rid of you. I'll bet they'll be congratulating themselves that they managed to dispel any suspicion.'

'That's why you must go back, Alan,' said Colbeck.

Hinton smiled. 'I was hoping you'd say that, sir.'

'Next time, however, you must go in disguise.'

'Yes,' said Leeming with a grin. 'You can dress up as a gardener as you did when we were in the Cotswolds. That disguise would fool anybody.'

'It had the authentic reek of the countryside,' teased Colbeck.

'We could smell you from ten yards away, Alan.'

'Don't remind me,' said Hinton, grimacing. 'Oh, there is something I need to ask you, Inspector.'

'What is it?'

'Brannigan talked about a race that had been lost because someone caught a crab? Who would fish for a crab when he was supposed to be rowing?' Colbeck laughed. 'Have I said something funny, sir?'

'No, you haven't, and I apologise for laughing. Catching

a crab is a technical term used in rowing. It means dipping the oar in the water at the wrong time. The result is that the oar is flipped parallel to the boat. The blade must always remain perpendicular,' explained Colbeck, 'so that it can provide power, and it must always do so in time with the other oarsmen. Someone who catches a crab is letting the rest of the crew down. The boat will be unbalanced.'

'Oh, I see.'

'It's a serious mistake.'

'So was my question,' said Hinton.

'Anyway,' Leeming put in, 'you won't find many crabs in the Thames.'

'I suppose not. Right, what are my orders, Inspector?'

'The first thing you must do is to enjoy your drink and hear about our adventures in Cambridge from the sergeant. I, meanwhile,' said Colbeck, 'will slip off to my room and write a report which you can be deliver to the superintendent first thing in the morning.'

'Will there also be a letter for Mrs Colbeck?'

'Do you really need to ask that?'

'When do I go back to Oxford?'

'As soon as you've been to Scotland Yard,' said Colbeck. 'Tell the superintendent that you may have to spend at least one night there. He'll give you some cash to cover your expenses.'

'That will be welcome.'

'Don't forget your disguise,' warned Leeming. 'You don't want to be recognised by either of the two people you've already met.'

'I know how to change my appearance.'

Colbeck rose to his feet. 'I'll disappear and write that report,' he said.

He was about to move away when he saw a man in railway uniform coming into the bar. Before the newcomer could speak to the landlord, Colbeck went swiftly across to him.

'Have you come from the telegraph station?'

'Yes, sir,' said the other.

'Then you probably have something for me. I'm Inspector Colbeck.'

'I was told to put this into your hands, Inspector.'

Colbeck took the telegraph from him. 'Let me put something into *your* hands,' he said, taking a few coins from his pocket.

'Thank you, sir,' said the man, delighted with his tip.

Returning to the table, Colbeck sat down again and opened the telegraph.

'I know what that is,' said Leeming, confidently. 'It's your invitation to speak to the Prime Minister, isn't it?'

'No,' replied Colbeck, reading the short message, 'but it may turn out to be equally valuable to us. It's from Constable Bullen. He's seen that man again.'

'Which man is that?' asked Hinton.

'It's the one we believe to be the killer.'

Alone in his house, Caleb Andrews looked again at the painting of a locomotive that hung on the wall of his living room. It was his most treasured gift, all the more so because his daughter had painted it for him. Love, artistic talent and a lot of hard work had gone into it. As he studied it now, he began to feel guilty at the way he'd actually hidden from Madeleine, cowering in his bedroom while she was knocking on his door. It was wrong of him. She'd obviously come to make an apology. If he'd let her in, he would have taken the first step towards reconciliation.

Yet he'd somehow been unable to do that. It was as if an invisible hand was holding him back. Andrews now realised that the hand bore a name – Elsie Gurr. It was she who'd counselled him to stay apart from Madeleine for a while in order to convey his hurt feelings. That way his daughter would learn to show him more respect and consideration. Elsie had made a difference in his life. Though their friendship was still at a comparatively early stage, he was eager for it to blossom. Since the death of his wife, he'd never found any woman whose company he could really enjoy for any length of time. Then he met Elsie and found that he could, without the slightest discomfort, spend any amount of time with her. She was kind, warm-hearted, attentive and fiercely loyal to him. As he looked back over their relationship, he saw that she'd changed his life.

Madeleine would always be his daughter and he'd love her in spite of her faults, but there was someone else to consider now. Elsie had committed herself to him. Her opinions had to be taken into account. There would be a time, he hoped, when he felt able to introduce her to Madeleine. At the moment, it was too soon. He needed to restore his position in the Colbeck household first. If he had to make Madeleine wait, so be it. She needed to be brought to heel.

Seeing him standing apart from everyone else, Malcolm Henfrey-Ling went across to Nicholas Thorpe and gave him a friendly pat on the back.

'Can I get you another drink?' he asked.

'No, thanks, Malcolm – I haven't finished this one yet.'

'How are you feeling?'

'Do I really need to tell you that?' asked Thorpe. 'I feel completely bereft. The only time when I functioned as a normal human being was when we were out on the water. It was a wonderful escape.'

'You rowed well. We *all* did. It was exhilarating.'

'Andrew tells me that the press has been troubling you.'

'It wasn't so much troubling,' said the other, 'as irritating. They all wanted to pry into Bernard's private life, and I refused to discuss that. I also made it clear that I didn't want any of the crew put under any pressure. Concentration is a vital aspect of rowing. I'm not having reporters distracting us all the time.'

'Have they spoken to Inspector Colbeck?'

'I heard that he was going to make a statement to them at the police station.'

'That should help,' said Thorpe. 'He knows how to talk to reporters. He's also very industrious. Since they've been here, he and Sergeant Leeming have gathered a surprising amount of information about Bernard.'

'They'll never fully know the person that *we* did.'

'He was unique.'

Henfrey-Ling glanced around to make sure that they were not overheard.

'What do you make of the suspects who've been named?' he asked.

'Well, I'd remove Andrew's name for a start. After the way he spoke to me earlier, I could see how genuinely horrified he was at his behaviour when you announced that someone else would take over as cox.'

'Yes, he spoke to me with evident sincerity. He went off in a fit of pique and regrets it now. Andrew is still very much part of this club.'

'That brings us to Professor Springett.'

'Ah, yes.'

'He's the person Bernard hated most. Did you know that Springett did his damnedest to get Bernard sent down?' Henfrey-Ling blenched. 'How petty can you get? Just because someone dared to criticise an article of his, the professor wanted to have him ejected from Cambridge altogether.'

'In a sense,' said the other, darkly, 'Bernard *has* been ejected.'

'Springett is probably rubbing his hands with glee. Not that that means he had a hand in his death,' he added. 'There's still Simon Reddish to consider. When he realised that Bernard could act him off the stage, he was fuming. He kept saying that Bernard was obstructing his destiny.'

'What destiny?'

'You'll have to ask him. I couldn't bear to speak to the man.

Whenever Bernard was near him, Reddish was throbbing with spite and envy.'

'It sounds to me as if Reddish had a stronger motive than Springett,' said Henfrey-Ling. 'He and Bernard must have been in a state of continuous hostility towards each other whereas the professor only clashed with him once.'

'That's not strictly true, Malcolm.'

'Oh?'

'I'll say no more.' Thorpe drained his tankard in one last gulp. 'But I will accept your kind offer of another drink.'

Having waved Hinton off when he caught a train to London, they had boarded one that took them on the branch line. A full compartment precluded any private conversation so Colbeck and Leeming were each left alone with their own thoughts. When they reached Bury St Edmunds, they were among a sizeable crowd that alighted. To their dismay, there was no sign of Arthur Bullen. They waited until the bulk of the passengers had disappeared, then began a search for the railway policeman.

The stationmaster suddenly popped up from nowhere.

'Bullen is off duty, Inspector,' he said.

'Do you have his address?' asked Colbeck.

'Oh, he won't be at home.'

'Why not?'

'He has somewhere important to go to first – The Black Horse.'

Moult excused himself and went off to despatch the waiting train.

* * *

It had never occurred to Madeleine that her father had been at home when she called there. They'd had arguments before, but he'd never actually avoided his daughter. That would have been unthinkable. There were servants in the house, but Madeleine suddenly felt alone and vulnerable. Her daughter had been put to bed and would wake up next day expecting to see her grandfather. What if he didn't turn up? How could Madeleine explain his absence to a small child? Worse still, what if he *did* call at the house but refused to speak to his daughter, spending all his time in the nursery with Helena Rose? That would be intolerable.

Something had happened. Looking back over the past few weeks, she saw that subtle changes had taken place in her father's behaviour. He still came to the house every day, but he left earlier than usual. On the few occasions when he dined with her and Lydia Quayle, his mind seemed to wander off from time to time. Could that be the explanation? Was he beginning to show his age and lose concentration? That might account for the tetchiness he'd started to show. It was an attempt to cover the deficiencies he was now displaying.

At all events, decided Madeleine, she was at fault. If he came the following day, she'd make an abject apology. If he stayed away, then she would take a cab to his house with her daughter. That would be the way to sweep aside his hurt feelings. She believed that Helena Rose Colbeck would come to the rescue.

Having taken directions from a porter, the detectives walked the short distance to The Black Horse, an establishment frequented mainly by cab drivers and railway employees. If he hadn't been wearing a frock coat and a top hat, Leeming would have felt comfortable in the pub's noisy atmosphere. As it was, he and Colbeck attracted the kind of stares that marked them out as invaders. Still in uniform, Bullen had been drinking at the bar with a fellow railway policeman. He walked across to the detectives and took them aside.

'You got my telegraph, I see,' he said.

'Yes,' replied Colbeck, 'we came as soon as we could. It was welcome news.'

'I wish I could've said I had the man in custody, but I recognised him too late. By the time I realised who he was, he'd disappeared.'

'Are you sure it was *him?*' asked Leeming.

'I'm positive, Sergeant.'

'Then why didn't you spot him immediately?'

'You've seen how many passengers get off a train,' said Bullen. 'It's difficult to pick anyone out. Also, he was clever. He had different clothes from the ones he wore yesterday, and he had a cap pulled down over his face.'

'Yet you still feel certain that it was the same man,' said Colbeck.

'Yes, Inspector, I do.'

Bullen's confidence was reassuring. The man they wanted had not just been an anonymous face in the crowd. The railway policeman had remembered his build and his distinctive gait. Once he'd done that, he gave chase.

'I was too slow,' he admitted. 'By the time I got to the cab rank, he'd been driven away. He knew that I'd identified him. That's why he took to his heels. An innocent man wouldn't have run away like that.'

'Why didn't you take a cab and follow him?' said Leeming.

'He'd had the only one at the rank. By the time another cab turned up, it was too late. We'd have no idea in which direction to go.'

'Of course,' said Colbeck. 'I take it that you spoke to the cab driver who *had* driven him off.'

'Yes, sir, I did. I waited until he came back. His passenger asked to be dropped off in the town centre. The cab driver didn't see which way he went when he got out of the cab. He was too eager to get back here to pick up another fare.'

'We can't blame him for that,' said Leeming. 'When you first noticed the man, what was he carrying?'

'Nothing but a small valise,' said Bullen.

'That might mean he could be staying the night here.'

'It might,' said Colbeck, nodding in agreement, 'but it could equally well indicate that he's only here for the day and intends to leave the town later on.'

'He certainly hasn't got a return train yet,' said Bullen. 'I know that because I gave a detailed description of him to a policeman still on duty at the station. If the man turns up again, he'll be arrested.'

'It may be that you frightened him off so he won't dare to come anywhere near the station. On the other hand, we can't ignore the possibility that he'll catch a later train back to wherever he came from, working on the possibility that the station will be deserted at that time of night.'

'It won't be, Inspector. When I've had my pint, I'm going

home to change out of uniform and have a bite to eat with my wife. Then I'll come straight back to wait on the platform as if I'm just another passenger.'

'We'll wait with you,' said Colbeck.

'But we haven't had *our* bite to eat,' wailed Leeming.

'I daresay they'll serve you a meat pie or something of the sort right here. When you've finished eating it, come and join me on the platform.'

'What about you, sir? You must be famished.'

'Going without food is a small price to pay for the chance to catch a killer. Now then,' he went on, turning to Bullen, 'you described him to the sergeant when he first questioned you. I'd like even more detail about him, please. What sort of clothing was he wearing this time?'

'Before you answer that,' said Leeming, interrupting, 'there's something *I* need to know. Do they serve meat pies here?'

Madeleine hadn't realised how quickly the time had passed. Retiring to the drawing room after dinner, she had tried to read the book that Lydia had given her but simply couldn't concentrate. That was no reflection on its elegant prose. She was simply in no mood to enjoy *North and South*. While her father continued to occupy her mind, there was no room for anything else.

In the end, she forced herself to get up and leave the room. She was just coming into the hall when she saw something dropping through the letterbox. Rushing to pick it up, she recognised Colbeck's distinctive hand. It prompted her to open the door and step out.

'Wait!' she called, peering into the gloom at a departing figure. 'Is that you, Alan?'

'Yes, it is,' he said, stopping in his tracks.

'Come inside for a moment.'

'I didn't mean to disturb you, Mrs Colbeck.'

'It's all right. I was wide awake.'

Accepting the invitation, he stepped into the house and was taken into the drawing room. To save her the trouble of asking, he explained that he'd been told to deliver the letter when he got back to London.

'That's so kind of you, Alan,' she said.

'I'm just a messenger boy. The kindness is displayed by the inspector. You have a caring husband, Mrs Colbeck.'

She smiled. 'I've had unlimited proof of that. Wait a moment,' she added as a thought prodded her. 'I thought you were going to Oxford – not Cambridge.'

'I've been to both.'

'Why?'

'There's a short answer to that – the Boat Race.'

He gave her a highly abridged version of his visit to Oxford and explained that he'd felt duty-bound to report immediately to Colbeck at the rival university.

'I daresay that the inspector will have told you in his letter how he and Victor Leeming have fared. They always work so hard on a new case.'

'Robert commits himself wholeheartedly.'

'I'm sorry that I can't be with them in Cambridge. Watching the inspector at work is a real treat. I learn so much from him.'

'Let's go back to Oxford,' she said. 'Didn't you say that you'd be in disguise when you return there tomorrow?'

'Yes, that will add more spice to the trip.'

'Have you decided what you're going to wear?'

'I'm still considering the possibilities.'

'May I make a suggestion?'

'Yes, of course,' he said. 'Any advice from you is doubly welcome.'

'Then I think you should take no risks, Alan.'

'I don't intend to. The president and coach of the Oxford University Boat Club both had a good look at me. Whatever I wear must make me look very different.'

'There's something you could do that would deflect attention from you completely. On your own, you take a risk. If you had company, however . . .'

'I don't understand.'

'Lurk alone beside the river and you'll be picked out. But if you walk along the towpath with a woman on your arm, nobody will give you a second look.'

He was startled. 'Are *you* offering to come with me, Mrs Colbeck?'

She laughed. 'I wish I could, Alan, but I'm needed here. Lydia isn't, however. What better disguise could you have than her?'

His brow wrinkled. 'Is this some kind of joke?'

'I was never more serious. Lydia would jump at the opportunity.'

'If the superintendent knew that I'd taken a woman to Oxford while I was on duty, he'd have me dismissed on the spot. It's strictly forbidden.'

'Then you have to be discreet about it. I was involved in more than one of my husband's cases, working silently in the background and going to places that only a woman could reach. Lydia wouldn't be doing that,' she argued. 'She'd simply be there to make you look less like a detective and more like a young man taking his betrothed for a pleasant walk.' She grinned. 'Aren't you at least tempted?'

A light came into his eye.

CHAPTER THIRTEEN

The first thing that Colbeck did when he returned to the station was to introduce himself to the railway policeman who'd been primed by Bullen to act as a lookout. They agreed to stand well apart from each other on the platform so that – if the man did turn up – they could wait until he was in between them before they tried to apprehend him.

Since he lived so close to his place of work, it didn't take Bullen long to go home, gobble down a meal and change out of his uniform. When he returned to the railway station, he looked so different that at first Colbeck didn't recognise him. It meant that the man they were after would also be fooled by the radical change of appearance. Bullen mingled with the other passengers as if he were one of them. The first train came in, several people got out and their places were taken by those waiting on the platform.

It was a process repeated three times in a row before Leeming eventually arrived with an air of deep satisfaction. He ambled over to Colbeck.

'You look disgustingly well-fed,' said the inspector.

'The meat pie was delicious, sir.'

'It must also have been enormous. It's taken you well over an hour to eat it.'

'I got into conversation,' said Leeming. 'You've always told me to pick up information whenever I could, so I chatted with two men who live here. They told me a lot about Bury St Edmunds. It's a sleepy market town with a slow pace of life. You can't say that about London.'

'Are you eyeing it as a place for your retirement?'

'That depends, sir. If and when I do retire, I'd need to know that The Black Horse was still serving such tasty food. Why don't you slip off and try it yourself?'

'I'd rather stay here.'

'But there are already three of us looking out for him.'

'Four gives us an even better chance of an arrest – if he comes, that is.'

Alan Hinton was in a quandary. He was standing in the hall at the Colbeck residence as he considered Madeleine's suggestion. It was an alluring one. If he took Lydia Quayle to Oxford with him, she would act as a form of camouflage. More enticingly, he'd be able to walk around with her on his arm and revel in the pleasure of doing so. Set against the appeal of the idea was the fact that he could be imperilling his career in the Metropolitan Police Force. If he were caught, he could expect no mercy from Superintendent Tallis. Instant dismissal would be accompanied by a blistering tirade. He was consoled by the thought that Colbeck had disobeyed the rules in the past by involving Madeleine in the investigative process. Not a whisper of his actions had ever reached the superintendent's ears.

Hinton came to his decision. Since the inspector had set an example, he felt able to follow it. There was only one problem.

'Do you think that Lydia will agree to the plan?' he asked.

'She most certainly will,' said Madeleine, confidently. 'Even though it's a last-minute request, Lydia will be thrilled.'

'But how do I make contact with her?'

'You won't need to, Alan. I'll do it for you. I'll write her a letter, giving all of the details. One of the servants can take a cab to her house and deliver it by hand. All I need to know from you is what time you'd like her to be waiting for you at Paddington Station in the morning?'

'What if Lydia already has commitments for tomorrow?'

'She'll cancel them immediately,' said Madeleine. 'That's what *I'd* do in her position.' She saw the hesitation coming into his eyes. 'What's the problem now?'

'It's the inspector – do you think *he'd* approve?'

'Robert would congratulate you on your initiative.'

'But it was *your* idea.'

She raised an eyebrow. 'There's no need to mention that, is there?'

* * *

191

They remained on the station until the last train was due. Only a few passengers were waiting for it. Leeming decided that their quarry would not be coming.

'He knows there'll be a trap set for him,' he said.

'Don't give up hope,' advised Colbeck. 'If he *is* intending to catch this train, he'll leave it until the last moment to make an appearance.'

'We have to be on the train ourselves, Inspector. There's no other way to get back to Cambridge at this hour.'

'Be patient. There's still ten minutes to go.'

In fact, the train was late, so they had to wait for almost half an hour. When it finally steamed into the station, they stayed on the platform until the last possible moment, then jumped quickly into a compartment.

'He's staying the night here,' decided Colbeck.

'I wish that *we* were,' said Leeming, using a palm to stifle a yawn. 'I'm tired and you must be starving.'

'I daresay that the landlord will rustle up some kind of supper for me. I don't need much. Well, I'm sorry that our long wait was futile, Victor, but it's not the first time we've been in this position.'

'It certainly isn't. What a pity!' he exclaimed. 'We may have lost our last chance to catch the devil. While we're going back to Cambridge with our tails between our legs, he's probably tucked up in a nice, warm bed.'

The man took no chances. He was hiding on a platform at Newmarket Station. When the last train from Bury St Edmunds finally came into view, he waited until it was on the point of departure before running out and leaping into an empty compartment.

Nicholas Thorpe endured another largely sleepless night. He knew that he needed rest in order to restore his energy for rowing, but all that he could manage were short bursts of slumber. His mind was in turmoil. He and Bernard Pomeroy had been so inseparable that James Webb, the coach, had called them the Siamese twins. One of those twins had now, in effect, been hacked off, leaving the survivor weakened, dispirited and in constant pain. Why had Pomeroy been in Bury St Edmunds? What possible reason could have taken him there at a time when he should have been on the river with the rest of the crew? Whom was he going to see? Was there someone in his life whose existence he'd been keeping from Thorpe?

He kept asking the same unanswered questions time and again until he dozed off out of sheer fatigue. But there was no rest for him there. Thorpe was soon caught up in a dream that was so dark and frightening that it made him thresh around in the bed. Awakening with a cry of alarm, he saw that he was covered in perspiration yet shivering with cold.

A new question now taxed his brain. Pomeroy had once told him something, then sworn him to secrecy. Should he divulge the information to Colbeck? It might or might not have any relevance to the case. Since Pomeroy had extracted a promise from him, Thorpe felt that he could say nothing. Then he began to wonder if his friend's death absolved him of keeping the promise. Should he speak or stay silent? By the time that the first rays of light were poking around the edges of the curtains, he was still unable to decide.

'Good morning,' said Hinton, raising his hat in greeting.

'Good morning,' replied Lydia, smiling broadly.

'I'm sorry that the invitation came at such short notice.'

'That only added to the excitement.'

'I'm so pleased that you were able to come, Lydia.'

'I wouldn't have missed an opportunity like this,' she said. 'When I woke up this morning, I couldn't wait to get to Paddington.'

'What exactly did Madeleine put in her letter to you?'

She laughed gaily. 'That would be telling.'

He gazed fondly at her and realised yet again what a striking young woman Lydia was. Having her company for a whole day was a treat that he'd never expected. When he got the opportunity, he intended to shower Madeleine with heartfelt thanks. For the moment, however, Lydia was all his.

'I must say,' he said, appraising her. 'You look wonderful.'

'Thank you.'

'But then, I knew that you would be.'

Lydia had dictated his own appearance. Knowing how smart she would be, he'd discarded all the ideas he'd had of a disguise and dressed to match her. He wore a light frock coat with rounded edges, a short, single-breasted waistcoat, a bow tie instead of his more usual cravat and a pair of dark trousers. He'd opted for a grey top hat. Lydia ran an approving eye over him.

'Given the name of our destination,' she said, 'I'd assumed that you'd wear your normal *Oxford* cravat.'

'The bow tie is one of a number of subtle changes.'

'Madeleine's letter mentioned that you were anxious to avoid recognition.'

'It's important, Lydia.'

She was wearing a dress that was as pretty as it was colourful. The bodice had balloon-like pagoda sleeves, narrow shoulders and a large open bell at the elbow. Her white blouse was attached to the wide, hooped, many-flounced skirt by ribbon braces and sashes. In the latest fashion, the skirt was drawn up in four places to show the outer of a number of petticoats. The outfit was completed by a flower-trimmed poke bonnet tied under the chin by a ribbon, and by a cashmere shawl, edged in silk and fringed. Both of them wore elastic-sided boots.

In the middle of a bustling Paddington Station, Hinton just stood there and marvelled. His expression made her giggle politely.

'I take it that you *do* have the train tickets?' she said.

'Oh, yes. I got them before you arrived.'

'Then you can conduct me to the correct platform, please.'

'With the greatest of pleasure,' he said, offering his arm.

'Our adventure begins.'

They linked arms. After enjoying that first, stimulating moment of contact, they sailed happily across the crowded concourse.

The Jolly Traveller had excelled itself. When they got back late the previous day, Leeming had mentioned that Colbeck hadn't eaten for several hours. Though in his dressing gown, the landlord had insisted on going off into the kitchen and making an impromptu meal for him so that the inspector could retire to bed with a full stomach. An excellent breakfast next morning was made and served by the landlord's wife, leaving both men feeling well-fed and positive.

Leeming went off to the river, hoping to get there early enough to see the crew setting off. In view of what Hinton had told them about Oxford's spying activities, he wanted to see if they were still keeping the Cambridge boat under surveillance. That would involve walking nonchalantly along the towpath while keeping an eye out for strangers taking an undue interest in what was happening on the river. It was the kind of assignment that appealed to him.

Colbeck, meanwhile, had gone back to Corpus Christi College to speak once again to Jack Stott. Cheerful and polite, the porter was also wary.

'Don't worry,' said Colbeck, noting his caution, 'I haven't come to ask you about Professor Springett. I understand your reservations about him.'

Stott relaxed visibly. 'Thank you, Inspector.'

'I wanted to ask about security.'

'That's part of our responsibility.'

'Presumably the gates are locked at a certain time.'

'Yes,' said Stott. 'Whoever is on duty will lock them at eleven o'clock at night and they'll be reopened at seven in the morning.'

'What happens if undergraduates get back here in the small hours? Is it easy for them to climb in?'

Stott cackled. 'It might be if they were sober, but they never are. We've had some nasty accidents. More than one of them has been impaled on the railings and dozens have fallen off the ropes that have been dangled out of windows by their friends.'

'Then there are the patrols, I suppose.'

'Yes, Inspector,' said Stott. 'If they're caught in the act, they could face heavy fines. When they're caught trying to smuggle a woman into the college, then they're in serious trouble.' His eyelids narrowed. 'Why are you interested in our security?'

'I think that someone may have got into the college a few nights ago and slipped a message under Mr Pomeroy's door. It's the only way to explain his sudden flight to Bury St Edmunds. The message must have contained a summons.'

'He went running out of here as if his life depended on it.'

'I think it was somebody else's life,' said Colbeck to himself.

He remembered the edition of *Doctor Faustus* they'd found on Pomeroy's desk. In all likelihood, it was left by the intruder who had put the message under the door. The man, he realised, hadn't necessarily had to climb in after dark. It would have been much easier to enter the college during the day when the gates were open and hide somewhere until it was time to leave the message. Once Pomeroy had charged out of his room, the intruder could have gone in to leave the book open at a specific page, then bided his time until a number of undergraduates were leaving the premises, allowing him to use them as cover.

'How soon after Mr Pomeroy had left,' he asked, 'did people start to drift past the lodge?'

'It'd be the best part of an hour, Inspector,' said Stott.

'And would you have recognised everybody who went out?'

'As a rule, I would have, but it was pouring down, remember. Some had umbrellas, others had coats and hats. I couldn't swear that everyone who went out that morning was a member of the college.'

'Thank you,' said Colbeck. 'That's all I need to know.'

'I'm sorry I can't give you more help,' said Stott. 'I'm only a porter, not a policeman. I'm here to help everyone, not to keep watch on their comings and goings. They *trust* me, Inspector.'

'You're very worthy of that trust.'

'Mr Pomeroy treated me as a friend.'

'He was clearly right to do so.'

'Catch him, Inspector,' urged the porter. 'Catch the devil what killed him.'

'We're getting closer all the time,' said Colbeck.

While he was watching the boat skim across the water, Leeming had to keep one eye out for James Webb, the coach, who liked to keep pace with them on his horse and bellow orders as he did so. As the animal cantered along, everyone on the towpath had to jump out of the way. The sergeant was impressed by how smoothly and swiftly the boat moved along. What he couldn't hear, however, were the numbers called out by the cox when he wanted the rate to be changed. Further up the river was a place wide enough for the boat to be turned so that it could head back to its starting point.

When it finally came into view in the middle distance, Leeming spotted something glinting beside a willow tree that genuflected towards the riverbank. As he walked stealthily towards the tree, he saw that the momentary dazzle was caused by the impact of the morning sun on a telescope attached to a tripod. Someone was keeping the boat under scrutiny. Deciding that it had to be a spy from Oxford, he quickened his pace, ready to give the man a fright by clamping a hand on his shoulder. As it happened, however, his intervention was not needed. Reaching the willow tree, he realised that the person with the telescope was an artist, perched on a stool, watching the boat approach before committing what he saw into his sketchbook.

In less than a minute, the boat flashed past with rhythmical ease.

Alan Hinton was also beside a river, discovering that Lydia Quayle's company was both a help and a hazard. While she gave him effective cover, she was also a distraction. He was enjoying the novelty of having her beside him so much that she broke his concentration. Instead of trying to gather intelligence, he was luxuriating in a situation that he'd only ever dreamt about. Thanks to a suggestion from Madeleine Colbeck, his dream had become a reality. As the Oxford boat shot past them, he tried to impress his companion.

'Do you know what catching a crab means?' he asked.

'Yes, I do.'

He was deflated. 'Oh, I see.'

'It happened to my elder brother. He was rowing in the school eight and got his timing wrong. Stanley had to lift the oar right up in the air so that he could twist the blade into the right angle again. He was very unpopular with the rest of the crew.'

'Ah, so you know a bit about rowing.'

'Both of my brothers were keen oarsmen. When they were at school, I watched them a number of times.'

'Then you're a better judge of standards than I am, Lydia.'

'Not really – the only sport I know anything about is lawn tennis.'

'Did you play it yourself?'

'Yes,' she said, 'we had our own court. It was good fun.' Her face clouded as she thought of the family from whom she was estranged. 'But that was a long time ago. My playing days are over. Walking is the only exercise I'm capable of now.'

'You're still a fit young woman.'

'I don't always feel that, Alan.'

As they turned a bend in the river, he brought them to a sudden halt. Standing on the bank not far away was Liam Brannigan, talking earnestly to some other members of the Boat Club. Hinton turned to face Lydia.

'What's the matter?' she asked.

'I don't want the coach to recognise me.'

'Is he the man you told me about?'

'Yes, he and the president are the two under suspicion,' said Hinton, 'but others may be involved.'

'Would they *really* resort to murder?'

'That's what I'm here to find out, Lydia.'

'Thank you so much for inviting me to join you.'

'The person to thank is Madeleine. It was she who made it possible. I'd forgotten that she actually helped the inspector on some of his cases.'

'That was how I came to meet her in the first place.'

'Yes, of course.'

'As a result, it's *my* chance to be a detective for the day.'

He squeezed her arm. 'Let's walk on, shall we?'

'I thought you were afraid of being seen by the Oxford coach.'

'Oh, I won't get a second glance from him,' he said, airily. 'If we stroll past him, Brannigan will be far too busy looking at *you*.'

Madeleine was quietly alarmed. It was well past the time when her father was due, yet he'd failed to arrive. While she was restive, her daughter was quite distressed. Helena kept asking where her grandfather was. After a long wait, Madeleine feared that he was deliberately staying away. She therefore decided to take her daughter to her father's house by cab. As soon as she opened the front door, however, she saw Caleb Andrews marching towards the house. Breaking away from her mother, Helena ran to him and was lifted up into his arms.

'We thought you weren't coming,' said Madeleine.

'I was held up.'

'We were about to go in search of you.'

'Why?' asked Andrews. 'I couldn't let Helena down.'

'No, of course you couldn't.'

'Let's go up to the nursery, shall we?'

Hugging the child, he took her into the house and went straight upstairs. There was no customary embrace or kiss for Madeleine. She felt snubbed.

'I'm sorry, Inspector,' said Reddish, crouched over a desk strewn with papers, 'but you've come at a rather inconvenient time.'

'I make no apology for that,' said Colbeck, who'd just entered the room.

'I have to hand in my essay at the end of the afternoon.'

'Then you've left it rather late, sir.'

'Couldn't you come back in three or four hours?'

'Murder investigations can't be postponed at the whims of undergraduates.'

'It's not a whim,' said Reddish, getting to his feet. 'It's a case of necessity. You've obviously never had to write an essay under stress.'

'That's where you're wrong, Mr Reddish. When I was at Oxford, I wrote a countless number of essays, though not always under stress, I must admit. I usually had the sense to allow plenty of time for any work. It saved me from the last-minute panic that you seem to be in.'

Colbeck had been given a frosty reception when he called at Simon Reddish's college. In order to get a positive response from him, Colbeck had had to be firm.

'Why are you bothering me?' asked Reddish. 'I've already

spoken to that sergeant of yours and I have nothing else to add.'

'Let me be the judge of that, sir. First of all, however, allow me to say how much I've enjoyed your father's career over the years.'

Reddish blinked. 'You go to the theatre?'

'Not as much as I'd wish,' said Colbeck. 'I blame the criminal fraternity for that. But I treasure your father's performances as Richard III, as Malvolio in *Twelfth Night* and as Volpone. More recently, I admired his Iago. He managed to hold his own against Nigel Buckmaster, as powerful an Othello as I've ever seen.'

'Iago is a role *I* covet.'

'The same can be said of Doctor Faustus, I gather.'

Reddish winced. 'Why are you here, Inspector?'

'I came to see why you told my sergeant so many lies.'

'I'm not aware of any lies.'

'To start with,' said Colbeck, 'you were *not* a friend and admirer of Bernard Pomeroy. He was your greatest rival as an amateur actor.'

'Rivalry brought out the best in both of us.'

'Yet he was the one who always seemed to win any contest between you. We've heard that you felt undervalued. That must have rankled.'

'I have the opportunity to blossom now.'

'How was that opportunity created?'

Reddish smirked. 'That's for you to find out.'

'I'm sorry that you view the death of a so-called friend as a source of amusement, sir. When you spoke to Sergeant Leeming, you evinced a token sympathy. You can't even manage that pretence now.'

'I was not pretending.'

'Then what were you doing?'

'In spite of our differences, Bernard and I respected each other.'

'I've seen little sign of respect for him in your manner or in your actions. Let me ask you this,' Colbeck went on. 'Have you ever been to Mr Pomeroy's college?'

'Yes, I've been to Corpus a number of times.'

'And did you ever go to his room?'

'That was one of my reasons for being there. When the auditions for *Hamlet* were over, those of us in the principal roles met in Bernard's room for readings of the play and discussions of how it could best be staged.'

'So you obviously know your way around the college.'

'Is that a crime?'

'No, Mr Reddish, but it is a valid piece of information.'

'What are you talking about?'

'Have the patience to listen,' said Colbeck, 'and you'll find out.'

Leeming had spent a few moments looking over the shoulder of the artist at his sketchbook. The man was clearly talented. His sketch of the approaching boat was remarkably lifelike, its eight oarsmen bent double over the oars while its cox sat bolt upright. Leeming wondered how it would look when transferred to the canvas. Reminding himself that he was there as an observer, he left the willow tree and walked towards the boat which had now pulled into the bank. On his way there, he kept his eyes peeled for anyone lurking in the shadows to watch the morning outing on the river. From what he himself had seen, it had been very successful, but Webb was not satisfied. When he got close enough, Leeming could hear the coach criticising the oarsmen and demanding more effort. The only person who escaped his censure was the cox, Colin Smyly.

When they'd been dismissed, the crew, clearly exhausted by their efforts, began to melt away. Malcolm Henfrey-Ling took the coach aside to get a more detailed analysis of their shortcomings. Nicholas Thorpe headed for Leeming.

'I'm so glad to see you, Sergeant,' he said.

'I enjoyed watching. In my opinion, it was impossible to fault in you, yet your coach was full of complaints.'

'James is always like that. He knows that we rowed well this morning, but he has to demand more of us each time. It's the way that he works.'

'Oh, I see.'

'Anyway,' said Thorpe, 'I need to know when I can speak to the inspector.'

'How important is it?'

'It could be very important.'

'Then I'll ask him to come to your room early this afternoon.'

'Thank you.'

'Can I tell him what it's about?' asked Leeming.

'It's . . . a private matter.'

Painting was not simply a delight and a source of income for Madeleine, it sometimes acted as a solace. When her husband was away, she could lose herself in her work and keep loneliness at bay. It was the same that morning. Troubled by the friction between herself and her father, she went off to her studio and found the perfect antidote to her anxieties. The problem was that she revelled in her work so much that she didn't keep check of the time. When she eventually remembered her father, she went straight to the nursery to catch him before he left the house.

But he was no longer there. The nanny was playing with Helena.

'What's happened to my father?' she asked.

'He left ten minutes ago, Mrs Colbeck,' said the other.

'Was there any message for me?'

'No, he simply said that he was in a hurry.'

'I see.'

'But Helena had a lovely time with him.'

'Did my father say where he was going?'

'No, he didn't.'

Helena got to her feet with a doll in her arms and ran to her mother. Lifting her up, Madeleine held her tight and spun round in a circle to make the girl laugh. She admired the way that Helena had dressed the doll and told her what a clever little daughter she had. Madeleine's mind, however, was fixed on a family member of an older generation and she could find no words of approval for him.

Simon Reddish was not only evading questions, he was still simmering with exasperation at being interrupted. Colbeck therefore adopted a different approach, shifting the conversation to the theatre because he knew that it would secure his companion's interest and draw him out.

'Your father has a prodigious memory,' said Colbeck, 'and, at any given time, can hold more than one major role in his head. That's a vital asset for an actor. Do *you* have a retentive memory?'

'I most certainly do,' boasted the other.

'Like father, like son.'

'From an early age, my father made me learn famous speeches from plays. It became second nature. That's what I found so disappointing about the auditions for *Hamlet*. I'd learnt every one of the soliloquies yet Bernard – who'd done no preparation at all – walked off with the title role.'

'Why were you cast as Horatio?'

Reddish snorted. 'You may well ask,' he snapped. 'It was demeaning. I could have played Polonius or Claudius far better than those to whom the roles were allotted but I was palmed off with Horatio.'

'You could always have refused it.'

'And miss a chance to appear on a stage?' said Reddish in disbelief.

'Spoken like a true actor,' said Colbeck.

'That's what I am, Inspector,' said the other, earnestly. 'The rest of the cast took an interest in drama because it helped them escape the tedium of their studies. I was the only person who committed himself wholeheartedly.'

'We were told that Mr Pomeroy was a brilliant Hamlet. A performance of that quality requires full commitment.'

'Drama was just a pleasant diversion in Bernard's life.

His ambition was to be a politician and get his hands on the levers of power.'

'Parliament is full of theatricality, sir, so performing in plays is a good apprenticeship for it. I suspect that Mr Pomeroy took it as seriously as you do.'

'I dispute that.'

'I had a feeling that you would,' said Colbeck, evenly. 'Well, I won't keep you from your essay any longer.'

'Thank you.'

'Incidentally, what are you reading?'

'Divinity.'

'Really? That's hardly the ideal choice for an actor.'

'It was the subject that Marlowe chose.'

'I suppose that the church is also a kindred profession to the theatre.'

'In what way?' asked Reddish.

'Well, I wouldn't dare say this to a clergyman, but his work does involve wearing a costume and repeating lines that have been learnt by heart. That's no reflection on the importance of church services,' he added, quickly. 'I've attended them regularly throughout my life and found them, in the main, immensely reassuring.'

'I thought you were going to let me write my essay.'

'What would happen if you gave it in late?'

'I'd be severely reprimanded by my tutor.'

'And who might that be?'

'Professor Springett.'

Colbeck felt that he had just learnt something important.

* * *

Elsie Gurr poured two cups before putting the teapot down and covering it with a cosy. After adding milk and sugar to each of the cups, she sat down opposite her visitor.

'I think you made your point, Caleb,' she said.

'So do I,' he said. 'When she saw that I'd left, Maddy would have realised that I'm still angry at being accused of lying.'

'Don't leave it too long.'

'What do you mean?'

'Well, you'll have to accept her apology sooner or later. If this goes on and on, the distance between you will get wider and wider.'

'That's what I'm afraid of.'

'Joe and I were very happy together,' she recalled with a smile, 'but we did fall out from time to time. Before we went to bed, we always kissed and made up. "Never let the sun go down on your anger." That's what Joe always said.'

'But I am still angry.'

'Enough is enough.'

'If you say so . . .'

'I do, Caleb. How can I meet your daughter if you're still not really talking to each other? I want us all to be friends – don't you?'

'Yes, I do.'

'Then sort everything out tomorrow,' she said, stirring her tea. 'Now, then, you told me that you had something important to ask me and the answer is "yes".'

'But you don't know what I was going to say.'

'Of course, I do, you silly man. Ever since we met, you've

wanted to invite me to *your* house, but you were afraid I might say "no". That's right, isn't it?' He nodded. 'I'll come tomorrow, Caleb, *and* any other day you invite me.'

Andrews laughed with relief, reaching out to squeeze her hands.

CHAPTER FOURTEEN

There was safety in numbers. Bright sunshine had brought untold dozens of people out for a walk beside the river. Alan Hinton and Lydia Quayle were anonymous in the crowd. It gave them confidence. When they saw someone coming out of the Oxford University Boat Club, therefore, they felt able to approach the man. While he did not look like one of the oarsmen, he was clearly an enthusiastic member of the club. He was a young man in his early twenties with a friendly smile that broadened when they intercepted him. His eyes settled on Lydia.

'Can I help you?' he asked.

'We've been watching the boat,' she replied.

'Then you've come at a good time. We're close to our best now.'

'Does that mean you'll win the Boat Race?' said Hinton.

'We hope so,' said the man, flicking his gaze to Hinton, 'but there's no such thing as a foregone conclusion. That's what makes the Boat Race so exciting. Anything can happen. We've entered the Race before with what was by far the better crew, yet we still lost because of some unforeseen hazard. By the same token, I once watched a raw and inexperienced Oxford boat surprise us all by winning because the Cambridge eight came close to sinking as a result of a disastrous mistake by their cox.'

'When it comes to the cox,' said Hinton, 'you'll have a definite advantage this year.'

'Yes,' said Lydia, 'I read about that in the newspaper. The Cambridge cox died on the platform of a railway station.'

'He didn't die – he was murdered, apparently.'

'Either way,' said the man, 'we're grateful. Bernard Pomeroy gave Cambridge a definite advantage. That's disappeared now. When the news first broke, we were sorry – then we cheered the fact that Pomeroy was no longer a problem for us. Getting him out of the contest was a boon to us.'

He walked off with an air of complacence.

'No,' said Leeming, 'I didn't find any spies making notes about the Cambridge crew. In fact, the only person taking any real interest in them was an artist who was drawing a sketch of the boat as it approached. It was a very good sketch as well. I got close enough to see it.'

'You're missing something,' said Colbeck.

'Am I?'

'Yes, Victor. Did it never occur to you that he wasn't only there to draw a sketch? Posing as an artist could have been a clever disguise.'

'But he *was* an artist, Inspector.'

'That doesn't preclude his being there on behalf of Oxford.'

'No,' agreed Leeming. 'I suppose not.'

They'd met up at the pub that had now become their headquarters. The sergeant had been interested to hear of the connection between Simon Reddish and Professor Springett. He was impressed by the way that Colbeck's knowledge of the theatre had allowed him to get more out of Reddish than he himself had managed. When he talked about his time on the towpath, however, Leeming's account was being questioned.

'What happened to this artist?' asked Colbeck.

'He left his pitch by the willow tree.'

'Which way did he leave?'

'Why do you want to know?'

'Did he go *away* from the boat or towards it?'

'I didn't really notice,' admitted Leeming, 'but I have a vague memory that he went past it. Yes,' he added, 'now that I think of it, he did.'

'So he'd have been able to hear what the coach was saying to the crew.'

'I suppose that he would.'

'That might be useful information to Oxford. Their president and coach would love to know how their rivals were faring in the wake of Pomeroy's death.'

213

'I still think he was an artist,' said Leeming, 'and nothing else. There's a very easy way to find out.'

'Is there?'

'Yes, I spoke to Thorpe afterwards. He told me he needed to speak to you as a matter of urgency.'

'Did he say why?'

'No, sir – it is a private matter, he said. I told him you'd go to his college this afternoon.'

'What state was he in?'

'He was very tired and glistening with sweat. Pulling on that heavy oar is hard work. I wouldn't fancy doing it.'

'Did he seem anxious, depressed, excited?'

'He was gasping for breath. That's all I can tell you.'

'Thank you for passing on his message.'

'You won't forget to ask him about that artist, will you?' said Leeming. 'I still think he was harmless.'

Jack Stott was alone in the lodge, taking advantage of a quiet period to glance at the local weekly newspaper. The murder of Bernard Pomeroy was announced in bold type on the front page. Before he could begin to read the article, the porter was disturbed by the arrival of Terence Springett.

'Good day to you, Professor,' he said.

'The same to you, Stott,' replied the other. 'Has he been here today?'

'Who do you mean, sir?'

'I'm talking about Inspector Colbeck.'

'He called here earlier this morning.'

'Did he come to see anyone in particular?'

'Actually,' said Stott, 'he wanted a chat with me.'

'What was it about?'

'He asked about the college security and wanted to know if it was easy to climb in after dark when the place was locked up.'

'Why?' said the professor with heavy sarcasm. 'Is he planning to join us for a midnight feast?'

'The inspector believes that Mr Pomeroy could only have raced out of here if he'd had some kind of summons. It would have to have been slipped under his door during the night.'

'That's idle supposition.'

'I think there's something in the idea. Why would someone as polite and friendly as Mr Pomeroy charge in here, thrust a note into my hand, then run off at top speed without another word? He was like someone possessed. There must have been a reason why he behaved like that.'

'Pomeroy was always inclined to be headstrong.'

'I've never seen him in that state before.'

'He could be unduly excitable,' said Springett. 'Let's go back to Inspector Colbeck. Did he ask about *me*?'

'No, he didn't.'

'Are you certain of that?'

'He just wanted to know what time we locked up at night and when we unlocked everything in the morning.'

'Remember what I told you,' warned Springett.

'I will, Professor.'

'Say *nothing* to either of the detectives about Pomeroy and me.' The porter nodded. 'Your job here depends on it. Is that clear enough for you?'

'I know where my loyalties lie.'

'Don't let me down as the other porter did or you'll suffer the same fate.'

'I heard your instructions the first time, sir,' said Stott, meeting his gaze. 'I'll obey them to the letter.'

James Webb called on Malcolm Henfrey-Ling early that afternoon. It had become the custom for coach and president to discuss in more depth the morning's performance on the river. Webb always began with the same question.

'Are all the places in the boat allocated?'

'I think so,' said Henfrey-Ling.

'Does that mean you're happy with our choices?'

'We've got the best men in the correct positions, James.'

'So that is the crew to take on Oxford. It's settled.'

'Unless you have any doubts,' said Henfrey-Ling.

'The only question mark for me is over Dangerfield,' said Webb. 'If we have a potential weakness, it must be him. Should we give Pusey a chance?'

'There's little to choose between Pusey and Dangerfield. I'd stick with the latter on the grounds of experience. He's rowed in the Race before. Neil Pusey is an equally good oarsman but has never had to stand up to real pressure.'

'Let's stick with Dangerfield then.'

'He stood up well to your criticism this morning whereas some of the others wilted a little. You were unduly harsh on all of us, James, yet you let Colin Smyly off scot-free even though our cox made some bad mistakes.'

'He won't make those again, Malcolm. He needs

encouragement. That's why I left him off my list of complaints. If I'd yelled at him in front of the others, it would have affected his confidence. I took him aside afterwards for a quiet word.'

'Ah, I didn't know that.'

'I wished I could've done that with Nick as well.'

'Why?'

'He was trying *too* hard,' said Webb. 'Commitment is one thing, but he was almost manic. Since you had your back to the rest of the crew, you couldn't see him, straining as if he was powering the boat entirely on his own. I need to tell him to pace himself.'

'Nick is still dazed by what happened to Bernard.'

'Poor man – he's lost his Siamese twin.'

'He told me that the river is the only place where he can forget the horror of it all. Left alone, he's close to despair. When he's back in the boat, he pretends that Bernard is still with us, guiding our destiny.'

'If only he were, Malcolm.'

'Nick will be all right, I'm sure. He just needs our moral support. When he's on the river,' said Henfrey-Ling, 'he's one of the strongest links in our chain. That's why we must help Nick during this difficult period. We rely on him.'

When he got to the room, Colbeck found that the door had been left wide open. Thorpe was lying on the floor with his eyes closed and with a book under his head acting as a pillow. As soon as Colbeck entered the room, the eyes flickered open. Thorpe then got to his feet very slowly.

'Thank you for coming, Inspector,' he said, stepping past him to close the door. 'Do sit down, please.'

'The sergeant said that you had something to confide to me,' said Colbeck, lowering himself into an armchair. 'He wondered why you were being so secretive.'

'You'll soon understand.' Thorpe sat opposite him on the sofa. 'I'd given Bernard my word that I'd never tell anyone about it, but things are different now.'

'He's not here to stop you.'

'I believe that he'd *want* me to speak out.'

'I'm all ears.'

Before saying another word, Thorpe seemed to grapple with some last-minute reservations about doing so. He eventually overcame the resistance.

'Bernard was an Apostle,' he said.

'You mean that he belonged to some religious order?'

'No, Inspector, the Apostles are members of a secret society that was founded over forty years ago by a man who went on to become the bishop of Gibraltar.'

'What was its avowed aim?'

'It was essentially a debating society that met to discuss such topics as truth, God and ethics. Originally, it had only twelve members, hence the name. It's still highly exclusive. To be invited to join is a signal honour. One has to have shown exceptional intelligence.'

'Evidently, Mr Pomeroy had that.'

'He was up against another problem,' explained Thorpe. 'Historically, the society drew most of its members from St John's, Trinity and King's. Bernard was probably the first from Corpus.'

'What happens when the members cease to be undergraduates and venture out into the wider world?'

'Apostles become Angels and organise secret meetings of their own.'

'And, presumably, they're all men of some standing.'

'Oh, yes. As well as bishops, there are eminent scholars, captains of industry and Members of Parliament in their number.'

'Your friend was clearly in illustrious company,' remarked Colbeck, 'though I have to say that he seems an unlikely Apostle. Secret societies tend to recruit quiet, moderate, trustworthy members. Mr Pomeroy was surely too flamboyant.'

'Bernard loved the cut and thrust of debate.'

'Where did the meetings take place?'

'It was usually in a room belonging to one of the members. Bernard hosted one in Corpus.'

'Well, an interesting new side of Mr Pomeroy has been revealed, but I can't at the moment see that it has any relevance to the investigation.'

'Bernard wasn't the only person from Corpus eager to join the society. In his day, there was someone even more desperate to be invited.'

'Ah,' said Colbeck, understanding. 'Might that person be Professor Springett?'

'It might indeed, Inspector.'

'If Pomeroy had been courted while he was rejected, the professor would have been mortified.'

'It was a wound that never healed,' said Thorpe. 'Springett

was turned down when he was an undergraduate at Corpus all those years ago, yet he behaved as if it had been last week. Then a brilliant newcomer turns up and is invited to become part of what was, in effect, a privileged circle.'

'How did the professor respond?'

'I'm sure you can imagine.'

'Was that the cause of this feud between them?'

'Not exactly . . .'

'Then what was?'

'Bernard was an intensely serious person at heart,' said Thorpe, 'but there was a vein of impishness in him.'

'How did it manifest itself?'

'I'm afraid that he couldn't resist baiting Professor Springett.'

Victor Leeming had been alarmed at the suggestion that the artist whom he'd seen on the riverbank had been sent there by the Oxford University Boat Club. Colbeck had asked him to take a closer look that afternoon at Andrew Kinglake as a potential suspect, but the sergeant realised that he could kill two birds with one stone. If he spoke to Malcolm Henfrey-Ling, he could not only discover a lot more about Kinglake, he could ask him if he was aware of an artist making sketches of the Cambridge boat. To that end, he went along to the president's college and found him chatting in his room to James Webb.

The two men sat up with interest when he came in. Leeming shook his head.

'No,' he said, 'I'm afraid that we haven't made an arrest yet, but we have a number of people who've aroused our interest.'

'May we know who they are?' asked Webb.

'I've come to talk to you about one of them.'

'Oh – who is that?'

'Andrew Kinglake.'

'Yes,' said Henfrey-Ling, 'we had our own suspicions about Andrew because he expected to profit by Bernard's disappearance. As it turned out, we'd selected someone else ahead of him, so he flounced off.'

'Being in your boat means everything to him,' said Leeming. 'Did you know that his father was the Cambridge cox in the first ever Boat Race?'

'Andrew never stops talking about it,' moaned Webb. 'He said he was carrying on a family tradition.'

'But only if he proved himself worthy of the opportunity,' said Henfrey-Ling. 'He had that opportunity last year and, if truth be told, made rather a mess of it. However,' he went on, 'Andrew did make a point of apologising for his behaviour in stalking off.'

'Was it a sincere apology?' asked Leeming.

'I believe so.'

'What's his position now?'

'Well, he's the reserve cox. We must cover every eventuality. If something happens to Colin Smyly, we have a replacement at hand.'

'Does that mean Mr Smyly may be in danger?'

'No, Sergeant, I think you can forget about Andrew Kinglake as a killer. It was an idea that flitted into our heads, but it's flitted out again now.'

'There's additional proof of that,' said Webb.

'Is there?' asked Leeming.

'What's the best way to damage our prospects in the Race?'

'Killing your cox?'

'There's a much simpler but equally devastating way.'

'Oh?'

'Instead of targeting a member of the crew,' said Webb, 'they could have destroyed our boat. It's a new design and it cuts through the water beautifully. If it were badly damaged in some way, we'd have to revert to our old boat and that would mean we were handicapped.'

Leeming was puzzled. 'I don't see the connection with Mr Kinglake.'

'Our new boat is kept under guard day and night. We've had to call on a number of volunteers to maintain a vigil. Each stint is four hours. Andrew Kinglake has just volunteered to take his turn at the night shift.'

'Will he be there on his own?'

'No, Sergeant, there'll be two other people with him.'

'In short,' added Henfrey-Ling, 'he wants to make amends for his bad behaviour. For most volunteers, protecting our boat is just something that has to be done. For Andrew, it's a kind of penance.'

'It could also be a smokescreen,' suggested Leeming. 'Mr Kinglake is hiding his crime behind a show of helping you out. I'm not rushing to take his name off our list of suspects. He made a commitment to his father. One way or another, he means to honour it.'

'I disagree, Sergeant.'

'So do I,' said Webb. 'We know him better than you.'

'That's true,' conceded Leeming. 'Rowing is a closed book to me. Anyway, let's put Mr Kinglake aside for a moment. I want to ask you about someone else.'

'Who is it?'

'I don't know his name, sir, but he was standing near a willow tree this morning as the boat approached. He had a telescope on a tripod so that he could watch the boat while trying to draw a sketch of it.'

'There's nothing to stop him doing that,' said Webb.

'What if he was there to keep an eye on you as well?'

'If he's a spy from Oxford, good luck to him. All that he can report is that we're in fine fettle and determined to beat them.'

'So he didn't *ask* you if he could sketch you?'

'Why should he?' replied Henfrey-Ling. 'We've had artists drawing pictures of us before. It does no harm. We don't object to people who admire us enough to go to all the trouble of spending hours watching us from the riverbank.'

'That's the least of our worries,' said Webb.

'What's the biggest of them, sir?' asked Leeming.

'Oh, that's an easy question to answer.'

'Is it?'

'Our biggest worry is that we'll lose. We have the better boat, the better crew, the better coach . . .'

'And by far the better president,' said Henfrey-Ling with a laugh. 'If all goes well, we *should* be first past the post but . . . well, we have to be realistic. The result is in the lap of the gods.'

*   *   *

Madeleine Colbeck was feeling lonely. At a time when she most needed a close friend, there was nobody available. The one person to whom she could have turned had gone off for the day to Oxford – and all because Madeleine had suggested it. The irony of it all had not escaped her. As she sat in her studio, she was sad and listless, unable to lift her brush, let alone resume work on her latest painting. The rift with her father preoccupied her because she could see no easy way to repair it. Their only point of contact at the moment was her daughter.

Making an effort to concentrate on her work, she reached for her palate and studied the canvas. After a desultory attempt at working, however, she soon broke off. Painting was over for the day. Madeleine went off to the bathroom to wash her hands properly. On her way there, she passed a window at the front of the house and saw something out of the corner of her eye that made her stop. When she looked down, she noticed a short, plump woman in her sixties staring at the property through her spectacles as if it were a thing of wonder.

Madeleine had never seen her before. The visitor didn't linger. When she saw the face in the front window, she scurried away.

As he listened to the description of what had happened at the meeting of the Apostles in Pomeroy's room, Colbeck could see why the undergraduate had antagonised people so easily. It was almost as if Pomeroy gloried in doing so. The debate on that occasion had been about the worth of theological study and Pomeroy had used it to launch a personal attack on Professor Springett.

'It was deliberately wounding,' said Thorpe. 'Once he was in his stride, Bernard was a brilliant speaker. He had everyone roaring with laughter at the professor's expense. You can imagine Springett's reaction when he heard about it.'

'I thought these meetings were secret.'

'Things sometimes seep out.'

'Who actually told the professor?'

'It was the Master,' replied Thorpe. 'I should perhaps explain that he and Springett vied for the post of running the college. It was another blow to the professor's self-esteem when Sir Harold Nellington was appointed ahead of him.'

'How did Sir Harold become aware of the debate?'

'Bernard made sure of it, Inspector. He knew that the Master would be bound to pass it on and – I daresay – take pleasure in doing so. Incidentally, it was Bernard who coined the nickname for the Master.'

'What was it?'

'Death Knell.'

Colbeck smiled. 'I won't ask you what his nickname for the professor was,' he said. 'It was probably even less flattering.'

'Springett was hopping mad. He demanded an apology.'

'Did he get one?'

'Bernard never apologised,' said Thorpe as if it were a virtue. 'It was an iron rule for him.'

'*You* might forgive his behaviour,' said Colbeck, 'but

I think that the professor was unfairly traduced. He had a perfect right to protest. Was Mr Pomeroy aware that the professor had once been rejected by the Apostles?' Thorpe nodded. 'Your friend no doubt used it as a means of goading him.'

'It was all in fun, really.'

'I fail to detect any cause for mirth.'

'Debate was at once serious and light-hearted.'

'I thought the Apostles were famed for their intellectual prowess.'

'They were, Inspector, but beer flowed freely at the meetings. Bernard said that they sometimes ended in drunken hilarity.'

Colbeck was glad that he'd been given a new insight into the sometimes tempestuous relationship between Pomeroy and Professor Springett. Locked into hero-worship of his friend, Thorpe approved of everything he'd said and done. The inspector took an impartial view, noting that it was Pomeroy who'd initiated the attacks on a respected don. In doing so, had he unwittingly created a vengeful enemy bent on having him killed?

'Thank you, Mr Thorpe,' he said. 'What you've told me is illuminating.'

'I hoped that it would be.'

'Professor Springett seems to have been a hapless victim.'

'Far from it,' argued the other, hotly. 'Bernard felt that he was a spiteful, manipulative toad and worthy of attack. My opinion is that the professor could stand it no longer and retaliated.'

'I'll weigh everything in the balance before I reach a conclusion,' said Colbeck, stoutly. 'If you don't mind my saying so, you're assigning guilt far too recklessly. That's unwise. I need to amass a lot more evidence about *all* the suspects before I even consider making an arrest.' Thorpe looked suitably chastened. 'Now, then, there's another matter I'd like to raise with you,' resumed Colbeck. 'When you were on the river this morning, were any of you aware that someone was drawing a sketch of the boat?'

It was mid afternoon before Brannigan was able to pop into Oriel College. After a successful morning on the river, the coach was in a buoyant mood when he went into Vincent Pinckney's room. The latter was at his desk, making a list.

'You're just in time, Liam,' he said, offering him a sheet of paper. 'This would be *my* choice for the dark blue boat.'

'Let's have a look,' said the other, running an eye down the names. 'Ah, we have a problem, I see.'

'I've plumped for Tom Unsworth as bow.'

'What – in spite of the fact that he's not fully fit?'

'He's been working hard on that.'

'We need eight supremely fit oarsmen, Vince. Tom is *almost* there, but that's not good enough for me. He was puffing and blowing this morning.'

'We *all* were, Liam. You really pushed us.'

'That's what you asked me to do.'

'I say that we stay with Tom for the time being.'

'Maurice Matthews is in better condition,' said

Brannigan. 'Why don't we give him a turn as bow tomorrow and see how he measures against Tom?'

'Fair enough,' agreed Pinckney. 'If you only question *one* of my choices, the rest of the crew is agreed on. Good – I'm glad we think the same way.'

'That's important. Coaches and presidents should always be of one mind.'

'Then why were you so bloody argumentative at the start?' demanded Pinckney. 'In your view, we couldn't do anything right. Literally and metaphorically, you rocked the boat, Liam.'

'It worked,' said the Irishman.

'You're such a devious bastard.'

'I'll do whatever it takes.'

'You've proved that,' said Pinckney. 'We've both gone to extremes we'd never have thought possible. Now that Pomeroy is out of our way, we're in the perfect position.'

'Cambridge will be rowing with a novice cox.'

'How do you know?'

'It's because I make it my business to know. They've got a fresh-faced young lad named Colin Smyly. I had him watched this morning.'

'But there's no point, is there? Once Pomeroy was removed, we knew that we had a clear advantage. Why keep them under surveillance?'

'I want to be doubly sure, Vince. The man I sent there is a wonderful artist. When he delivers his report later today,' said Brannigan, 'we'll get a drawing of the Cambridge crew as well.'

'What do we do with it?'

'Stick it on a dartboard and see how many of their oarsmen we can hit.'

They laughed together at the prospect.

CHAPTER FIFTEEN

When he retired, Caleb Andrews suddenly had long hours to fill and a new pattern of living slowly emerged. Regular visits to his daughter and her husband were of paramount importance, even more so when Helena Rose Colbeck came into existence. He coveted his role in the family and – until recently – felt comfortable in it. As for leisure time, he felt most at home in the company of railwaymen, whether retired from, or still at work for, the London and North Western Railway. At a public house near Euston Station, he and his friends would meet regularly to chat, reminisce, argue, complain, discuss the latest developments in the design of locomotives and pour scorn on the rivals of the LNWR.

On his walk to the pub early that evening, he reflected on the difference that meeting Elsie Gurr had made on his life. She'd not only offered warm and uncritical friendship, she had brought him alive again in ways that even his family couldn't match. In the short time they'd known each other, Elsie had been unobtrusively caring and affectionate. Offering much, she seemed to demand nothing in return. Pleasant thoughts of her filled his mind as he strolled towards Euston. By agreeing to come to his house for tea on the following afternoon, she'd signalled a definite move forward in their relationship. It put a decided spring into his step.

When he got within reach of his destination, he saw a tall, thin, hunched figure coming out of the pub with a walking stick tapping on the pavement. Gilbert Parry was moving slowly and carefully towards him, his teeth clenching from time to time.

'Is that hip of yours still causing you trouble, Gil?' asked Andrews.

'The pain comes and goes.'

'You look as if you need that walking stick.'

'I fought hard against it, Caleb, but, in the end, I had to give in.'

'You were always so lively in the old days.'

'That was then,' said Parry, sadly. His face brightened. 'How are things?'

'Oh, things are fine. Thanks for asking.'

'You didn't understand my question. How are . . . *things*?'

Andrews beamed. 'They've never been better, Gil.'

'I was hoping you'd say that.'

* * *

When their train stopped at Didcot, the other passengers got out, leaving Alan Hinton and Lydia Quayle alone together in the compartment and able to talk freely at last.

'There was no need for you to escort me back to London,' she said.

'There was every need. I couldn't let you go on your own. You deserve to be taken all the way to Paddington.'

'But you'll have to go straight back to Oxford and spend the night there.'

'There's still more to do, Lydia,' he said. 'Thanks to you, we learnt a lot simply by keeping our ears open, but there's much more intelligence to gather.'

'It's been an intriguing day for me.'

'I'm glad that you enjoyed it.'

'If that's what being a detective amounts to, I'll help you whenever you like.'

'It's rarely as easy and trouble-free as today. Most of the criminals we chase are nasty, violent people who need locking away. They always resist arrest. I wouldn't let you anywhere near real villains.'

'If members of the Oxford Boat Club are involved in what happened to the Cambridge cox, they *are* real villains,' she pointed out. 'They just happen to speak differently to the dangerous thugs you usually deal with.' She put a hand on his arm. 'You will take care, won't you, Alan?'

'I always keep my wits about me.'

'Good.'

'I'll have so much to tell Madeleine when I get back.'

'Please give her my warmest regards.'

'I will, Alan.'

'And tell her that I've enjoyed the services today of a budding detective.'

She laughed. 'All that I did was to *listen* to people.'

'That's a vital part of the job.'

The president and coach of the Cambridge University Boat Club might have absolved Andrew Kinglake from any involvement in the murder, but Leeming still had lingering doubts about the cox. As a result, he decided to call on him a second time. He was given an even more hostile reception than on the previous occasion. When the sergeant entered the undergraduate's room, Kinglake was relaxing in a chair with a book in his hands.

'What is it *this* time?' he demanded.

'I just wanted a few words, sir.'

'Make sure that it is only a few.'

'I've been speaking to the president and the coach.'

'Does that mean you were checking up on me?'

'Your name did . . . come up, Mr Kinglake.'

'Then I hope you were told about my commitment to the Boat Club. I'm on sentry duty there every night.'

'I was impressed by that.'

'We spent a lot of money on that new boat. It has to be protected.'

'Do you really think that someone from Oxford might damage it?'

'We're not giving them the chance, Sergeant. Instead

of hassling people like me, you should be conducting investigations there.'

'We already are, sir.'

Kinglake was taken aback. 'Oh, I see.'

'We're trying to examine all possibilities.'

'What's been discovered in Oxford?'

'That information is private,' said Leeming. 'I came to talk about you.'

'Why?'

'I'm told that you apologised for going off in a huff when you discovered that you would not be the Cambridge cox this year.'

'It was a nasty shock,' said Kinglake, 'and I admit that I should have accepted the decision with more grace. Anyway, that's all behind me now. It's water under the bridge.'

'Did you watch the crew in action this morning?'

'Of course, I did.'

'What did you think of the cox's performance?'

'It was competent. Colin did a few things that I'd have done differently, perhaps, but he seemed to have a firm control of the crew.'

'Did you happen to notice an artist sketching the boat?'

'No, I didn't. I was positioned near the point where the boat had to be turned around. That's a real test for the cox.'

'It's been suggested that the artist might have been there on behalf of Oxford. He made a point of walking past when the coach was yelling at the crew. He would have heard about any mistakes they'd made.'

'We've had spies here before,' said Kinglake, unworried. 'It's inevitable. As for James, he doesn't feel happy until he's had a good yell at us.'

'Why do you think he left you out of the boat?'

'It would've been a joint decision between him and Malcolm.'

'Both of them preferred Mr Smyly.'

'That was their decision yesterday,' said the other, 'but there's still a fair amount of time before the Boat Race. As we get closer to that, they may start to think differently.'

'Does that mean you still have hope of being in the Cambridge boat?'

'I've set my heart on it.'

'Do you expect your rival to falter?'

'I'm ready for any eventuality, Sergeant.'

Kinglake did his best to hold back a smirk.

Terence Springett was just about to pour himself a glass of cordial when there was a tap on the door. In response to the invitation, Simon Reddish came into the study with a sheaf of papers in his hand.

'I'm sorry that my essay is slightly late, Professor,' he said, 'but I was held up by Inspector Colbeck. Apart from taking up valuable time, he disturbed my train of thought. Anyway,' he went on, handing over the essay, 'here it is.'

'Thank you, Simon.'

'I didn't want you to think that I was letting you down.'

'I'd never think that,' said Springett, 'and I sympathise with you. I had the inspector in here so I know how intrusive he can be. If there was an award for badgering innocent people, he'd be a clear winner.'

'I agree. I couldn't get rid of the man.'

'Nor me – he was like a limpet.'

'I was glad when he finally left.'

'That makes two of us,' said Springett, putting the essay down and reaching for a decanter. 'I was going to have a non-alcoholic drink but perhaps you'd like to join me in a sherry.'

'Thank you, Professor. I will.'

'It might help you cope more easily with the effects of your interrogation.'

Reddish sighed. 'Yes, there was a whiff of the Spanish Inquisition about it.'

After pouring two glasses, Springett offered one to his visitor and gestured towards a chair. The professor sat opposite him and had a first sip.

'That's better!' he said, licking his lips. 'What exactly did Colbeck want?'

'He kept harping on about my so-called feud with Bernard Pomeroy. When I told him we were friends, he refused to believe me. He claimed I had an obsession about taking on the title role in *Doctor Faustus*.'

'It's a legitimate ambition, Simon. The part was written for you.'

'When I shave in the morning, I recite the major speeches in the play. It's a trick that my father taught me. Rehearse on a daily basis – that was his mantra. To be fair to the inspector,' he continued, 'he knows a lot about theatre and has actually seen some of my father's most celebrated performances.'

'Did he ask you about *me*?'

'He had no reason to do so.'

'That's a relief.'

'But your name did come into the conversation at the end.'

Springett tensed. 'Oh? Why was that?'

'He asked me what I was reading and who my tutor was.'

'I see. That's unfortunate.'

'He didn't say anything about you, but I could see that he was interested that we met each other on a regular basis.'

'That means he'll probably want to corner me again.'

'I found him less of a nuisance than Sergeant Leeming.'

'Yes,' said Springett, 'and the inspector *is* well-mannered. That's something, I suppose. I just hate the feeling of being under the microscope, so to speak. I don't know why. After all, we've nothing to hide.'

'No,' agreed the other with a sly grin, 'we don't, do we?'

They raised their glasses in a toast.

Madeleine Colbeck was overjoyed when Lydia turned up on her doorstep that evening. She whisked her visitor into the drawing room and demanded to know everything that had happened on the latter's visit to Oxford. Lydia duly obeyed and gave her a fairly comprehensive account of what she and Alan Hinton had done.

'Go on,' urged Madeleine. 'Tell me what I *really* want to know.'

'I've just done that.'

'No, you haven't, Lydia. You've only talked about the Oxford crew. You haven't said a single word about your day out with Alan.'

'It wasn't a day out – it was a search for evidence.'

'That's what I want to hear about, you silly woman. Tell me what evidence there was of Alan's fondness for you. Was he hopelessly distracted?'

'Of course not,' said Lydia. 'He concentrated hard on his work.'

'Did he say what a valuable asset you'd been?'

'He didn't *need* to say it. Alan obviously enjoyed having me on his arm and it was something that I savoured as well.'

'And so you should – he's besotted with you.'

'He's a dedicated detective. His work comes first – as it does for Robert.'

'Yes,' said Madeleine, 'Alan and my husband are two of a kind. But that doesn't stop Robert from showing his affection for me. What about Alan?'

'I've told you all that I'm going to.'

'Ah, so something meaningful *did* happen.'

'We had a pleasant day together – nothing more. In any case,' said Lydia, 'that's enough of *my* adventures. Tell me about your father. Has he forgiven you yet?'

Madeleine's face fell. 'No, he hasn't.'

'Did you apologise?'

'He didn't give me the chance. He refused to kiss me when he arrived, and he left without telling me that he was going.'

'That sounds bad.'

'It was like a slap in the face. I've spent so much time worrying about him that I haven't been able to work. How long is this going to go on?'

'That's up to you, Madeleine.'

'I've been to his house, I've tried to apologise, I've made it clear that I accept I was in the wrong – yet none of it works.'

'Be more assertive.'

'That would upset him even more.'

'At least you'd get his attention.'

'I'm not so sure about that. He's shutting me out, Lydia, and it hurts.'

'Mr Andrews can't be that unreasonable, can he?'

'As a rule, he isn't. But he won't even listen to me this time.'

'Why is that?'

'Without meaning to, I insulted him.'

'Yet all you did was to challenge him about something.'

'It was as if I'd touched a nerve. He was fuming – and he still is. The thing that worries me most,' said Madeleine, gloomily, 'is that I don't understand why.'

Seated in the pub with his friends, Caleb Andrews roared with laughter at a joke someone had just told, even though he'd heard it before. It was wonderful to be back among people who thought, spoke and acted like him. They were united by a shared experience of working on the railway. That meant everything to Andrews. He counted his blessings. He had wonderful friends, the most beautiful granddaughter in the world and a blossoming romance with Elsie Gurr. His life had never been happier.

Colbeck and Leeming had agreed to meet up on the riverbank so that they could walk along it to the place where the sergeant had seen the artist. Light was starting to fade slowly but there was still enough of it for them to see fairly clearly. Leeming talked about his conversation with the president and coach of the Boat Club, then described what happened when he paid a second visit to Andrew Kinglake.

'It was as if he was certain he'd be in the Boat Race, after all,' he said.

'Anything can happen between now and then, Victor. The new cox might get injured somehow or turn out to be unequal to what is, after all, a formidable task.'

'The coach admitted that Smyly had made some mistakes this morning, but he didn't want to criticise him in front of the rest of the crew. He's trying to build the cox's confidence.'

'Then he's doing his job properly.'

'I suppose that's true,' said Leeming. 'You went to see Thorpe, didn't you? What did he have to say for himself?'

Colbeck tailored his reply. He saw no point in telling the sergeant about the secret that Pomeroy had entrusted to his best friend. Thorpe had seen the invitation to become an Apostle as both a triumph for Pomeroy and a stick that he could use to beat Professor Springett.

'Oh,' said Colbeck, 'he just wanted to tell me that Pomeroy and Springett had had an earlier clash over something. Their antagonism towards each other didn't only arise from the biting criticism that Pomeroy directed at Springett's article. They were sworn enemies before that.'

'Whose fault was it?'

'Thorpe blamed the professor.'

'He would,' said Leeming. 'Pomeroy could do nothing wrong in his eyes.'

'The icon may be shattered when the truth finally comes out,' said Colbeck. 'Disillusion could be lying in wait for Thorpe.'

Leeming put out a hand to stop him and pointed to the nearby willow tree.

'That's where he was standing, sir.'

'What an odd place to choose. Some of those fronds hanging down would have obscured his view, surely.'

'Maybe he just wanted to be out of the sun.'

'It's more likely that he wanted to be out of sight,' said Colbeck. 'Thorpe didn't even see him. Did you ask Webb and Henfrey-Ling about the artist?'

'Yes, I did. Neither of them was really worried if he *had* been a spy. Webb pointed out that all he could report back to Oxford was that the Cambridge crew were on good form. That might actually unsettle them.'

'It might, indeed,' said Colbeck.

'You mentioned that you were going to speak to that porter.'

'And I did just that. He told me that the college was locked all night.'

'So, if someone wanted to deliver a message to Pomeroy, then he'd have had to climb in somehow.'

'No, Victor – he'd have stayed the night there.'

Leeming was surprised. 'Would a complete stranger have got away with that?'

'He might not have been a stranger,' said Colbeck. 'He might have been one of the Fellows.'

'Springett?'

When I was in his study, I noticed that he had a bedroom leading off it. If he'd spent the night there, he would have been in the ideal position to deliver a summons.'

'And he wouldn't have aroused the slightest suspicion.'

'There's another possibility. The Master mentioned to me that the professor had a house in Cambridge. Perhaps he went home at the end of the day as usual, allowing someone else to make use of his bedroom at the college. Can you guess who that person might have been?'

'Simon Reddish!'

They said the name in unison.

'Curst be the parents that engendered me!
No, Faustus, curse thyself. Curse Lucifer,
That hath deprived thee of the joys of heaven.
O, it strikes, it strikes! Now, body, turn to air,
Or Lucifer will bear thee quick to hell.
O, soul, be changed into little water drops
And fall into the ocean, ne'er be found!
My God, my God, look not so fierce on me!
Adders and serpents, let me breathe a while!
Ugly hell, gape not. Come not, Lucifer!
I'll burn my books. Ah, Mephistopheles!'

Terence Springett was entranced. His visitor had not merely quoted the doctor's final lines in the play, he'd acted them with great passion. Simon Reddish's performance had been riveting. It would have been impressive in a large theatre. In the confines of a small study, it was overwhelming.

'How could anyone choose Pomeroy over you?' asked the professor.

'You may well ask.'

'Depriving you of the role was a heinous crime.'

'Thank you,' said Reddish with a bow. 'It has now been restored to its rightful owner. I'll play it to the hilt. Marlowe will rise from his grave to lead the applause.'

By the time they'd walked all the way back to The Jolly Traveller, they'd exchanged every scrap of information that each had gathered in the course of the afternoon. It was time for a restorative meal before they continued their investigation. That, at least, had been Colbeck's plan. As he entered the pub, however, he discovered that his plan had been rewritten. The moment the landlord saw the inspector, he handed him a telegraph that had been delivered earlier. Colbeck opened it at once.

'I bet that's a demand from the superintendent,' said Leeming.

'He sent it, Victor, but it's not a demand. He's passing on a request from the Prime Minister.'

'Will you be able to speak to him, after all?'

'I will, indeed. I must call on Lord Palmerston at nine tomorrow morning.'

'Then you'll have to be up at the crack of dawn to catch the early train back to London.'

'I prefer the last train this evening,' decided Colbeck. 'That will enable me to give my wife a pleasant surprise and to fit in a visit to Superintendent Tallis early tomorrow before I go on to Downing Street.'

'What am I to do while you're away?'

'I'll give you a long list of instructions, don't worry. First of all, we've earned a hearty meal.' He read the telegraph again. 'I was starting to lose hope, but it turns out that Lord Palmerston is eager to see me. That sounds promising.'

Jack Stott was about to go off duty when he was accosted by someone he recognised. Nicholas Thorpe had turned up at Corpus Christi College.

'Good evening, sir,' said the porter.

'I need to ask you a favour, Stott.'

'What is it?'

'I want to borrow the key to Bernard's room.'

'I'm sorry, Mr Thorpe, but I'm not allowed to part with it.'

'But there's some personal property there that I'd like to reclaim. It will only take me two minutes. I know that you keep spare keys to all the rooms. Please give me the one to Bernard's.'

'I'm under strict orders, sir.'

'Don't be ridiculous, man. I was his closest friend.'

'That makes no difference. The Master insisted that nobody apart from the detectives was to be allowed in there. My hands are tied, sir.'

'I can't believe you're being so obstructive,' said Thorpe, angrily. 'Now stop playing games and give me the key.'

Stott was firm. 'I can't do that, sir. I might lose my job.'

'Who cares about that?'

'I do, sir. I have a family to feed.'

'Look,' said Thorpe, trying to control his temper, 'if you let me have that key for a few minutes, I'll make it worth your while.'

'I can't do it, sir, whatever you offer me.'

'Damn and blast you!'

'There's no need for that kind of language, sir.'

Thorpe pointed a finger at him. 'I'll report you to the Master.'

'He'll support me. I'm obeying his orders.'

Thorpe was about to give vent to his rage when he saw Professor Springett approaching. Turning instantly on his heel, he stalked off. Stott was relieved.

'What was all that shouting about?' asked Springett.

'The young gentleman wanted something I couldn't give him, sir.'

'It was Thorpe, wasn't it?'

'Yes, Professor.'

'I thought so. Why was he arguing with you?'

'He wanted the key to Mr Pomeroy's room.'

'But he's not even a member of the college.'

'Even if he was,' said the porter, 'I'm not allowed to give it to him. Mr Thorpe was insistent, but I had to turn him away.'

'Well done, Stott.'

'Thank you, Professor.'

'You did the right thing.'

Springett went out into the street, leaving the porter to savour a rare compliment from him.

Madeleine Colbeck was unable to settle. After putting her daughter to bed, she'd dined alone and wondered how she could best make peace with her father. Trying to keep herself occupied, she made a vain attempt to work in her studio but found that the oil lamp cast unsuitable light on the canvas. She abandoned her painting and retired to the study to write a series of letters to friends. Even that task didn't really occupy her mind. It was filled with echoes of the arguments she'd had with her father. How had they fallen out so quickly, and why had he put himself beyond her reach? A chasm had opened up between them.

As the evening wore on, she began to tire. Madeleine decided that she needed to turn her attention to something entirely different, if only to get some stimulus from it. She reached for the book that Lydia Quayle had recommended. It turned out to be a wise decision. *North and South* captivated her from the first page. The transformation in the heroine's life reminded her of her own. Margaret Hale was the daughter of a parson whose doubts about his religion caused him to resign his living in Hampshire and take his family to a grim, noisy, malodorous northern city known for its cotton-spinning. Margaret was at first horrified to be in a world dominated by trade.

Madeleine had moved in the opposite direction, leaving a tiny, terraced house in a working-class district to go into an infinitely more comfortable, middle-class environment. She'd been forced to adapt to what was, in essence, foreign territory. The sheer power of the narrative kept her reading. It was only when fatigue set in that she began to falter, eventually drifting off to sleep with the book open on her lap.

She was awakened by the soft touch of a hand on her shoulder.

'Madeleine . . . wake up, darling. It's me.'

Her eyelids fluttered, then she managed to half open an eye. She realised that her husband was bending solicitously over her.

'Robert!' she cried in amazement.

'Don't be so surprised. I do live here, you know.'

'Is it really you?'

He grinned. 'Who else are you expecting?'

As she struggled to bring herself fully awake, Colbeck sat beside her and put an arm around her. With the other hand, he lifted the book from her lap.

'What are you reading?' he asked.

'It's a book that Lydia lent me. It held me spellbound.'

'It can't have been that spell-binding or it wouldn't have sent you off to sleep. I read *North and South* years ago. It's a fine novel and proof that women can write every bit as well as men. Would you like me to tell you what happens at the end?'

'No,' she protested. 'That would be cruel.'

'Then I'll let you read at your own pace.'

Sitting up, she wiped the sleep from her eyes and studied him carefully.

'I thought you were in Cambridge.'

'I was, but now I'm back in London.'

'Why?'

'Given the choice between sleeping with my wife and having a room in a pub next to Victor Leeming's, I made the obvious decision. Also, I have two rather important appointments tomorrow morning.'

'Appointments?'

'The first is a courtesy visit to Superintendent Tallis to bring him up to date with the investigation. The second appointment,' he said, affecting indifference, 'is rather less interesting.'

'Why – who are you going to see?'

'I have a meeting with the Prime Minister.'

Madeleine's jaw dropped. 'Lord Palmerston?'

'Yes, he's asked to see me.'

'That's wonderful news, Robert.'

'I suppose that it is mildly exciting.'

'Stop teasing me,' she said, punching him playfully. 'I want to know how you came to get an invitation from the Prime Minister.'

Putting the book aside, he gave her a succinct account of their activities in Cambridge, explaining how they'd culminated in the meeting with Palmerston. Thrilled by his news about the Prime Minister, Madeleine was however disappointed that he and Leeming had not made any substantial progress.

'That's my report on the Cambridge front,' he said at length. 'I'm waiting to hear if Alan Hinton's second trip to Oxford has borne fruit.'

'I can tell you that, Robert.'

'How?'

'Ah, well . . .' She took a deep breath. 'I have to make a confession.'

'I'm listening.'

'Don't look so solemn. I only did what you've encouraged me to do.'

'And what's that?'

'You urged me to take an interest in your work – an *active* interest.'

His brow crinkled. 'And just how active have you been, Madeleine?'

There was no sense in keeping it from him. Her husband was bound to find out in the end. Madeleine gave him a full explanation of what had happened, undaunted by the fact that his expression became ever more disapproving.

'Did I do wrong?' she asked, meekly.

'Yes and no,' he replied.

'What do you mean?'

'In acting as a matchmaker, you were interfering in the lives of two people who are old enough to make up their own minds. Let them be, Madeleine. If Alan and Lydia are destined for each other,' he said, 'it will happen. Think of the time when you and I first met. How would *you* have felt if someone else had tried to engineer our courtship?'

'I'd have told them to mind their own business,' she replied.

'Lydia is too fond of you to say that, but she must think it sometimes.'

'I know, Robert,' she confessed. 'I see it in her face.'

'On that score, I'm afraid that you were very wrong.'

'What about the idea of using Lydia as camouflage?'

'It was brilliant,' he said, smiling. 'It must have given Alan Hinton the confidence to stroll around Oxford without fear of recognition. On that score, you were triumphantly right, Madeleine. Employing a woman in law enforcement may be anathema to Superintendent Tallis but I applaud it.'

'Then let me tell you about today in Oxford.'

'How do you know what happened there?'

'Lydia called in here when she got back and gave me chapter and verse.'

Colbeck sat back and listened intently, making the occasional remark but doing nothing to interrupt the full flow. At the end of her recitation, Madeleine paused to catch her breath.

'How on earth did I remember all that?' she asked.

'It was because you knew each detail was important. Thank you.'

'I pressed Lydia to stay for dinner, but she was exhausted. She went home in a cab and promised herself an early night.'

'I wish that *I* could afford one of those.'

'What time is it now?'

'Didn't you hear the clock chime? It's past midnight.'

'Goodness!' she exclaimed.

Rising to his feet, he offered his hand and helped her up.

'I think that it's time for bed, Mrs Colbeck, don't you?'

'I have a complaint to make first.'

'Why – what have I done?'

'You can't count. When you woke me up, you told me that you had two important appointments tomorrow.'

'It's the truth.'

'Oh, no, it isn't.'

'What are you talking about?'

'I'm talking about a *third* important appointment. It's with a precious little girl who's been asking after her father ever since he left the house. The superintendent may be important, and Lord Palmerston is even more important, but there's someone who loves her father dearly and who wants to see him the moment she wakes up.'

'I'm rightly corrected,' he said, laughing. 'Helena will always come first.'

With an arm around her shoulders, he led her upstairs to bed.

In the early hours of the morning, Cambridge lay under a blanket of darkness. The figure picking his way through the streets needed no light to guide him. He was on a well-trodden route. As he walked past a shop, someone stepped out of the doorway.

'Would you like some company, sir?' she asked.

'No,' he snarled, pushing her away.

He didn't hear the vile language the prostitute hissed after him because he was concentrating on his objective. When he reached the railings at the rear of the college, he first checked that nobody was about before climbing up with the ease of someone who'd entered by that means on more than one occasion. After balancing on the top of the railings, he jumped off and landed soundlessly on the ground. He crouched low and ran towards the Old Court.

When he reached the doorway he sought, he went through it and crept up the stairs until he reached the room at the top. Out came the knife he'd brought with him and he inserted it carefully in the lock. No matter how much he jiggled it, however, it could not do what he'd hoped it might. His weapon took on a more violent role, pushed between the door and the jamb so that it could act as a lever. He applied pressure slowly but firmly until there was definite movement. Suddenly, without warning, there was a loud bang and the door opened. He waited for a few minutes until he was certain that nobody had been roused by the noise.

He then went swiftly into the room, crossed to the desk and felt for the lever that would open the secret drawer. His fingers closed gratefully around the key. Using it to open the box beneath the bed, he grabbed the item that he'd come for.

After locking the box and returning the key to its hiding place, he left the room. Because the lock was broken he simply pulled the door shut. Then he descended the stairs on tiptoe.

He was soon climbing over the railings again.

CHAPTER SIXTEEN

Seated behind his desk, Edward Tallis read the report he'd just been handed and gave a grunt of approval.

'You and Leeming have done well,' he said.

'The case is growing in complexity, sir,' explained Colbeck, still on his feet. 'It poses a real challenge for us.'

'So I see.' Tallis clicked his tongue. 'Can this Professor Springett *really* be a plausible suspect?'

'He most certainly can,' said Colbeck. 'There's a direct link with another suspect, Simon Reddish. Individually, I don't believe that either of them would be capable of arranging a murder. Together, however, each would bolster the other. Once they'd decided to act, they'd have done so with fierce determination.'

'What about Andrew Kinglake?'

'He wasn't involved with either of them.'

'Could he *afford* to hire an assassin on his own?'

'He's a wealthy young man with money to burn, apparently. He boasted to Sergeant Leeming that his father is in royal service.'

'Heavens!' exclaimed Tallis. 'This gets more and more bizarre. Your suspects consist of a Professor of Divinity, the son of a famous actor and someone whose father consorts with Her Majesty. Who else will you add to your list – the Archbishop of Canterbury, Charles Dickens, the Queen of Sheba?'

'You're very droll this morning, sir,' said Colbeck with a smile. 'By the way, you forgot the two suspects from the Oxford University Boat Club.' Taking a watch from his waistcoat pocket, he glanced at it. 'I'd best be off. I have to get to Downing Street by nine.'

'You're not going anywhere near it.'

'But I thought that—'

'You didn't think, Inspector,' said Tallis, interrupting him. 'You *assumed* and that was a mistake. Cabinet meetings are held at Ten Downing Street, but Lord Palmerston prefers to operate from his townhouse in Piccadilly.'

'I didn't realise that. Thank you for telling me. May I say how grateful I am to the commissioner for arranging the interview on my behalf?'

'It may turn out to be a waste of time.'

'I'm cautiously optimistic.'

'Why? All you have to go on is a letter written in Italian. You haven't a clue what it says or what significance can be attached to it.'

'The Prime Minister regards it as being important enough to discuss it with me. That reinforces my belief that it may be of real value.'

'I remain sceptical.'

'It accords with your personality, Superintendent.'

Tallis's eyes ignited. 'Are you being disrespectful?'

'That would never cross my mind,' said Colbeck, face impassive. 'Might I ask for Lord Palmerston's address?'

'He lives in Cambridge House.'

Colbeck was startled. 'How appropriate!'

'It's merely a coincidence.'

'I've learnt to take coincidences seriously, sir,' said Colbeck. 'They crop up so often in the course of my work. Dismiss this one as irrelevant, if you wish, but I regard it as worthy of interest.'

'Suit yourself, Inspector,' said Tallis, irritably. 'Off you go, then, and make sure that you call back here afterwards to tell me what you've learnt.'

'I promise that I will, sir.'

'There's one last thing.'

'What is it?'

'The victim's body has been in that hospital for days and we still don't have precise details of how he died.'

'I'm very conscious of that, sir. It's the reason I asked the sergeant to go to Bury St Edmunds this morning. My guess is that he'll be on his way there right now.'

Victor Leeming was pleased with his first assignment of the day. It would give him the chance to see Arthur Bullen again and enjoy a few words with him. Also, as he left the station, he'd catch a glimpse of The Black Horse and rekindle fond memories of the delicious pie he'd eaten there. In the event, neither of those things happened. When the sergeant alighted from the train, Bullen was on the opposite platform and obscured by the stationary train, so Leeming was unaware of his presence. As he left the station, he found that a steady drizzle was falling, making him scurry to the cab rank. The Black Horse didn't even merit a backward glance.

Arriving at the hospital, he asked to see Dr Nunn and was conducted to his office. When the sergeant explained why he'd come, the doctor was apologetic.

'Yes,' he said, 'I know that it's taken a lot of time but our post-mortem is still incomplete. Someone from St Thomas's Hospital in London arrived yesterday. After an initial examination of the deceased, he took samples from the stomach to look at more carefully in his laboratory. When his analysis is complete, he'll contact Scotland Yard.'

'Good.'

'There's one thing I need to ask you.'

'What is it?' asked Leeming.

'Have you heard from any member of the family?'

'Not yet, Doctor. By now, word will have reached the sister who lives in Ireland, but the message that the inspector sent to Florence will take longer. You've met Mr Thorpe, I think. He was the victim's friend. He feels the family will almost certainly want the body sent to Italy.'

'I see.'

'Getting him there will be a problem.'

'So I can imagine.'

'I just hope that *I'm* not involved,' groaned Leeming.

'Wouldn't you like to see the delights of Florence?'

'Brighton is good enough for me. They speak English there.'

'Italian is a beautiful language.'

'Have you been to the country, Dr Nunn?'

'No,' said the other, 'but then, I don't need to. I've had a number of Italian patients over the years. Bury has had its share of immigrants, you know.'

'Really?'

'Go to St Edmund's on a Sunday and you'll hear Italian, French and Spanish voices among the English ones. It's a Roman Catholic Church.'

'Yes,' said Leeming, thoughtfully. 'It is, isn't it?'

Because he was determined to end the estrangement with his daughter, Caleb Andrews went to the house earlier than usual that morning. On his way there, he rehearsed what he was going to say. He genuinely regretted what had happened and felt guilty at the way that he'd behaved. Now that he was ready to put their tiff behind him, he realised how much he loved Madeleine and how reliant he'd been on her over the years. It was time to put their differences aside.

When he got to the house, however, no words were needed. Madeleine had glanced through the window and seen him coming so she flung the front door open in a gesture of welcome. He gave her a warm smile and spread his arms. With tears streaming down their faces, they hugged each other until they became aware that they were arousing the interest of passing pedestrians. Madeleine took her father into the house, closed the door behind them and led him to the drawing room.

'I'm so sorry for what happened,' she said.

'Don't take all the blame, Maddy. I deserve my share.'

'We must never let this happen again.'

'I agree.'

'Now dry your eyes and go up to your granddaughter. She'll be delighted that you've come so early.'

'Am I forgiven, then?'

'Am *I*?'

'Well . . .'

After an awkward moment, they embraced each other again.

'Have you heard anything from Robert?' he asked.

'I've heard a lot,' she replied, happily. 'He spent the night here.'

'Wonderful! I want all the details.'

'You'll have to wait until later. There one thing that I can tell you now, however. Your son-in-law has a very important appointment this morning.'

'Oh – who is he going to see?'

'The Prime Minister.'

Madeleine laughed at the expression of incredulity on her father's face.

Cambridge House had been built just over a century earlier for the Earl of Egremont and was known at the time as Egremont House. More recently it had been the London residence of the Duke of Cambridge, so the name was changed. When it was bought by Henry Temple, 3rd Viscount Palmerston in 1850, therefore, he let it continue as Cambridge House. As he took a first look at it, Colbeck saw that it was a large, imposing edifice with three main storeys. Built in the Palladian style, it was a fitting abode for a Prime Minister.

Arriving ten minutes before the time of his appointment, Colbeck expected a lengthy wait while Palmerston attended to the affairs of the nation because they would obviously have a prior claim. Palmerston also had a reputation for keeping foreign visitors waiting for long periods. Colbeck was amazed and delighted that he was conducted immediately to the Prime Minister's office, passing, on the way, other visitors waiting to be called and resentful at the sight of a newcomer jumping the queue. The secretary who had escorted him there tapped on the door, then opened it wide to usher him into the room. Colbeck felt honoured. During his long career, he knew Palmerston had not only occupied most of the major offices of state and led a previous administration, but his reputation as a fearless Foreign Secretary was unrivalled. Colbeck was about to meet a political titan.

He was therefore surprised to find himself confronted by a dapper individual in his mid seventies with curling grey hair and sculptured sideboards reaching down to his chin. There was nobility in Palmerston's bearing and unmistakable authority in his manner. He offered his hand.

'Good morning, Inspector,' he said, affably.

'Good morning, Prime Minister,' replied Colbeck,

accepting the firm handshake. 'It's good of you to see me.'

'I wanted to satisfy my curiosity. I've enjoyed reading about your exploits in the newspapers. In fact, you seem to get more sympathetic coverage than I do. Some of the articles about me are unkind and all of the cartoons in *Punch* are verging on criminality, albeit undeniably comical.'

'I, too, have been lampooned in *Punch* on occasion.'

'Then we are fellow sufferers,' said Palmerston. 'Let's sit down.'

While Colbeck chose a high-backed chair, the Prime Minister sat behind his desk. They took a moment to study each other carefully. Invited to explain why he wanted the interview, the inspector gave the relevant facts as crisply yet as fully as he could. Palmerston listened with a furrowed brow and gleaming eyes. At the end of the report, he made a hissing sound through his teeth.

'This is a bad business,' he said, 'a very bad business. It was a shock when I read about Bernard Pomeroy's murder. It beggars belief that he should have his life snuffed out prematurely like a candle. I knew his father well, you know.'

'So I was led to understand.'

'Alexander Pomeroy and I had much in common. Our fathers were both born in Sligo and owned land not far from each other. They were good friends and so were we. Alex was quite a bit younger than me, but that didn't matter. We got on famously and shared a love of Italy.'

'You became fluent in the language, I believe.'

'No disrespect to our dear Queen and her late husband,' said Palmerston, 'but it's far more euphonious than German.

The words flow so sweetly. As a young boy, I had an Italian tutor and I've been eternally grateful to my parents for providing me with such a wondrous gift. Now,' he went on, seriously, 'you discovered a letter I'd written to Bernard.'

'That's correct.'

'And you're honest enough to admit that you don't know what it means.'

'I know that it was of great importance to him or he wouldn't have kept it locked away.'

'You deduce correctly. It was an invitation.'

'Of what kind, may I ask?'

'It was an invitation to come and see me.'

'Why was it written in Italian?'

'I was replying to a request framed in that divine language.'

It was Eric Ayres who made the discovery. He was one of the scouts who saw to the needs of the undergraduates in Corpus Christi College. When he began his daily routine in the Old Court, he liked to start at the top of a staircase, clean and tidy each room and work his way down. Since he'd been told that Bernard Pomeroy's room was locked, he was surprised to see the door moving slightly in the wind that was blowing up the staircase. As soon as he'd investigated, he hurried downstairs and headed for the lodge. The porter had never seen him in such a state of distress.

'You look flustered, Eric,' said Stott.

'It's Mr Pomeroy's room. It's been broken into.'

'Are you sure?'

'I know a burglary when I see one. That lock was forced open.'

'Was anything stolen?'

'That's the funny thing, Jack. As far as I could see – and I know that room very well – nothing had been touched.'

'Is there anything of value in there?'

'Lots of things – and they're still there.'

'So why would anyone want to get into the room?'

Ayres shrugged. 'God knows.'

'All right, Eric,' said the porter. 'Thanks for telling me. I'll get someone to repair the door. You can get on with your work.'

'Something odd is going on,' muttered the scout as he withdrew.

In reporting the break-in, he'd put Stott in an awkward position. It was easy for him to identify the burglar. Since he'd demanded to be let into Pomeroy's room the previous day, Nicholas Thorpe had to be responsible. Unable to get into it by legal means, he'd resorted to illegality. It was the porter's duty to pass on his name to the police, but something stopped him. Thorpe had, after all, been Pomeroy's closest friend. In a sense, he had a right to access. According to Ayres, nothing of value had been taken from the room. Everything seemed to be untouched. Had Thorpe gone in search of something that was not actually there? Or did he just wish to enjoy being in a room that held so many pleasant memories for him?

Stott's loyalties were being tested. His first duty was to the college, but he had been known to turn a blind eye to undergraduates he'd seen climbing into the college at night. It was a rite of passage, he'd told himself and let them get on with it. Because he was not a member of the college, Thorpe's case was slightly different. He was guilty of trespass and, at the very least, should be forced to pay for the damage he'd done to the door of Pomeroy's room. After agonising over the problem for several minutes, the porter saw that there might be a way out of his dilemma. He was able to relax.

Though he took his family to church on a Sunday whenever he could, Victor Leeming was not an ardent worshipper. He never felt entirely comfortable in the House of God and approached this one with trepidation. St Edmund's Church had been founded by the Jesuits exactly a century earlier. Situated on Westgate Street, it was at the centre of the town. The current church had been built less than thirty years earlier, yet it had a sense of permanence. It had been constructed in the Grecian style with an impressive facade that featured two tall marble pillars. When he looked up at it, Leeming found it slightly daunting.

Two elderly women drifted into the church for silent worship, their heads bent and well-covered. After reminding himself how important his visit might be, Leeming removed his hat and went in through the main door. He stood in the gloomy interior, picking up the smell of the lighted candles stationed throughout. Feeling conspicuous, he sat down. He was not alone for long. After hearing footsteps behind him, he felt a gentle hand touch his shoulder.

'Welcome to St Edmund's,' said a soft voice. 'I sense that you're a newcomer. Are you here to pray or simply to look?'

'To be honest,' said Leeming as he rose to his feet, 'I'm not

263

here for either of those things. I'm a detective sergeant from the Metropolitan Police Force.'

'Saints preserve us! Have we done something wrong?'

'Not at all, Father . . .'

'Father O'Brien.'

'Is there somewhere more private where we could talk?'

'Come into the vestry.'

He led the sergeant down the nave towards the altar. When they got to the vestry, the extra light from several large candles enabled Leeming to see his companion more clearly. Father O'Brien was a white-haired old man wearing clerical garb and a black biretta with a tuft on the top of it. A crucifix hung from the chain around his neck. His manner was pleasant and confiding.

'How may we be of help to you?' he asked.

'It's in connection with a murder investigation.'

'Ah, of course. I read about it in the newspapers. The victim was a Cambridge undergraduate. He had some link with the Boat Race.'

'We're trying to find out what brought him to Bury St Edmunds on the day of his death. We know that he made some earlier visits when he was met by a beautiful young Italian woman. They had lunch at The Fox Inn, then they came here.'

'Do you have the name of the young lady?'

'Isabella.'

'What about her surname?'

'We don't know it, Father. I'm hoping that you might.'

'We have more than one Isabella in the congregation.

264

One of them is Italian but she's even older than I am so she can't have been the person you want.'

'I'm told that our Isabella was very striking. If you'd seen her, you'd certainly have remembered her.'

'I'm a celibate priest,' reminded the other, 'and I don't judge a woman by the prettiness or otherwise of her physical features. Besides, those who come in here have their heads covered and bowed in respect. What I can tell you is that the young woman of whom you speak is not a regular visitor to St Edmund's. I may well have seen her and the young man you mention but they made no imprint on my memory. Our door is always open. Strangers come and go all the time.'

'If you *do* happen to recall something about them . . .'

'I'll get in touch with you at once, Sergeant.'

'We're staying at a pub named The Jolly Traveller,' Leeming told him. 'A message addressed to Inspector Colbeck and sent to the telegraph station in Cambridge is bound to reach us.'

'I'll bear that in mind,' said O'Brien, 'and I wish you the very best of luck in tracking down the killer.' He became pensive. 'Something drew Mr Pomeroy and Isabella into this church. I'd like to think that it was a religious impulse.'

Leeming was realistic. 'We may never find out.'

The Prime Minister spoke very fondly about the Pomeroy family. Notwithstanding the many claims on his attention, he'd maintained a fitful correspondence with Alexander Pomeroy over the years. During the latter's time as Consul in the Grand Duchy of Tuscany, Palmerston, who'd been Foreign Secretary at the time, had gone out of his way to visit him at the family home and been very impressed by the youthful Bernard.

'He was no more than ten or eleven at the time,' he recalled, 'but he spoke with the unassailable confidence of an adult. When I asked him what his ambition was, he said that he intended to become a politician and serve the nation as well as *I'd* done.' He chuckled at the memory. 'I liked him. He was ebullient and precocious. When he got nearer to the time of taking up a political career, I told him, he was welcome to contact me for advice. A fortnight or so ago, he did just that. The letter of his that you found in his room was my reply.'

'I see,' said Colbeck.

'The Pomeroys were a charming family. Bernard's sisters were delightful young creatures, and his mother was a woman with the kind of breathtaking beauty that would ensnare a Pope. My heart goes out to her. Losing her husband was a crushing blow, but Alexander had at least had a full and rewarding life. Bernard, alas, had only just come into full bloom.'

'His achievements at Cambridge were outstanding, academically and in other ways.'

'I was looking to him to help my alma mater win the Boat Race this year.'

'The crew certainly had great faith in him,' said Colbeck.

'I daresay that they've transferred their faith to *you* now, Inspector. Until the murder is solved, it will hang over them like a black cloud. Don't let them down.'

'I'll do my best, Prime Minister.'

'I'm sure that you will.'

'What you've told me about the family has been interesting. We've reason to believe that his killer may have been Italian, leading to the possibility that Bernard Pomeroy was assassinated as a result of some sort of vendetta with another family.'

'I think it unlikely, Inspector. If they'd lived in the south of Italy – especially if it had been Sicily – then a vendetta would be something to consider. Blood runs hot in such places. Family feuds abound. There's also a great deal of banditry blighting the area. You'll find little of that in Tuscany, I can assure you. What put the idea of a vendetta into your head?'

'Bernard Pomeroy had secret meetings in Bury St Edmunds with an attractive Italian woman.'

'Is that surprising?' asked the other with a knowing smile. 'Undergraduate life can seem quite oppressive at times. Vigorous young men quite naturally need a way of spicing up their dull routines.'

Even in his late seventies, the Prime Minister retained much of the spirit that had earned him the nickname of Lord Cupid. Rumours about his antics on the social scene had been in circulation for decades. Colbeck had noted the way that his face glowed when he'd first mentioned Bernard Pomeroy's mother. The inspector shifted the conversation in another direction.

'What difference has *Risorgimento* made to Italy?' he asked.

'It's made *every* difference,' replied Palmerston with

relish. 'It's set in motion the long-overdue process of unification The *Risorgimento* – the Resurgence – has been the country's salvation . . .'

Though he'd had a busy morning, Jack Stott nevertheless found time to write a short note and ask one of the college scouts to deliver it for him. News of the broken lock on the door of Pomeroy's room had worried the porter. While he had no wish to get Nicholas Thorpe into trouble, he couldn't just brush the matter aside. A formal report would have to be made to the college authorities, if not to the city's police. He just hoped that word of the crime didn't reach the ears of Professor Springett because he was bound to take an unwelcome interest.

Early that afternoon, Stott was relieved to see Victor Leeming appear at the lodge. The sergeant was responding to the message he'd received when he returned to The Jolly Traveller. It had made him head straight for the college.

'Your note claimed that you had news for us,' he said.

'That's right, Sergeant.'

'Is it good news or bad?'

'It's . . . awkward news.'

He explained what had happened and why he felt certain that the culprit was Nicholas Thorpe, who, having failed to get into his friend's room the previous day, had taken the law into his own hands. Leeming understood the predicament, but he also had a sneaking sympathy for Thorpe.

'He must have been desperate,' he said.

'Yet nothing was taken from the room.'

'How do you know?'

'Eric Ayres swore blind that nothing had been touched.'

'Is he the scout you mentioned?' Stott nodded. 'Then what could Mr Thorpe have been after?'

'Search me, Sergeant. I'd just like the problem sorted out, only I don't want to name Mr Thorpe. He and Mr Pomeroy were so close.'

'Leave it to us,' said Leeming.

'Will you speak to Mr Thorpe?'

'I'll leave that to the inspector. He'll know what to do. With luck, he's on his way back to Cambridge right now. I'm dying to hear his news.'

'Why is that?'

'He had an appointment with the Prime Minister.'

Stott gaped. 'Is *he* involved in this case?'

'That's what I'm waiting to find out.'

The train journey gave Colbeck the opportunity to look back gratefully on his stay in London. It had started with a joyful reunion with his family, then moved on to a standard confrontation with the superintendent. Apart from his time with his wife and daughter, the real treat was the generous amount of time he'd spent alone with Lord Palmerston. Colbeck had been duly flattered by the information that the Prime Minister had followed his career by reading newspaper reports of his cases. He was interested to meet the man face-to-face and to find him so approachable.

Palmerston had not only spoken fondly of the Pomeroy family, he'd given his visitor an insight into the kind of life that a British Consul in Italy enjoyed and the formative effect it would have had on his only son. Bernard Pomeroy must have been an unusual child if he could impress the British Foreign Secretary when the latter visited his home. But it was the father who intrigued Colbeck. Joining the diplomatic service after graduating from Cambridge, he'd had a few minor appointments before being moved to Tuscany. It had become his spiritual home, so much so that he converted to Roman Catholicism and married a beautiful young woman of noble birth. Alexander Pomeroy seemed to have had an idyllic life.

Colbeck was bound to wonder from which of his parents their son had inherited his character traits. Diplomacy required tact, moderation and an ability to hide one's feelings. Bernard Pomeroy seemed to have been lacking in all of those qualities. He was reputedly a gifted young man who took a delight in being in the public eye and who would be ideally suited to the rough and tumble of political life. His father may have worked quietly and effectively behind the scenes, but that form of existence held no appeal for the son. He longed to be at the centre of the stage. From whom had he inherited such a lust for attention?

The inspector's visit to London had ended with a second visit to Scotland Yard. Edward Tallis had been an attentive listener, pleased with the amount of relevant information Colbeck had gained from his meeting with Palmerston and actually congratulating him for once. As a result of what the inspector had learnt, he felt the investigation had suddenly moved into a new phase.

* * *

Alone in his office, the superintendent went through the notes he'd made when Colbeck delivered his report of the visit to Cambridge House. He marvelled at the way that the inspector had drawn so much out of the Prime Minister and was honest enough to admit that he could never have done that himself. It was the reason he'd not been troubled by envy. At certain things, he accepted, Colbeck was considerably better than him.

A tap on the door interrupted his reflections. The constable who entered told him that he had a visitor with a pressing desire to see him.

'Who is this person?'

'A Mr Lambert.'

'Let me introduce myself properly,' said the visitor, sweeping into the room before being invited to do so. 'I'm Bernard Pomeroy's brother-in-law, and I have a number of questions to ask.'

'Do come in, Mr Lambert,' said Tallis, drily, 'and take a seat.'

Francis Lambert lowered himself into a chair. He was a big, handsome man in his early thirties with an unambiguous air of wealth about him. When he spoke, there was no trace of an Irish brogue. He seemed to swing between forthrightness and grief.

'We were shocked when the letter came,' he said, lowering his head. 'Bernard was dead? It was impossible to believe.' His voice hardened. 'My wife and I came as soon as we could, and we want the truth.'

'There is no intention to deceive you, Mr Lambert.'

The head came up again. 'There had better not be.'

'However,' said Tallis, sitting down, 'when Inspector Colbeck wrote that letter, he didn't wish to alarm you even more by voicing his suspicions.'

'What do you mean?'

'It's now clear that your brother-in-law did not die by natural means.'

'How else could he die?'

'He was murdered, sir. To be more exact, he was poisoned to death.'

'Poisoned? Who on earth would want to poison Bernard?'

'If you have any suggestions, Mr Lambert, I'd be glad to hear them.'

'Are you *sure* that the victim was my brother-in-law?'

'The body was identified by his closest friend.'

'That would be Thorpe,' said the other with obvious displeasure. 'I never knew what Bernard saw in that man.'

'He was able to make a positive identification.'

'Where is the body now?'

'It's in the hospital in Bury St Edmunds.'

'Then we need to reclaim it at once.'

'I'm afraid that you can't do that yet, sir.'

'My wife is adamant, Superintendent. Her brother will be buried under Italian soil. As soon as we've secured the necessary visas, we'll take Bernard back to the country in which he was born.'

'You'll have to be patient for a short while.'

'I'm not used to being thwarted,' warned Lambert.

'And I'm not used to being threatened,' countered Tallis. 'You can bluster all you like but there's a process to follow.

Frustrating as it may be, you and your wife must follow it.'

'I demand to speak to Inspector Colbeck.'

'You'll speak to me first because I am his superior. Besides, I'm not having anybody getting in the inspector's way when he's deep into an investigation. It would hamper him unnecessarily. Now, why don't we begin this conversation again and do so in a more civilised way? I'm prepared to answer any questions you may put to me, Mr Lambert,' said Tallis, levelly, 'then I'd like to ask *you* a few things.'

Lambert squirmed in his seat. He'd met his match.

CHAPTER SEVENTEEN

Since he no longer had Lydia Quayle to render him almost invisible, Alan Hinton was not quite so bold on his walk beside the river in Oxford that morning. Even in a change of clothing by way of a disguise, he felt slightly vulnerable. On the credit side, he was more alert than he had been on the previous day's promenade and picked up details he might have missed had he still had Lydia on his arm. Every so often he'd stopped to consider what would happen if Tallis ever became aware of what he'd done in using a female accomplice in a police investigation. It was only now that the experiment was over that he realised the immense danger he'd courted.

By dint of loitering near the boathouse and keeping his ears open, Hinton had learnt where some of the onlookers went off to lunch. He followed two of them to a pub in the High Street and bided his time. While the others remained standing as they consumed their beer, Hinton found a table nearby and, while picking at his food, hid behind the newspaper he was pretending to read. Undergraduate chatter filled the bar, but he was only interested in the discussion between the two men. It was not long before the Boat Race came into the conversation.

'It's in the bag,' said one of them. 'Cambridge will be trailing in our wake from start to finish.'

'Does that mean you're going to bet on the result, Ralph?'

'I certainly am,' said Ralph with enthusiasm. 'I'm betting everything I can lay my hands on. Unfortunately, that doesn't amount to a great deal.'

'Why not?'

'Father has cut my allowance.'

'The mean bastard!' exclaimed the other.

'To be fair to him, I did ask for it.'

'Ah, yes,' said the other, remembering. 'It was that business at The White Swan, wasn't it? You did rather cut loose, Ralph. I've seen you drunk out of your mind before, but you've never been so wild and aggressive. How many glasses did you smash?'

'Too many, I'm afraid.'

'You broke all those chairs as well. It looked as if a herd of buffalo had stampeded through the bar. No wonder you were banned.'

'I did apologise to the landlord the next day.'

'What did your father say?'

'He was livid. He paid for the damage, then he gave me a stern lecture and halved my allowance. If I'm honest, I have to admit I deserved it.' Ralph brightened. 'That's why I'm so grateful the Boat Race is on the horizon. It's my chance to repair my finances.'

'We can both make a killing.'

'It's a foregone conclusion.'

'It is now, Ralph,' said his friend. 'A week ago, we couldn't have been quite so confident. The Cambridge eight was doing well. That cox of theirs was nothing short of a genius. I remember our coach saying that Pomeroy was their talisman. Brannigan knew that our task would be a lot easier if their cox was disabled in some way.'

'He's been more than disabled. Pomeroy is dead.'

'Don't ask me to shed any tears. I want us to win and win well.'

'But he was *murdered.*'

'Cambridge should have looked after him properly,' said the other. 'When you have an asset like Pomeroy, you have to protect him. Liam Brannigan was right. There were two ways to get the advantage. One was to destroy that amazing new boat of theirs. Unfortunately, they were guarding it around the clock.'

Ralph was shocked. 'Are you saying that   ?'

'I'm saying nothing,' said his friend with a grin.

'You *know* something, don't you?'

'My lips are sealed.'

'This is serious. You're implying that—'

'I'm implying nothing,' said the other, firmly. 'I just

know the way that Brannigan's mind works. He's promised an Oxford victory. When you count your winnings after the Race, you won't care how that victory was achieved.'

When the train deposited him in Cambridge, Colbeck went straight to the telegraph station to see if there were any messages for him. He was pleased to find one sent by Superintendent Tallis, informing him that Francis Lambert and his wife were on their way to Cambridge to view the body of Bernard Pomeroy. Colbeck was instructed to take them to Bury St Edmunds. The superintendent had obviously consulted Bradshaw's train timetable because he'd been able to say exactly when the visitors would arrive. A glance at the clock in the telegraph station told Colbeck that he had just over an hour before the couple were due. That gave him enough time to take a cab to The Jolly Traveller and make contact with Victor Leeming.

The sergeant was delighted when he saw him coming into the pub.

'Welcome back, sir!' he said. 'I've got some news for you.'

'Good,' replied the other. 'I've brought tidings of my own. My time is limited so you'd better tell me what *you* found out.'

Leeming told him about his trip to the hospital in Bury St Edmunds and how a stray comment from Dr Nunn had made him go to the Roman Catholic Church there. Colbeck was impressed by the way he'd shown initiative.

'When I got back here,' said Leeming, 'I had an urgent message from Stott.'

'What did the porter have to say?'

'They've had a break-in at the college.'

Leeming explained what had happened and how it seemed clear that Nicholas Thorpe had been the culprit. The porter had been surprised that nothing had been taken from Pomeroy's room. Colbeck believed that it had been. He felt certain that Thorpe had been eager to reclaim a letter he'd once sent and which was kept in a secret drawer in his friend's desk. When he passed on his theory to Leeming, the sergeant was perplexed.

'Why was he so desperate to get the letter back?'

'It was couched in terms of great affection. He didn't want a very personal message to fall into the wrong hands and be misinterpreted. I'm far too busy to see him at the moment,' said Colbeck, 'so I delegate the task to you. Go to Thorpe and remember to treat him gently. He's very vulnerable at the moment.'

'I know,' said Leeming, 'but don't keep me waiting any longer, sir. I'm dying to know how you got on with the Prime Minister.'

'You'll have to be patient. Something more important cropped up.'

'What can be more important than speaking to Lord Palmerston?'

'Taking Pomeroy's sister to view the body of her brother,' said Colbeck. 'She's come all the way from Ireland to do so. Please mention it to Mr Thorpe. I know that he's met Mrs Lambert.'

'Do you have any advice about the break-in last night?'

'Yes, Victor – make absolutely sure that it was Thorpe's doing.'

'And then what do I do?'

'You showed initiative earlier today. Show it again.'

As the train clattered on, Caroline Lambert sat alone with her husband in a first-class compartment. Dressed in mourning attire, she sat with her head bowed, body bent forward, veil pulled down and gloved hands clasped tightly together. Her husband knew better than to attempt any conversation with her. When he'd married her, Caroline had been a highly attractive woman with a vivacity that appealed to him and a love of riding that he shared. From the moment they'd received Colbeck's letter, she'd become a different person. Her brother's untimely fate was at the forefront of her mind. Nothing else mattered.

After the long, heavy silence, she spoke in a whisper.

'What did the superintendent say to you?' she asked.

'I've told you, Caroline. He acceded to my demand that we be taken to the hospital.'

'Did he give you any details about the cause of my brother's death?'

'Don't vex yourself over things like that.'

'I want to know the truth, Francis.'

'Inspector Colbeck is the best person to tell you that.'

'You're hiding something from me,' she said, grabbing his arm.

'Don't be silly.'

'You were in that office a very long time. I want to know why.'

'All will be explained in due course,' he promised. 'Rely on me, Caroline. I'll make sure that we are told *everything*.'

Caleb Andrews had never felt quite so nervous before. All that was happening was that he was expecting a friend for afternoon tea. He'd been up early to clean and tidy the downstairs of his house, then he'd gone out to buy a selection of cakes from the baker's shop. His hands were still trembling slightly when he went off to see his granddaughter, and he was glad that Madeleine didn't notice the state he was in. Back in his own house again, he had a simple lunch, then cleaned the downstairs all over again. Elsie Gurr was punctual. The moment she used the knocker, he rushed to open the door.

'Come on in,' he said with a lordly sweep of his hand.

'Thank you, Caleb.'

'I'm so pleased to see you.'

Once inside, she cast a shrewd eye around the living room. When it landed on the painting, she gasped in surprise.

'Isn't it wonderful?' he said. 'I used to drive that engine. It was painted for me by Maddy. She gave it to me as a present.'

'That was very nice of her,' she muttered.

He was disappointed. 'Is that all you can say?'

'Oh, it's very well done. I can see that. Your daughter is a real artist. But why does she spend her time painting a dirty old steam engine? It's not the sort of thing a young woman should do.'

'Maddy is a railwayman's daughter.'

'Our Pauline is a sailor's daughter but that didn't make her want to paint a picture of a filthy old ship for Joe and me.

280

I mean – that engine is so *big*. You can't take your eyes off it.'

'I never tire of looking at it,' he said.

'Well, I've seen enough of it already,' she admitted, turning her back on the painting. 'I couldn't be doing with it at all. I don't mean to be rude, Caleb, but it's so . . . unsettling.'

Andrews gnashed his teeth. 'I'll make some tea.'

The architectural glories of King's College were wasted on Leeming. He was there on business and paid them no heed. He was grateful to find Nicholas Thorpe in his room and, importantly, alone.

'May I have a few words, sir?' he asked.

'Well, yes,' said the other, surprised to see him. 'If you must, that is.'

'I was sent for by the porter at Corpus Christi College. He told me that someone had broken into Mr Pomeroy's room.'

'That's dreadful news! Whoever would do that?'

'I won't beat about the bush, sir. The porter believes that it might have been you.'

'Damn the fellow!' exclaimed Thorpe. 'He has no right to make such an accusation. Who is going to listen to a mere porter's word?'

'*I* am, sir,' said Leeming with emphasis. 'You went to the college yesterday, I believe, and asked him for the key to the room. The porter obeyed his orders and refused to part with it. You were very angry.'

'I'm even angrier now, Sergeant. You go back to Corpus and tell him that, if he makes allegations about me again, I'll report him to the Master.'

'I don't think you'll do that, sir,' said Leeming, quietly.

'Why not?'

'It's because you know that you *did* go there last night. You were so desperate to reclaim something of yours that you were prepared to break the law and force a way into that room.'

'I deny it.'

'In that case, the crime will be reported to the police and you'll be questioned by someone who is not quite as sympathetic as me. I know it's a difficult time for you, Mr Thorpe, and I admire the way you've kept going. I've watched you rowing and been struck by the energy you put into it. The president and the coach know what a valuable member of the crew you are. Now then,' said Leeming, gently, 'what would they think if you were prosecuted for a crime? I doubt very much if you'd be in this year's Boat Race, sir.'

'This is complete nonsense,' gabbled Thorpe. 'Why on earth would I want to break into Bernard's room in the middle of the night?'

'So it was during the night, was it? Thank you for telling me. To answer the question,' said Leeming, 'you wanted to get your hands on a letter you'd once written to him.'

Thorpe flinched. 'However do you know that?'

'Inspector Colbeck is very thorough, sir When we searched that room, he discovered the secret drawer in Mr Pomeroy's desk and found the key to that box under the bed.'

'That was private correspondence. He had no right to read it.'

'I'm not sure that he did, Mr Thorpe. He put it straight back in the box and closed it.' He leant in closer. 'Now, sir, can you imagine anyone else climbing into that college last night in search of a letter? Apart from the inspector and me, only one person knew where it was hidden, and that person was you.'

Thorpe was terrified. When he reclaimed something precious to him, he didn't consider the possible consequences. He'd committed a crime and put his involvement in the Boat Race in jeopardy. Instead of telling lies to Leeming, he ought to be grateful to him for trying to deal with the matter discreetly.

'What must I do?' he asked.

'The first thing is that you must be honest. *Was* it you, sir?'

The words took a full minute to come out. 'Yes, it was.'

'Now we're getting somewhere,' said Leeming.

'You don't know what that letter means to me.'

'I don't *want* to know, sir. It's none of my business. You need to understand the danger you're in. By doing what you did, you've dug yourself into a large hole.'

'How do I get out of it?' whispered Thorpe.

'Well, your only hope is to make a clean breast of it,' advised Leeming. 'Go to the college, admit that you caused the damage to the door of that room and say the item you were after was not, in fact, there. Apologise sincerely and insist on paying for the repairs to the door.'

'Do you think they'll accept that explanation?'

'The sooner you make it, the more likely you are to get sympathy. Jack Stott, the porter, hasn't reported the break-in yet. I asked him to delay it until one of us had spoken to you. Get round there immediately.'

Thorpe was on his feet at once. 'I will, Sergeant – and thank you.'

'One last thing,' said Leeming, 'and this is advice that, as a policeman, I shouldn't really be giving you. Don't admit that you climbed into the college. Say that you timed your visit late in the evening so that you could get into Mr Pomeroy's room, then leave the college shortly before the gates were locked. In other words, you were not trespassing.'

'I'll get round there straight away.'

'Good luck, Mr Thorpe. If all goes well, don't forget that you owe the porter an apology. You were very harsh on him yesterday.'

When they arrived at Cambridge railway station, Francis Lambert and his wife were met by Colbeck. His appearance and manner impressed them immediately. He'd not only bought three return tickets to Bury St Edmunds, he'd arranged to make use of the stationmaster's office while they were waiting for their train. The newcomers were pleased to have a measure of privacy.

Lambert was blunt.

'We'd like to hear full details of Bernard's death.'

'Everything I can tell you,' warned Colbeck, 'is second-hand. There is, however, someone who was there at the time. His name is Arthur Bullen and he's a railway policeman working at Bury St Edmunds. You may wish to speak to him.'

'I'll insist on doing so,' said Lambert.

'What about you, Mrs Lambert? The details may be upsetting. If you'd rather not hear them, your husband can talk to Bullen alone.'

'Bernard was my brother,' she said. 'I want to know the truth. Don't worry about me, Inspector. I'm not as frail as I look.'

'Right,' said Colbeck. 'I've already sent a telegraph to make the arrangements. You'll be able to listen to Bullen in the stationmaster's office. It's very similar to this one,' he went on, looking around. 'It's not ideal but it's serviceable.'

'Thank you for taking the trouble.'

'Yes,' added Lambert, 'the superintendent told me how considerate you'd be.'

'How did you get on with him?'

'Let's just say that I'd hate to work for the man.'

Colbeck smiled inwardly. 'What exactly has he told you?'

'He told me that you'd been to see the Prime Minister.'

'Yes, that's correct. I have. My visit was extremely worthwhile . . .'

Madeleine Colbeck broke off from work that afternoon so that she could welcome Lydia Quayle for tea. She was pleased to see her friend again.

'This time yesterday,' she observed, 'you were enjoying yourself in Oxford.'

'Alan and I were there on business, Madeleine.'

'You don't need to tell *me* that. I was the one who suggested it.'

'Are you going to tell Robert what we did?'

'I've already done so.'

'Oh?' said Lydia in surprise.

'He came home unexpectedly last night. I'd dozed off with that copy of *North and South* in my lap. I couldn't deceive him. I told him everything.'

'Was he angry with you?'

'He was and he wasn't, Lydia.'

'That doesn't make sense.'

'At first, he was very cross. Robert said that I should stop trying to find ways to push you and Alan together. I had no right to interfere.'

'I don't see it as interference.'

'What he said was true and it made me feel guilty. I owe the both of you an apology.' Madeleine smiled. 'As for the idea of using you to act as a shield, Robert was all in favour of it. He was pleased with me for suggesting it and grateful to *you* for getting involved in the investigation.'

'I wouldn't have missed the chance for anything,' said Lydia. 'I wonder how Alan is managing alone.'

'He'll find a chance to tell you, I'm sure. You see?' said Madeleine, scolding herself. 'I'm doing it again. It's none of my business. Let's talk about something else, shall we? Ah, yes,' she continued, 'I have good news at last about my father.'

'Are the two of you reconciled?'

'Yes, Lydia – we hugged each other on the doorstep until we realised that people were stopping to watch us. We've put our problems behind us and resolved to be very nice to each other.'

'I'm delighted to hear it.'

'With all his faults, I love him dearly – and so, of course, does Helena.'

'You're a happy family once again,' said Lydia, a hand on her arm. 'I'm pleased for you and I'm also pleased for your father.'

After a sticky start, the tea party got steadily better. Elsie Gurr made admiring comments about the house and she was amazed when she learnt that Andrews had made the little table beside the sofa.

'I didn't know you were a carpenter, Caleb.'

'Oh, I can turn my hand to most things.'

'And you look after your garden?'

'I wouldn't let anyone else touch it, Elsie,' he said. 'Growing vegetables is an art. I've learnt the knack of it. There's something very satisfying about eating food you've planted yourself.'

'Your garden's bigger than ours.'

'Do you want a closer look at it?'

'Not at the moment,' she replied. 'To be honest, I'm ready for another cup of tea. Would you like me to help you—?'

'Stay where you are,' he said, interrupting politely. 'You're the guest. I do all the work. I just wanted you to feel completely at home.'

While he went into the kitchen, she settled back in her armchair.

'That's exactly what I *do* feel, Caleb,' she murmured.

* * *

Led by Arthur Bullen, the visitors went into the stationmaster's office in Bury St Edmunds. As they were sitting down, Stanley Moult peered enviously through the window, annoyed that he'd had to make way for them. He had little time to feel dispossessed because he was soon needed to despatch the train on the next stage of its journey. After introductions had been made, Bullen took over, giving a clear, measured account of what had happened when Bernard Pomeroy had visited the station for the last time.

Caroline Lambert listened carefully. Colbeck had feared that some of the details might have distressed her but she remained calm throughout. When the railway policeman had finished, it was she who asked the first question.

'Did my brother die in pain?'

'I don't believe so,' said Bullen.

'What makes you say that?'

'I've seen people who've died from severe injuries, Mrs Lambert. They're usually hunched up in agony. That wasn't the case with your brother.'

'Thank you. I'm relieved to hear it.'

'Why didn't you arrest the man who killed him?' asked Lambert, accusingly.

'I didn't know that he was dead when I first bent over him, sir. While I was examining Mr Pomeroy, the man disappeared in the crowd.'

'Bullen is not at fault here,' said Colbeck, coming to his defence. 'He acted swiftly and effectively. And when the same person visited the town again, he alerted me at once. Unfortunately, we got here too late to catch him.'

After a few more questions, it was time to leave. Lambert left the office without a word, but his wife stopped to lift her veil and looked at Bullen.

'Thank you very much for what you did,' she said.

'I wish that I could have done more, Mrs Lambert.'

'We were fortunate that *you* were on duty that day,' said Colbeck. 'Goodbye.'

'Goodbye, Inspector,' said Bullen.

Jack Stott was pinning an advertisement on the noticeboard when he received a visitor. Nicholas Thorpe was very subdued. He cleared his throat before speaking.

'I owe you an apology,' he said.

'I don't think so, sir.'

'When I called here yesterday, I was unduly rude.'

'I took no offence, Mr Thorpe. I know the pressure you must be under.'

'I've just been to see the Master. I admitted that I broke into Mr Pomeroy's room in search of something, but it wasn't there. He accepted my explanation and my offer to pay for the repair to the door. Sir Harold said that, as far as he was concerned, the matter is closed.'

'I won't mention it again, sir.'

'There is one thing I'd like to make clear,' resumed Thorpe. 'I'm not a thief. I didn't climb into Corpus in the dead of night. I came here a quarter of an hour before the gates were locked and, after I'd forced my way into the room, I left quietly.'

Stott's face was motionless. 'Have you talked to Sergeant Leeming, sir?'

'I have, as a matter of fact.'

'Did he give you any advice?'

'He merely condoned the course of action I'd decided upon.'

'That's very much to your credit, Mr Thorpe,' said the porter. 'But since you had a particular need to get into the room, it might have been better if you'd appealed to the Master before doing what you did. It would have saved us a lot of bother.'

'I agree. I was too headstrong.'

'It's good of you to admit that, sir.'

'Well,' said Thorpe, 'I must be off. But I couldn't leave without apologising for my behaviour to you. Bernard had great regard for you, Stott,' he added, slipping something into the porter's hand. 'I share that regard.'

He walked off abruptly. Stott opened his palm and saw that he was holding a five pound note. To a man in his position, it was like gold dust.

'Thank you, sir,' he said. 'I believe *some* of what you've told me.'

Only one cab was waiting when they got to the rank so Colbeck suggested that he should take it in order to reach the hospital first and warn Dr Nunn that he had visitors coming. Lambert and his wife agreed to wait. When he reached the hospital, Colbeck explained the situation. Pleased to have a member of the family to identify the body, Nunn wished that he'd had more time to prepare.

'There'll be some delay while we get everything ready,' he explained.

'It will give them time to control their nerves.'

'Will you be accompanying them, Inspector?'

'I've seen what I needed to see.'

Dr Nunn went off. It was only minutes before the others arrived. Colbeck waved them to seats in the waiting room. He was worried about Pomeroy's sister. She looked extremely tense.

'Are you sure that you wish to go ahead with this?' he asked.

'That's why I'm here, Inspector,' she said.

'It could be a harrowing experience, Mrs Lambert.'

'Don't worry about my wife,' said Lambert. 'She can take a horse over a five-barred gate without batting an eyelid. Caroline has remarkable courage.'

'This *is* rather different, sir,' said Colbeck.

'My wife will manage.'

There was a complacence about the man that irked Colbeck. Lambert spoke to him as if he were an employee of his rather than the head of a murder investigation. He showed the inspector no respect. His wife, by contrast, was both grateful and well-mannered. During a wait of almost twenty minutes, the three of them sat there in silence. They were eventually joined by Dr Nunn. Apologising for the delay, he told them that the post-mortem had taken place but was as yet incomplete. Like Colbeck, he wanted to be certain that Caroline Lambert felt able to confirm the identification.

'My wife is more than able,' said Lambert. 'Let's get on with it.'

'Follow me, please.'

Nunn led the way. Colbeck had expected Lambert to offer his arm to his wife, but he didn't do so and she obviously preferred to walk unaided, back straight and head erect. Left alone, Colbeck went through some of the information he'd gathered from Lord Palmerston about Bernard Pomeroy's early life. The father, too, must have had outstanding talent if he could maintain a friendship with the man who was now Prime Minister. From his brief acquaintance with Caroline Lambert, he could see that she had an inner strength that would carry her through her ordeal.

It was not a lengthy wait. When they reappeared, Lambert was pallid and in considerable discomfort. Instead of bringing him back to the waiting room, Nunn helped him along a corridor. Colbeck was on his feet to welcome Caroline.

'I'm sorry to see the effect on your husband,' he said.

She lowered herself into a chair. 'He'll soon recover, Inspector.'

'Would you like a moment alone, Mrs Lambert?'

'No,' she replied. 'I just want to sit here quietly with you. Seeing my brother like that was a hideous experience. I couldn't believe that it was him at first. Bernard had such an inexhaustible fund of energy. Nothing is left of it now. He's just an empty shell.'

'Fond memories of him still remain, Mrs Lambert.'

'Yes, that's true and I'll treasure them. I'll try to forget what I saw in there and remember Bernard as he was – a happy, bubbling, clever, mischievous brother who brought so much fun into our lives. Largely because of him and his antics, we had the most wonderful childhood.'

'Do you miss Italy?'

'Yes, I do,' she confessed. 'I certainly miss that glorious sunshine. I now live in the middle of four thousand acres of Irish farmland. It can be heavenly – but we do seem to have more than our fair share of rain. When Bernard visited us there—'

She came to an abrupt halt as a vivid memory made her purse her lips and bring a hand up to her mouth. Colbeck could see that, behind the veil, she was fighting back tears. When he tried to speak, she waved him into silence.

'Leave me be, Inspector,' she murmured. 'Just leave me be.'

After their second cup of tea, Caleb Andrews and Elsie Gurr had sat contentedly opposite each other and exchanged reminiscences about their late marital partners. It brought them closer together. Andrews was not blind to her faults, but they faded away when he looked at her. In his eyes, she was a lovely, well-preserved, interesting woman who had filled a gap in his life that he hadn't really noticed was there. The question he kept asking himself was how close to her she would like him to get. Meanwhile, he could simply enjoy the pleasure of her company.

When the clock on his mantelpiece chimed, the mood was suddenly broken. 'Oh dear!' she exclaimed. 'Is that the time?'

'Stay as long as you wish.'

'I'd love to, Caleb, but I have to be back home by five-thirty. My daughter is going to call in.'

'We can't have you being late for her,' he said, rising to his feet. 'I'll walk you back to your house.'

'There's no need to do that. I can manage on my own.'

'I *insist*, Elsie.'

'In that case,' she said with a laugh, 'I'll accept your kind offer.'

He helped her on with her coat and they left the house, setting off on a journey that would take them less than fifteen minutes. Andrews felt privileged to be escorting her in public. He wanted to offer his arm but felt that that would be a mistake. They hadn't quite reached that stage yet. As they strode along through a warren of streets, they talked fondly about the mutual friend who'd introduced them. Eventually, they were standing outside the front door of Elsie's house.

'Well,' she said. 'Here we are.'

'I've delivered you safely to your home.'

'You're a real gentleman, Caleb.'

'Thank you.'

After taking the key out of her handbag, she looked up at him.

'I did enjoy coming to tea with you.'

'You're welcome any time, Elsie.'

'I'll remember that,' she said, 'but next time, it's my turn.'

'I look forward to it.'

'Would Monday afternoon suit you?'

'*Any* Monday afternoon would suit me,' he said, gallantly.

She tittered. 'You do know how to pay a compliment, Caleb.'

'Be warned. There'll be a lot more of them coming.'

'I can't wait.' Putting the key in the lock, she opened the door, then turned to face him again. 'There's just one favour I'd like to ask.'

'Whatever it is, you can have it.'

'It's that picture of the steam engine your daughter painted for you. Next time I come to tea, could you turn it to the wall while I'm there?'

'Well, yes,' he said, wounded by what was to him a brutal request. His voice dwindled to a whisper. 'I suppose so, Elsie.'

'Thank you so much. It's such a distraction.'

CHAPTER EIGHTEEN

Caroline Lambert did not stay silent for long. After a short while, she inhaled deeply, then looked around to see exactly where she was. Once she had her bearings, she turned to Colbeck.

'I'm sorry, Inspector,' she said.

'You're perfectly entitled to do as you wish, Mrs Lambert.'

'It was very rude of me.'

'Not at all,' he said. 'What you did was quite understandable.'

'Brooding about Bernard's death solves nothing. It only makes me feel even gloomier. He wouldn't want that. I should draw strength from the good times we shared as children.'

'Do you remember the visit of Lord Palmerston?'

'How could I forget it? Daddy told us that someone important was coming to see us and that we had to be on our best behaviour. It was only when our visitor arrived that we realised he was the British Foreign Secretary.'

'He told me how much he'd enjoyed meeting you all.'

'Bernard kept trying to attract his attention by showing off. My brother was like that. At one point, he did his favourite trick, which was vaulting over a fence. Lord Palmerston clapped. Then,' she went on, 'to our amazement, he took off his coat, ran at the fence and vaulted over it himself with ease.'

'I can well believe it. Lord Palmerston is famed for his physical fitness. There was a time when he used to swim in the Thames every morning and he's a very accomplished horseman. You and he have a love of riding in common.' Colbeck was pleased to see a smile flit across her face. 'He's still remarkably active for his age.'

'He made us feel important,' she recalled. 'Most adults don't make the effort to do that to children. They expect them to sit there quietly and behave.'

Before she could continue, she saw her husband coming back towards them with Dr Nunn in tow. Lambert looked faintly embarrassed at his reaction to the sight of his brother-in-law. He was anxious to leave the hospital and get some fresh air. After thanking the doctor, the visitors departed.

When they walked to the cab rank, there were no vehicles there. Colbeck consulted his watch.

'We've plenty of time before the next train to Cambridge,'

he said. 'You and Mrs Lambert can take the first cab, sir. I'll meet you in the waiting room.'

'As you wish,' mumbled Lambert.

'Thank you, Inspector,' added Caroline. 'You've been so helpful.'

A cab arrived within minutes and they climbed into it. After waving them off, Colbeck thought about the visit that Palmerston had made to the family house in Florence. The former Foreign Secretary had clearly held Alexander Pomeroy in high esteem. He wondered why.

Jack Stott was relieved that the crime had been solved and that payment would be made by the interloper for the repair of the damaged lock. He was glad that he'd involved one of the detectives in the case. The porter guessed that Leeming had been both discreet and practical, advising Thorpe to confess to his illegal entry to Pomeroy's room while offering a full apology. It meant that Stott was no longer involved. In effect, Leeming had done both him and Thorpe a favour. The porter hoped that he could forget all about the incident.

His hope was soon shattered. He saw two figures heading for the lodge. One was Professor Springett and his companion was an undergraduate from another college who attended tutorials with him. Though he didn't know the young man's name, Stott recognised him from his regular visits.

Springett led the way with a look of determination on his face.

'What's this I hear about a break-in?' he demanded. 'When I spoke to the Master earlier on, he told me that someone had forced his way into Pomeroy's room.'

'That's correct,' said Stott.

'This person is from another college, apparently.'

'I heard the same thing, Professor.'

'Whoever it was,' said Reddish, 'he must have been very strong. The door is made of solid oak and had a stout lock.'

'What happened is insupportable,' added Springett. 'Complete strangers being allowed to walk in here and commit a crime like that – it's very alarming. And, of course, it just had to be *that* particular room.'

Reddish nodded. 'Even after he's dead, Pomeroy is causing trouble.'

'I don't think you can blame Mr Pomeroy for what happened, sir,' said Stott. 'That's unfair. Besides, from what I hear, nothing was taken from the room.'

'It doesn't matter,' claimed Springett. 'A crime is a crime. How would you feel if someone broke into your house even though he didn't steal anything?'

'That's not quite the same thing, Professor.'

'It's a pertinent question.'

'I agree,' said Reddish.

'What it shows is that porters ought to be more vigilant.'

'We do our best,' said Stott, stung by the criticism.

'Clearly, it's not enough. I told the Master that names ought to be taken at the lodge of any strangers entering the college. That way we can police the premises.'

'It's a good idea, Professor, but it's not foolproof. How

can we be sure that the names we were given were correct? I take note of any undergraduates, like your companion here, who come to Corpus for tutorials. But we also have lots of visitors,' Stott reminded him. 'We simply don't have the legal right to demand proof of identity from them.'

'That's true,' conceded Reddish. 'My father would be outraged if anyone tried to stop him walking into *my* college until he'd provided identification.'

'I still think that we should exercise more care,' said Springett. 'I intend to take up the matter again with the Master. Far be it from me to criticise Sir Harold, but I do feel that he's been found wanting here. If *I'd* been in his position,' he declared, 'steps would have been taken to monitor visitors more carefully.'

Stott made no comment. He was very much aware of the bitterness felt by Springett at being passed over as the Master. Like every other college employee, however, he'd been delighted that the Professor of Divinity had not been given power over all their livelihoods.

'Have you any idea who the thief might have been?' asked Springett.

'I'm afraid not,' said Stott. 'Didn't the Master tell you?'

'He refused to do so.'

'Then Sir Harold must have had good reason to do that.'

'I feel that I'm entitled to know.'

'I'd feel the same if I was you,' said Reddish.

'This can't simply be brushed under the carpet.'

'What was the thief *after*? That's what puzzled me.'

'Reddish has a special interest here,' explained Springett. 'He was a friend of Pomeroy's and had acted in a play with him.'

'I've been in Bernard's room a number of times,' said Reddish. 'The most valuable things in there were his books. Only another undergraduate would be interested in those.'

'You're probably right, sir,' said Stott.

'He *is* right,' decided Springett, 'and there's one obvious candidate. It's that friend of Pomeroy's from King's – Nicholas Thorpe. Only yesterday you quite rightly refused to give him the key to Pomeroy's room. I suspect that he crept back here at some point in search of whatever it was that he was after. Don't you agree?'

'It's possible, I suppose, but there's no evidence.'

'That confrontation with you is all the evidence I need.'

'I remember Nick Thorpe,' said Reddish. 'Whenever I visited Bernard, he was usually there. They were in the Boat Club together.'

'Not any longer,' said Springett under his breath.

'I didn't like him. Thorpe used to hang on his every word.'

'There's no harm in that, sir,' said Stott. 'They were friends. Even though I had that argument with Mr Thorpe, I admire him. He was a young man with a generous nature,' he went on, thinking of his five pound note. 'Most of the undergraduates I deal with are nowhere near as considerate.'

While waiting for his cab, Colbeck was able to take stock of his conversations with Pomeroy's sister and her husband. He would have liked to have more time alone with Caroline so that he could learn more about her brother's life before he came to Cambridge, but he knew that he couldn't do that without the looming presence of Francis Lambert. He also knew that Caroline would soon lose her composure. Having steeled herself to undergo the ordeal of viewing the corpse of her brother, she would be unable to hold back the tide of anguish indefinitely. It was best that the couple returned to their hotel in London that evening. Lambert could keep in touch with any developments in the investigation by going to Scotland Yard.

The cab arrived and Colbeck climbed in. He decided to make a point of speaking to Bullen when he got to the station and thanking him properly for the way he'd given his report to the Lamberts. He soon discovered that he had no need to search for the railway policeman. When Colbeck appeared on the platform, Bullen came quickly across to him.

'I've been waiting for you to turn up, Inspector,' he said.

'Why – has something happened?'

'Yes. It was when I was talking to Mr and Mrs Lambert.'

'Go on.'

'When Mrs Lambert lifted her veil to thank me,' said Bullen, 'I was quite taken aback. She looked a bit like an older version of that young woman who used to meet her brother here. It was only a faint resemblance, I suppose, but it did surprise me a bit at the time.'

'Thank you, Bullen,' said Colbeck. 'That's very interesting.'

Nicholas Thorpe was so deep in thought that he didn't hear the knock on the door of his room. He was therefore shocked to find Malcolm Henfrey-Ling suddenly standing in front of him.

'Hello, Nick,' said the newcomer.

'Where did you spring from?'

'I thought I'd pop in for a chat.'

'Yes, yes, of course,' said Thorpe. 'You're very welcome. Sit down.'

Henfrey-Ling dropped into a chair and looked closely at him.

'How are you?' he asked.

'I'm fine. In fact, I've never felt in better physical condition.'

'I'm not talking about that. James has watched you carefully when we've been on the river. He says that your strength and stamina are exemplary. You row with real commitment.'

'We must all do that, Malcolm. It's what we pledged at the very start.'

'What worries me – and James, for that matter – is what happens when you're not pulling on your oar like the rest of us. As soon as you get out of the boat, you go off into a private world and we all know who you're thinking about.'

'That's nobody else's business but mine,' said Thorpe, sharply.

'It is our business if it has an impact on how you perform under pressure.'

'The impact is a positive one, Malcolm.'

'We won't really know that until the Boat Race itself.'

Thorpe was anxious. 'You're not thinking of replacing me, are you?' he asked. 'I've earned my place in that boat. I've sweated blood for you, Malcolm.'

'We have no plans to replace you,' the president assured him, 'but there are rumblings of discontent. More than one person feels that there's a question mark over your mental attitude. Needless to say, they all hope to take over from you.'

'That always happens. Someone starts a whispering campaign against the oarsman they'd like to replace. It happened with Bernard. Look at the way that Andrew Kinglake tried to build up his own group of supporters. They kept badgering you and James.'

'We sent them packing with a flea in their ears,' said Henfrey-Ling.

'Then you can do the same to my detractors.'

'I just wanted you to be aware of what's being said.'

'Thanks for the warning, Malcolm.'

'One way to stop the sniping is for you to be more approachable. You haven't joined us for a drink for a couple of days. Don't lock yourself away and mope.'

'I'm not moping,' insisted Thorpe. 'I'm just . . . remembering the good times that Bernard and I had together. It would be unnatural if I didn't.'

'I'm just trying to give you a gentle warning, Nick.'

'I know and I'm grateful.' He got to his feet and inhaled deeply. 'Perhaps I *have* been too introspective of late. Let me take you down to our beer cellar right now. You won't find a better pint in Cambridge.'

'Lead the way,' said the other, happily. 'I'm right behind you.'

The three detectives had found a quiet table in The Jolly Traveller where they could eat their meal and discuss the latest developments. Alan Hinton repeated the story he'd already told Leeming, emphasising that the two undergraduates he'd heard chatting had been keen members of the herd of supporters of the Oxford University Boat Club. They picked up all the gossip about their heroes.

'That's the problem,' said Colbeck, 'it *is* only gossip.'

'One of them seemed to be a friend of the Oxford coach,' argued Hinton, 'and, having met Brannigan, I could believe what was said about him.'

'It was an opinion, Alan, and not an established fact.'

Hinton was deflated. 'I thought you'd be interested, sir.'

'I *am* interested. I'd just like more flesh on the bone of what you heard.'

'Does that mean I'm wasting my time going back there?'

'Of course not,' said Colbeck, giving him an encouraging pat. 'I want you back on the towpath in Oxford tomorrow, watching the crew on the river and listening to the two people you've told us about. If one of them is close to the coach, he might let something slip that can be construed as firm evidence.'

'Very good, sir,' said Hinton, mollified.

Leeming took over, describing how he'd been to see Thorpe and persuaded him to own up to what he'd done when trying to gain entry to the room once occupied by his friend. Colbeck pretended to be shocked.

'You urged him to admit one crime and lie about another?' he asked.

Leeming was hurt. 'It seemed like the best advice to give him.'

'If the superintendent heard what you'd done,' said Hinton, 'he'd have you hanged, drawn and quartered.'

'Thorpe was in an awkward position. I was only trying to save his skin.'

'You did the right thing, Victor,' said Colbeck, grinning. 'It's more or less exactly what I'd have done. You got him off the hook.'

'I *thought* I had, sir.'

'What do you mean?'

'The porter sent another note to me. He warned me that Professor Springett had taken an interest in the case and was eager to get all the details. He cornered Stott outside the lodge. Oh, and he had an undergraduate with him called Reddish.'

'That must be Simon Reddish.'

'I guessed it had to be him.'

'It might be worth having another word with Thorpe in order to warn him that Springett is on the warpath. If the Master has decided that the matter is closed, then he won't have named the person who broke into that room. The professor will no doubt hassle Sir Harold in the hope of getting that name out of him.'

'I agree, sir,' said Leeming. 'But I can't speak to Thorpe until he's been up and down the River Cam with the rest of the crew. I'll try to fall in beside him when he walks back to his college. Right, sir,' he went on, spearing a potato with his fork. 'Alan and I have told you *our* stories. What's yours?'

* * *

Caleb Andrews was at once elated and dejected, suffused with joy at having found Elsie Gurr yet shocked by her reaction to a painting he revered. As he sat and admired it once again, he could see the effort that had gone into it. Madeleine's talent was allied to her industry. She'd recreated an important part of his life on canvas, and he could feast his eyes on it whenever he wished. At least, that had been the case in the past. If Elsie was in the house, he couldn't even have it on display.

He did his best to see it from her point of view. A painting of a steam engine was hardly the thing to appeal to a woman, even though a female hand had actually created it. Elsie's own house was adorned with pretty watercolours depicting rural scenes. Andrews found them insipid, but he accepted that they had great sentimental value for her. It would never occur to him to insist that she should turn the paintings to the wall whenever he visited. That would be unkind. Yet it was exactly what the woman he cared for had requested.

Andrews did his best to find excuses for her behaviour. She was a woman who spoke her mind – he liked that. Where art was concerned, she had her own standards and preferences. He felt that that was surely permissible. And she was making no demand on him. Elsie was only asking for a favour when she said that something she found an eyesore should be put out of sight when she was there. Considered objectively, it seemed a reasonable thing to ask. If he refused, Andrews knew, he might lose her friendship altogether and that thought troubled him.

As an experiment, he lifted the painting carefully off the wall and turned it over. When he hung it up again, he found himself looking at a large plain rectangle. He imagined what his daughter would say if she realised what he was agreeing to do for his new friend. It was an insult to Madeleine. Andrews quickly restored the painting to its original position and took a few moments to enjoy studying it again. Whatever happened, his daughter's work would not be turned over. By way of a compromise, he would cover it with a cloth when Elsie Gurr came to tea.

When Colbeck had finished telling them about his meeting with the Lamberts, and with the Prime Minister, he sent Hinton back to Oxford to continue his search for clear evidence of its Boat Club's involvement in the murder. Left alone with Leeming, he passed on an additional piece of information.

'Bullen said something worth noting,' he recalled.

'What was it, sir?'

'When he'd given his account of what had happened when Pomeroy collapsed on the platform, Mrs Lambert lifted her veil briefly to thank him. Bullen was taken aback.'

'Why?' asked Leeming.

'He thought he saw a resemblance to Isabella.'

'How could he do that? Isabella is Italian and Mrs Lambert is English.'

'She has an Italian mother.'

'That explains it. Italian women all look much the same.'

'That's a ridiculous generalisation,' said Colbeck. 'Bullen did admit that it was only a faint likeness.'

'I think he was mistaken, sir.'

'I doubt that somehow.'

'How would *you* describe Mrs Lambert?'

'Well, I didn't get a proper look at her because she was in mourning attire with a veil pulled down. I wish I'd had more time to question her about her time in Italy. In particular, I'd have asked if she remembered Simon Reddish.'

'Oh, yes. His family owned a property in Tuscany, didn't they?'

'It was near Lucca. That's no great distance from Florence.'

'Reddish tried to give the impression that he was a friend of Pomeroy's.'

'That may have been true in their younger days. Mrs Lambert would have been able to confirm it. She did speak well of Thorpe, however, unlike her husband.'

'What did *he* say?'

'It was only a chance remark. When Thorpe's name cropped up, Lambert said that he had no time for him. He didn't explain why.'

'I'm not sure I like the sound of Mr Lambert.'

'He does like to throw his weight about.'

'Why did Pomeroy's sister marry him?'

'Who knows?' said Colbeck. 'The fact that he's a wealthy gentleman farmer with a stable of fine horses might have something to do with it. And, of course, in moving from Italy to Ireland, Pomeroy's sister was shifting from one Roman Catholic country to another. That might have been a factor.'

'It's strange, isn't it?' mused Leeming.

'What is?'

'I was thinking of the way that people are attracted to each other.'

'Well, it's easy to see what happened in *your* case. You and Estelle are ideal for each other. That's why it's such a happy marriage.'

'It was the same for you, sir.'

'Not exactly,' said Colbeck. 'You and Estelle were neighbours. You grew up together and got closer and closer over the years. In the normal course of events, I'd never have met Madeleine. It was only because I led the investigation into a train robbery that she came into my life. Her father was badly injured in that incident.'

'I remember it well.'

'Luckily, he recovered in time. When Mr Andrews thanked me for what we'd done, he didn't realise that he was talking to his future son-in-law.' Colbeck smiled. 'To be honest, neither did I.'

When they'd finished their meal that evening, they adjourned to the drawing room. Lydia Quayle began to laugh.

'I can't believe that we did that, Madeleine,' she said.

'Did what?'

'We spent the whole of dinner talking about *North and South.*'

'It's a fascinating novel,' said Madeleine. 'I'm gripped by it. Besides, I was determined not to bring Alan Hinton into the conversation, so I made sure that we talked about something else.'

'You could always have invited your father to join us. Mind you, I don't think he'd have let us go on and on about Mrs Gaskell. He probably doesn't believe that women can write novels.'

'Don't underestimate him, Lydia. Father is not as old-fashioned as you might think. He has a female artist in the family, remember. I'm slowly bringing him round to the idea that women can do things just as well as men.'

'Does that include driving a steam engine?'

'Why not?'

'Would *you* want to do it?'

'To be honest, I wouldn't – but only because I know how dirty I'd get. You wouldn't believe the filth on my father's clothes after a day on the footplate. I'll stick to working in my studio. All I get there is paint on my hands.'

'But you do have something to show for your efforts.'

'That's true, I suppose.'

After a brief pause, Lydia changed the conversation and lowered her voice.

'I don't really mind,' she said. 'When you tease me about Alan, I rather like it. The simple fact is that without what you call your "interference", I'd never get to see him. I owe you my thanks – and I'm sure that Alan said the same.'

'I was too nosey,' said Madeleine. 'That was naughty of me.'

'You're my closest friend. You're entitled to be nosey.'

'Robert was right. I mustn't make decisions for you.'

'That depends what those decisions are.'

'I think you know only too well, Lydia.' Her visitor nodded. 'Let's get back to *North and South*, shall we? We're on safer ground there.'

Colbeck and Leeming had an early breakfast together so that the latter could get down to the river on time. The inspector had been studying his notebook.

'What were the two things that puzzled us at the start?' he asked.

'There's a lot more than two in my case, sir.'

'We wondered why Pomeroy had been poisoned in public, so to speak. It would surely have been much easier to kill him somewhere in private.'

'I don't agree,' said Leeming. 'He never seemed to be alone. When he wasn't rowing, he was taking part in a play. When he was not doing that, he always had people around him. Then there were lectures he had to go to. And don't forget Thorpe,' he added. 'He more or less lived with Pomeroy. That's why the victim had to be lured out into the open on his own.'

'An urgent summons from Isabella might have done that.'

'How did she get in touch with him?'

'Someone did it for her, Victor. My guess is that he got into the college and delivered the message.'

'How could the killer have done that?'

'Quite easily, I fancy, if he knew where the room was. Thorpe had no difficulty climbing into the college in the dark. His problem was that he had the force the door open. All that the killer had to do was to slip an envelope underneath it.'

'But where did he come from in the first place?'

'That's what I've been asking myself,' said Colbeck. 'I sort of assumed that he'd come from London because there was nowhere better for an Italian immigrant to hide than in the capital. But I'm questioning that assumption.'

'Why?'

'It's because he'd need to have familiarised himself with Cambridge and put Pomeroy under close surveillance. In short, he had to do a lot of homework.'

'So?'

'I think he's been here for some time and may still be.'

'Why would he be stupid enough to hang about?'

'Perhaps he just wanted to enjoy watching us make mistakes,' said Colbeck. 'One thing we do know, however, is that he's not stupid. Meticulous planning went into Pomeroy's death.'

'I agree,' said Leeming. 'So, what are we going to do?'

'You are going to watch Thorpe in action on the river and I'm going to call on the chief constable again.'

'Why?'

Colbeck drained his coffee cup. 'I think we need to change direction.'

Alan Hinton went down to the river in Oxford to watch the Boat Race crew at work yet again. He didn't linger there. Now that he knew how long it took, he was able to go for a walk in the meadows and end up close to Magdalen College. The time when he needed to be back on the towpath was when the morning's practice was over and the crew were being welcomed ashore by a knot of supporters. In the middle of them were the two undergraduates he'd overheard the previous evening. He missed the company of Lydia Quayle but consoled himself with warm memories of their time together in the ancient seat of learning.

Professor Springett was nothing if not persistent. During a lull in his commitments that morning, he went to challenge the Master. Since he could hardly turn away a senior member of the college, Sir Harold agreed to see him.

'How is the investigation going?' asked Springett.

'Inspector Colbeck has everything under control.'

'I can't say that I've seen any visible signs of progress, Master.'

'It is nevertheless being made, I assure you. First thing today,' said Sir Harold, 'I had a letter from the inspector to inform me that Pomeroy's eldest sister had been in Cambridge yesterday. She wished to view her brother's body.'

'That must have been a grim assignment for her.'

'I'm told that she preserved her equanimity throughout.'

'Let's go back to the break-in, if we may,' said Springett, fussily.

'I've already told you, Terence. The matter is closed.'

'I merely wish you to confirm or dismiss a theory of mine.'

'What is it?'

'Two days ago, I happened to approach the lodge when the porter was having an argument with an undergraduate from King's. The young man insisted on being given the key to Pomeroy's room and the porter – Stott – quite properly refused to hand it over.'

'I'm glad to hear it.'

'The undergraduate in question was Nicholas Thorpe. It's my belief that he was the person who confessed to having forced his way into Pomeroy's room. Am I correct or mistaken?'

'You are mistaken, Terence.'

Springett sagged. 'Oh, that's disappointing.'

'You are mistaken in thinking that you can come in here and bully the name out of me. When I told you that the matter was closed, I meant just that. Everything has been settled to my satisfaction. The incident does not require a post-mortem.' He rose from behind his desk. 'Good day to you.'

It was time for the Professor of Divinity to beat a retreat.

Colbeck was pleased to meet the chief constable again and Captain Davies was equally glad to see him. After an exchange of pleasantries, they adjourned to the latter's office and sat down.

'You've been ubiquitous, Inspector,' said Davies. 'My men have reported seeing you here, there and everywhere.'

'I go where the evidence leads me.'

'I marvel at the way that you evade the press. They just can't keep up with you. I've had reporters in here to complain that they can't question you properly.'

'I'm here to solve a murder,' said Colbeck, 'not to write

lurid headlines for the London newspapers. If they bother you again, please quote me.'

'I will.' Davies sat back. 'So, what's brought you here today?'

'I've come to ask for your help.'

'It's yours for the taking, Inspector.'

'Thank you, sir. We've toyed with the idea that the killer must have come from London. I now believe that he may be right under our noses. Do you have many Italian immigrants in Cambridge?'

'We have a decent share. In the most recent census, our population was well over 26,000 and that includes 7,000 people attached to the university. We're a large, busy, thriving city set in a beautiful part of the country. As a result, we attract immigrants from all over Europe and beyond.'

'I see.'

'We have Italian barbers, shopkeepers, artists, singers, labourers and so on. Whenever my grandchildren come to stay with us, we take them to a place that sells the most wonderful Italian ice cream. The shop is run by a family from Umbria.'

'So it would be easy for a newcomer from Italy to conceal himself here?'

'If he had friends who live in Cambridge, it would be very easy.'

'What if he had no contacts here?'

'This is a city with lots of places to hide, Inspector.'

Davies told him how people from some of the poorer places in Europe had come to the city in the hope of improving their lives and those of their families. Other foreigners were there for academic reasons. Immigrants were an established part of the social scene.

'Unfortunately,' said Davies, 'they haven't all come here with the best of intentions. We get the bad as well as the good.'

'Every city has that problem.'

'Criminals of various nationalities – Italians among them – have tried to infiltrate us. They see Cambridge as a source of easy pickings. We've had to disabuse them of that fantasy. My officers have arrested people from a number of different countries. Only last month, we arrested some Dutch criminals who'd been stealing expensive items from local farms.'

'I hadn't realised that the city was so cosmopolitan.'

'Then you haven't walked around the backstreets in the suburbs and seen the names above some of the shops.'

'Perhaps it's time to do so, Captain.'

'I don't follow.'

'Our man is still here.'

'Killers don't usually hang around near the scene of the crime, Inspector. In my experience, they tend to get far away from it.'

'I agree, but this case is different somehow. For some reason, the killer is still in the area. He was spotted in Bury St Edmunds recently. He's here somewhere. I *sense* it.'

'That means you're relying on instinct?'

'It rarely lets me down,' said Colbeck. 'May I ask you a favour?'

'Of course – if you need extra officers, have as many as you wish.'

'I only need one man, actually. Perhaps you can give me his address.'

Davies was baffled. 'Who is this person?'

'He's the man who sells wonderful Italian ice cream to your grandchildren,' said Colbeck. 'I'd like to meet him.'

CHAPTER NINETEEN

While keeping an eye on the Cambridge boat, Leeming kept the other free to look out for what he thought might be spies from Oxford. There was no artist with a telescope this time, but one of two rather odd individuals did lurk along the towpath. Since he had no proof that they were doing anything wrong, Leeming didn't feel able to approach them. When the oarsmen were climbing out of the boat, he moved within earshot of the coach's comments.

James Webb was much more restrained than usual. While he had plenty to criticise, he had far more to commend and was particularly appreciative of the way that Colin Smyly had coxed the boat. As the coach was heaping praise on Smyly, the sergeant glanced across at Andrew Kinglake, forced to watch enviously from the bank. Realising that he was being watched, Kinglake produced a broad smile of approval at what was being said.

Leeming waited until the speech was over and the oarsmen began to disperse. He fell in beside Nicholas Thorpe.

'You looked better than ever today.'

'Thank you, Sergeant. We achieved real coordination.'

'I really wanted a word about what happened yesterday.'

'Ah, yes,' said Thorpe, still panting slightly from his exertions. 'I took your advice and went to see the Master.'

'I know that, sir.'

'He accepted my version of events and drew a line under the incident.'

'That line is not as final as it should be,' Leeming explained. 'I had a message from the college porter. He warned me that Professor Springett is determined to find out who the interloper was. He believes it was you because he came to the lodge when you were having that argument with Stott.'

'Sir Harold won't betray a confidence.'

'All I'm telling you is that you should be careful. Because of your friendship with Mr Pomeroy, you're tainted as far as the professor is concerned. If he can establish that you climbed into the college and forced your way into that room, he's likely to go to the police.'

'That would be a disaster,' cried Thorpe. 'I'd be dropped from the crew.'

'What you need is an alibi, sir.'

'Where would I get that from?'

'I can make a few suggestions,' said Leeming. 'But that wasn't the only reason I wanted to speak to you. Mr Pomeroy's eldest sister was here yesterday. She and her husband wanted to view the body.'

'Are they still in Cambridge?'

'No, they went back to London.'

'That's a shame,' said Thorpe. 'I'd have liked to have seen Caroline again. Of the three sisters, she was Bernard's favourite – though he never let the others know that, of course. Caroline was mad about horses,' he recalled. 'She was in the saddle every day. I'm so sorry I missed her.'

'What about her husband?'

'I'm sure that Francis Lambert has his good qualities, but I've never caught sight of them. He's always treated me as if I was nothing but a hanger-on. Bernard had a row with him about it.'

'What did Mr Pomeroy's father make of his son-in-law?'

'He never got to meet him. He died over a year before the wedding.'

'Do you think that he'd have liked Mr Lambert?'

'No, I don't, Sergeant. He'd have found him too brash and self-centred.'

'That was the inspector's estimate of him. He told me that he wished he'd been able to talk much longer with Mrs Lambert. He wanted to know more about her father. How much did she see of him when she was growing up, for instance?'

'I can answer that question.'

'Why?'

'It's because it was the same for all of the children. Mr Pomeroy was a very busy man. He was rarely at home. That's why Bernard had no interest in joining the diplomatic service. It was wreathed in secrecy. In all the time he knew his father,' said Thorpe, 'Mr Pomeroy never once explained to his son what he actually did at the Consulate. For someone as inquisitive as Bernard, it must have been maddening. I asked him once if he could sum his father up in three words.'

'What was his reply?'

'The Invisible Man.'

Alan Hinton knew the routine now. Liam Brannigan sent the crew off at more or less the same time and there was a set period for their practice up and down the river. The detective was able to saunter towards the boat as the oarsmen were taking it in turns to climb out. He never got close enough to hear what Brannigan was saying to the crew, but he could see from the way they cowered before him that he was not pleased with what he'd witnessed.

After delivering his comments, the coach sent them on their way. Hinton watched them go off to their respective colleges without making any attempt to follow one or more of them. His interest was in the two undergraduates he'd overheard on the previous day. After dallying on the towpath for a while, Ralph and his friend set off. Hinton tailed them from a safe distance until they went into their usual pub. Anxious not to give himself away, Hinton walked up and down the High Street for twenty minutes to kill time, then he drifted into the pub and ordered a beer. He felt sure that Ralph and his friend didn't even know that he was there. Hinton inched slowly in their direction until he was able to pick up snatches of their conversation.

Before he could get even closer, however, he felt that someone was standing directly behind him. He turned round to find Liam Brannigan. The coach had a mocking smile on his face, but his tone was threatening.

'Ralph told me I might find you here, Constable Hinton,' he said. 'We don't like eavesdroppers. We usually throw them in the river. I know you've had orders to watch us, but we're finding you a bit of a nuisance.' He leant in close. 'If I wasn't in a public place, I'd use more appropriate language.'

'I'm entitled to come in here for a drink, Mr Brannigan.'

'Of course, you are. Now drink up and get yourself out of here. Understand?'

While he was not intimidated, Hinton realised that his time in Oxford was over. He'd been seen and unmasked. It might even be that Ralph and his friend had deliberately led him astray when they'd talked about what Brannigan had been ready to do to ensure an Oxford victory. When he glanced across at their table, the two supporters sniggered and raised their tankards at him.

Marco Pedroni was a stocky man of middle years with a gleaming bald head and a smile as big as the Adriatic Sea. He was arranging the display in the window of his toyshop when Colbeck arrived. Though he smiled at the newcomer, he didn't expect him to come into the shop because it didn't sell anything that could possibly interest him. It was essentially an emporium for children stacked with colouring books, crayons, sets of water paints, toys, puzzles, musical instruments and a gallimaufry of items that might appeal to the younger mind.

Ice cream was advertised on a board in the shop window, but there was no sign of it when Colbeck walked in.

'Good day to you, Mr Pedroni,' he said.

'Welcome to my shop, sir.'

'I'm Inspector Colbeck of the Metropolitan Police.'

Pedroni was worried. 'You come to arrest me?'

'Is there any reason why I should?'

'No, no,' said the other. 'I obey law and follow rules, but some people, they don't like that my shop do better than theirs. They tell me I will be shipped back to Italy in chains.'

'Don't listen to them, sir. We need businessmen like you to bring some colour to our drab streets. I'm here because Captain Davies recommended your ice cream.'

'Yes, is right,' said the other, laughing. 'The captain, he comes in here with his grandchildren. Pedroni ice cream is finest in county. You like some?'

'Not at the moment,' said Colbeck. 'The other reason I'm here is that I'm told you speak English very well.'

'I try, Inspector. When you move to new country, I think, is only good manners to learn language. No?'

'I couldn't agree more.' Colbeck lowered his voice. 'Is there somewhere we could talk in private, please? I feel I'm in the way here and might put your genuine customers off.'

'No worry, sir. My wife, she will take over.' He cupped his hands around his mouth. 'Lina!'

'*Sì, sì!*' said a loud voice from the back of the shop.

Within seconds, a middle-aged woman came into view and looked in surprise at Colbeck because he was not typical of their customers. Pedroni introduced her to their visitor and, like her husband, she was apprehensive.

'No need to worry, my love,' said her husband. 'The inspector, he is not here to send us back to Umbria in chains.' Her frown blossomed into a grin. 'You mind the shop, please. We go talk.'

'I don't see any ice cream,' said Colbeck, looking around.

'It has to be kept cold at the back of the shop.'

'Did your wife make it?'

'No,' replied Pedroni, tapping his chest. 'I make it with secret recipe. You ask the children who come here. They will tell you, is delicious.'

'Is true,' confirmed his wife. 'Marco has a gift.'

'*You* are my gift, Lina!' he said, one hand to his heart.

She laughed merrily and went to stand behind the counter.

Victor Leeming had found the chat with Thorpe illuminating. After walking back to King's College with him, he veered off to Corpus Christi so that he could have a word with the porter. Stott was pleased to see him.

'I'm glad you've come, Sergeant,' he said. 'I owe you my thanks.'

'Why?'

'Mr Thorpe apologised for the way he behaved towards me the other day. I think he was only doing what you told him to do.'

Leeming winked at him. 'I'm saying nothing.'

'The money was a lovely surprise.'

'What money?'

'Mr Thorpe gave me a five pound note.'

'Well done! It's the least you deserve.'

'When I got home yesterday evening, I put it on the mantelpiece so that my wife and I could stare at it. We've got all sorts of ideas for how to spend it.'

'I bet you have,' said Leeming with a grin. 'As it happens, I came here to say thank you as well, but I'm afraid there's no five pound note this time. A detective's pay rate doesn't allow me to be quite so generous. Your warning about Professor Springett was very timely, by the way. I passed it on to Mr Thorpe earlier this morning.'

'With luck, the danger may have been passed.'

'Really?'

'In my job, Sergeant,' said the porter, 'I get to hear most things that happen in this college. When he went to see the Master, the professor had a face like thunder. He came out even looking angrier. I think it was because the Master refused to name Mr Thorpe.'

'I hoped he would.'

'Oh, I've just remembered. That friend of his was here again this morning.'

'What friend?'

'He goes to the professor for tutorials. They only happen once a week, but Mr Reddish is here more often than not. I don't know why. When he walked past today, he didn't even look at me. Mr Reddish was talking to himself and waving his arms about.'

'Could you hear what he was saying?'

'It sounded like some lines from a play – flowery stuff with words I didn't understand. Yet he didn't go to the professor's study. He went in the direction of the room where our famous playwright used to live.'

'Christopher Marlowe?'

'That's the one. Mr Pomeroy was very partial to him. He told me once that he worshipped Marlowe though he never said why.' He gave an expressive shrug. 'Lads of their age have funny ideas, don't they?'

When he was taken into the storeroom at the back of the shop, Colbeck saw that it was a paradise for children. Wherever he looked, there were games, dolls, jigsaws hoops, skipping ropes and a bewildering variety of other toys. Before he could question Pedroni, he was forced to listen to the history of ice cream making. The Italian began by claiming that the Emperor Nero had been fond of it and had blocks of ice brought from the Apennines so that his cook could make a kind of sorbet.

'The first ice cream parlour,' said Pedroni, 'it was opened in New York City in 1776. Since then, many others come along.'

'We can't claim to have gone back that far,' admitted Colbeck, 'but I do remember a man named Carlo Gatti setting up the first ice cream stand in London in 1851, the year of the Great Exhibition. It was outside Charing Cross railway station.'

'With a name like that, Carlo Gatti, he must have come from Italy.'

'Actually, I think he was Swiss. However, before we go any further, tell me a little more about yourself. Captain Davies said that you came from Umbria.'

'Is right, Inspector.'

'What made you want to leave Italy?'

'Is not something we *wanted*,' said Pedroni. 'Is something we *had* to do.'

His face crumpled. Colbeck listened with interest as the shopkeeper told his story. Pedroni had been born in the beautiful hilltop city of Spoleto, a place with a colourful history. The Italian was brought up in a family that had been in trade for many years. Having started with a stall in the market, Pedroni's father had been so successful that he'd been able to buy a shop and – as his fortunes flourished even more – find additional premises. All was going well until the old man died. Pedroni's older brother then became the head of the family. He treated his siblings badly, reserving the more flourishing areas of the business for himself and consigning his three brothers to a life of low expectation and growing resentment.

'Is not all Luigi's fault,' stressed Pedroni. 'He is my brother, and I must love him. But we had rivals, cold, ruthless men who envied what we'd built up and tried to take it from us. We fight back. Blood, it was spilt. To my shame, I spilt some of it. But at least we drove off our rivals.'

'Didn't the police try to intervene?'

'They did, Inspector, and they were close to arresting me. I had just married Lina. She was afraid I'd be locked away a long time even though everything I do, it was to defend the honour of the Pedroni family.'

'What did your elder brother suggest?'

'He say I have to leave for our safety. He give me money and tell us to go out of the reach of the police. We leave

Spoleto in tears. Lina only stops crying when we reach England and she sees something she likes. Umbria is full of hills. We prefer a place like this – very flat.'

'It was a brave decision to leave your native country.'

'We have to escape,' explained Pedroni, arms wide in supplication. 'That was years ago when things were bad for us. Now, everything is good. I have lovely wife, beautiful children. People like us. They buy our toys, they eat our ice cream. What more we want?'

It was impossible not to warm to the man though Colbeck suspected he'd been guilty of something fairly serious back in Spoleto. Clearly, it had been put firmly behind him. He shook Pedroni's hand in gratitude.

'Thank you,' he said. 'You told me exactly what I'd hoped to hear.'

'Why? You wish to go to Umbria?'

'I'd love to, Mr Pedroni, but I have too many commitments here.'

'Is there anything else I can do for you?'

'No, thank you.'

'Are you *sure*?' he asked as he saw the look in Colbeck's eye.

'Well . . .'

Pedroni chortled. 'I get you the ice cream right away.'

'Another time, perhaps,' said Colbeck. 'Having come to such a lovely toyshop, however, I can't possibly leave without buying something for my daughter.'

Edward Tallis was pleased to see the change in his visitor's manner. When Francis Lambert entered the superintendent's room, he did so in a more respectful mood. Having been slapped down hard during his previous visit, he'd learnt his lesson.

'I understand that you and Mrs Lambert viewed the body,' said Tallis.

'We did, Superintendent.'

'It's a grim business, I know. I hope that your wife wasn't too distressed.'

'She bore up well,' said Lambert, his stomach lurching slightly as he recalled his own response. 'And it was important for a member of the family to identify Bernard. The word of a friend is not enough.'

'I agree, sir. Unfortunately, you were in Ireland and other members of the Pomeroy family are in Italy. Getting any of you here instantly was not possible.'

'I understand that.'

'What brought you here today?'

'I want to know if any progress has been made yet,' said Lambert.

'Inspector Colbeck will have answered that question, sir.'

'He mentioned that the post-mortem was incomplete.'

'That's because they were unable to identify the poison used. We had to call in someone from St Thomas's Hospital here in London. His report was delivered earlier. The date of the inquest will be set for the near future. You and Mrs Lambert will be able to attend it.'

'Only if my wife is up to it,' said Lambert. 'The effort of bearing up at the hospital yesterday took its toll. When we got back to the hotel, the full force of her loss suddenly hit her. We had to get a doctor to prescribe a sedative.'

'I'm sorry to hear that.'

'She and Bernard were very close.'

'I sympathise with both of you, sir,' said Tallis. 'What are your plans?'

'Now that we know the inquest is at hand, I can contact a funeral director who is able to transport the body back to Tuscany with the necessary reverence. Cost is no obstacle. We want the best person for the task.'

'I may be able to offer you a suggestion or two.'

'We'd be very grateful,' said Lambert. 'And thanks are also due to the inspector for looking after us yesterday. He's obviously fully committed to this investigation. It's just a pity that it's moving so slowly.'

'Murder cases are never easy to solve. There's so much work involved. Inspector Colbeck once had a case that dragged on for all of nine months, but he stuck at it doggedly and eventually caught the killer. That's something to bear in mind, Mr Lambert.'

'Yes, it is.'

'However long it takes, we never give up.'

'That's . . . commendable.'

'There's something else that might reassure you,' said Tallis. 'I have several detectives under my command. They are all good, well-trained, dedicated officers. The very best of them is Robert Colbeck.'

There was so much laughter coming from the nursery that Madeleine was tempted to put her paintbrush aside to join her father and her daughter. What stopped her was the thought that she'd be trespassing on them. She could see Helena Rose almost any time she wished, but Andrews had a life outside the house. He came and went at set times every morning. If he returned for dinner, it was often after his granddaughter had been put to bed. Madeleine reminded herself that her father was the only grandparent that Helena had. That made it more important for the girl to form a strong bond with him. As a child, Madeleine had enjoyed the luxury of four grandparents, all of whom had doted on her. Colbeck's parents had died years ago and Madeleine's mother had also passed away. Helena never had the chance to know them.

Turning back to her easel, Madeleine started to work on the painting again. It was one that she hadn't allowed her father to see at any stage because, unknown to him, it was intended as a gift for his forthcoming birthday. One of her paintings already hung in the family house. The new one would also be put on display because it would stir up so many memories for her father. Having restricted herself to painting locomotives and railway scenes, she'd tried something far more ambitious this time. After visits there to make a series of sketches, Madeleine was bringing Euston Station to life before her.

It was both the starting point and return destination for countless journeys that her father had made in the service of the LNWR. Since she was less skilled at creating figures, she set the painting early in the morning when very few people were about and when pigeons were able to land with impunity to forage. Euston was slowly coming to life on the canvas. It was a scene that her father would know well, having often arrived for work when the sun was not really up and the station was dappled with shadows. As she stood back to appraise her work, Madeleine wondered if it would replace the painting of hers that already hung in her father's living room.

Elsie Gurr was also looking at a painting. She had just dusted it and replaced it on the wall where it belonged. It was a landscape that her husband had bought for her when they'd once stayed in a village nearby. A local artist had it on display in her window. Elsie stood back to admire it.

'Don't worry,' she said, soothingly. 'I won't ever turn *you* to the wall.'

Much as he'd have liked to sample Pedroni's famous ice cream, Colbeck had declined the offer on the grounds that he was hardly dressed to eat it in public. Ice cream was best consumed, he felt, on a hot day at a holiday resort on the south coast. There was a secondary reason to turn it down. He knew that, if Leeming ever found out what he'd done, he would tease the inspector mercilessly. Leaving the shop, he hailed a cab and asked to be taken to the railway station. His arrival there was timely. When he checked at the telegraph station, he discovered that a courier was about to be sent to The Jolly Traveller with two messages for him. Colbeck read both messages with interest.

The first one was brief. It had been sent from Oxford by Hinton to say that his time there was over. He was returning to London. The second telegraph was longer but equally disappointing. Tallis had paraphrased the report from St Thomas's Hospital. Pomeroy had been killed by a compound of drugs. Unfortunately, the main ingredient was unidentifiable.

To give himself thinking time, Colbeck ignored the cab rank and walked towards the city. The fresh air helped to clear his mind. He went over the evidence so far gathered and subjected it to close scrutiny. It enabled him to discard some lines of enquiry and concentrate on what remained. What struck him about the fatal poison was that the main ingredient was one that a British toxicologist had never heard of. It had, therefore, to be a foreign import. The assassin had brought it from overseas and given two doses of it to Bernard Pomeroy. They had been enough to kill him. Since the various poisons were not available over the counter, Colbeck wondered how they'd been obtained. Were they looking for an assassin with medical knowledge?

When he glanced up, he saw the first signs of the university, poking its head above the houses with an amalgam of towers, spires, pinnacles and other architectural features that set it apart from the city itself. It spurred him on to lengthen his stride. He was not the only person in a hurry. As he got within sight of The Jolly Traveller, he saw Leeming converging speedily on the pub as well. The sergeant waved to him.

'How did you get on, sir?'

'Come to my room and I'll tell you,' said Colbeck.

* * *

Alan Hinton was not looking forward to giving his report to the superintendent. He could imagine the searing criticism he'd receive. His failure in Oxford had to be admitted, however, and Hinton was brave enough to tell the truth. The only thing he would omit from his account was the fact that, for one whole day, he'd used Lydia Quayle as his decoy. During the train ride back to London, he had ample time to plan what he would say. His fear was that, when he went into Tallis's office, he might come out again having been demoted. He'd be reduced ignominiously to the ranks of uniformed constables.

Arriving at Scotland Yard, he decided to get the ordeal over as quickly as possible and went straight to the superintendent. Delivering bad news to Tallis was akin to standing in front of a one-man firing squad, but it had to be done. Hinton was honest, detailed and highly apologetic. Closing his eyes, he waited for the first bullet.

'Right,' said Tallis, calmly, 'the first thing I'll need is the bill for your time at the Eastgate Hotel in Oxford. We won't need you to stay there any more.'

'I kept strictly within the figure you allowed me, sir,' said Hinton, taking the bill from his pocket to put on the desk. He regarded the other quizzically. 'Excuse me, Superintendent, but I thought you'd be annoyed.'

'I'm being practical, Hinton.'

'Oh, I see.'

'You did your best and that's all I can ask. Colbeck was right to look into the possibility that Oxford might somehow be involved in the crime. That's why I seconded you to the investigation. Things have moved on since then.'

'Have they, sir?'

'Yes,' said Tallis. 'I had a telegraph from the inspector less than an hour ago. He's on his way back to London because he's firmly of the opinion that our interest must be focussed on Italy. The arrival of Pomeroy's sister has changed everything.'

'I'm delighted to hear it, sir.'

'You'll return at once to normal duties.'

'Yes, sir – and thank you for being so understanding.'

'You say that as if it's a rare event. I *always* understand.'

'Well . . .'

'Get out, man!'

Hinton almost ran out of the room.

Before leaving for London, Colbeck had sent the sergeant off to St John's College again. Victor Leeming was happy to have a second confrontation with Simon Reddish because he felt that he could get the upper hand over the young actor. As on his previous visit, he climbed the staircase to Reddish's room and heard an explosion of brittle laughter coming from within. Once again, Reddish was holding forth in front of his cronies. Irked at being interrupted by the sergeant, he dismissed his friends and turned on his visitor.

'What is it *this* time?' he asked.

'I thought you'd be pleased to see me, sir,' said Leeming. 'We had such an interesting talk when I came here before.'

'That's not how I'd describe it. At least you didn't disturb me while I was trying to finish an essay. That's what the inspector did.'

'What did the professor think of your essay?'

'He said what he always said,' boasted Reddish. 'It was an outstanding piece of scholarship.'

'You see a lot of Professor Springett, don't you?'

'What are you implying?'

'I'm not implying anything. It's just that, according to the inspector, you'd only have one tutorial a week at Corpus Christi College yet you're there more often than that. Mr Thorpe has noticed you a number of times.'

'Ha!' said the other, curling his lip. 'He's a fine one to talk. Thorpe more or less lived at Corpus. You don't need telling why.'

'You haven't answered my question, sir.'

'I don't see its relevance.'

'Then I'll have to ask the professor instead.'

'No, no,' said Reddish, quickly, 'there's no need to do that. The explanation is quite simple. The relevant texts for my studies are in short supply in the college library. We have to take it in turns to borrow them. It's so irritating. Because of the quality of my essays, Professor Springett has given me unlimited access to the library in his study. Others might call it an example of favouritism, but I see it as a deserved reward for the efforts I put in.'

'How many others can use the professor's books?'

'I'm the only one.'

'Then you must be an outstanding scholar, Mr Reddish.'

'I know how to apply myself.'

'Yet all you want to do is to become an actor like your father. The inspector told me that most people who study Divinity do so because it gets them ready for a life in Holy Orders. All you want to do is to stand on a stage and be applauded.'

Reddish was insulted. 'Don't show your ignorance, Sergeant,' he retorted. 'Acting is a noble profession. I won't demean myself by explaining why.'

'Let's move on,' said Leeming. 'You claim to be a friend of Mr Pomeroy's. When did you first meet him?'

'It was in Italy some years ago. I was visiting Florence when I saw there was a play on at the theatre there. I bought a ticket immediately. Bernard and I were the only two Englishmen there, so we drifted together. You can imagine how delighted I was when he told me about his ambition to come to Cambridge. That was exactly the path *I'd* chosen.'

'Did you see much of him in Italy?'

'Yes,' said Reddish. 'I went to Florence and he came over to Lucca from time to time. He was thrilled to meet my father, one of the leading actors in the English theatre. Bernard had the soul of a thespian.' He lifted his chin. 'Unlike you, he understood that there was far more to performing on stage than receiving applause.'

'I believe you, sir. I don't get to see plays in my job.'

'That's a shame – they might educate you.'

Leeming grinned. 'I've arrested a lot of educated people in my time, sir,' he said. 'But why is your memory different to Mr Thorpe's? He told us that you did meet Mr Pomeroy in Italy, but you spent very little time together.'

'I was *there*, Sergeant. Thorpe wasn't.'

'He did stay with Mr Pomeroy in Florence now and again.'

'I think his visits were quite rare. I'd spend part of the summer in Tuscany.'

'The truth will out, sir.'

'What do you mean?'

'Inspector Colbeck has gone to London to speak to Mr Pomeroy's elder sister again. She'll remember how often you visited the house. Yesterday the inspector took Mrs Lambert and her husband to view the body. Naturally, the lady was in no mood for a long conversation. Her mind was elsewhere. Things may be different today.'

'I . . . hope they are,' said Reddish.

'We're exploring every avenue in order to catch those involved in the murder,' said Leeming. 'The inspector has even talked to the Prime Minister.'

'Why?'

'It turns out that he was a friend of Mr Pomeroy's father and recalled visiting him in Florence. Lord Palmerston offered to give Bernard Pomeroy some advice about taking up a career in politics. You see?' added Leeming. 'We're getting help from the most unlikely sources.'

Reddish was too startled to do anything but gape.

CHAPTER TWENTY

Though he'd been feted in the newspapers many times after solving a murder case, Robert Colbeck knew that the credit was never entirely due to his efforts. Luck always played a crucial role. It was the same in the present investigation. He was fortunate enough to have met individuals who gave him significant help. The first was Arthur Bullen, the railway policeman, who'd supplied vital evidence. The second was Jack Stott, the porter, whose experience and discretion had been of great use to them. Surprisingly, the third was no less a person than the Prime Minister, who'd given Colbeck some idea of the background from which Bernard Pomeroy had come.

As he made his way across London in a cab, Colbeck wondered if his greatest stroke of luck might have been in meeting Marco Pedroni, the exiled Italian, a man forced to flee his native Umbria because of the way he'd defended the name of his family. After starting with a stall in the market, he now owned a toyshop and served what was reportedly magical ice cream. Simply by being the amiable extrovert that he was, Pedroni had made an impression on the inspector. It remained to be seen how positive it had been.

His luck continued. When he reached the hotel, he discovered that Francis Lambert was not there but that his wife was still in their room. Caroline Lambert would be far more likely to confide in him without a husband hovering over her. The only problem was that she might be too distraught to receive visitors. Her love for her only brother had been deep and unconditional. Having weathered the trial of viewing her brother's corpse, Caroline might prefer to be left alone to mourn in private.

The fact that the couple were staying in one of the finest hotels in the city told him how wealthy Francis Lambert must be. He was a man who expected the best and he'd chosen a wife on that basis. Colbeck sent a message up to their room, asking if they might have a quiet conversation somewhere. It was some time before a reply arrived. Caroline agreed to meet him in the lounge when she was ready. Delighted with her response, he didn't mind the fact that it was almost half an hour before she finally appeared. They sat in high-backed leather chairs that helped to screen them off from other residents of the hotel.

Colbeck was struck by her appearance. She was calm, poised and alert. If she was still struggling with her loss, there was no hint of it in her manner.

'I thought you'd still be in Cambridge,' she said.

'I was anxious to meet you again, Mrs Lambert.'

'You've missed my husband, I'm afraid. He went to Scotland Yard this morning and learnt that Bernard's body will soon be released. Francis has gone to the premises of some funeral directors whose names were kindly given to him by the superintendent. We need someone capable of transferring the body to Florence.'

'Wouldn't it have been easier to employ a funeral director in Bury St Edmunds itself?' asked Colbeck. 'That's where your brother's body is being kept.'

'My husband wouldn't even consider it, Inspector. He said that an ordinary little market town like that wouldn't be able to provide the service we needed. As usual, he's in search of perfection. Now,' she said, settling back in her chair, 'what would you like to ask me about Bernard?'

'First of all, Mrs Lambert, I'd like you to talk about your father. Nicholas Thorpe told my sergeant that Mr Pomeroy was a man whose work always came first. Your brother, apparently, called him The Invisible Man. Is that a fair description?'

'Yes,' she replied, sadly. 'I'm afraid that it is.'

'What's your memory of him?'

'When he was there, he was everything you'd want in a father.'

'But he was frequently absent.'

'He lived for his work, Inspector – to the detriment of family life.'

'How did your mother react to that?'

'She was understanding and very loyal,' said Caroline. 'Whenever we complained – and we did that on a regular basis – Mother would always defend him and say that we had to be patient.'

'And *were* you?'

'My sisters and I made token efforts, but Bernard didn't bother. We only ever saw Father for a few minutes after supper. My brother demanded more attention. Looking back,' she went on, 'I have to admit that Bernard could be quite beastly at times.'

She was there again. Madeleine was certain. Having agreed to go to Lydia Quayle's house for tea that afternoon, she went to the bedroom and opened the wardrobe to choose what to wear. Something made her swivel towards the front window and glance out. On the opposite side of the road, she saw the person who'd been staring at the house once before. It was more than casual interest. The little old woman, in the same coat and the same feathered hat, seemed to be spellbound. Madeleine watched her for minutes. She was about to pull back the curtains to take a closer look at the woman when the latter suddenly turned away and walked off along the pavement. Why had she been so curious? On the first occasion, thought Madeleine, the woman could have been passing by and stopped to look at the house out of interest. She wouldn't have done so twice unless there was a good reason.

Madeleine was worried. She needed to discuss the matter with Lydia.

* * *

It was the look on his face that made Victor Leeming pay him a second visit. Beside the river that morning, he'd seen Andrew Kinglake simmering with jealousy at being displaced from the Cambridge boat in favour of someone who was younger, less experienced and, in Kinglake's view, less resourceful in an emergency during a race. Leeming feared that it remained more than possible that he might wish to do something about the glaring injustice. While the investigation was tilting in a new direction, he nevertheless felt that it was still worth keeping one of their initial suspects under scrutiny. The mysterious death of one coxswain might yet have involved another.

He got to the college to find Kinglake chatting to some friends in the main quadrangle. Seeing the sergeant approaching, the undergraduate came forward to meet him so that he was out of earshot of his companions.

'I wasn't expecting to see you again, Sergeant,' he said, pointedly.

'I didn't want you to feel that you're being ignored, sir.'

'If you needed to speak to me,' said Kinglake, 'why didn't you do so down by the river this morning?'

'You were too busy wincing at what your coach was saying about Mr Smyly.'

'That's arrant nonsense.'

'Is it?'

'I agreed with every word that James said. Colin Smyly did well.'

'But not as well as *you* might have done.'

'He's still not fully-fledged.'

344

'Whereas you are, I suppose.'

'How much do you know about coxing an eight?' asked Kinglake with disdain. 'What do you know about rowing of any kind, for that matter?'

'I'm a tug-of-war man myself,' replied Leeming, affably. 'It's a sport where you keep your feet on dry land.'

'All that you saw this morning were the likely eight oarsmen and cox who will represent Cambridge in the Boat Race. Had you stayed a little longer, you'd have seen me coxing members of the reserve eight.'

'I didn't know that there was one, sir.'

'What do you think happens if someone drops out?' asked Kinglake. 'He has to be replaced by someone who is equally fit and who has been on the river in that boat on a regular basis. We take no chances.'

'How did you get on today, sir?'

'We did extremely well. In fact, Webb said that we were in excellent form and he picked me out for additional praise.'

'How did that make you feel, Mr Kinglake?'

'It made me feel good.'

'Yet the coach still prefers Mr Smyly.'

'He does at the moment.'

'Do you think you can change his mind?'

Kinglake smiled. 'We'll see.'

There was a smug quality about him that irritated and amused Leeming in equal measure. The cox had clearly not given up his ambition to be in the Cambridge boat on the one day of the year when it mattered.

'Look,' said the other, 'I can't waste any more time

talking to you, I'm afraid. I've a tutorial fairly soon. What are you doing here, anyway? I thought you were more or less based at Corpus.'

'What makes you say that, sir?'

'My brother has seen you talking to the porter a number of times.'

'Your brother?'

'He's at Corpus, reading Divinity.'

'I didn't know that,' said Leeming, wishing that he'd had the information earlier.

'May I go now?'

'Not just yet, Mr Kinglake. There's something else I'd like to know. How did your father take the news that you'd been replaced?'

'I *haven't* been replaced, Sergeant. I've simply been rested while another cox is being tried out. The Boat Race is still some time away. I predict that one or two people will make way for someone else by the time the big day arrives.'

'Will one of them be the cox?'

'That depends on how fit Colin is.'

'He looked in good condition to me,' said Leeming.

'I'm talking about his mental fitness. The pressures on a cox are immense. He has to goad his oarsmen on, set the rate at which they pull on the oars and make strategic decisions at short notice. It's open warfare on Boat Race day.'

Leeming studied him. 'When did you first cox a boat?'

'It was when I was at school. I loved the feeling of control, of getting the oarsmen to do exactly what I needed them to do.'

'So you'd had years of practice before you came here.'

'Five or six at least,' said Kinglake.

'How many years of experience did Mr Pomeroy have?'

'None.'

Leeming was astonished. 'None at all?'

'He'd rowed on a river from time to time, I daresay, but he'd never coxed an eight. Nick Thorpe boasted that Bernard would be brilliant at whatever he took up and urged him to try coxing.' Kinglake glowered. 'You know the rest of the story.'

'He turned out to have a natural talent at it.'

'That was only one element to it.'

'What were the others?'

'The main one was Thorpe. His position in the boat was secure so he set about getting Bernard into it as well. He leant on Malcolm, our president, and never stopped whispering in our coach's ear.'

'What are you trying to tell me, sir?'

'He should never have been in our boat as cox,' said Kinglake with blistering derision. 'Bernard was too erratic, too pleased with himself and too prone to make the wrong decisions out of sheer bravado. Yes, he had flair, I'll grant him that. However, he was also a risk-taker and that can be fatal.' He took a deep breath. 'I regret what happened to him, of course,' he went on, 'but I must be candid. We have far more chance of winning the Boat Race *without* Bernard Pomeroy.'

Caroline Lambert took time to relax completely. Once she'd done so, there was no longer a need for Colbeck to ply her with questions. Her memories provided all the answers he needed. She emphasised the fact that she and her siblings had grown up at a time when Italy was a patchwork of different governments and that it suited the Austrian Empire, in particular, to keep the country disunited. Caroline admitted that she and her sisters took very little interest in political affairs, though their brother watched developments carefully. What the whole family did realise was that there was increasing volatility in the Grand Duchy of Tuscany.

'Father was caught up in the middle of it,' she explained. 'He was always rushing off to important meetings. It was difficult for us to decide on a date for any family gatherings because we couldn't guarantee that he'd be available.'

'Where were you married?' asked Colbeck.

'It was in Florence, almost two years ago.'

'You'd have had plenty of choices of venue, I should imagine. I'm told that the city has a large number of churches.'

'There's one on almost every corner.'

'I'm sorry that your father was no longer alive to attend the wedding.' He studied her for a moment. 'Did he have no interests outside of his diplomatic duties?'

'He adored art and architecture,' said Caroline. 'That's why he was delighted to be sent to Florence. It's a feast for the eye, Inspector. If and when you go there, you'll wander around in a daze.'

'I'm too much of a policeman to do that, Mrs Lambert. Visitors who marvel at the city's wonders are tempting targets for pickpockets.'

'You're right. They flock to places like Florence.'

'Let me ask you something else, if I may,' he said. 'Your brother befriended Simon Reddish, a young man who stayed near Lucca occasionally. Do you remember meeting him?'

'Yes, but it was only a couple of times.'

'Mr Reddish insisted that he and your brother met whenever possible.'

'That's ridiculous.'

'Are you sure of that?'

'Bernard may have gone to Lucca once or twice, but he never really liked Simon and neither did we. He is horribly competitive. We were glad when Bernard fell out with him. His real friend was Nick Thorpe. We love him.'

Madeleine always enjoyed a visit to Lydia's home because it got her out of the house and liberated her from the nagging fear that she ought to be working in her studio. Over tea that afternoon, she told her friend about the two occasions when she'd noticed an old woman watching the property.

'That's twice, Lydia,' she said. 'For all I know, there may have been other instances. Why take such an interest in *our* house?'

'It's an attractive property.'

'Yes, but it's virtually identical to the houses either side of it.'

'That's true, but they don't have a wonderful artist and a famous detective living in them. You and Robert are what make the place so special.'

'It's a lovely idea,' said Madeleine, laughing, 'but how could a complete stranger have any idea that we *did* live there?'

'The first time you spotted her there,' said Lydia, thoughtfully, 'she realised that she'd been seen and scurried away. The second time she was on the other side of the road and unaware that you were watching her.'

'Yes, Lydia, that's right. Before I could catch her eye, she moved off. I'd seen her outside for some minutes, but she might have been there much longer.'

'Did you feel threatened in any way?'

'No, not really, but it did make me feel uneasy. I don't like being spied on.'

'Is that what she was doing?'

'I don't know.'

'And you say that she was a harmless old lady?' Madeleine nodded. 'In that case, I shouldn't worry about it. She wasn't breaking any law. Perhaps she had some connection with your house,' suggested Lydia. 'It may be that she used to live there.'

'Judging by her appearance,' said Madeleine, 'I think that's very unlikely.'

'Then maybe she worked there as a servant. Staring at the place may have revived pleasant memories for her. Whatever the truth, I don't think it's anything to worry about.'

'I suppose that it isn't, really.'

'Let's talk about something more serious, shall we?' said Lydia. 'Have you finished *North and South* yet?'

Leeming had become so familiar with Trumpington Street that he believed he could find his way to Corpus Christi College blindfolded. When he turned into the entrance, the first thing he saw was a cluster of young men around Jack Stott, each of them with a problem to be solved. The porter handled the battery of enquiries with his customary speed and skill. He knew the names of every one of the undergraduates. Before moving in, the sergeant waited until they'd all disappeared.

'Good afternoon to you,' he said, cheerily.

'Welcome back,' replied Stott. 'You seem to be in a good mood.'

'I found out something that interested me, that's all,' said Leeming. 'It concerns Simon Reddish. I now know why he comes here so often.'

'Please tell me, Sergeant.'

'It seems that the professor allows him to use the books in his study. That means he must have a key to it. Professor Springett must have a lot of commitments. He can't be here every time that Reddish decides to pop in.'

'That's true,' said Stott. 'In fact, he's only here four days a week and he sometimes disappears altogether during the weekend.'

'I wish *I* had that kind of job.'

'Me, too – I'm on duty seven days a week.'

'What happens in the holidays?'

'Most of the undergraduates go back home and several of the Fellows disappear as well. Porters stay on duty to look after visitors.'

'Does the professor disappear?'

'Oh, yes,' said the other. 'He's always abroad in August.'

'Do you know where he goes?' asked Leeming.

'He usually starts off in France.'

'Does he spend the whole holiday there?'

'Oh, no,' said Stott. 'I can tell you where he finishes up because he usually complains about the heat when he gets back here. I mean, it's not the place to go when it's baking hot, is it?'

'It depends what reason he has for going there.'

'He told me it was for research, whatever that means. One thing is certain, though. The professor would never miss his annual visit to Italy.'

Colbeck returned to Scotland Yard. After his long and informative conversation with Caroline Lambert, he had to report to the superintendent. He found him in a more placid mood for once. Prone to interrupt him during such encounters, Tallis just sat there and listened, nodding his head from time to time. He waited patiently until Colbeck had finished.

'What's your abiding memory of Mrs Lambert?' he asked.

'She's a beautiful and highly intelligent woman,' replied Colbeck. 'I suspect that she takes after her mother. Mrs Lambert is the child of an Anglo-Italian marriage and that fact has coloured her existence.'

'Did she enjoy living in Italy?'

'Yes, sir, she did.'

'Then why did she marry a man who took her away from there?'

'I can only guess.'

'Her husband is one of those men who think that his wealth entitles him to hold sway over lesser mortals like us.'

Colbeck grinned. 'Nobody would dare to call *you* a lesser mortal, sir.'

'That, in effect, was what Lambert did so I had to put him firmly in his place. From what you've told me, his wife has a very different temperament.'

'She certainly does, Superintendent. Mrs Lambert loves Ireland and settled down there very well. Italy, I fancy, is more exotic, but perhaps she's outgrown its charms. Besides, I don't think that her husband would have considered moving to Tuscany to live. He wants to be among his own.' Colbeck became reflective. 'It was interesting to see the way that Mrs Lambert changed.'

'What do you mean?'

'At the start of her conversation, she was very much the wife of a rich Irish farmer. As time passed, however, the Italian side of her character began to appear. She became more animated and started to gesticulate. Also,' he went on, 'she began to use Italian phrases from time to time. I was reminded of Marco Pedroni.'

'Who, in God's name, is he?'

'He runs a toyshop in Cambridge and sells ice cream.'

'I sent you there to solve a murder,' complained Tallis bitterly, 'not to buy toys and eat ice cream.'

'I did neither, I assure you,' said Colbeck, concealing the fact that he had bought something for his daughter. 'The name was given to me by the chief constable. Meeting the gentleman – Pedroni, that is – turned out to be a most enlightening experience.'

'You're not making much sense, Inspector.'

'He made me realise what it means to be Italian. Family is at the very heart of their lives. As Catholics, they're enjoined to increase the size of that family. Most of the time, they're happy, hard-working, convivial people. If there's a threat to their family, however,' said Colbeck, 'they pull together to destroy it at whatever cost.'

'Excuse me for asking,' said Tallis, sarcastically, 'but does this have the slightest bearing on the case in hand?'

'I believe that it does, sir.'

'Is that what this ice cream seller told you?'

'He didn't need to tell me,' said Colbeck. 'I saw it in his eyes and heard it in his voice. Marco Pedroni taught me something about the nature of an Italian family.'

To wipe away the memory of their brief estrangement, Madeleine had invited her father for dinner that evening. Andrews arrived in time to read some nursery rhymes to his granddaughter and watch her being put to bed. Over the meal itself, neither he nor Madeleine said a word about the rupture in their relationship. They were closer than ever to each other now.

It was when they moved to the drawing room that she told him about her unwelcome visitor. Madeleine expected him to advise her to forget all about it, but his reaction was markedly different.

'When exactly was this, Maddy?'

'Yesterday was the first time,' she said. 'Today was the second.'

'And she just stood there and stared at the house?'

'Yes.'

'Describe her to me.'

'I've told you, Father – she was a short, rather plump old woman in a brown coat and a feathered hat. Oh, yes, and she wore spectacles.'

'Can you remember anything else?'

'When I caught her the first time,' said Madeleine, 'she more or less broke into a run. I think that's why she stood on the opposite side of the road today – so that she wouldn't give herself away. I told Lydia about it and she wonders if the woman had some link with the house.'

'What sort of link?'

'Perhaps she'd been in service here at one time.'

'Oh, I don't think so,' he said, quietly. He made a conscious effort to shake off his fears. 'I don't think it's anything to worry about.'

'That's what Lydia told me.'

Anxious to get off the subject, Andrews changed tack.

'How is Robert's investigation going?' he asked.

'It's taken a new turn, Father.'

He was hopeful. 'Is he ready to call on *me* yet?'

Back in Cambridge again, his son-in-law was eating a meal with Victor Leeming at the pub where they were staying. Colbeck had described his meeting with Caroline Lambert and the subsequent exchange with Edward Tallis.

'He doesn't believe in the value of serendipity,' he said.

'I know what that means, sir – picking up a good thing where you find it.'

'Marco Pedroni is a perfect example. To the superintendent, he's simply an immigrant shopkeeper who has no relevance at all to this investigation. In my view, Pedroni was invaluable.'

'I like the sound of that ice cream of his.'

'The chief constable's granddaughter has given it the seal of approval and that's good enough for me.' Colbeck set aside his knife and fork. 'Tell me about Reddish.'

'He wasn't exactly pleased to see me,' said Leeming.

He described his meeting with the undergraduate, stressing that he was given free access to Professor Springett's own library and must therefore have a key to it. Moving on to Andrew Kinglake, he insisted that the cox shouldn't be ruled out yet, especially as he had a brother at Corpus Christi.

'That could be significant, Inspector.'

'Yes, I agree. Since he was living in college, the brother might conceivably have delivered the message that we believe made Pomeroy leave the college in such a panic.'

'Shall I speak to the brother?'

'Not yet – but we'll bear him in mind. The important thing is that Kinglake clearly hasn't lost his determination to be part of the Cambridge crew for the Boat Race. You were right to tackle him again, Victor.'

'Thank you, sir.'

'I'm also impressed that you went on to question Jack Stott about the movements of Professor Springett, discovering that the man has a regular summer holiday in Italy. It's another example of serendipity, Victor.'

'That means the superintendent would dismiss it out of hand.'

'Forget him. We must put on our thinking caps.'

Leeming sighed. 'Mine is a bit frayed at the edges, sir.'

'Your opinions always have value,' said Colbeck. 'The question we haven't yet answered is this: why do I feel that the killer is still here?'

'I don't know, but I'm getting that same feeling myself.'

'He broke cover to go to Bury St Edmunds. Why?'

'It must have been to see that young woman, Isabella.'

'Why did he take that risk?'

'If he can kill someone in broad daylight,' argued Leeming, 'then he's not afraid to take chances. Besides, he didn't think that Bullen would recognise him.'

'So, who is he and where is he hiding?'

Leeming lifted his shoulders. 'My mind is a blank, sir.'

'Do you know what I'm beginning to think?'

'Yes, you regret turning down that ice cream.'

'Not exactly,' said Colbeck, smiling. 'Treats of any kind must wait. What we're seeing at the moment,' he continued, 'is a case of unfinished business.'

'Unfinished?' echoed Leeming. 'The man killed his victim. What more does he need to do?'

'I don't know.'

He took a moment to ponder. Leeming took advantage of the silence to finish his meal and wash it down with a long drink of his beer.

'Perhaps,' said Colbeck at length, 'he wants to add a further insult when the body is moved from the hospital.'

'But he can't possibly know when that could be.'

'Yes, he can.'

'You said that he's living here.'

'Isabella isn't. She's in Bury St Edmunds. Suppose that she is staying there in order to keep the place under surveillance. It may be the reason the man went to see her there. He wants an advance warning of when the coffin is within his reach so that he can desecrate it in some way.'

Leeming was shocked. 'What sort of man would want to do that?'

'One who has something to avenge,' said Colbeck.

Caleb Andrews was so tense when he left the house that he walked for ten minutes so that he was able to absorb the full implications of what he'd been told. While he'd been in Madeleine's company, he'd somehow managed to keep his anger bottled up inside him. Alone at last, he was able to release it. He swore fluently under his breath. Then he forced himself to decide on a course of action. Once his mind was made up, he summoned a cab and gave the driver directions.

When he got to the house, he was pleased to see that a light was still on in the living room. He just hoped that Elsie didn't have a visitor. What he had to say to her was solely for her ears. After paying the driver, he stood outside the house and made an effort to remember the good things that she'd brought into his life. There were a number of them, but they paled beside the bad things such as pouring scorn on a painting that he loved and insisting that it was turned to the wall when she next visited his house. Until that evening, Andrews would have done anything to appease her. He'd now shifted his position radically.

He knocked on the door and waited. Footsteps could be heard coming along the passageway. There was alarm in Elsie's voice.

'Who is it?' she demanded.

'It's Caleb,' he replied.

'Whatever are you doing here?'

'I need to speak to you, Elsie.'

'But I was about to go to bed. Can't it wait until tomorrow?'

He was firm. 'No, it can't.'

'Have I done something wrong?'

'Open the door, please. I'll stay out here until you do.'

'What's got into you, Caleb?'

He bit back his reply and stood in silence. Elsie retreated to the living room and tugged back the curtain so that she could see him. The last time he'd come to the house it was after escorting her there. He'd been kind, gentle and considerate. There was no hint of those qualities now. Gritting her teeth, she went back to the door and raised her voice to speak through it.

'You'd better have a good reason for giving me such a fright,' she warned.

'Why have you been spying on my daughter's house?'

'I don't know what you mean, Caleb.'

'Maddy saw you there two days running. How many other times were there? And why did you do it?'

'You've been drinking, haven't you?' she said, accusingly. 'Joe was the same. He was the soul of sweetness when he was sober but, as soon as he'd been to the pub, he came home looking for a fight.'

'I don't want a fight, Elsie,' he said, his tone softening. 'For the sake of the happy times we've had together, I'll control my temper. Now, please don't lie to me. Maddy gave me a very clear description. It was as if she was showing me a photograph of you. At least have the decency to admit it.'

'It wasn't me, Caleb,' she vowed. 'I swear it.'

'Open the door, please.'

'Come back in the morning and we'll discuss this properly.'

'I'm going nowhere.'

'You can't stay outside. What will the neighbours think?'

'That's up to them,' said Andrews.

There was silence on the other side of the door.

Victor Leeming had just drained the last of his beer. He looked across at Colbeck, who was so deep in thought that he seemed unaware that he had company. The sergeant knew the situation of old. When an idea seized his companion, he went off into a trance that could last indefinitely. It was the end of the evening and Leeming was tired. He wondered if he should slip away quietly to bed or wait until Colbeck became conscious of him again. In the end, he yielded to the promise of a good night's sleep and rose silently from his chair.

'Sit down again, Victor,' said the inspector.

Leeming obeyed. 'Yes, sir.'

'I need to tell you something.'

'You'll have to wake up first.'

Colbeck opened an eye. 'I hadn't dozed off. I was deep in contemplation.' Opening the other eye, he sat up. 'I apologise for leaving you like that.'

'I'm used to it, sir.'

'Then you'll know that it sometimes pays dividends.'

'Is that what it's done this time, Inspector?'

'I'm not sure.'

Colbeck summoned the barmaid and ordered another tankard of beer for Leeming and a glass of malt whisky for himself. The sergeant was glad that he hadn't sneaked off to his room.

'What were you thinking about, sir?' he asked.

'Christopher Marlowe.'

'Oh, him again,' groaned the other.

'I wonder if I chose the wrong play.'

'Do you mean that one about Doctor So-and-So?'

'*Doctor Faustus* or, to give it its full title, *The Tragical History of the Life and Death of Doctor Faustus*.'

'That's him,' said Leeming. 'He sounds like a really nasty sort of man.'

'Yet he exerts a strange appeal to anyone who reads the play – even more so if they witness a performance. I was beginning to see Bernard Pomeroy as a Faustian figure, a man with the suicidal urge to sell his soul to the Devil. Everything in his life came so easily to him,' said Colbeck. 'He revelled in his good fortune.'

'You've lost me, sir.'

'Then his luck finally runs out. His fate is sealed. Lucifer comes to claim him in the end. But I was forgetting that there's a *second* Devil.'

'I'm more confused than ever now,' said Leeming.

'*The Jew of Malta.*'

'Who on earth is he?'

'It's the title of another of Marlowe's plays,' said Colbeck, 'and Barabas the Jew is another character with a devilish streak. Among his crimes is the murder of his daughter, Abigail, who converts to Christianity and enters a nunnery. Barabas not only poisons her, he kills her fellow nuns by the same means.' He glanced at Leeming. 'Do you see what I'm getting at, Victor?'

'Not really, sir.'

'How was Pomeroy murdered?'

'He was poisoned. Ah,' he added, 'I think I follow you now. The killer's name must be Barabas and he's Jewish.'

'No, he isn't.'

'But you just told me that . . .'

'It's a clue I should have picked up earlier,' said Colbeck, seriously. 'Both of us wondered why the killer had gone to such trouble to murder a man in public when he could more safely have done so in private.'

'And I *still* can't understand it, sir.'

'The crime was carefully stage-managed, Victor. Don't you see? There's a theatricality about it that confirms the involvement of one of our suspects.'

'Simon Reddish?'

'Yes – he must be an accomplice.'

'But he may never have heard of *The Jew of Malta*.'

'I'd bet every penny I own that he knows it well,' said Colbeck, laughing.

'How can you be so certain?'

'There are two reasons. First, he's as passionate about

362

Marlowe's plays as Bernard Pomeroy was. Second, I once saw Reddish's father take the role of Barabas in a production of the play at the Strand Theatre. He was brilliant and I guarantee that his son would have been there to watch him on the opening night.'

Leeming was excited. 'Can we arrest Simon Reddish right now?'

'I'm afraid not.'

'But you've just explained what happened.'

'All I did was to offer a theory,' warned Colbeck. 'I'm fairly certain that it has some bearing on the truth, but we don't as yet have the evidence to support it. We need to flush Reddish and the killer out into the open.'

'How can we possibly do that, sir?'

'Fortune may favour us at last. What day is it tomorrow?'

'Sunday.'

'Then a devout Catholic like Isabella will almost certainly attend a service at St Edmund's Church in Bury St Edmunds. We'll be there as well.'

'But we don't really know what she looks like.'

'Constable Bullen does.'

Having retreated into her living room, Elsie Gurr had sat there in silence and hoped that her unwanted caller would go away. She was too frightened to check if Caleb Andrews was still there. It was only when she could hear rain drumming hard against the window that she changed her mind. She inched the curtain aside so that she could peer out. The sight that greeted her made her blood run cold. Arms folded,

Andrews was standing there defiantly, ignoring the rain and determined to stay all night if necessary. Her resolve weakened. Rushing to the door, she opened it and ushered him inside. After looking up and down the street to make sure that nobody was about, she shut it behind her. When they went into the living room, she stared at him.

'You're soaked to the skin, Caleb,' she said.

'I don't care.'

'You should go home and get out of those wet clothes.'

'There's something we must sort out first,' he said. 'Did you or did you not go to my daughter's house twice in a row?'

'No, I didn't,' she replied. 'I give you my word.'

'I'd rather you gave me the truth, Elsie.'

'That *is* the truth.'

'Please don't lie to me,' he said. 'Maddy is an artist. That means she has an eye for detail. She described your hat and coat perfectly. She also described the way you walked. It simply had to be you. Who else would have a reason to stand there and stare at the house?'

Her discomfort increased. She searched desperately for a way to placate him.

'I . . . may have glanced at the house when I happened to be in the area,' she admitted, 'because you'd told me what a lovely place it was to live. But it was only once. If your daughter thought I was there a second time, she made a mistake. In any case,' she went on, attempting an emollient smile, 'why are we arguing about it? I'm entitled to be curious, surely.'

'Oh, I think it was more than curiosity.'

'There's no need to be so angry with me, Caleb.'

'It's not anger I feel,' he said. 'It's sadness – real sadness.'

'Why?'

'I've lost something that I was enjoying very much.'

'You asked for honesty,' she told him, 'so I'll give it to you. In the short time I've known you, I've been drawn closer and closer.' She smiled lovingly. 'You've changed my life, Caleb. It's as simple as that. After Joe died, I couldn't believe that I'd find someone like you. I cherish every moment I've spent with you.'

'Unless it was at my house,' he said, sharply, 'where you couldn't bear to look at the picture Maddy painted for me. You wanted me to turn it to the wall next time you visited.'

'I was only teasing.'

'Oh, no, you weren't.'

'I *was*, I promise you.'

'You were laying down rules.'

'Well, you did once say you'd do anything for me.'

'Within limits,' he replied. 'Telling me what I can hang on the wall in my own home is outside those limits. And so is spying on Maddy's house. We both know why you were doing that.'

'I was only being practical,' she said, persuasively. 'Let's face facts, Caleb. Neither of us will live for ever. In the short time we have left, why not spend it in the best possible place?'

'Elsie—'

'Please don't interrupt.'

'But—'

'You've told me how often your daughter has pressed you

to move in with them. It's true, isn't it?' He gave a grudging nod. 'That lovely basement of theirs is bigger than our two houses joined together. It would be ideal. I'd make new curtains and do all sorts of things to turn it into a perfect home for us. We'd have use of a big garden and we could see Helena Rose whenever we wanted to. In fact—'

'Stop!' he cried, raising a palm. 'Nobody and nothing will make me leave my own home while I'm still fit and able. I love it there and I look at Maddy's painting with pride every day. Yes,' he agreed, 'we've had good times together, but that's all they were to me, Elsie. You were a friend, and I was fond of you.' His voice darkened. 'But that was before I realised you were using me to get out of this little rabbit hutch and into a much bigger house in a far better area. Helena Rose is *my* granddaughter,' he reminded her, 'not yours. I wouldn't dream of letting you anywhere near her. And I certainly wouldn't dream of sharing my life with someone who tells me bare-faced lies the way that you did. Goodnight, Elsie!'

Before she could stop him, Andrews went out through the front door and marched off into the pouring rain. All that she could do was to collapse into her chair under the sheer weight of her shattered dreams.

The rain continued throughout the night and into the morning. It was another reason why Leeming wished that he was still in a warm bed back in Cambridge.

'Why did we have to be here so early?' he complained.

'I didn't want to miss the first service of the day,' said Colbeck.

'But she didn't come to it, sir. She may not come to any of the other services. For that matter, she may not be in Bury St Edmunds at all.'

'I'm glad to find you brimming with optimism, Victor.'

'It could be a terrible waste of time.'

'Arthur Bullen didn't think so. He respected my judgement and answered the call immediately. If Isabella turns up – as I hope she will – Bullen will recognise her.'

'But if she doesn't,' said Leeming, gloomily, 'then he won't.'

They were standing under their respective umbrellas close to St Edmund's Church. People had streamed in for the early morning service, then streamed out again. Bullen had taken up a vantage point from which he could see the faces of all the worshippers as they entered the building. In place of his uniform, he was wearing his best suit. Since the next service was hours away, he strolled across to the detectives.

'Do you think she'll come alone, Inspector?' he asked.

'I hope not,' said Colbeck. 'Ideally, I'd like them both to turn up. It would enable us to catch the pair of them.'

'It seems funny to me.'

'Why is that?'

'Well, most of the people I've arrested don't go to church on a Sunday at all unless it's to steal something. Think of what this young woman has done,' said Bullen. 'Isabella was involved in a cruel murder. How can she have the gall to go to church after doing something like that?'

'You'll have to ask her.'

'If she ever turns up,' said Leeming, despondently.

'Have faith, Sergeant,' said Colbeck. 'There are two more services yet.'

'That means we'll be standing out here in the rain for hours.'

'We'll have a stroll until it's time to come back again.'

'Oh,' said Bullen, 'there's one thing I meant to ask. If and when they do arrive together, do we arrest them *before* they go into church or when they come out?'

'I think we should let them say their prayers first, don't you?' said Colbeck. 'There is one precaution we ought to take, however. The killer was clever enough to commit murder in full public view and get away with it. He'll be alert and cautious. If he senses danger as he goes into the church, he may not leave by the main door.' He turned to Leeming. 'That's a job for you, Sergeant. Have a quiet word with your friend Father O'Brien. Find out how many other exits there are. We need to watch them all. Having got this chance, we must take full advantage of it.'

It was not the first time that her father had arrived at the house so early. Madeleine could see that he was in a sombre mood. It sounded a warning bell inside her head. She gave him her usual welcome, then took him into the drawing room. They sat beside each other on the sofa. Having thought carefully about what he should say, Andrews blurted it out without pausing for breath.

'I've got a confession to make, Maddy, so please don't interrupt me. I misled you. I was upset when you questioned my honesty about where I went the other evening because I really *did* go to Gil Parry's house. But it wasn't for the reason

I gave you. Not long ago, Gil introduced me to his cousin's widow, Mrs Gurr. She seemed to be a very nice woman and I . . . I got on very well with her. I went to Gil's house that night with this new friend of mine. Elsie – Mrs Gurr, that is – let me take her home as well. I liked her . . .'

On he went until he came to Elsie's visits to the house. Learning about them, he explained, had made him see her very differently. He had gone straight to her house to challenge her about them and got soaking wet into the bargain.

Madeleine was torn between anger and sympathy, annoyed that he'd lied to her, after all, yet sorry that he'd been the victim of a woman like Elsie Gurr. She was outraged at the comments made about her painting of a locomotive and shocked that anyone could ask her father to turn it to the wall whenever she visited the house.

'I thought we were friends,' he said. 'I feel so stupid now, Maddy.'

'You solved one mystery, anyway,' she said. 'At least I can look out of the window again without seeing her sizing up the house before she moves in. Mrs Gurr was exploiting you, Father.'

'I see that now.'

'How long were you standing out in the rain last night?'

'Far too long,' he said, producing a handkerchief from his pocket. 'I think I have a cold coming – and I deserve it.' Standing up, he walked away from her so that he could blow his nose. He turned back and spread his arms. 'I'm sorry, Maddy. You didn't know that your father was such a silly old fool, did you?'

'Oh, yes, I did,' she said.

Bursting into laughter, she got to her feet and hugged him.

Since there was only one other exit from the church, Leeming was given the task of standing outside it. He consoled himself with the fact that the rain had finally stopped and that he was able to take his umbrella down before shaking some of the water off it. Still convinced that it was unlikely that the two suspects would arrive together, he relieved his aching legs by walking around in small circles. It was like being back on the beat again.

Colbeck, meanwhile, was stationed outside the main door, watching the members of the congregation as they began to arrive. They tended to come in families, though there was the occasional lone worshipper. Bullen scrutinised everyone who passed him. Hoping that their targets would arrive together, they were disappointed. The bell kept tolling and the people kept arriving but there was no sign of Isabella or her accomplice. Then, at the very last moment, a smartly dressed young woman came bustling along and went into the church.

Bullen lifted his cap slightly. It was the signal for which Colbeck had been waiting. It was her. The earlier description of Isabella had been accurate. She was slim, dark-haired, elegant and strikingly beautiful. There was also an extraordinary self-possession about her. She was no accomplice in a murder on her way to confess her sins. Isabella was a devout Roman Catholic, doing what she always did on a Sunday. Colbeck was intrigued. Leaving the railway policeman outside, he slipped quickly into the building and sat down in the row behind Isabella. Her head was bent in prayer. Colbeck had the feeling that she was not praying for the salvation of Bernard Pomeroy's soul.

Victor Leeming couldn't believe that a church service could go on for so long. It seemed interminable. He could hear the organ booming out from time to time, rising above the voices of the congregation. Extended silences followed, periods when he began to wonder if the service was over and if everyone had departed through the main door. Whenever he was tempted to go to the front of the church, he remembered his orders and remained where he was.

Eventually, the service did end, and he could hear the babble of voices as people came out of the main door and dispersed. He was about to abandon his vigil when he was distracted by the noise of an iron bolt being drawn back on the door right in front of him. It was suddenly flung wide open. A swarthy man in his thirties ran out. Finding someone in his path, he pushed Leeming away so that he could escape, but the sergeant responded quickly. After staggering back a few yards, he used the handle of his umbrella like a shepherd's crook and hooked it around the man's ankle, causing him to fall flat on the ground.

Leeming was on him at once. He dived onto his back and used his weight to hold him down while trying to twist his arms behind his back.

'You're under arrest, sir,' he said.

'*Scendete!*' yelled the man.

371

Fear gave him power and determination. He reared up like a horse and dislodged his assailant. Recovering instantly, Leeming grabbed him before the man could get away and the two of them grappled on the ground. They rolled over and over, each struggling hard to get an advantage. Unable to escape, the man became desperate and tried to end the fight. He slipped a hand inside his coat and produced a dagger. As the man raised his arm to strike, however, Leeming got a firm grip on his wrist and held the weapon at bay. But he was very much on the defensive now, twisting and turning wildly in an effort to shake him off. The dagger inched slowly towards his chest and he was left in no doubt about the man's murderous intent. Two blazing eyes told him all he needed to know.

Leeming gathered his energy for a final attempt at getting free, but the effort was unnecessary. Before the dagger could be plunged into his chest, the man was suddenly yanked off him altogether, deprived of his weapon and knocked unconscious with a vicious blow to his chin. Arthur Bullen offered his hand.

'Can I help you up, Sergeant?' he asked.

'No, thank you,' said Leeming, getting quickly to his feet and handcuffing the man who'd almost killed him. He picked up the dagger and examined it. 'You saved me from being stabbed with this.'

'It could have been worse, Sergeant. He might have used a syringe.'

'Is this the man who injected Bernard Pomeroy?'

'Yes, it is,' said Bullen. 'I cursed myself for not spotting him when he arrived. He must have sneaked past me by joining a large family group. When the inspector arrested Isabella, the first thing she did was to look anxiously over a shoulder. That meant she wasn't alone. The killer was here as well.'

'I'm so glad you realised he might leave by this exit.'

'They came to church separately but I daresay they'd planned to meet somewhere in private later on.'

'Right,' said Leeming as he heard a groan of pain from the man on the ground. 'Let's arrest him properly.' He pulled his prisoner unceremoniously to his feet. 'Come on, sir. It's time you started your long walk to the gallows.'

When accosted by the inspector, Isabella had made no attempt to escape. She was far more concerned about her accomplice's safety than about her own. Colbeck questioned her politely, but she was evasive and would admit nothing. He told her about the evidence that had been amassed against her and her face fell. She rallied at the thought that her partner in crime had eluded arrest, but her face betrayed her terror when she saw him being dragged to the front of the church by two burly men.

'Has she confessed, sir?' asked Leeming.

'Not yet,' replied Colbeck. 'She hasn't told me why they killed Pomeroy.'

'I think our first guess might have been right.' The sergeant turned to Isabella. 'He was your lover, wasn't he?'

'No!' she retorted with a snort of disgust.

'Then what *was* he to you?'

'Bernard was my brother.'

* * *

373

When the letter was delivered to King's College, it was taken at once to Nicholas Thorpe's room. He was seated at his desk, poring over an essay that he'd finally finished. The letter was delivered, and he opened it immediately to read Colbeck's message. Realising that the killer and his accomplice were at last in custody, he was overcome with such a sense of relief that he all but fainted.

Colbeck delivered his message to Simon Reddish in person. Through the door of the latter's room, he could hear the young actor declaiming Marlowe's poetry. Without waiting to be invited in, Colbeck opened the door and entered the room.

'What the devil do you mean by barging in here?' demanded Reddish.

'I've come to make an arrest, sir.'

'Don't be absurd.'

'Two friends of yours are already cooling their heels in police cells. It's time for you to join them.'

'I haven't a clue what you're talking about, Inspector.'

'Do you deny knowing Isabella and Paulo Vaccari?'

'I certainly do,' retorted Reddish. 'I've never heard those names before.'

'That's strange, sir. I'm told that the Vaccari family own a pharmacy in Lucca. It's one that you've used often in the past.'

'Don't believe a word they've told you.'

'Why not, sir?'

'They're hot-blooded Italians. They'll tell you all sorts of lies.'

'A few moments ago, you denied even knowing them.'

'Paulo Vaccari is in *trade*, Inspector,' said the other with scorn. 'Can you imagine that I'd deign to associate myself with someone like that?'

'Revenge is a powerful impulse, Mr Reddish. It unites the most unlikely bedfellows.'

'Have either of them had the cheek to name me?'

'They didn't need to. When they told me they hailed from Lucca, you leapt immediately into my mind.' He pointed to the door. 'Shall we go, sir?'

Reddish stood his ground. 'I've no intention of going anywhere.'

'Then let me offer you alternatives. We can either leave this college as if we were merely acquaintances or – if you prefer – I will overpower you and drag you across the quadrangle in handcuffs.' He took a step closer. 'I've arrested bigger and stronger criminals than you, sir. Some of them had dangerous weapons. When you've disarmed a man holding a meat cleaver, you're hardly likely to quail at the sight of someone with a book of poetry in his hand.'

'Look,' said Reddish, panic showing at last, 'let me be honest with you. It was never *my* idea. It was something I once floated by way of a joke. I never suspected for one moment that Paulo and his sister would take me seriously. I give you my word that I was not involved in . . .'

His voice tailed off into silence. It was impossible to talk himself out of his predicament. He accepted defeat. Reddish's world suddenly caved in on him. There would be no stirring performance as Doctor Faustus and no illustrious career on the professional stage. He would simply leave an ugly stain on the reputation of his college. Family and friends would be appalled. He'd be seen in his true light.

He fell to his knees in despair and gibbered uncontrollably.

It was Monday morning. Jack Stott was polishing one of the windows of the lodge when he saw Professor Springett hurrying towards him. It was the moment for which the porter had been waiting.

'Good morning, Professor,' he said.

'Is there any mail for me?' asked the other.

'I gave it to you when you first arrived.'

'I was just wondering if there was a message from Mr Reddish. He should have been here half an hour ago. He's always punctual. If he was indisposed, he'd certainly have sent an apology.'

'He's in no position to do so, I'm afraid.'

'Why not?'

'Simon Reddish was arrested yesterday on a charge of murder.'

Face ashen, Springett began to totter.

Having delivered a long report to Edward Tallis, he'd been congratulated on his success. Colbeck left the superintendent's office with a smile for once. Back at home that evening, he had a less critical audience. Leeming was there as were Alan Hinton and Lydia Quayle. Madeleine had decided not to invite her father, knowing that he was badly bruised by the collapse of his friendship with Elsie Gurr and preferred to be on his own.

'In essence,' said Colbeck, 'it was a family tragedy. Alexander Pomeroy had seduced the wife of a leading pharmacist who operated in Florence at the time. When she was with child, she pretended that it was her husband's baby and he welcomed Isabella, as she was called, into the world. Soon afterwards, they moved to larger premises in Lucca. They already had a son, Paulo, who was years older than Isabella. To all outward appearance, they were a happy family. The children grew up to be lively and well-educated. Everything seemed fine until their father suddenly and unaccountably went berserk. He strangled his wife to death, then took his own life. You can guess how he did that.'

'Poison,' said Leeming.

'He left no explanation behind, so the children were utterly bemused at first. Then they found letters confirming that their mother had had a liaison with the British Consul in Florence.'

'What a dreadful shock it must have been for them!' said Lydia.

'Their parents had been raising another man's child all those years.'

'Yes,' said Leeming. 'No wonder Bullen saw a likeness between Isabella and Bernard Pomeroy's eldest sister. Both women had the same father.'

'What a monster he seems to have been,' said Madeleine. 'He betrayed his wife, wreaked havoc in the life of his mistress's family and put his only son in danger. Bernard Pomeroy was the chosen victim.'

'Did they *have* to kill him?' said Lydia.

'They believed so,' said Colbeck. 'Paulo and Isabella had a perverted idea of revenge. In their minds, he'd inherited the sins of his father. The honour of the Vaccari family, they felt, could only be upheld by the death of the one man in the Pomeroy family. It became their obsession.'

'At first,' said Leeming, taking over, 'there was nothing they could do. They didn't know where Bernard Pomeroy was living or how they could possibly stalk him. The one thing they did find out was that he was at Cambridge University.'

'Then Simon Reddish came into their lives,' resumed Colbeck. 'He was staying with his parents at their second home near Lucca. Since he was a famous actor, Oliver Reddish was approached to put on some sort of performance in the city. Quite naturally, he involved his son and they acted scenes from plays by Shakespeare and Marlowe. As it happened, Paulo and Isabella were in the audience. They were struck by the brilliance of the actors, but it was the programme that proved to be a revelation. It named both actors and described them in detail. They knew enough English between them to translate the description of the son.'

'It told them that Simon Reddish was studying at Cambridge.'

'They made a point of befriending him and discovered that he, too, had a reason to despise Bernard Pomeroy.'

Colbeck went on to describe how they'd hatched a plot to kill their common enemy. As a pharmacist himself, Paulo Vaccari had concocted a lethal poison. Isabella was used as bait. Moving to Bury St Edmunds, she'd written to Pomeroy and told him that they shared a father. Once he'd absorbed the shock, he agreed to see her in secret to verify her claim and discuss what he could do for her. Deeply embarrassed by the turn of events, he'd confided nothing to close friends like Nicholas Thorpe.

'May I ask a question?' said Madeleine.

'Please do,' replied her husband.

'If they'd agreed to kill him, why didn't Isabella administer the poison in some way? She'd obviously won his confidence.'

'That's what *I* was thinking,' added Lydia.

'Yes,' said Hinton. 'Why arrange a murder that was so difficult to bring off? How could they guarantee that Isabella's plea would make Pomeroy charge off like that? And how could Paulo get close enough to him to inject the poison?'

'You're forgetting something,' said Colbeck. 'The plan was conceived by Simon Reddish, so it was like a scene in a play. What do actors do before they put on a performance, Alan?'

'They rehearse.'

'Yes, they do. That was why Isabella lured Pomeroy to those meetings in Bury St Edmunds. Every time he boarded the train in Cambridge, he was trailed by Paolo Vaccari, who was working out how best he could kill him. It wasn't a spontaneous murder,' stressed Colbeck. 'It was well-rehearsed.'

'That's what Reddish admitted to us,' said Leeming.

'I have another question,' said Hinton. 'Where exactly was the murder committed? The first injection was given in Cambridge and the second lethal one on the platform in Bury St Edmunds.'

'I know the answer to that,' said Leeming with a grin. 'It was a case of tragedy on the branch line.'

'I'm sorry to be pedantic, Victor,' said Colbeck, 'but I'd qualify that verdict. I believe that it was a tragedy on the branch line of the Pomeroy family.' The others laughed. 'Now let's turn to the burning question of the day, shall we?' he continued. 'Who is going to win this year's Boat Race?'

AUTHOR'S NOTE

In 1863, the Boat Race was won by Oxford in a time of twenty-three minutes six seconds. The Cambridge cox that day was F. H. Archer, King's School, Canterbury and Corpus Christi College.

EDWARD MARSTON has written well over a hundred books. He is best known for his hugely successful Railway Detective series and his other series include the Bow Street Rivals series featuring twin detectives set during the Regency, as well as the Home Front Detective series.

edwardmarston.com